Praise for
The House in the Cerulean Sea

'I loved it. It is like being wrapped up in a big gay blanket. Simply perfect'   **V. E. Schwab**

'*The House in The Cerulean Sea* is a modern fairy tale about learning your true nature and what you love and will protect. It's a beautiful book'   **Charlaine Harris**

'*1984* meets *The Umbrella Academy* with a pinch of Douglas Adams thrown in. Touching, tender and truly delightful, *The House in the Cerulean Sea* is an utterly absorbing story of tolerance, found family and defeating bureaucracy'   **Gail Carriger**

'Sweet, comforting and kind, this book is very close to perfect . . . I cannot recommend it highly enough'   **Seanan McGuire**

'A witty, wholesome fantasy that's likely to cause heart-swelling'   ***Washington Post***

'Quirk and charm give way to a serious exploration of the dangers of complacency in this delightful, thought-provoking Orwellian fantasy from Klune . . . This tale of found family is hopeful to its core. Readers will revel in Klune's wit and ingenuity'   ***Publishers Weekly*, starred review**

'Smart and sincere and brilliantly romantic . . . This is the book we all need to be reading right now'   ***Locus***

THE HOUSE IN THE CERULEAN SEA

TJ Klune is the *New York Times* and *USA Today* bestselling, Lambda Literary Award-winning author of *The House in the Cerulean Sea*, *The Extraordinaries* and more. Being queer himself, TJ believes it's important – now more than ever – to have accurate, positive, queer representation in stories. You can find out more at tjklunebooks.com

By TJ Klune

The House in the Cerulean Sea
Under the Whispering Door

THE HOUSE IN THE CERULEAN SEA

TJ KLUNE

First published 2020 by Tom Doherty Associates

First published in the UK in paperback 2021 by Tor
an imprint of Pan Macmillan
The Smithson, 6 Briset Street, London EC1M 5NR
EU representative: Macmillan Publishers Ireland Ltd, 1st Floor,
The Liffey Trust Centre, 117–126 Sheriff Street Upper, Dublin 1, D01 YC43
Associated companies throughout the world
www.panmacmillan.com

ISBN 978-1-5290-8794-9

5 7 9 8 6

A CIP catalogue record for this book is available from the British Library.

Printed and bound by CPI Group (UK) Ltd, Croydon, CR0 4YY

MIX
Paper from
responsible sources
FSC® C116313

Visit **www.panmacmillan.com** to read more about all our books
and to buy them. You will also find features, author interviews and
news of any author events, and you can sign up for e-newsletters
so that you're always first to hear about our new releases.

For those who have been with me since the beginning: look at what we've made. Thank you.

THE HOUSE IN THE CERULEAN SEA

ONE

"Oh dear," Linus Baker said, wiping the sweat from his brow. "This is most unusual."

That was an understatement. He watched in rapt wonder as an eleven-year-old girl named Daisy levitated blocks of wood high above her head. The blocks spun in slow, concentric circles. Daisy frowned in concentration, the tip of her tongue stuck out between her teeth. It went on for a good minute before the blocks slowly lowered to the floor. Her level of control was astounding.

"I see," Linus said, furiously scribbling on his pad of paper. They were in the master's office, a tidy room with government-issued brown carpet and old furniture. The walls were lined with terrible paintings of lemurs in various poses. The master had showed them off proudly, telling Linus painting was her passion, and that if she hadn't become the master of this specific orphanage, she'd be traveling with a circus as a lemur trainer or even have opened up a gallery to share her artwork with the world. Linus believed the world was better off with the paintings staying in this room, but he kept the thought to himself. He wasn't there to engage in amateur art criticism. "And how often do you—er, you know? Make things float?"

The master of the orphanage, a squat woman with frizzy hair, stepped forward. "Oh, not often at all," she said quickly. She wrung her hands, eyes darting back and forth. "Perhaps once or twice . . . a year?"

Linus coughed.

"A month," the woman amended. "Silly me. I don't know why I said a year. Slip of the tongue. Yes, once or twice a *month*. You know how it is. The older the children get, the more they . . . do things."

"Is that right?" Linus asked Daisy.

"Oh yes," Daisy said. "Once or twice a month, and no more." She smiled beatifically at him, and Linus wondered if she'd been coached on her answers before his arrival. It wouldn't be the first time it'd happened, and he doubted it'd be the last.

"Of course," Linus said. They waited as his pen continued to scratch along the paper. He could feel their gazes on him, but he kept his focus on his words. Accuracy demanded attention. He was nothing but thorough, and his visit to this particular orphanage had been enlightening, to say the least. He needed to jot down as many details as he could to complete his final report once he returned to the office.

The master fussed over Daisy, pulling her unruly black hair back, fixing it in place with plastic butterfly clips. Daisy was staring forlornly at her blocks on the floor as if she wished they were levitating once more, her bushy eyebrows twitching.

"Do you have control over it?" Linus asked.

Before Daisy could open her mouth, the master said, "Of course she does. We'd never allow her to—"

Linus held up his hand. "I would appreciate, madam, if I could hear from Daisy herself. While I have no doubt you have her best interests in mind, I find that children such as Daisy here tend to be more . . . forthright."

The master looked to speak again until Linus arched an eyebrow. She sighed as she nodded, taking a step back from Daisy.

After scribbling a final note, Linus capped his pen and set it and the pad of paper back in his briefcase. He stood from his chair and crouched down before Daisy, knees groaning in protest.

Daisy gnawed on her bottom lip, eyes wide.

"Daisy? Do you have control over it?"

She nodded slowly. "I think so? I haven't hurt anyone since I was brought here." Her mouth twisted down. "Not until Marcus. I don't like hurting people."

He could almost believe that. "No one said you did. But sometimes, we can't always control the . . . gifts we're given. And it's not necessarily the fault of those with said gifts."

That didn't seem to make her feel better. "Then whose fault is it?"

Linus blinked. "Well, I suppose there are all sorts of factors. Modern research suggests extreme emotional states can trigger instances such as yours. Sadness. Anger. Even happiness. Perhaps you were so happy, you accidentally threw a chair at your friend Marcus?" It was the reason he'd been sent here in the first place. Marcus had been seen in hospital in order to have his tail looked after. It'd been bent at an odd angle, and the hospital had reported it directly to the Department in Charge of Magical Youth as they were required to do. The report triggered an investigation, which was why Linus had been assigned to this particular orphanage.

"Yes," Daisy said. "That's exactly it. Marcus made me so happy when he stole my colored pencils that I accidentally threw a chair at him."

"I see," Linus said. "Did you apologize?"

She looked down at her blocks again, shuffling her feet. "Yes. And he said he wasn't mad. He even sharpened my pencils for me before he gave them back. He's better at it than I am."

"What a thoughtful thing to do," Linus said. He thought about reaching out and patting her on the shoulder, but it wasn't proper. "And I know you didn't mean him any harm, not really.

Perhaps in the future, we will stop and think before we let our emotions get the better of us. How does that sound?"

She nodded furiously. "Oh yes. I promise to stop and think before I throw any more chairs with nothing but the power of my mind."

Linus sighed. "I don't think that's quite what I—"

A bell rang from somewhere deep in the old house.

"Biscuits," Daisy breathed before running toward the door.

"Only *one*," the master called after her. "You don't want to spoil your supper!"

"I won't!" Daisy shouted back before slamming the door behind her. Linus could hear the little pitter-patter of her footsteps as she raced down the hall toward the kitchen.

"She will," the master muttered, slumping down in her chair behind her desk. "She always does."

"I believe she's earned it," Linus said.

She rubbed a hand over her face before eyeing him warily. "Well, that's it, then. You've interviewed all the children. You've inspected the house. You've seen that Marcus is doing well. And while there was the . . . incident with the chair, Daisy obviously means no harm."

He believed she was right. Marcus had seemed more interested in having Linus sign his tail cast rather than getting Daisy into any trouble. Linus had balked, telling him it wasn't his place. Marcus was disappointed, but bounced back almost immediately. Linus marveled—as he sometimes did—how resilient they all were in the face of everything. "Quite."

"I don't suppose you'll tell me what you're going to write in your report—"

Linus bristled. "Absolutely not. You will be provided with a copy once I've filed it, as you know. The contents will be made clear to you then, and not a moment before."

"Of course," the master said hastily. "I didn't mean to suggest that you—"

"I'm glad you see it my way," Linus said. "And I know DICOMY will certainly be appreciative as well." He busied himself with his briefcase, rearranging the contents until he was satisfied. He closed it and snapped the locks in place. "Now, unless there is anything else, I'll take my leave and bid you—"

"The children like you."

"I like them," he said. "I wouldn't do what I do if I didn't."

"That's not always how it is with others like you." She cleared her throat. "Or, rather, the other caseworkers."

He looked at the door longingly. He'd been so close to making his escape. Clutching his briefcase in front of him like a shield, he turned back around.

The master rose from her chair and walked around the desk. He took a step back, mostly out of habit. She didn't come any closer, instead leaning back against her desk. "We've had . . . others," she said.

"Have you? That's to be expected, of course, but—"

"They don't see the children," she said. "Not for who they are, only for what they're capable of."

"They should be given a chance, as all children should. What hope would they have to be adopted if they're treated as something to be feared?"

The master snorted. "Adopted."

He narrowed his eyes. "Something I said?"

She shook her head. "No, forgive me. You're refreshing, in your own way. Your optimism is contagious."

"I am positively a ray of sunshine," Linus said flatly. "Now, if there's nothing else, I can show myself—"

"How is it you can do what you do?" she asked. She blanched as if she couldn't believe what she'd said.

"I don't know what you mean."

"Work for DICOMY."

Sweat trickled down the back of his neck into the collar of his shirt. It was awfully warm in the office. For the first time in a long time, he wished he were outside in the rain. "And what's wrong with DICOMY?"

She hesitated. "I mean no offense."

"I should hope not."

"It's just that . . ." She stood from her desk, arms still folded. "Don't you wonder?"

"Never," Linus said promptly. Then, "About what?"

"What happens to a place like this after you file your final report. What becomes of the children."

"Unless I'm called to return, I expect they continue to live as bright and happy children until they become bright and happy adults."

"Who are still regulated by the government because of who they are."

Linus felt backed into a corner. He wasn't prepared for this. "I don't work for the Department in Charge of Magical Adults. If you have any concerns in that regard, I suggest you bring it up with DICOMA. I'm focused solely on the well-being of children, nothing more."

The master smiled sadly. "They never stay as children, Mr. Baker. They always grow up eventually."

"And they do so using the tools that one such as yourself provides for them should they find themselves aging out of the orphanage without having been adopted." He took another backward step toward the door. "Now, if you'll excuse me, I have to catch the bus. It's a rather long trip home, and I don't want to miss it. Thank you for your hospitality. And again, once the report is filed, you will be sent a copy for your own records. Do let us know if you have any questions."

"Actually, I do have another—"

"Submit it in writing," Linus called, already through the door. "I look forward to it." He shut it behind him, the latch clicking in place. He took a deep breath before exhaling slowly.

"Now you've gone and done it, old boy. She'll send you hundreds of questions."

"I can still hear you," the master said through the door.

Linus startled before hurrying down the hall.

He was about to leave through the front door when he paused at a bright burst of laughter coming from the kitchen. Against his better judgment, he tiptoed toward the sound. He passed by posters nailed to the walls, the same messages that hung in all the DICOMY-sanctioned orphanages he'd been to. They showed smiling children below such legends as WE'RE HAPPIEST WHEN WE LISTEN TO THOSE IN CHARGE and A QUIET CHILD IS A HEALTHY CHILD and WHO NEEDS MAGIC WHEN YOU HAVE YOUR IMAGINATION?

He stuck his head in the kitchen doorway.

There, sitting at a large wooden table, was a group of children.

There was a boy with blue feathers growing from his arms.

There was a girl who cackled like a witch; it was fitting seeing as how that's what her file said she was.

There was an older girl who could sing so seductively, it brought ships crashing onto the shore. Linus had balked when he'd read that in her report.

There was a selkie, a young boy with a fur pelt resting on his shoulders.

And Daisy and Marcus, of course. Sitting side by side, Daisy exclaiming over his tail cast through a mouthful of biscuit. Marcus grinned at her, his face a field of rusty freckles, tail resting on the table. Linus watched as he asked her if she would draw him another picture on his cast with one of her colored pencils. She agreed immediately. "A flower," she said. "Or a bug with sharp teeth and stinger."

"Ooh," Marcus breathed. "The bug. You have to do the bug."

Linus left them be, satisfied with what he'd seen.

He made his way to the door once more. He sighed when he realized he'd forgotten his umbrella once again. "Of all the—"

He opened the door and stepped out into the rain to begin the long journey home.

TWO

"Mr. *Baker*!"

Linus groaned to himself. Today had been going so well. Somewhat. He'd gotten a spot of orange dressing on his white dress shirt from the soggy salad he'd purchased from the commissary, a persistent stain that only smudged when he'd tried to rub it away. And rain was thundering on the roof overhead, with no signs of letting up anytime soon. He'd forgotten his umbrella at home yet again.

But other than that, his day had been going well.

Mostly.

The sounds of clacking computer keys stopped around him as Ms. Jenkins approached. She was a stern woman, hair pulled back so severely that it brought her unibrow up to the middle of her forehead. He wondered every now and then if she had ever smiled in her life. He thought not. Ms. Jenkins was a dour woman with the disposition of an ornery snake.

She was also his supervisor, and Linus Baker didn't dare cross her.

He nervously pulled on the collar of his shirt as Ms. Jenkins approached, weaving her way between the desks, her heels snapping against the cold, stone floor. Her assistant, a despicable toad of a man named Gunther, followed close behind her, carrying a clipboard and an obscenely long pencil he used to keep tally of those who appeared to be slacking on the job. The list would be totaled at the end of the day, and demerits would be added to an ongoing weekly tally. At the end of the week, those with five or more demerits would have them added to their personal files. Nobody wanted that.

Those whom Ms. Jenkins and Gunther passed by kept their heads down, pretending to work, but Linus knew better; they were listening as best they could to find out what he'd done wrong, and what his punishment would be. Possibly he'd be forced to leave early and have his pay docked. Or perhaps he'd have to stay later than normal and still have his pay docked. At worst, he'd be fired, his professional life would be over, and he wouldn't have any pay to get docked ever again.

He couldn't believe it was only Wednesday.

And it was made worse when he realized it was actually Tuesday.

He couldn't think of a single thing he'd done out of order, unless he'd gotten back a minute late from his allotted fifteen-minute lunch, or his last report had been unsatisfactory. His mind raced. Had he spent too long trying to get the dressing stain off? Or had there been a typo in his report? Surely not. It'd been pristine, unlike his shirt.

But Ms. Jenkins had a twisted look on her face, one that didn't bode well for Linus. For a room he always thought was frigid, it was now uncomfortably warm. Even though it was drafty—the miserable weather only making things worse—it did nothing to stop the sweat from trickling down the back of his neck. The green glow from the screen of his computer felt over-bright, and he struggled to keep his breathing slow and even. His doctor had told him his blood pressure was too high at his last physical, and that he needed to cut the stressors from his life.

Ms. Jenkins was a stressor.

He kept that thought to himself.

His small wooden desk was almost at the center of the room:

Row L, Desk Seven in a room comprising twenty-six rows with fourteen desks in each row. There was barely any space between the desks. A skinny person would have no trouble getting by, but one who carried a few extra pounds around the middle (few being the operative word, of course)? If they'd been allowed to have personal knickknacks on their desks, it'd probably end in disaster for someone like Linus. But seeing as how that was against the rules, he mostly ended up bumping into them with his wide hips and apologizing hastily at the glares he received. It was one of the reasons he usually waited until the room was mostly empty before he left for the day. That and the fact he'd recently turned forty, and all he had to show for it was a tiny house, a crusty cat that would probably outlive everyone, and an ever-expanding waistline his doctor had poked and prodded with a strange amount of glee while bloviating about the wonders of dieting.

Hence the soggy salad from the commissary.

Hung high above them were dreadfully cheery signs proclaiming: YOU ARE DOING GOOD WORK and ACCOUNT FOR EVERY MINUTE OF YOUR DAY BECAUSE A MINUTE LOST IS A MINUTE WASTED. Linus hated them so.

He put his hands flat on the desk to keep from digging his fingernails into his palms. Mr. Tremblay, who sat in Row L, Desk Six, smiled darkly at him. He was a much younger man who seemed to relish his work. "In for it now," he muttered to Linus.

Ms. Jenkins reached his desk, her mouth a thin line. As was her wont, she appeared to have applied her makeup rather liberally in the dark without the benefit of a mirror. The heavy rouge on her cheeks was magenta, and her lipstick looked like blood. She wore a black pantsuit, the buttons of which were closed all the way up to just under her chin. She was as thin as a dream, made up of sharp bones covered in skin stretched too tightly.

Gunther, on the other hand, was as fresh-faced as Mr. Tremblay. Rumor had it, he was the son of Someone Important, most likely Extremely Upper Management. Though Linus didn't talk much to his coworkers, he still heard their gossipy whispers. He'd learned early on in life that if he didn't speak, people often forgot he was there or even existed. His mother had told him once when he was a child that he blended in with the paint on the wall, only memorable when one was reminded it was there at all.

"Mr. Baker," Ms. Jenkins said again, practically snarling his name.

Gunther stood next to her, smiling down at him. It wasn't a very nice smile. His teeth were perfectly white and square, and he had dimples in his chin. He was handsome in a chilling way. The smile should have been lovely, but it didn't reach his eyes. The only times Linus could say he'd ever believe Gunther's smile were when he'd perform surprise inspections, long pencil scratching against the clipboard, marking demerit after demerit.

Maybe that was it. Maybe Linus was going to get his first demerit, something he'd miraculously been able to avoid since the arrival of Gunther and his point system. He knew they were monitored constantly. There were large cameras hanging from the ceiling recording everything. If someone was caught doing something wrong, the large speaker boxes affixed to the walls would crackle to life, and there would be shouts of demerits for Row K, Desk Two or Row Z, Desk Thirteen.

Linus had never been caught mismanaging his time. He was far too smart for that. And too fearful.

Perhaps, however, not smart or fearful enough.

He was going to get a demerit.

Or maybe he was going to get *five* demerits, and then it would go into his personal file, a mark that would sully his seventeen years of service in the Department. Maybe they'd seen the dressing stain. There was a strict policy regarding professional attire. It was listed in great detail on pages 242–246 of the *RULES AND REGULATIONS*, the employee handbook for the Department in Charge of Magical Youth. Perhaps someone had seen the stain and reported him. That wouldn't surprise Linus in the slightest. And hadn't people been sacked for smaller things?

Linus knew they had.

"Ms. Jenkins," he said, voice barely above a whisper. "It's nice to see you today." This was a lie. It was never nice to see Ms. Jenkins. "What can I do for you?"

Gunther's smile widened. Possibly *ten* demerits, then. The dressing was orange, after all. He wouldn't need a brown box. The only things that belonged to him were the clothes on his back and the mouse pad, a faded picture of a white sandy beach and the bluest ocean in the world. Across the top was the legend DON'T YOU WISH YOU WERE HERE?

Yes. Daily.

Ms. Jenkins didn't seem inclined to respond to Linus's greeting. "What have you done?" she demanded, eyebrows near her hairline, which should have been physically impossible.

Linus swallowed thickly. "Pardon me, but I don't think I know what you're referring to."

"I find that hard to believe."

"Oh. I'm . . . sorry?"

Gunther scratched something on his clipboard. He was probably giving Linus yet another demerit for the obvious sweat stains under his arms. He couldn't do anything about those now.

Ms. Jenkins didn't seem as if she accepted his apology. "You must have done *something*." She was very insistent.

Perhaps he should come clean about the dressing stain. It would be like ripping off a bandage. Better to do it all at once rather than drag it out. "Yes. Well, you see, I'm trying to eat healthier. A diet, of sorts."

Ms. Jenkins frowned. "A diet?"

Linus nodded jerkily. "Doctor's orders."

"Carrying a bit of extra weight, are you?" Gunther asked, sounding far too pleased at the idea.

Linus flushed. "I guess so."

Gunther made a sympathetic noise. "I noticed. You poor dear. Better late than never, I suppose." He tapped his own flat stomach with the edge of the clipboard.

Gunther was odious. Linus kept that thought to himself. "How wonderful."

"You have yet to answer my question," Ms. Jenkins snapped. "What is it you could have possibly done?"

Might as well get it over with. "A mistake. Clumsy me. I was trying eat the salad, but apparently kale has a mind of its own, and slipped from my—"

"I have no idea what you're prattling on about," Ms. Jenkins said, leaning forward and putting her hands on his desk. Her fingernails were painted black, and she tapped them against the wood. It sounded like the rattling of bones. "Stop talking."

"Yes, ma'am."

She stared at him.

His stomach twisted sharply.

"You've been requested," she said slowly, "to attend a meeting tomorrow morning with Extremely Upper Management."

He hadn't expected that. Not in the slightest. In fact, of all the things Bedelia Jenkins could have said at this exact moment, that had been the least likely option.

He blinked. "Come again?"

She stood upright, crossing her arms underneath her breasts, gripping her elbows. "I've read your reports. They're marginally adequate, at best. So imagine my surprise when I received a memo that Linus Baker was being summoned."

Linus felt cold. He'd never been asked to meet with Extremely Upper Management in his entire career. The only time he'd actually *seen* Extremely Upper Management was during the holidays when the luncheon occurred, and Extremely Upper Management stood in a row at the front of the room, dishing out dried-up ham and lumpy potatoes from foil trays, grinning at each of their underlings, telling them they'd earned this fine meal for all their hard work. Of course, they had to eat it at their desks because their fifteen-minute lunch break had been used up by standing in line, but still.

It was *September*. The holidays were still *months* away.

Now, according to Ms. Jenkins, they wanted him personally. He'd never heard of that happening before. It couldn't possibly mean anything good.

Ms. Jenkins looked as if she were waiting for a response. He didn't know what to say, so he said, "Maybe there's been a mistake."

"A mistake," Ms. Jenkins repeated. "A *mistake*."

"Ye-es?"

"Extremely Upper Management doesn't make mistakes," Gunther simpered.

There was that, yes. "Then I don't know."

Ms. Jenkins wasn't pleased by his answer. It struck Linus then that *she* didn't know any more than she was telling him, and for reasons he didn't want to explore, the very idea gave him a nasty little thrill. Granted, it was tinged with unimaginable terror, but it was there nonetheless. He didn't know what kind of person that made him.

"Oh, Linus," his mother had told him once. "It's never polite to revel in the suffering of others. What a terrible thing to do."

He never allowed himself to revel.

"You don't know," Ms. Jenkins said, sounding as if she were gearing up to strike. "Perhaps you lodged a complaint of some kind? *Perhaps* you don't appreciate my supervisory technique and thought you could go above my head? Is that it, Mr. Baker?"

"No, ma'am."

"*Do* you like my supervisory technique?"

Absolutely not. "Yes."

Gunther scratched his pencil along his clipboard.

"What *exactly* do you like about my supervisory technique?" Ms. Jenkins asked.

Conundrum. Linus didn't like to lie about anything. Even little white lies caused his head to ache. And once one started lying, it became easier to do it again and again until one had to keep track of *hundreds* of lies. It was easier to be honest.

But then there came times of great need, such as this one. And it wasn't like he had to lie, not completely. A truth could be twisted and still resemble the truth. "It's very authoritative."

Her eyebrows rose to her hairline. "It is, isn't it?"

"Quite."

She lifted a hand and snapped her fingers. Gunther shuffled through some of the papers on his clipboard before handing a cream-colored page over to her. She held it between two fingers as if the thought of it touching any other part of her could cause a blistering infection. "Nine o'clock sharp tomorrow, Mr. Baker. God help you if you're late. You will, of course, make up the time you missed after. On the weekend, if necessary. You aren't scheduled to be in the field for at least another week."

"Of course," Linus agreed quickly.

She leaned forward again, dropping her voice until it was barely a whisper. "And if I find out you've complained about me, I will make your life a living hell. Do you understand me, Mr. Baker?"

He did. "Yes, ma'am."

She dropped the paper on his desk. It fluttered to a corner, almost falling to the floor. He didn't dare reach out and grab it, not while she still stood above him.

Then she was spinning on her heels, shouting that everyone had *better* be working if they knew what was good for them.

Immediately, the sound of clacking keyboards resumed.

Gunther still stood near his desk, staring at him strangely.

Linus fidgeted in his chair.

"I don't know why they would ask for you," Gunther finally said, that terrible smile returning. "Surely there are more . . . *suitable* people. Oh, and Mr. Baker?"

"Yes?"

"You have a stain on your shirt. That's unacceptable. One demerit. See that it doesn't happen again." Then he turned and followed Ms. Jenkins down the rows.

Linus held his breath until they reached Row B before he exhaled explosively. He would need to wash his shirt as soon as he got home if he had any hopes of getting the sweat stains out. He scrubbed a hand over his face, uncertain of how he was feeling. Vexed, to be sure. And most likely frightened.

At the desk next to him, Mr. Tremblay wasn't even trying to hide the fact he was craning his neck to see what was written on the page left by Ms. Jenkins. Linus snatched it away, careful not to crumple the edges.

"Had it coming, didn't you?" Mr. Tremblay asked, sounding far too cheerful at the prospect. "I wonder who my new desk neighbor will be."

Linus ignored him.

The green glow from his computer screen backlit the page, making the thick script of the words that much more ominous.

It read:

DEPARTMENT IN CHARGE OF MAGICAL YOUTH
MEMO FROM EXTREMELY UPPER MANGEMENT

CC: BEDELIA JENKINS

MR. LINUS BAKER IS TO REPORT TO THE OFFICES OF EXTREMELY UPPER MANAGEMENT AT NINE A.M. ON WEDNESDAY, SEPTEMBER 6.

ALONE.

And that was all.

"Oh dear," Linus whispered.

That afternoon, when the clock chimed five, the people around Linus began to shut down their computers and pull on their coats. They chatted as they filed out of the room. Not a single person said good night to Linus. If anything, most stared at him as they left. Those who had been too far away to hear what Ms. Jenkins had said were most likely filled in via speculative whispers around the water cooler. The rumors were probably wild and completely inaccurate, but since Linus didn't know why he'd been summoned, he couldn't argue with whatever was being said.

He waited until half past five before he, too, began to wrap up for the day. The room was mostly empty by then, though he could still see the light on in Ms. Jenkins's office at the far end. He was thankful he wouldn't have to pass by it as he left. He didn't think he could handle another face-to-face with her today.

Once his computer screen was dark, he stood and lifted his coat from the back of his chair. He pulled it on, groaning when he remembered he'd left his umbrella at home. From the sound of it, the rain still hadn't let up. If he hurried, he'd still be able to make the bus.

He only bumped into six desks in four different rows on his way out. But he made sure to put them back into their places.

It would have to be another salad for him tonight. No dressing.

He missed the bus.

He saw its taillights through the rain as it rumbled down the street, the advertisement on the back of a smiling woman saying SEE SOMETHING, SAY SOMETHING! REGISTRATION HELPS EVERY-ONE! still clear even through the rain.

"Of course," he muttered to himself.

There would be another one in fifteen minutes.

He held his briefcase above his head and waited.

He stepped off the bus (which had, of course, been ten minutes late) at the stop a few blocks from his house.

"It's a wet one out there," the driver told him.

"A fine observation," Linus replied as he stepped onto the sidewalk. "Really. Thank you for—"

The doors snapped shut behind him, and the bus pulled away. The back right tire hit a rather large puddle, splashing up and soaking Linus's slacks up to his knees.

Linus sighed and began to trudge his way home.

The neighborhood was quiet, the streetlamps lit and inviting, even in the cold rain. The houses were small, but the street was lined with trees covered in leaves that were beginning to change colors, the dull green fading to an even duller red and gold. There were rosebushes at 167 Lakewood that bloomed quietly. There was a dog at 193 Lakewood that yipped excitedly whenever it saw him. And 207 Lakewood had a tire swing hanging from a tree, but the children who lived there apparently thought they were far too old to use it anymore. Linus had never had a tire swing before. He'd always wanted one, but his mother had said it was far too dangerous.

He turned right down a smaller street, and there, sitting on the left, was 86 Hermes Way.

Home.

It wasn't much. It was tiny, and the back fence needed to be replaced. But it had a lovely porch where one could sit and watch the day pass by if one were so inclined. There were sunflowers in the flowerbed at the front, tall things that swayed in the cool breeze, though they were closed now against the coming evening and dreary rain. It'd been raining for weeks on end, mostly an uncomfortable drizzle interspersed with a tedious downpour.

It wasn't much. But it belonged to Linus and no one else.

He stopped at the mailbox out front and grabbed the day's mail. It looked as if it were all advertisements addressed impersonally to RESIDENT. Linus couldn't remember the last time he'd received a letter.

He climbed up onto the porch and was uselessly shaking the water from his coat when his name was called from the house next door. He sighed, wondering if he could get away with pretending he hadn't heard.

"Don't you even think about it, Mr. Baker," she said.

"I don't know what you mean, Mrs. Klapper."

Edith Klapper, a woman of an undiscernible age (though he thought she'd gone past *old* into the fabled land of *ancient*) sat on her porch in her terry cloth bathrobe, pipe lit in her hand as it usually was, smoke curling up around her bouffant. She hacked a wet cough into a tissue that probably should have been discarded an hour before. "Your cat was in my yard again, chasing the squirrels. You know how I feel about that."

"Calliope does what she wants," he reminded her. "I have no control over her."

"Perhaps you should *try*," Mrs. Klapper snapped at him.

"Right. I'll get on that immediately."

"Are you sassing me, Mr. Baker?"

"I wouldn't even dream of it." He dreamed of it often.

"I thought not. Are you in for the night?"

"Yes, Mrs. Klapper."

"No dates again, huh?"

His hand tightened around the handle of his briefcase. "No dates."

"No lucky lady friend?" She sucked on her pipe and blew the thick smoke out her nose. "Oh. Forgive me. It must have slipped my mind. Not one for the ladies, are you?"

It hadn't slipped her mind. "No, Mrs. Klapper."

"My grandson is an accountant. Very stable. Mostly. He does have a tendency toward rampant alcoholism, but who am I to judge his vices? Accounting is hard work. All those numbers. I'll have him call you."

"I'd prefer if you didn't."

She cackled. "Too good for him, then?"

Linus spluttered. "I don't—I'm not—I don't have *time* for such things."

Mrs. Klapper scoffed. "Perhaps you should consider making time, Mr. Baker. Being alone at your age isn't healthy. I'd hate to think of what would happen if you were to blow your brains out. It'd hurt the resale value of the whole neighborhood."

"I'm not depressed!"

She looked him up and down. "You aren't? Why on earth not?"

"Is there anything else, Mrs. Klapper?" Linus asked through gritted teeth.

She waved a hand dismissively at him. "Fine, then. Go. Put on your pajamas and that old record player of yours and dance around the living room as you do."

"I *asked* you to stop watching me through my window!"

"Of course you did," she said. She sat back in her chair and stuck her pipe between her lips. "Of course you did."

"Good night, Mrs. Klapper," he called as he slid the key into the doorknob.

He didn't wait for a response. He shut the door behind him and locked it tight.

Calliope, a thing of evil, sat on the edge of his bed, black tail twitching as she watched him with bright green eyes. She started purring. In most cats, it would be a soothing sound. In Calliope, it indicated devious plotting involving nefarious deeds.

"You aren't supposed to be in the yard next door," he scolded her as he slid out of his suit coat.

She continued purring.

He'd found her one day almost ten years back, a tiny kitten under his porch, screeching as if her tail were on fire. Thankfully, it wasn't, but as soon as he'd crawled underneath the porch, she'd hissed at him, black hair on her back standing on end as she arched. Rather than waiting to get a face filled with kitten scratch fever, he'd backed quickly out and returned to his house, deciding that if he ignored her long enough, she'd move on.

She hadn't.

Instead, she spent most of that night yowling. He'd tried to sleep. She was too loud. He pulled the pillow over his head. It didn't help. Eventually, he grabbed a flashlight and a broom, bent on poking the cat until she left. She was waiting for him on the porch, sitting in front of the door. He was so surprised, he dropped the broom.

She walked into his house as if she belonged.

And she never left, no matter how many times Linus had threatened her.

Six months later, he'd finally given up. By then, the house was filled with toys and a litter box and little dishes with CALLIOPE printed on the sides for her food and water. He couldn't quite be sure how it'd happened, but there it was.

"Mrs. Klapper will get you one day," he told her as he slid out of his wet clothes. "And I won't be here to save you. You'll be feasting on a squirrel, and she'll . . . Okay, I don't know what she'll do. But it'll be *something*. And I won't feel sad in the slightest."

She blinked slowly.

He sighed. "Fine. A little sad."

He put on his pajamas, buttoning up the front. They were monogrammed with an *LB* on the breast, a gift from the Department after fifteen years of service. He'd selected them out of a catalogue he'd been given on the day of. The catalogue had two pages inside. One page was the pajamas. The second page was a candleholder.

He'd selected the pajamas. He'd always wanted to own something monogrammed.

He picked up the wet clothes and left the room. The loud thump behind him told him he was being followed.

He dropped his soiled work garments in the washing machine and set it to soak while he made dinner.

"I don't need an accountant," he told Calliope as she wound between his legs. "I have other things to think about. Like tomorrow. Why is it that I must always worry about tomorrows?"

He moved instinctively to the old Victrola. He flipped through the records sitting in the drawer underneath before finding the one he wanted. He slid it out of its sleeve and set it on the turntable before bringing down the needle.

Soon, the Everly Brothers began to sing that all they had to do was dream.

He swayed back and forth as he headed toward the kitchen.

Dry food for Calliope.

Salad from a bag for Linus.

He cheated, but just a little.

A splash of dressing never hurt anyone.

"Whenever I want you," he sang quietly. "All I have to do is dream."

If one were to ask if Linus Baker was lonely, he would have scrunched up his face in surprise. The thought would be foreign, almost shocking. And though the smallest of lies hurt his head and made his stomach twist, there was a chance he would still say no, even though he was, and almost desperately so.

And maybe part of him would believe it. He'd accepted long ago that some people, no matter how good their heart was or how much love they had to give, would always be alone. It was their lot in life, and Linus had figured out, at the age of twenty-seven, that it seemed to be that way for him.

Oh, there was no specific event that brought along this line of thinking. It was just that he felt . . . dimmer than others. Like he was faded in a crystal-clear world. He wasn't meant to be seen.

He'd accepted it back then, and now he was forty with high blood pressure and a spare tire around his middle. Sure, there were times when he'd stare at himself in the mirror, wondering if he could see what others could not. He was pale. His dark hair was kept short and neat, though it seemed to be thinning on the top. He had lines around his mouth and eyes. His cheeks were full. The spare tire looked as if it'd fit on a scooter, though if he weren't careful, it'd turn into one that belonged on a lorry. He looked . . . well.

He looked like most everyone else by the time they reached forty.

As he ate his salad with a drop or two of dressing in his tiny kitchen in his tiny house while the Everly brothers began to ask for Little Susie to wake up, wake up, Little Susie, worrying about what tomorrow would bring with Extremely Upper Management, the thought of being lonely didn't even cross Linus Baker's mind.

After all, there were people with far less than what he had. There was a roof over his head and rabbit food in his belly, and his pajamas were monogrammed.

Besides, it was neither here nor there.

He didn't have time to sit in silence and think such frivolous thoughts. Sometimes, silence was the loudest thing of all. And that would not do.

Instead of allowing his thoughts to wander, he lifted the copy he kept at home of *RULES AND REGULATIONS* (all 947 pages of it, purchased for nearly two hundred dollars; he had a copy at work, but it seemed right to have one for his house as well), and began to read the tiny print. Whatever tomorrow would bring, it was best to be prepared.

THREE

The next morning, he was early to the office by nearly two hours. No one else had yet arrived, most likely still tucked away safely in their beds without a care in the world.

He went to his desk, sat down, and turned on his computer. The familiar green light did nothing to comfort him.

He tried to get as much work done as he could, constantly aware of the clock above ticking by each and every second.

The room began to fill at a quarter till eight. Ms. Jenkins arrived at precisely eight o'clock, heels clicking on the floor. Linus slunk down in his seat, but he could feel her eyes on him.

He tried to work. He really did. The green words were a blur on the screen in front of him. Even the *RULES AND REGULATIONS* couldn't calm him down.

At exactly eight forty-five, he stood from his chair.

The people in the desks around him turned and stared.

He ignored them, swallowing thickly as he picked up his briefcase and walked down the rows.

"Sorry," he muttered with every desk he bumped into. "Apologies. So sorry. Is it just me or are the desks getting closer together? Sorry. So sorry."

Ms. Jenkins stood in the doorway to her office as he left the room, Gunther beside her, scratching his long pencil on the clipboard.

The offices of Extremely Upper Management were located on the fifth floor of the Department in Charge of Magical Youth. He'd heard rumors about the fifth floor, most of them downright alarming. He'd never been there himself, but he assumed that at least *some* of the rumors had to be true.

He was alone in the elevator as he pressed a button he never expected to.

The bright gold five.

The elevator started to rise. The pit of Linus's stomach seemed to stay in the basement. It was the longest elevator ride of Linus's life, lasting at least two minutes. It didn't help that it stopped on the first floor, opened, and began to fill with people. They asked for two and three and four, but nobody ever asked for five.

A handful got off on the second floor. Even more at the third. And it was at the fourth that the remaining exited. They glanced back at him curiously. He tried to smile but was sure it came off as more of a grimace.

He was alone when the elevator began to rise again.

By the time the doors opened on the fifth floor, he was sweating.

It certainly didn't help that the elevator opened to a long, cold hallway, the floor made of stone tile, the gold sconces on the wall casting low light. At one end of the hall was the bank of elevators where he stood. At the other end was a shuttered pane of glass next to a pair of large wooden doors. Above them was a metal sign:

EXTREMELY UPPER MANAGEMENT
BY APPOINTMENT ONLY

"Okay, old boy," he whispered. "You can do this."

His feet didn't get the message. They remained firmly stuck to the floor.

The elevator doors began to shut. He let them. The elevator didn't move.

At that moment, Linus gave very real thought to going back to the first floor, exiting the DICOMY building, and perhaps walking until he could walk no longer, just to see where he ended up.

That sounded good.

Instead, he pressed the five again.

The doors opened.

He coughed. It echoed down the hallway.

"No time for cowardice," he scolded himself quietly. "Chin up. For all you know, maybe it's a promotion. A *big* promotion. One with higher pay and you'll finally be able to go on that vacation you've always dreamed about. The sand on the beach. The blue of the ocean. Don't you wish you were there?"

He did. He wished it greatly.

Linus began to walk down the hallway slowly. Rain lashed against the windows to his left. The lights in the sconces to his right flickered slightly. His loafers squeaked on the floor. He pulled at his tie.

By the time he reached the opposite end of the hallway, four minutes had passed. According to his watch, it was five till nine.

He tried the doors.

They were locked.

The window at the side of the doors had a metal grate pulled down on the inside. There was a metal plate next to it, with a small button on the side.

He debated briefly before pressing the button. A loud buzzer sounded on the other side of the metal grate. He waited.

He could see his reflection in the window. The person staring back at him looked wide-eyed and shocked. He hastily smoothed down his hair from where it had started sticking up on the side as it always did. It didn't do much. He straightened his tie, squared his shoulders, sucked in his belly.

The metal grate slid up.

On the other side was a bored-looking young woman snapping gum behind her bright red lips. She blew a pink bubble, and it popped before she sucked it back into her mouth. She cocked her head, blond curls bouncing on her shoulders. "Help you?" she asked.

He tried to speak, but no sound came out. He cleared his throat and tried again. "Yes. I have an appointment at nine."

"With whom?"

That was an interesting question, one that he didn't have an answer to. "I . . . don't quite know."

Ms. Bubblegum stared at him. "You have an appointment, but you don't know with whom?"

That sounded about right. "Yes?"

"Name?"

"Linus Baker."

"Cute," she said, tapping perfectly manicured fingernails against the keyboard. "Linus Baker. Linus Baker. Linus—" Her eyes widened. "Oh. I see. Hold one moment, please."

She slammed the metal grate down again. Linus blinked, unsure of what he was supposed to do. He waited.

A minute passed.

And then another.

And then another.

And then—

The metal grate slid back up. Ms. Bubblegum looked far more interested in him now. She leaned forward until her face was almost pressed against the glass separating them. Her breath caused the window to fog up slightly. "They're waiting for you."

Linus took a step back. "Who is?"

"All of them," she said as she looked him up and down. "All of Extremely Upper Management."

"Oh," Linus said weakly. "How delightful. And we're sure it's me they want?"

"You *are* Linus Baker, aren't you?"

He hoped so, because he didn't know how to be anyone else. "I am."

Another buzzer sounded, and he heard a click from the doors next to him. They swung open on silent hinges. "Then yes, Mr. Baker," she told him, cheek bulging slightly from her gum. "It's you they want. And I would hurry, if I were you. Extremely Upper Management doesn't like to be kept waiting."

"Right," he said. "How do I look?" He sucked in his stomach a little farther.

"Like you have no idea what you're doing," she said before she slammed down the metal grate again.

Linus glanced back longingly at the elevators at the other end of the hall.

Don't you wish you were here? they asked him.

He did. Very much so.

He stepped away from the window toward the open doors.

Inside was a circular room with a rotunda overhead made of glass. There was a fountain in the center of the room, a stone statue of a man in a cloak, water spilling in a continuous stream from his outstretched hands. He was looking toward the ceiling with cold, gray eyes. Around him, clutching at his legs, were little stone children, water splashing on the tops of their heads.

A door opened to Linus's right. Ms. Bubblegum stepped out from her booth. She smoothed down her dress, snapping her gum loudly. "You're shorter than you look through glass," she told him.

Linus didn't know how to respond to that, so he said nothing at all.

She sighed. "Follow me, please." She moved like a bird, her

steps tiny and quick. She was halfway across the room before she looked back at him. "That wasn't a suggestion."

"Right," Linus said, nearly tripping over his own feet as he hurried to catch up with her. "Apologies. I've . . . I've never been here before."

"Obviously."

He thought he was being insulted, but he couldn't figure out how. "Are they . . . *all* of them?"

"Odd, isn't it?" She blew another bubble, which popped daintily. "And for you, of all people. I didn't know you existed until this moment."

"I get that a lot."

"I can't imagine why."

Yes, definitely insulted. "What are they like? I've only seen them when they serve me lumpy potatoes."

Ms. Bubblegum stopped abruptly and turned to look back at him over her shoulder. Linus thought she could probably spin her head all the way around if she put her mind to it. "Lumpy potatoes."

"For the holiday luncheon?"

"I make those potatoes. From *scratch*."

Linus blanched. "Well, I—it's a matter of taste—I'm sure you—"

Ms. Bubblegum harrumphed and moved forward again.

Linus wasn't off to a good start.

They reached another door on the other side of the rotunda. It was black with a gold nameplate fastened near the top. The plate was blank. Ms. Bubblegum reached up and tapped a fingernail against the door three times.

There was a beat, and then another, and then—

The door swung open slowly.

It was dark inside.

Pitch-black, even.

Ms. Bubblegum stepped to the side as she turned to face him. "After you."

He peered into the darkness. "Hmm, well, perhaps we could reschedule. I'm very busy, as I'm sure you know. I have many reports to complete—"

"Enter, Mr. Baker," a voice boomed through the open doorway.

Ms. Bubblegum smiled.

Linus reached up and wiped his brow. He almost dropped his briefcase. "I suppose I shall enter, then."

"Looks like," Ms. Bubblegum said.

And he did just that.

He should have been expecting the door to slam shut behind him, but he was still startled, nearly jumping out of his skin. He held his briefcase against his chest as if it could protect him. It was disorienting being in the dark, and he was sure this was a trap, and he would spend the rest of his days wandering around sightlessly. It would almost be as bad as getting sacked.

But then lights began to shine at his feet, illuminating a pathway before him. They were soft and yellow, like a brick road. He took a tentative step away from the door. When he didn't trip over anything, he took another.

The lights led him much farther than he expected, before forming a circle at his feet. He stopped, unsure of where he was supposed to go. He hoped he wouldn't need to flee anything terrible.

Another light, this one much brighter, flicked on overhead. Linus looked up, squinting against it. It looked like a spotlight, shining down on him.

"You may set down your briefcase," a deep voice said from somewhere above him.

"That's quite all right," Linus said, clutching it tightly.

Then, as if a switch had been flipped, more lights began to glow above him, shining up into the faces of four people that Linus recognized as Extremely Upper Management. They were seated far above Linus at the top of a large stone wall, peering down from their perches with varying expressions of interest.

There were three men and one woman, and though Linus had learned their names early on in his career at DICOMY, for the life of him, he couldn't remember them presently. His mind had come to the decision that it was experiencing technical difficulties and was broadcasting nothing but fuzzy snow.

He looked at each of them, beginning left to right, nodding as he did so while trying to keep his expression neutral.

The woman's hair was cut into a petite bob, and she wore a large brooch in the shape of a beetle, the carapace iridescent.

One of the men was balding, his jowls hanging off his face. He sniffled into a kerchief, clearing his throat of what sounded like quite a bit of phlegm.

The second man was rail thin. Linus thought he would disappear if he turned sideways. He wore spectacles far too large for his face, the lenses shaped like half-moons.

The last man was younger than the others, possibly around Linus's age, though it was hard to tell. His hair was wavy, and he was intimidatingly handsome. Linus recognized him almost immediately as the one who always served the dried-out ham with a smile.

He was the one who spoke first. "Thank you for taking this meeting, Mr. Baker."

Linus's mouth felt dry. He licked his lips. "You're . . . welcome?"

The woman leaned forward. "Your personnel file says you've been employed in the Department for seventeen years."

"Yes, ma'am."

"And in all that time, you've maintained your current position."

"Yes, ma'am."

"Why is that?"

Because he had no prospects for anything else and no desire for Supervision. "I enjoy the work I do."

"Do you?" she asked, cocking her head.

"Yes."

"Why?"

"I'm a caseworker," he said, fingers slipping slightly on his briefcase. "I don't know that there is a more important position." His eyes widened. "Other than what you do, of course. I wouldn't presume to think—"

The bespectacled man shuffled through papers in front of him. "I have here your last six reports, Mr. Baker. Do you want to know what I see?"

No, Linus didn't. "Please."

"I see someone who is very thorough. No nonsense. Clinical to a startling degree."

Linus wasn't sure if that was a compliment or not. It certainly didn't sound like one. "A caseworker must maintain a degree of separation," he recited dutifully.

Jowls sniffled. "Is that so? Where is that from? It sounds familiar."

"It's from *RULES AND REGULATIONS*," Handsome said. "And I should hope you recognize it. You wrote most of it."

Jowls blew his nose into his kerchief. "Indeed. I knew that."

"Why is it important to maintain a degree of separation?" the woman asked, still staring down at him.

"Because it wouldn't do to get attached to the children I work with," Linus said. "I'm there to make sure the orphanages I inspect are kept in tip-top shape, and nothing more. Their welfare is important, but as a whole. Individual interaction is frowned upon. It could color my perception."

"But you do interview the children," Handsome said.

"Yes," Linus agreed. "I do. But one can be professional while dealing with magical youth."

"Have you ever recommended the closing of an orphanage in your seventeen years, Mr. Baker?" the bespectacled man asked.

They had to already know the answer. "Yes. Five times."

"Why?"

"The environments weren't safe."

"So, you do care."

Linus was getting flustered. "I never said I didn't. I merely do what is required of me. There's a difference between forming attachments and being empathetic. These children . . . They have no one else. It's the reason they're in the orphanages to begin with. They shouldn't have to lay their heads down at night with an empty stomach, or worry about being worked to the bone. Just because these orphans must be kept separate from normal children doesn't mean they should be treated any differently. All children, no matter their . . . disposition or what they're capable of, must be protected regardless of the cost."

Jowls coughed wetly. "Do you really think so?"

"Yes."

"And what became of the children in the orphanages you closed?"

Linus blinked. "That's a matter for Supervision. I make my recommendation, and the Supervisor handles what comes next. Most likely they're placed in the schools that DICOMY runs."

Handsome sat back in his chair. He looked at the others around him. "He's perfect."

"I agree," Jowls said. "There's really no other choice for something so . . . sensitive."

The bespectacled man stared down at Linus. "Do you understand discretion, Mr. Baker?"

Linus felt insulted. "I work with classified youth on a daily basis," he retorted, more sharply than he intended. "I'm a vault. Nothing gets out."

"And it appears nothing gets in," the woman said. "He'll do."

"Forgive me, but might I ask what *exactly* you're talking about? I'll do for *what*?"

Handsome rubbed a hand over his face. "What is said next doesn't leave this room, Mr. Baker. Do you understand? This is classified level four."

Linus took in a stuttering breath. Classified level four was the highest classification. He'd known it existed in theory, but was unaware that it was actually in use. He'd only had a classified level three case once before, and it been most troubling. There'd been a girl in an orphanage who had turned out to be a banshee, a herald of death. DICOMY had been summoned once she started telling all of the other children they were going to die. The problem turned out to be, of course, that she'd been right. The master of the orphanage had decided to use the children as part of a pagan sacrifice. Linus had barely escaped with the children and his life. He'd been given a two-day vacation after that one, the most time off he'd had in years.

"Why me?" he asked, voice barely above a whisper.

"Because there's really no one else we can trust," the woman said simply.

That should have filled Linus with a sense of pride. Instead, he felt nothing but dread curling in his stomach.

"Think of this as more of a checkup," the bespectacled man said. "We haven't received word of any wrongdoing, but the orphanage you'll be going to is . . . It's special, Mr. Baker. The orphanage is nontraditional, and the six children who live there are different than anything else you've seen before, some more than others. They're . . . problematic."

"Problematic? What's that supposed to—"

"Your job will be to make sure everything is on the up-and-up," Handsome said, a small smile on his face. "It's important, you see. The master of this specific orphanage, one Arthur Parnassus, is certainly qualified, but we have . . . concerns. The six children are of the more extreme variety, and we must make sure that Mr. Parnassus continues to be capable of managing them. One would be a handful, but six of them?"

Linus wracked his brain. He was sure he'd heard of *all* of the masters in the region, but—"I've never heard of Mr. Parnassus."

"No, I don't suppose you have," the woman said. "But that's

why it's classified level four. If you had, it would mean we had a leak. We don't do well with leaks, Mr. Baker. Is that understood? Leaks need to be plugged. Swiftly."

"Yes, yes," he said hastily. "Of course. I would never—"

"Of course you wouldn't," Jowls said. "It's part of the reason why you were chosen. One month, Mr. Baker. You will spend one month on the island where the orphanage is located. We will expect weekly reports. Anything that raises alarms must be reported immediately."

Linus felt his eyes bulge. "A *month*? I can't leave for a *month*. I have duties!"

"Your current caseload will be reassigned," the bespectacled man said. "In fact, it's already being done." He flipped to another paper. "And it says here you are quite alone. No spouse. No children. No one to miss you if you had to leave for any extended length of time."

That stung more than it should have. He was aware of such things, of course, but to have them so blatantly laid bare caused his heart to stutter. But still—"I have a cat!"

Handsome snorted. "Cats are solitary creatures, Mr. Baker. I'm sure it won't even know you're gone."

"Your reports will be directed to Extremely Upper Management," the woman said. "They will be overseen by Mr. Werner, though we will all be involved." She nodded toward Handsome. "And we expect them to be as thorough as the ones you've done in the past. In fact, we insist upon it. More so, if you deem necessary."

"Ms. Jenkins—"

"Will be informed of your special assignment," Handsome—Mr. Werner—assured him. "Though the details will be kept at a minimum. Think of this as a promotion, Mr. Baker. One that I believe is a long time in coming."

"Don't I have a say in this?"

"Think of this as a *mandatory* promotion," Mr. Werner corrected. "We expect big things from you. And who knows where this could lead for you if it all goes well? Please don't let us down. Now, feel free to take the rest of the day to get your affairs in order. Your train leaves tomorrow, bright and early. Do you have any questions?"

Dozens. He had *dozens* of questions. "Yes! What about—"

"Excellent," Mr. Werner said, clapping his hands. "I knew we could count on you, Mr. Baker. We look forward to hearing from you about the state of affairs on the island. It should be interesting, to say the least. Now, all this blathering on has left my throat parched. I do think it's time for tea. Our secretary will show you out. It was lovely to meet you."

Extremely Upper Management stood as one, bowed down at him, and then all the lights went out.

Linus squeaked. Before he could begin to fumble in the dark, a light switched back on at the top of the wall. He blinked up at it. Mr. Werner stared down at him, a curious expression on his face. The others were already gone.

"Something else?" Linus asked nervously.

Mr. Werner said, "Beware, Mr. Baker."

That was certainly ominous. "Beware?"

Mr. Werner nodded. "You must prepare yourself. I cannot stress enough how important this assignment is. Leave no detail out, no matter how small or inconsequential it may seem."

Linus bristled. It was one thing to question his readiness, but it was something else entirely to question the thoroughness of his reports. "I always—"

"Let's just say I have a vested interest in what you find," Mr. Werner said, ignoring Linus's spluttering indignation. "It goes beyond mere inquisitiveness." He smiled, though it didn't quite reach his eyes. "I don't like being disappointed, Mr. Baker. Please don't disappoint me."

"Why this place?" he asked rather helplessly. "What brought this orphanage to your attention and requires the oversight of a caseworker? Has the master done something to—"

"It's rather what he *hasn't* done," Mr. Werner said. "His monthly reports are . . . lacking, especially in the face of who his charges are. We need to know more, Mr. Baker. Order only works if there is complete transparency. If we can't have that, then we run the risk of chaos. Is there anything else?"

"What? *Yes*. I've—"

"Good," Mr. Werner said. "I wish you luck. I think you'll need it."

And with that, the light went out yet again.

"Oh dear," Linus said.

The golden lights on the floor lit up once more.

"Are you quite finished?" a voice said near his ear.

He absolutely did not scream, no matter the evidence to the contrary.

Ms. Bubblegum stood behind him, gum snapping. "This way, Mr. Baker." She spun around, dress flaring at her knees, and marched toward the exit.

Linus followed her quickly, only glancing over his shoulder once into the darkness.

She waited for him just outside the chambers, tapping her foot with impatience. Linus was quite out of breath by the time he passed through the open door. He couldn't be sure what had just happened was anything more than a fever dream. He certainly *felt* feverish. It was possible Ms. Bubblegum was a hallucination conjured up by a previously undiagnosed illness.

A very *pushy* hallucination, to be sure, as she thrust a thick folder into his hands, causing him to fumble and almost drop his briefcase. "Train ticket is inside," she said. "In addition, you'll find a sealed envelope with the files you'll be needing. I don't know what it's about, and I don't care. I'm paid *not* to snoop, if you can believe that. You're not to open the envelope until you've stepped off the train at your final destination."

"I think I need to sit down," Linus said weakly.

She squinted at him. "Of course you can sit down. Just make sure you do it far away from here. Your train leaves at seven tomorrow morning. Don't be late. Extremely Upper Management will be most displeased if you're late."

"I need to go back down to my desk, and—"

"Absolutely not, Mr. Baker. I have been instructed to tell you that you are to exit the premises without delay. Speak to no one. I don't think that should be a problem for you, but it had to be said."

"I have no idea what's going on," he said. "I'm not even sure if I'm *here*."

"Yes," Ms. Bubblegum said sympathetically. "Sounds like quite the existential crisis. Perhaps consider having it somewhere else."

They were standing in front of the elevators. He hadn't even known they were moving. The doors slid open in front of him. Ms. Bubblegum shoved him in, and reached in to hit the button for the first floor. She stepped out of the elevator. "Thank you for visiting the offices of Extremely Upper Management," she said cheerfully. "Have a fantastical day."

The doors slid shut before he could speak another word.

It was still raining. He barely even noticed.

One moment, he was standing in front of the Department in Charge of Magical Youth, and the next, he was on the stone path that led to his porch.

He didn't know how he'd gotten there, but that seemed to be the least of his worries.

He was startled out of his daze when Mrs. Klapper called over to him. "You're home early, Mr. Baker. Did you get sacked? Or perhaps you received terrible medical news and need time to reconcile with your bleak future?" Smoke curled up around her bouffant from her pipe. "I'm so sorry to hear that. You'll be missed terribly."

"Not dying," he managed to say.

"Oh. More's the pity, I suppose. So that only leaves getting sacked. You poor dear. How will you go on? Especially in this economy. I suppose you'll have to sell your house and find a dismal apartment somewhere in the city." She shook her head. "You'll probably end up murdered. Crime is on the rise, you know."

"I didn't get sacked!"

She snorted. "I don't believe you."

Linus sputtered.

She sat forward on her rocker. "You know, my grandson is looking for a personal secretary at his accounting firm. This could be your in, Mr. Baker. I do believe I've read stories that started *exactly* like that. Think about it. Your life is at its lowest this very moment, and you need to start fresh, which leads you to finding your true love. It practically writes itself!"

"Good day, Mrs. Klapper!" Linus cried as he stumbled up his steps.

"Think about it!" she shouted after him. "If all goes well, we could be *family*—"

He slammed the door shut behind him.

Calliope sat in her usual spot, tail twitching, seemingly un-surprised at his early return.

Linus slumped against the door. His legs gave out, and he slid to the carpet.

"You know," he told her, "I don't know if I had a very good day. No, I don't think I had a good day at all."

Calliope, as was her wont, only purred.

They stayed that way for a long time.

FOUR

The train car emptied as it went into the country. People getting on and off stared with open curiosity at the somewhat schlumpy man sitting in seat 6A, a large plastic crate on the empty seat next to him. Inside, a large cat glared balefully out at anyone who bent over to coo at it. One child nearly lost a finger when he tried to stick it in between the slats of the crate.

The man, one Linus Baker of 86 Hermes Way, barely noticed.

He hadn't slept well the night before, tossing and turning in his bed before finally giving up and deciding his time was better spent pacing back and forth in the sitting room. His luggage, an old, scuffed bag with a broken wheel, sat near the door, mocking him. He'd packed it before attempting to sleep, sure he wouldn't have time in the morning.

As it turned out, he had all the time in the world, seeing as how sleep remained elusive.

By the time he boarded the train at half past six, he was in a daze, the bags under his eyes pronounced, his mouth curled down. He stared straight ahead, one hand resting atop the crate where Calliope fumed. She'd never done well with travel, but he didn't have a choice in the matter. He'd considered asking Mrs. Klapper to take care of her in his absence, but the squirrel debacle had most likely soured any chance of Calliope making it through the month unharmed.

He hoped none of the children were allergic.

Rain sluiced down the windows as the train chugged along through empty fields and forests with great, old trees. He'd been on the train for almost eight hours when he realized it was quiet.

Too quiet.

He looked up from the *RULES AND REGULATIONS* he'd brought from home.

He was the only one left in the train car.

He hadn't noticed when the last person had left.

"Huh," he said to himself. "Wouldn't that just beat all if I missed my stop? I wonder how far the train goes. Maybe it goes on and on, never reaching the end."

Calliope had no opinion of it one way or another.

He was about to start worrying that he *had* in fact missed his stop (Linus was nothing if not a consummate worrier), when an attendant in a snappy uniform slid open a door at the end of the car. He was humming to himself quietly, but it was cut off when he noticed Linus. "Hello," he said amiably. "I didn't expect anyone else to be here! Must be going a long way on this fine Saturday."

"I have my ticket," Linus said. "If you need to see it."

"If you please. Where are you headed?"

For a moment, Linus couldn't think. He reached into his coat for his ticket, the large tome in his lap almost falling to the floor. The ticket was slightly crumpled, and he attempted to smooth it out before handing it over. The attendant smiled at him before looking down at the ticket. He whistled lowly. "Marsyas. End of the line." He punched it with his clicker. "Well, good news, then. Two more stops and you're there. In fact, if you— Ah yes, look." He gestured toward the window.

Linus turned his head, and his breath caught in his throat.

It was as if the rain clouds had reached as far as they could.

The gray darkness gave way to a bright and wonderful blue like Linus had never seen before. The rain stopped as they passed out of the storm and into the sun. He closed his eyes briefly, feeling the warmth through the glass against his face. He couldn't remember the last time he'd felt sunlight. He opened his eyes again, and that's when he saw it, in the distance.

There was green. Bright and beautiful greens of waving grass, and what appeared to be flowers in pinks and purples and golds. They disappeared into white sand. And beyond the white was cerulean.

He barely noticed when the *RULES AND REGULATIONS* fell to the floor of the train with a loud thump.

Don't you wish you were here?

"Is that the ocean?" Linus whispered.

"It is," the attendant said. "Quite the sight, isn't it? Though, you act like you've never— Say, have you never *seen* the ocean before?"

Linus shook his head minutely. "Only in pictures. It's so much bigger than I thought it'd be."

The attendant laughed. "And that's only a small portion of it. I reckon you'll see a bit more when you depart the train. There's an island near the village. Takes a ferry to get to it, if you're so inclined. Most aren't."

"I am," Linus said, still staring at the glimpses of the sea.

"And who do we have here?" the attendant asked, bending over Linus toward the crate.

Calliope hissed.

The attendant stood quickly. "I think I'll leave her be."

"Probably for the best."

"Two more stops, sir," the attendant said, heading for the door at the opposite end of the train car. "Enjoy your visit!"

Linus barely heard him leave.

"It's really there," he said quietly. "It's really, really there.

I never thought—" He sighed. "Maybe this won't be so bad after all."

It wasn't bad.

It was worse.

But Linus didn't know that right away. The moment he stepped off the train, crate in one hand, luggage in the other, he smelled salt in the air and heard the call of sea birds overhead. A breeze ruffled his hair, and he turned his face toward the sun. He let himself breathe for a moment, basking in the warmth. It wasn't until the bell on the train rang out and it started chugging away that he looked around.

He stood on a raised platform. There were metal benches in front of him under an overhang. The overhang was painted in blue-and-white stripes. Along the edges of the platform and stretching as far as he could see was beach grass growing atop dunes of sand. He heard what sounded like waves crashing in the distance. He'd never seen anything looking so bright. It was as if this place had never seen a rain cloud.

The train disappeared around a corner, and Linus Baker realized he was completely alone. There was a small cobbled road that disappeared between the dunes, but Linus couldn't see where it led to. He hoped he wouldn't have to walk along it, not while carrying his luggage and an angry cat.

"What should we do?" he wondered aloud.

No one responded, which was probably for the best. If someone *had* responded, he probably would have—

A loud ringing noise startled him from this thoughts. He jerked his head.

There, hanging on the side of the train platform, was a bright orange phone.

"Should I answer it?" he asked Calliope, tilting his head toward the front of the crate.

Calliope turned around completely, presenting him with her rump.

He figured that was the best he was going to get.

He left his luggage where it was and walked toward the phone. He set the crate down in the shade. He stared at the ringing phone for a moment before steeling himself and picking it up.

"Hello?"

"Ah, finally," a voice said in response. "You're late."

"I am?"

"Yes. I've called four times in the last hour. Since I couldn't be sure you'd actually arrive, I didn't want to make the trip off the island until I was sure you'd be there."

"You're calling for Linus Baker, correct?"

She snorted. "Who else would I be calling for?"

He felt relieved. "I'm Linus Baker."

"Bully for you."

Linus frowned. "Pardon?"

"I'll be there in an hour, Mr. Baker." He heard a whispering in the background. "I'm told you have an envelope you need to open now that you've arrived. It would be best if you did so. Things will make more sense if you do."

"How did you know about—"

"Toodle-oo, Mr. Baker. I'll see you shortly."

The line cut off, and he was left with a dial tone.

He stared at the handset before hanging it back where it belonged. He stared at it for a moment more before shaking his head.

"Now, then," he said to Calliope as he sat on the bench with a huff. He pulled his suitcase toward him. "Let's see what all the secrecy is about, shall we?"

Calliope ignored him.

He unzipped his bag enough for him to reach inside for the envelope he'd placed on top. It was thick, nearly bursting at the seams. The seal on the back was made of bloodred wax, the word

DICOMY stamped into it. He broke the seal, the wax crumbling onto his lap and bouncing to the ground.

He pulled out the bundle of papers, held together by a leather strap.

On the top was a letter addressed to him, typed neatly and cleanly.

DEPARTMENT IN CHARGE OF MAGICAL YOUTH
OFFICES OF EXTREMELY UPPER MANAGEMENT

Mr. Baker,

You have been chosen for the most important of assignments. As a reminder, this is CLASSIFIED LEVEL FOUR. Any parties disseminating information to those who do not meet the required classification level will receive punishment beginning at immediate termination and up to incarceration for ten years.

Enclosed, you will find seven files.

Six belong to the children at the Marsyas Island Orphanage.

The seventh belongs to Master Arthur Parnassus.

Under no circumstances should you share any of the contents of these files with the residents of the Marsyas Island Orphanage. They are for your eyes only.

This orphanage is different than all the others you've been to, Mr. Baker. It is important that you do your best to protect yourself. You will be staying at the guest house on the island, and we suggest locking all the doors and windows at night to avoid any . . . disturbances.

"Oh dear," Linus breathed.

Your work on Marsyas is important. Your reports will provide us with the necessary information to see if this orphanage can remain open, or if it needs to be shut permanently. Arthur Parnassus has been entrusted with a great responsibility, but it remains to be seen if that trust is still warranted. Eyes and ears open, Mr. Baker. Always. We expect the searing honesty you're known for. If anything appears out of order, you must bring it to our attention. There is nothing more important than ensuring things are on the up-and-up.

And also make sure the children are safe, of course. From each other, and themselves. One, in particular. His file is the first you'll see.

We look forward to your extraordinarily thorough reports.

Sincerely,

CHARLES WERNER
EXTREMELY UPPER MANAGEMENT

"What on earth have I gotten myself into now?" Linus whispered as another breeze ruffled the letter in his hand.

He read through the letter a second time, trying to read between the lines, but he was left with more questions than answers.

He folded the letter and put it in his breast pocket before looking at the files in his hand. "No time like the present, I suppose," he told Calliope. "Let's see how big of a secret this actually is. I'm sure this is all blown out of proportion. The higher your expectations, the greater the disappointment."

He flipped open the first file.

Attached to the top was a photograph of a young boy of perhaps six or seven years of age. He was smiling rather devilishly. He was missing his two front teeth, his hair was a mess, sticking up all over the place, and his eyes were—

Well. They looked as if they were suffering from red-eye effect, the flash happening too quickly for the pupils to react. There was a ring of blue around the red. It was certainly chilling, but

Linus had seen it many times before. Just a trick of the light. That's all it was.

Underneath the photograph, in blocky letters, was a name. LUCY.

"A boy named Lucy," Linus said. "That's certainly a first. I wonder why they chose . . . the name . . . Lucy . . ."

The last word came out choked.

There, written in clear English, was exactly the reason why. The file read:

NAME: LUCIFER (NICKNAME LUCY)
AGE: SIX YEARS, SIX MONTHS, SIX DAYS (AT TIME OF THIS REPORT)
HAIR: BLACK
EYE COLOR: BLUE/RED
MOTHER: UNKNOWN (BELIEVED DECEASED)
FATHER: THE DEVIL
SPECIES OF MAGICAL YOUTH: ANTICHRIST

Linus Baker fainted dead away.

"G'way," he muttered when he felt a tapping against his cheek. "S'not time for your breakfast, Calliope."

"That's good to know," a voice that obviously did not belong to Calliope said. "Seeing as how it's afternoon. Unless they breakfast late in the city. I wouldn't know. I tend to avoid such places. Too much noise for my taste."

Linus opened his eyes, blinking slowly.

A woman peered down at him, silhouetted by the sun.

Linus sat up quickly. "Where am I!"

The woman took a step back, a look of cool amusement on her face. "Marsyas Train Station, of course. An odd place for a nap, but I suppose it's as good a place as any."

Linus pushed himself off the floor of the platform. He felt gritty and out of sorts. There was an ache in his head, and he seemed to have accumulated quite a collection of sand on his backside. He brushed himself off as he looked around wildly. Calliope sat in her crate, tail twitching as she watched him warily. His luggage sat near her.

And there, on the bench he'd been sitting on, was a pile of folders.

"Is this all you've got?" the woman asked, and Linus turned his attention back to her. He was immediately concerned when he couldn't quite get a grasp on her age. Her hair sat like a white fluffy cloud atop her head. Bright flowers had been woven in. Her skin was dark and lovely, but it was her eyes that confused Linus the most. They were the eyes of someone far older than the rest of her appearance suggested. It must have been a trick of the bright sunlight, but they looked almost violet. He couldn't place why he thought her familiar.

She wore a thin wispy shirt that hung loosely on her frame. Her trousers were tan and ended mid-calf. Her feet were bare.

"Who are you?" he demanded.

"Ms. Chapelwhite, of course," she said, as if he should have known. "Caretaker of Marsyas Island."

"Caretaker," he repeated.

"Is that all the luggage you've brought?" she asked again.

"Yes, but—"

"To each his own," she said. He stood dumbfounded as she pushed by him, lifting his suitcase as if it were filled with nothing but feathers. He'd broken out in a sweat lugging it onto the train, but she seemed to have no such issue. "Gather your papers and your gigantic cat, Mr. Baker. I don't like to dillydally, and you're already later than I expected. I do have responsibilities, you know."

"Now see here," he began, but she ignored him, moving toward the stairs at the edge of the platform. She descended the stairs gracefully, as if she were walking on air. It was only then that he noticed a small car idling on the road. The roof appeared to have been sheared off, leaving the seats exposed. A convertible, though he'd never actually seen one in person.

He gave very real thought to grabbing Calliope and fleeing down the train tracks.

Instead, he gathered his files and lifted the crate, following after the strange woman.

She'd already placed his luggage in the trunk by the time he reached the car. She glanced at him, then down at the crate. "Don't suppose you'd be fine with putting that thing in the back?"

"Absolutely not," he said, moderately offended. "That's just cruel."

"Right," she muttered. "Fine. You'll have to carry it on your lap, then. Or we can fasten it to the hood, if you think that'd work better."

He was scandalized. "She would be so *angry.*"

Ms. Chapelwhite shrugged. "I'm sure she'd get over it."

"I'm not tying her to the hood of the car!"

"Your choice. Get in, Mr. Baker. We'll need to hurry. I told Merle we wouldn't be long."

Linus's head was spinning. "Merle?"

"The ferryman," she said, opening the door and climbing into the car. "He'll take us to the island."

"I haven't decided if I even *want* to go to the island."

She squinted up at him. "Then why are you here?"

He sputtered. "It was—I was told—this isn't—"

She reached to the dash of the car toward a pair of oversize white sunglasses. "Either get in or don't, Mr. Baker. Frankly, I would prefer if you didn't. The Department in Charge of Magical Youth is a farce, and you seem to be nothing but a clueless lackey. I'd have no problem leaving you here. I'm sure the train will be back at some point. It always is."

That rankled him more than he expected. "What I do is most certainly *not* a farce!"

The car turned over with a rumbling cough before the engine smoothed out. Black smoke curled from the tailpipe.

"That," Ms. Chapelwhite said, "remains to be seen. In or out, Mr. Baker."

He got in.

Ms. Chapelwhite seemed to get far too much enjoyment from the way Linus screamed when they took a corner at a high rate of speed. She handled the car deftly, but Linus was convinced he'd entered the vehicle of a madwoman.

The wind whipped through their hair, and Linus thought she'd lose the ornamental flowers, but they snapped and swayed and stayed put. He held the folders flat against the top of the crate, not wanting to lose them over the back of the car.

They drove on a narrow road through dunes that rose and fell. When the mountains of sand were at their lowest, he caught glimpses of the ocean, now much closer than it'd been from the train. Linus tried not to be distracted by the sight of it, but failed miserably. Even though he was sure he was about to die, it was still a wonder to behold.

It wasn't until he was slammed against the door after yet another corner that he found his voice again. "Would you *slow down*?"

And wonder of all wonders, she did as he asked. "Just having some fun."

"At my expense!"

She glanced over at him, hair bouncing around her head. "You're wound up awfully tight."

He bristled. "Wanting to live is not being *wound up*."

"Your tie is crooked."

"It is? Thank you. I hate it when I look disheveled—that's not funny."

He saw a flash of teeth through her smile. "Maybe there's hope for you, after all. Not much, but a little." She looked at him again, for longer than Linus felt was safe. "You don't look like I expected."

He didn't know what to do with that. He'd never really been *seen* before. "What's that supposed to mean?"

"That you look unexpected."

"Do you often speak without saying anything at all?"

"Quite often. But not this time, Mr. Baker." She took another corner at a much lower speed. "I thought you would be younger. Your type usually is."

"My type?"

"Caseworkers. Been doing it long?"

He frowned. "Long enough."

"And do you enjoy your work, Mr. Baker?"

"I'm good at it."

"That's not what I asked."

"It's the same thing."

She shook her head. "Why were you sleeping on the platform? Couldn't you have done that on the train?"

"I wasn't sleeping. I was—" It hit him, then, what he'd forgotten since he'd been rudely awoken. "Oh my."

"What?"

"Oh *my*." He couldn't catch his breath.

Ms. Chapelwhite looked alarmed. "Are you having a heart attack?"

He didn't know. He'd never had one before, and he couldn't be sure what they felt like. But given that he was forty years old with extra pounds and high blood pressure, that certainly seemed like a possibility.

"Damn," he heard her mutter as she jerked the car to the side of the road, slamming the brakes.

Linus struggled to breathe, putting his forehead on the top of the crate. His vision had narrowed to pinholes, and there was a roaring in his ears. He was sure he was about to pass out again (or possibly die from a heart attack), when he felt a cool hand press against the back of his neck. He managed to suck in a deep breath as his heart rate slowed.

"There," he heard Ms. Chapelwhite say. "That's better. Another breath, Mr. Baker. That's it."

"The file," he managed to say. "I read the file."

She squeezed the back of his neck once before letting go. "About Lucy?"

"Yes. I didn't expect it."

"No, I don't suppose you did."

"Is it . . ."

"True?"

He nodded, face still pressed against the crate.

She didn't respond.

He lifted his head, looking over at her.

She was staring straight ahead, hands in her lap. "Yes," she finally said. "It's true."

"How on earth is this possible?"

She shook her head. "It's not—*he's* not what you think. None of them are."

That startled him. "I didn't even look at the other files." A terrible thought struck him. "Are the others worse?"

She ripped off her sunglasses, looking at him sharply. "It can't be any worse because there's nothing wrong with any of them. They're children."

"Yes, but—"

"No buts," she snapped. "I know you have a job to do, Mr. Baker. And I know you probably do it well. *Too* well, if you ask me. You would have to in order for DICOMY to send you here. We're not exactly orthodox."

"I should say not. You have the *Antichrist* on the island."

"Lucy isn't—" She shook her head, obviously frustrated. "Why are you here?"

"To ensure the safety of the children," he said as if it were second nature. "To see that they are being provided for. Cared for. And that they aren't in danger, either from themselves or others."

"And that goes for *all* children, correct?"

"Yes, but—"

"No *buts*. It doesn't matter where he came from. Or what he is. He is a child, and your job, as much as it is mine or Arthur's, is to protect him. And all the others."

He gaped at her.

She slid her sunglasses back on. "Close your mouth, Mr. Baker. You don't want to swallow a bug."

She gunned the engine again and pulled back onto the road.

"Seven files," he said a few minutes later after coming out of his daze.

"What?"

"Seven files. I was given seven files. Six children. The master of the orphanage. That's seven."

"Rudimentary counting a priority at DICOMY, is it?"

He ignored the barb. "There isn't one for you." He saw a sign in the distance, approaching on the right at the top of the next hill.

"Of course not. I'm not employed by DICOMY. I told you. I'm a caretaker."

"Of the house?"

"That. And also the island. Runs in the family. Has for generations."

Linus Baker had been in his job for a long time. And yes, he was good at it. He could think analytically, could notice the little cues that others could not. It was why, he thought, he'd been chosen for this assignment.

That being said, he should have recognized it the moment he opened his eyes on the platform. Fainting after receiving the shock of his life shouldn't have been an excuse.

The violet in her eyes should have given it away. It hadn't been a trick of the light.

"You're a sprite," he said. "An island sprite."

He'd surprised her. She tried to cover it up, and had he not known what to look for, he would've missed it. "What makes you think that?" she asked, voice even.

"You're a caretaker."

"That means nothing."

"Your eyes."

"Unusual, sure, but certainly not unique."

"You carried my luggage—"

"Oh, I apologize. Had I known I was destroying your toxic masculinity, I wouldn't have—"

"You're barefoot."

This caused her to pause. "I live near the ocean," she said slowly. "Maybe I'm always barefoot."

He shook his head. "The sun is high in the sky. The road must be extremely hot. And yet, you walked along it as if it were nothing. Sprites don't like shoes. Too confining. And nothing hurts their feet. Not even heated asphalt."

She sighed. "You're smarter than you look. That can't possibly be good."

"Are you registered?" he demanded. "Does DICOMY know that you're—"

She bared her teeth. "I was never in the system, Mr. Baker. My line is far older than the rules of men. Just because you have decided that all magical beings need to be tagged in the wild for tracking doesn't give you the right to question me or my legal status."

He blanched. "That's— You're right. I shouldn't have said that."

"Was that an apology?"

"I think so."

"Good. Don't ask about my status again."

"It's just— I've never met an island sprite before. A water sprite, yes. And even a cave one once. It's how I was able to recognize you. I didn't know you existed."

She snorted. "I'm sure there's much you don't know about existing, Mr. Baker. Look. There. We're almost to the ferry."

He followed where she was pointing. Up ahead, the sign he'd seen in the distance was approaching as they crested the hill. Above the picture of a palm tree and the waves of the ocean was the legend: VILLAGE OF MARSYAS.

"I've never heard of this place before," he admitted as they drove past. "The village. Is it nice?"

"Depends on your definition of nice. To you, probably. To me, no."

They reached the top of the hill. Below them, along the edges of the ocean, was a cluster of brightly colored buildings nestled amongst tall trees that had been bent over time with the winds. He could see houses spread out into the forest, all in pastels and thatched roofs. It looked like he always dreamed a place near the ocean would. It caused his heart to ache.

"We won't stop, so don't ask," she warned him. "They don't like it when we do."

"What do you mean?"

"Not everyone is as progressive as you, Mr. Baker," she said, and he *knew* he was being mocked. "The people of Marsyas don't appreciate our kind."

That surprised him. "Sprites?"

She laughed again, but the bitterness was heavy. "All magical beings, Mr. Baker."

It didn't take long to see what she meant. As soon as they pulled onto the main thoroughfare, heading through the village, people on the streets and in the shops turned toward the sound of the car. Linus had been on the receiving end of many looks of disapproval in his life, but never ones filled with so much hostility. People in board shorts and bikinis and rubber flip-flops turned to glare at them openly as they drove through. He tried waving at a few of them, but it didn't do any good. He even saw a man inside what looked to be a seafood shanty reach up and lock the door as they drove by.

"Well, I never," Linus said with a sniff.

"You get used to it," Ms. Chapelwhite said. "Surprisingly."

"Why are they like this?"

"I don't pretend to know the minds of men," she said, hands tightening on the steering wheel as a woman on the sidewalk appeared to shield her chubby, squawking children away from the car. "They fear what they don't understand. And that fear turns to hate for reasons I'm sure even they can't begin to comprehend. And since they don't understand the children, since they fear them, they hate them. This can't be the first time you've heard of this. It happens everywhere."

"I don't hate anything," Linus said.

"You lie."

He shook his head. "No. Hate is a waste of time. I'm far too busy to hate anything. I prefer it that way."

She glanced at him, her expression hidden behind her sunglasses. She opened her mouth—to say what, he didn't know—but appeared to change her mind. Instead, she said, "We're here. Stay in the car."

She parked at the edge of a pier. She got out before Linus could say another word. There was a man standing next to a small ferry, tapping his foot impatiently. Behind him, Linus thought he could see the faint outline of an island. "It's getting late," the man snapped at Ms. Chapelwhite as she approached, voice drifting over to Linus. "You know I can't be at the island after dark."

"It's fine, Merle. I wouldn't let anything happen to you."

"That's not as comforting as you seem to think it is." He spat over the edge of the pier into the water before looking over her shoulder at Linus. "That's him, then?"

She glanced back at him. "That's him."

"Thought he'd be younger."

"That's what I said."

"All right. Let's get on with it. And you tell Parnassus my rates have doubled."

She sighed. "I'll let him know."

Merle nodded, and with one last withering look at Linus he turned and jumped deftly onto the ferry. Ms. Chapelwhite turned back toward the car.

"I think we might have gotten into something bigger than we were led to believe," Linus whispered to Calliope.

She purred in response.

"All right?" he asked as the sprite climbed back inside the car. He wasn't sure it was; Merle seemed to be a troublesome fellow.

"All right," she muttered. The car turned over again, and she pulled forward as Merle lowered the gate onto the ferry. There was a moment when Linus's stomach dropped as the gate creaked and groaned under their weight, but it was over before he could react.

She put the car in park and pressed a button. Linus startled as the sounds of gears rumbled from the rear of the car. He looked back in time to see a vinyl roof rising up and over them. It locked into place with a terrible finality. She shut the car off before turning toward him. "Look, Mr. Baker. I think we got off on the wrong foot."

"You mean you're not always such a joy to be around? Could have fooled me."

She glared at him. "I'm a sprite, which means I'm very protective of what's mine."

"The island," Linus said.

She nodded. "And all its inhabitants."

He hesitated. Then, "Are you and this Mr. Parnassus . . ."

She arched an eyebrow.

He flushed as he coughed and looked away. "Never mind."

She laughed at him, though not unkindly. "No. Trust me when I say that would never happen."

"Oh. Well. Good to know."

"I know you have a job to do," she continued. "And you're finding out it's like nothing you've ever done before, but all I ask is that you give them a chance. They're more than what's in their files."

"Are you telling me how to do my job?" he asked stiffly.

"I'm asking for an ounce of compassion."

"I know compassion, Ms. Chapelwhite. It's why I do what I do."

"You really believe that, don't you?"

He looked at her sharply. "What's that supposed to mean?"

She shook her head. "You don't have a file on me because I'm not supposed to exist. Arthur—Mr. Parnassus—sent me as an act of good faith. To show you how serious he is. He knows the kind of person you can be. He hopes you can be that person here."

Linus felt a trickle of dread at the base of his spine. "How does he know a single thing about me? He can't know who was assigned. *I* didn't even know until yesterday."

She shrugged. "He has his ways. You should use the time you have left before arriving at the island to review the remaining files. It's best if you know what you're walking into before you do. It'll be safer, I think."

"For who?"

There was no answer.

He turned to find the driver's seat empty, as if she'd never been there at all.

"Bugger," he muttered.

He considered doing what she asked. Forewarned was forearmed and all that, but he couldn't bring himself to peruse the files after what he'd discovered in Lucy's, fearing that it would only get exponentially worse. Extremely Upper Management certainly hadn't made things any easier, given their dire warnings about how the inhabitants of the island were unlike anything he'd ever seen before. Ms. Chapelwhite had only seemed to confirm that. He wondered briefly if he'd said too much to her, or if she'd managed to peek inside the files while he'd been lying on the platform. Both seemed likely, and he reminded himself to be on his guard from here on in.

Not trusting himself to maintain consciousness, he sat with the files on his lap, fingers twitching, the urge to know what he was walking into shrinking in the face of the desire to keep his sanity firmly in place. He thought of all manner of things, from terrible monsters with wickedly sharp teeth to fire and brimstone. They were children, he told himself, but even children could bite if provoked. And if they happened to be worse than what he was imagining, he would rather not know about it beforehand in case he found himself unable to leave the ferry.

But still . . .

He shuffled through the files, looking for one in particular. He inhaled sharply when he saw Lucy's and skipped by it as quickly as possible until he found the one he wanted.

The master of the house.

Arthur Parnassus.

The file was thin, consisting of a blurry photograph of a spindly man against a blue background and a single sheet of paper. He certainly seemed . . . normal, but appearances could be deceiving.

The file (as much as it could be called that for something so sparse) didn't tell him much more, as certain parts were redacted and the rest were bits and pieces without rhyme or reason. Aside from learning his age (forty-five) and the fact that his tenure at Marsyas appeared to be without any significant issue, there wasn't much more Linus could glean from it. He didn't know whether he was disappointed or relieved.

The sun was beginning to set by the time a bell rang, signaling the arrival at the island. He was lost in thought when the ferry shuddered underneath him, and he looked out the back window to see the ferry gate lowering against a small dock.

A shadow stretched over the windshield as he turned around. "This is where you get off!" a voice shouted at him.

He peered up through the windshield.

Merle stood above him, hands on his hips. "Off," he repeated.

"But—"

"Get off my damn boat!"

"What an ass," Linus muttered. The key was still in the ignition, and Linus figured he should at least be thankful for that. He opened the passenger door and almost fell out. He was able to save himself and Calliope at the last second, though she wasn't appreciative of his acrobatics. He set her on the seat and shut the door against her hissing. He tipped a jaunty salute up to Merle as he rounded the back of the car.

Merle didn't respond.

"Certainly off to an auspicious start," Linus said under his breath. The driver's door creaked as he shut it behind him. It'd been a while since he'd driven. He'd never actually owned a car of his own. It was too much of a hassle in the city. He'd rented one once, years ago, planning on spending a weekend driving out to the country, but he'd been called into work at the last minute and ended up returning the car only an hour after he'd taken it out.

He pushed the seat back before turning the key.

The car rumbled to life around him.

"Okay, then," Linus said to Calliope, hands sweating against the steering wheel. "Let's see what we see, shall we?"

FIVE

There were no signs pointing in any direction, but since there was only one road, Linus figured he must be heading the right way. It only took a few minutes of driving away from the ferry landing before he found himself in an old forest, the trees massive, their canopies almost completely blocking out the sky streaked in pinks and oranges. Leafy vines hung from tree limbs, loud birds called from unseen perches.

"I don't suppose this is some sort of trap?" Linus said to Calliope as it grew darker the deeper into the forest they went. "Maybe this is where everyone goes after they've been sacked. They think they're getting a top assignment, but instead, they get sacrificed in the middle of nowhere."

It wasn't a pleasant thought, so he pushed it away.

He couldn't find the lever for the headlamps, so he leaned forward as close to the windshield as he could get. It was dusk. His stomach rumbled, but he hadn't felt like eating less in his life. He knew Calliope would probably be looking for a litter box soon, but he didn't want to stop until he had some idea where he was. His luck would have Calliope running off into the woods, forcing Linus to chase after her.

"And I probably wouldn't," he told her. "I'd leave you out here to fend for yourself."

He wouldn't, but she didn't need to know that.

The odometer had turned over two additional miles, and he was about to start panicking—after all, the island couldn't be *that* big, could it?—when the forest fell away around him, and he saw it.

There, ahead of him, set against the falling sun, was a house.

Linus had never seen one quite like it before.

It was set up a hill on a cliff overlooking the ocean. It looked as if it were at least a hundred years old. It was made of brick and had a large turret, of all things, set right in the middle of the roof. The side of the house facing Linus was covered in green ivy, growing around multiple white window frames. He thought he could see the outline of a gazebo set off next to the house and wondered if there was a garden. He would like that very much. He could walk through it, smelling the salt in the air and—

He shook his head. He wasn't here for such things. There would be no time for frivolities. He had a job to do, and he was going to do it right.

He turned the car toward what appeared to be a long driveway that led up to the house. The closer he got, the bigger it grew, and Linus couldn't be sure how he'd never heard of this place. Oh, not the orphanage, not if Extremely Upper Management didn't want anyone to know. But surely this island, this *house* should have been known to him. He wracked his brain, but came up empty.

The driveway widened near the top of the hill. There was another vehicle parked next to an empty fountain, overgrown by the same vines that latched on to the orphanage. It was a red van, surely big enough for six children and the master of the house. He wondered if they took many trips. Not into the village, of course, not if the people there weren't inviting.

But as he got closer, he saw the van appeared not to have been moved in some time. Weeds grew up through the wheel wells.

It appeared they didn't take many trips, if any at all.

For a moment, Linus felt a pang, something akin to sorrow. He rubbed a hand against his chest, trying to chase it away.

He'd been right, though. There was a garden. The last rays of sun seemed to be illuminating the flowers to the side of the house, and Linus blinked when he thought he saw movement, a quick flash before it was gone.

He rolled down the window a smidge, just enough to be heard. "Hello?" he called.

There was no answer.

Feeling slightly braver, he rolled the window down halfway. The thick scent of the ocean filled his nose. Leaves rustled on the branches of the trees. "Hello?"

Nothing.

"Right," he said. "Well. Perhaps we can just stay in here until tomorrow."

And then he heard the unmistakable giggle of a child.

"Or maybe we should leave," he said weakly.

Calliope scratched the front of the crate.

"I know, I know. But there appears to be something out there, and I don't know if either of us wants to be eaten."

She scratched again.

He sighed. She'd been good for the most part. The trip had been long, and it wasn't fair of him to leave her cooped up.

"Fine. But you will be quiet while I sit here and think and try to ignore childlike laughter coming from the strange house so very far away from everything I know."

She didn't put up a fight when he opened the crate and pulled her into his lap. She sat regally, staring out the window, eyes wide. She didn't make a sound when he stroked her back.

"All right," Linus said. "Let's review, shall we? I can either do what I was sent here to do, or I can sit here and hope a better idea comes to me, preferably where I keep all my bits and bobs as they are."

Calliope dug her claws into his thighs.

He winced. "Yes, yes. I suppose you're right. It *is* cowardly, but it also means we stay alive."

She licked her paw slowly before brushing it over her face.

"No need to be rude," he muttered. "Fine. If I must." He reached for the door handle. "I can do this. I *will* do this. You stay here, and I'll—"

He didn't have time to react. He opened the door, and Calliope leapt from his lap. She hit the ground and took off running toward the garden.

"Of all the— You stupid cat! I will leave you here!"

He would do no such thing, but empty threats were better than no threats at all.

Calliope disappeared beyond a line of perfectly maintained bushes. He thought he saw a flash of her tail, but then she was gone.

Linus Baker was not a fool. He prided himself in that regard. He was well aware of his limitations as a human being. When it was dark, he preferred to be locked safely inside his house, wearing his monogrammed pajamas, a record playing on the Victrola, holding a warm drink in his hands.

That being said, Calliope was essentially his only friend in the entire world.

So when he climbed out of the car, rocks crunching under his feet in the driveway, it was because he understood that sometimes, one had to do unsavory things for those one cared about.

He followed where she'd run off to, hoping she hadn't gotten far. The sun was almost gone, and while the house itself was still foreboding even though lights appeared to be on inside, the sky above was lit in colors he wasn't sure he'd ever seen before, at least not mixed together as they were. He could hear the waves crashing far down below the cliff, and seagulls screamed overhead.

He reached the line of bushes that Calliope had disappeared behind. There was a small stone path that led into what he thought was the garden, and he hesitated only briefly before entering.

The garden was far bigger than it had first appeared. The gazebo that he'd seen from the road was farther ahead, strung with red and orange paper lanterns that swung in the breeze. Their lights flickered softly, and there came the distant sound of chimes.

The garden itself was blooming wildly. He didn't see any sunflowers, but there were calla and Asiatic lilies. Dahlias. Celosias. Chrysanthemums, orange gerberas, and Chinese bellflowers. There were even beautyberries, something he hadn't seen since he was a child. The air was thick and redolent, and it made him slightly dizzy.

"Calliope," he called softly. "Come now. Don't make this difficult."

She didn't appear.

"Fine, then," he said irritably. "I can always make a new friend. After all, there are many cats who need to be adopted. A new kitten would fix this problem quite easily. I'll just leave you here. It's for the best."

He would do no such thing, of course. He continued on.

There was an apple tree growing near the house, and Linus blinked when he saw red and green and pinkish apples, all different varieties growing on the same limbs. He followed the trunk down toward the ground and saw—

A little statue.

A garden gnome.

"How quaint," he murmured as he moved toward the tree.

The statue was bigger than the ones he had seen before, the tip of its pointed cap about waist-high. It had a white beard, and its hands were clasped at its front. The paint job that had been done on the statue was remarkably detailed, almost lifelike in the fading light. The eyes were bright blue, and its cheeks were rosy.

"Strange statue, aren't you?" he said, hunkering down in front of it.

Had Linus been in his right mind, he would have noticed the eyes. However, he was tired, out of sorts, and worried about his cat.

Therefore, the noise that came out of him wasn't that surprising when the gnome statute blinked and said rather haughtily, "You can't just say something like that about a person. It's rude. Don't you know anything?"

His scream was strangled as he fell backward, hand digging into the grass underneath him.

The gnome sniffed. "You're awfully loud. I don't like it when people are loud in my garden. If you're loud, you can't hear the flowers talking." And she (because she *was* a she, beard and all), reached up and straightened her cap. "Gardens are quiet spaces."

Linus struggled to find his voice. "You're . . . you . . ."

She frowned. "Of course I'm me. Who else would I be?"

He shook his head, managing to clear the cobwebs before latching on to a name. "You're a gnome."

She blinked owlishly at him. "Yes. I am. I'm Talia." She bent over and picked up a small shovel that had been laying on the grass next to her. "Are you Mr. Baker? If you are, we've been expecting you. If not, you're trespassing, and you should leave before I bury you here in my garden. No one would ever know because the roots would eat your entrails and bones." She frowned again. "I think. I've never buried anyone before. It would be a learning experience for the both of us."

"I'm Mr. Baker!"

Talia sighed, sounding incredibly disappointed. "Of course you are. No need to shout about it. But is it too much to ask for a trespasser? I've always wanted to see if humans make good fertilizer. It seems like they would." She eyed him up and down hungrily. "All that flesh."

"Oh dear," Linus managed to say.

She huffed out a breath. "We don't get trespassers here. Unless . . . I saw a cat. Did you bring it as a gift for the house? Lucy will be excited about that. And maybe when he's done with it, he'll let me use what's left. It's not the same as a human, but I'm sure it'll work."

"She's not an offering," Linus said, aghast. "She's a *pet*."

"Oh. Darn."

"Her name is Calliope!"

"Well, we better find her before the others do. I don't know what they'll think of her." She grinned at him, her teeth large and square. "Aside from looking tasty, that is."

Linus squeaked.

She waddled toward him, her stubby legs moving quickly. "Are you going to lie there all night? Get up. Get up!"

He did. Somehow, he did.

He was sweating profusely as he followed her farther into the garden, listening as she muttered under her breath. It sounded as if she were speaking Gnomish, her grunts low and guttural, but Linus hadn't ever heard it spoken aloud before, so he couldn't be sure.

They reached the gazebo, which creaked as they stepped onto it. The paper lanterns were brighter now, swinging on their lines. There were chairs with thick, comfy cushions. Underneath them was an ornate rug, the edges of which were curled.

Talia went to a small chest that was set off to the side. She pushed open the lid and hung her shovel on a hook inside, next to other gardening tools. Once she seemed satisfied that everything was in place, she nodded and closed the lid.

She turned back toward him. "Now, if I were a cat, where would I be?"

"I . . . don't know."

She rolled her eyes. "Of course you don't. Cats are cunning and mysterious. That doesn't seem like something you'd understand."

"I beg your—"

She stroked her beard. "We need help. Fortunately, I know just who to ask." She looked at the ceiling of the gazebo. "Theodore!"

Linus frantically thought back to the files he hadn't looked at. Oh, what a fool he'd been. "Theodore. Who is—"

From somewhere above came a cry that sent shivers down Linus's spine.

Talia's eyes were sparkling. "He's coming. He'll know what to do. He can find anything."

Linus took a step back, ready to grab Talia and run if needed.

A dark shape swooped into the gazebo, landing artlessly on the floor. It squawked angrily as it tripped over its too-big wings, rolling end over end until it crashed into Linus's legs. Linus did his best not to shriek, but unfortunately, his best wasn't good enough.

A scaly tail twitched as its owner stared up at him with bright orange eyes.

Linus had never actually seen a wyvern in person before. They were quite rare and thought to be descended from ancient reptiles that once roamed the earth, though they were barely larger than a housecat. Many considered them to be nuisances, and for a long time, they were hunted down, their heads used as trophies, their skin made into fashionable shoes. It wasn't until laws were enacted protecting all magical creatures that the barbaric acts ceased, but by then, it'd almost been too late, especially in the face of empirical evidence that wyverns were capable of emotionally complex reasoning that rivaled even humans. Their numbers had dwindled alarmingly.

So, it was with fascination (tinged, of course, with horror) that Linus stared down at the wyvern at his feet, a tail beginning to wrap around his ankle.

It—*he*, Linus reminded himself—was smaller than Calliope, though not by much. His scales were iridescent, the light from the lanterns above casting a kaleidoscope of colors. His hind legs were thickly muscled, the claws at the tips of his feet black and wicked sharp. He didn't have front legs; instead, his wings were long and leathery like a bat's. His head was curved downward, the snout ending in twin slits. His tongue snaked out and flicked against Linus's loafers.

His orange eyes blinked slowly. He jerked his head up toward Linus, and . . . chirped.

Linus's heart was thundering in his chest. "Theodore, I presume?"

The wyvern chirped again. He wasn't unlike a bird. A very large, scaly bird.

"Well?" Talia asked.

"Well, what?" Linus croaked out, wondering if it was rude to try to kick the wyvern away. The tail was tightening around his leg, and Theodore's fangs were awfully big.

"He's asking you for a coin," Talia said, as if it were obvious.

"A . . . coin?"

"For his hoard," Talia said, as if he were daft. "He'll help you, but you have to pay him."

"That's not . . . I don't . . ."

"Ohhhh," Talia said. "Do you not have a coin? That isn't good."

He looked up at her frantically. "What? Why?"

"Perhaps I'll have human fertilizer after all," she said ominously.

Linus immediately reached for his pockets. Surely he had— there had to be *something*—

Aha!

He pulled his hand out triumphantly.

"There!" he crowed. "I have a . . . button?"

Yes, a button. It was small and made of brass, and for the life of him, Linus couldn't remember where it'd come from. It wasn't really his style. Linus tended toward muted colors, and this was bright and shiny and—

Theodore clicked in the back of his throat. He almost sounded as if he were purring.

Linus looked down again to see Theodore picking himself up from the floor. He seemed to have a bit of trouble; his wings were far too big for something of his size. His legs kept getting caught in them, causing him to stumble. Theodore chirped angrily, before using his tail wrapped around Linus's calf as support. He managed to right himself before letting Linus go, never taking his eyes off the button. As soon as he was upright, he began to bounce on his legs around Linus, opening and closing his jaws.

"Well, give it to him," Talia said. "You can't just offer a wyvern a gift and then keep it from him. The last time someone did that, he lit them on fire."

Linus looked up at her sharply. "Wyverns can't breathe fire."

She grinned again. "You're not as gullible as you look. And you look *really* gullible. I'll have to remember that."

Theodore was jumping higher and higher, trying to get his attention, wings fluttering. He was chirping loudly, and his eyes were blazing.

"All right, all right," Linus said. "You'll get it, but I won't have you making a scene. Patience is a virtue."

Theodore landed on the ground and spun himself in a circle before arching his neck up toward Linus. He opened his mouth and waited.

His fangs were very big. And very sharp.

"You have to put it in his mouth," Talia whispered. "Quite possibly your whole hand."

Linus ignored her. Swallowing thickly, he reached down and set the tip of the button in Theodore's mouth. The wyvern bit down slowly, taking the button. Linus pulled his hand away as Theodore fell onto his back, wings spreading out on the floor. His stomach was pale and looked soft. He raised his back legs to his mouth until he could clutch the button. Holding it in his claws, he lifted the button toward his head, studying it carefully, spinning it around to see either side. He chirped loudly as he flipped himself over. He glanced back at Linus before spreading his wings and clumsily taking off. He almost tripped, but at the last moment, managed to fly off toward the house.

"Where's he going?" Linus asked faintly.

"To put it with the rest of his hoard," Talia said. "Something you'll never find, so don't even think about it. A wyvern is very protective over his hoard and will maim anyone who tries to take it from him." She paused, considering. "It's underneath the sofa in the living room. You should go check it out."

"But you just said— Ah. I see."

She stared innocently at him.

"He was supposed to help us find Calliope," he reminded her.

"He was? I never said that. I just wanted to see what you'd give him. Why do you have buttons in your pocket? That's not where they go." She squinted at him. "Do you not know that?"

"I know where—" He shook his head. "No. I won't. I am going to find my cat with or without your help. And if I have to tromp through your garden to do it, I will."

"You wouldn't *dare*."

"Wouldn't I?"

She sniffed. "Phee."

"Bless you," Linus said.

"What? I didn't sneeze. I was— Phee!"

"Yeah, yeah," another voice said. "I heard you the first time."

Linus whirled around.

There was a dirty girl of perhaps ten years of age standing behind them. She had smudges of dirt on her face that almost covered the bright freckles dotting her pale skin. She blew out a breath, and a lock of fire-red hair fluttered off her forehead. She was wearing shorts and a tank top. She was barefoot, and her toenails had grime underneath them.

But it was the thin wings that rose from her back that caught Linus's attention the most. They were translucent, lined with veins, and they curled around her shoulders, much larger than he would expect from one her size.

A sprite, like Ms. Chapelwhite, though there were marked differences. There was an earthy scent emanating from her that reminded Linus of the drive through the trees to get to the house, dense and thick. He thought it was possible they were her doing.

A forest sprite.

Linus had only met a handful of sprites before. They tended to be solitary creatures, and the younger they were, the more dangerous. They weren't in full control of their magic. Once, Linus had seen the aftermath of a young lake sprite who had felt threatened by a group of people on a boat. The water level had risen almost six feet, and what remained of the boat had floated on the choppy surface in pieces.

He didn't know what had happened to that sprite after he filed his report. That information was above his pay grade.

This sprite however—Phee—reminded him of the lake sprite from years before. She was looking at him distrustfully, her wings twitching. "This him?" she asked. "Doesn't seem like much."

"He's not gullible," Talia said. "So he has that going for him at least. He brought a cat that escaped."

"Better not let Lucy find it. You know what he'll do."

Linus had to regain control of the situation. They were just children, after all. "My name is Linus Baker. And *her* name is Calliope. I'm—"

Phee ignored him as she walked by him, the tip of her left wing smacking him in the face. "It's not in the woods," she told Talia.

Talia sighed. "I didn't think so, but figured I'd ask."

"I need to go get cleaned up," Phee told her. "If you haven't found it by the time I'm done, I'll come back and help." She glanced back at Linus before walking out of the gazebo toward the house.

"She doesn't like you," Talia said. "Don't feel too bad about it, though. She doesn't like most people. It isn't personal, I don't think. She would just rather you weren't here. Or alive."

"I'm sure," Linus said stiffly. "Now, if you could point me toward—"

Talia clapped her hands in front of her beard. "That's it! I know where we need to look! They were supposed to be getting it ready for you, and I bet Sal's got her. He's good with strays."

She waddled toward the opposite end of the gazebo before looking over her shoulder at him. "Come on! Don't you want to get your cat?"

Linus did.

And so he followed.

Talia led them through the garden around the side of the house that he hadn't been able to see from the road. The light was fading, and he could see stars appearing overhead. The air was cool now, and he shivered.

Talia, for her part, pointed out every single flower they came across, telling him their names and when she'd planted them. She warned him not to touch them, or she'd have to hit him upside the head with her shovel.

Linus didn't dare try her. She obviously had a propensity for violence, and he needed to remember that for his reports. This investigation wasn't off to a great start. He had many concerns. Specifically, that all these children appeared to be scattered about.

"Where is the master of the house?" Linus asked as they left the garden behind. "Why isn't he keeping an eye out for you?"

"Arthur?" Talia asked. "Why on earth would he?"

"Mr. Parnassus," Linus insisted. "It's only polite to refer to him by a proper name. And he *should* be, because you're a child."

"I'm 263 years old!"

"And gnomes don't reach an age of maturity until they're five hundred," Linus said. "You may think me a fool, but that would be a mistake."

She grumbled something in what Linus was now convinced was Gnomish. "From five in the afternoon until seven, we're given time for personal pursuits. Arthur—oh, *excuse me,* Mr. Parnassus—believes we should explore whatever interests us."

"Highly unusual," Linus muttered.

Talia glanced at him. "It is? Don't you do things you like after you get done working?"

Well . . . yes. Yes, he did. But he was an adult, and that was different. "What if one of you gets hurt while in your personal pursuit? He can't be lazing about while—"

"He's not lazing about!" Talia exclaimed. "He works with Lucy to make sure he doesn't bring about the end of the world as we know it!"

It was about this time that Linus felt his vision gray yet again at the thought of—of this *child.* This *Lucy.* He couldn't believe that such a creature existed without his knowledge. Without the *world's* knowledge. Oh, he understood why there was secrecy and could even comprehend the need for it. But the fact that there was a weapon of mass destruction in the body of a six-year-old and the world wasn't prepared was simply shocking.

"You've gone awfully pale," Talia said as she squinted up at him. "And you're swaying. Are you ill? If you are, I think we should go back to the garden so you can die there. I don't want to have to drag you all the way back. You look really heavy." She reached up and poked his stomach. "So soft."

Strangely, that simple action managed to clear his vision. "I'm not ill," he snapped at her. "I'm just . . . processing."

"Oh. That's too bad. If your left upper arm starts to hurt, would you let me know?"

"Why would I—that's a sign of a heart attack, isn't it?"

She nodded.

"I demand you take me to Mr. Parnassus this instant!"

She cocked her head at him. "But what about your cat? Don't you want to find her before she gets eaten and all that's left is her tail because it's too fluffy to choke down?"

"This is very perturbing and irregular. If this is the way this orphanage is run, I will need to inform—"

Her eyes widened before she grabbed him by the hand and began to pull him. "We're fine! See? Everything is fine. I'm not dead, and you're not dead, and nobody is hurt! After all, we're on an island with no way on or off aside from a ferry. And the house has electricity and working toilets, something we're very proud of! What could possibly happen to any of us? And Zoe keeps an eye on us when Mr. Parnassus is otherwise detained."

"Zoe?" Linus demanded. "Who is—"

"Oh! I meant Ms. Chapelwhite," Talia said hastily. "She's wonderful. So caring. Everyone says so. And distantly related to a fairy king named Dimitri, if you can believe that! Though, he's not from around these parts."

Linus's mind was a whirlwind. "What do you mean, *fairy king*? I've never—"

"So you see, there is absolutely nothing to worry about. We're always monitored with everything we do, so no need to inform anyone of anything. And would you look at that! I *knew* Sal would have your cat. Animals love him. He's the best. See? Calliope looks so happy, doesn't she?"

And indeed, she did. She was rubbing up against the legs of a large black boy sitting on the porch of a small house set away from the big house, her back arched as he traced a finger down her spine, tail swishing lazily from side to side. The boy smiled down at her, and then wonder of all wonder, Calliope opened her mouth and *meowed,* a sound Linus couldn't ever remember hearing her make before. It was rusty and deep, and it nearly stopped him in his tracks. She purred, of course—usually her distaste—but she never *talked.*

"Yes," the boy said, voice low. "Such a good girl, aren't you? Yes, you are. Prettiest girl."

"Okay," Talia said quietly. "No sudden movements, okay? You don't want to—"

"That's my cat!" Linus said loudly. "You there, how did you get her to do that?"

"—scare him," Talia finished with a sigh. "Now you've gone and done it."

The boy looked up fearfully at the sound of Linus's voice. His big shoulders hunched as he appeared to sink *inward*. One moment, there was a handsome boy with dark eyes, and the next, the clothes he'd been wearing fell to the porch as if the body wearing them had disappeared from the face of the earth.

Linus stopped, jaw dropping.

Except even as he watched, the pile of clothes began to shift. There was a flash of white hair, and then the clothes fell away.

Sal, the large boy who had to weigh at least 150 pounds, was gone.

But not completely.

Because he had turned into a five-pound Pomeranian.

A *fluffy* five-pound Pomeranian. The hair around his head was white, shot with rusty orange that extended down his back and legs. His tail was curled up behind his back, and before Linus could process the fact that he'd seen an actual shifter change before him, Sal gave a high-pitched bark and turned and ran into the guest house.

"My word," Linus breathed. "That was . . ." He didn't know how to finish.

"I told you not to scare him," Talia said crossly. "He's very nervous, you know. He doesn't like strangers or loudness, and here you are being both."

Calliope seemed to agree, as she glared at Linus before she climbed the steps and disappeared into the house as well.

The house itself was tiny, even smaller than Linus's own. The porch wasn't big enough for a rocking chair, but it looked charming, flowers growing along the front underneath windows that had a warm and inviting light pouring out of them. It, too, was made of brick, much like the main house, but it didn't exude the dread Linus had felt upon arrival.

He could hear barking coming from inside the house. There was a response that sounded high-pitched and garbled, as if someone was throwing a wet sponge on the floor repeatedly.

"Chauncey's here too," Talia said, sounding delighted. "He probably grabbed your luggage for you while we were in the garden. He's very hospitable, you know. He wants to be a bellhop when he gets older. The uniform with the little hat and everything." She looked up at him with wide, innocent eyes that Linus distrusted immediately. "Do you think he'd be good at that, Mr. Baker?"

And because Linus believed in the power of positive thinking, he said, "I don't see why not," even though he wondered what Chauncey could possibly be.

Talia smiled sweetly as if she didn't believe a single word.

The inside of the house was just as endearing as the outside. There was a sitting room with a comfortable-looking chair in front of a brick fireplace, and a table sitting in a nook in front of one of the windows. The barking sound came from farther down the hall, and for a moment, Linus was slightly disoriented, because there didn't seem to be—

"Where's the kitchen?" he asked.

Talia shrugged. "There isn't one. Whoever owned the house before seemed to think everyone should eat together in the main house. You get to eat with all of us. Probably for the best, so you can see we eat only the healthiest foods and are civilized or whatever."

"But there's—"

"Sir!" a wet and warbled voice exclaimed from behind him. "Might I take your coat?"

Linus turned to see—

"Chauncey!" Talia said, sounding delighted.

There, standing (sitting?) in the hallway, a tiny dog peering out around him, was an amorphous green blob with bright red lips. And black teeth. And eyes on stalks that stuck high above his head, seemingly moving independently of each other. He didn't have arms so much as tentacles with tiny little suckers along their lengths. He was not quite see-through, though Linus could make out the faint outline of Sal hiding behind him.

"I'm not wearing a coat," Linus heard himself say, though he hadn't actually instructed his brain to say it.

Chauncey frowned. "Oh. That's . . . disappointing." His eyes wiggled around as he seemed to brighten. As in literally brighten, because he became a lighter shade of green. "No matter! I've already attended to your luggage, sir! It's been placed in your room, as has the barbaric cage I assume is for your cat that is now sleeping on your pillow." He held out one of his tentacles.

Linus stared at it.

"Ahem," Chauncey coughed, flipping the tip of his tentacle toward him twice.

"You have to pay him," Talia hissed from behind him.

Again, independent of any thought, Linus felt himself reach back for his wallet. He opened it up, found a single, and handed it over. It instantly soaked through as Chauncey's tentacle closed over it. "Wow," he whispered as he pulled the bill close, eyes drooping on their stalks to look it over. "I did it. I'm a bellhop."

Before Linus could respond to *that,* a chilling voice rang out, sounding as if it were coming from *everywhere.* The air, the floors, the very *walls* that surrounded them.

"I am evil incarnate," the dastardly voice said. "I am the blight upon the skin of this world. And I will bring it to its *knees.* Prepare for the End of Days! Your time has come, and the rivers will run with the blood of the innocents!"

Talia sighed. "He's such a drama queen."

SIX

Linus Baker, for what it was worth, did care about the children he was tasked with observing. He didn't think one could do what he did and lack empathy, though he couldn't understand how someone like Ms. Jenkins had ever been a caseworker before being promoted to Supervision.

And so when faced with a perceived threat, and even though everything felt topsy-turvy, Linus did the only thing he could: He moved to protect the children.

Talia squawked angrily as he shoved her behind him toward Sal and Chauncey. "What are you *doing*?"

He ignored her, the ringing in his ears he'd heard since he'd arrived on the island now turning into a full-blown roar. He took a step toward the open door, and he swore on everything he had that the darkness settling outside had somehow gotten *darker*. He believed if he stepped out onto the porch, the stars above would be blotted out, and all that would remain would be eternal night.

"What's going on?" Chauncey whispered behind him.

"I have no idea," Talia said irritably.

Sal barked nervously, a high-pitched yip.

"Probably," Talia said.

Linus took a step toward the door. He should have realized that accepting this assignment was going to be the last thing he'd do. He wondered if Lucy had already taken out Mr. Parnassus and whoever (or *what*ever) had been in the main house with them. He couldn't be sure if there were other things that Extremely Upper Management hadn't made him aware of. If there was a clear path, perhaps he could get the children to the car. He'd need to get Calliope into her crate, but he'd rather have an angry cat to deal with than a devil. He didn't know how he'd get them off the island, but—

He stepped onto the porch.

It *was* darker, perhaps darker than it'd ever been before. He could barely see the flowers just off the porch. Everything else was lost to the darkness. It was as if the night were a living thing and had consumed the world. Linus's skin felt electrified.

"Hello," a sweet voice said from beside him.

Linus gasped and turned his head.

There, standing at the edge of the porch, was a child.

Lucy looked exactly as he had in the photograph. His black hair was windswept, and his eyes were red and ringed with blue. He looked so *small*, but the smile on his face was twisted into a sneer, and his fingers were twitching at his sides, as if he were barely restraining himself from reaching out and tearing Linus limb from limb.

"It's nice to see you," Lucy singsonged before giggling. "I knew you'd come, Mr. Baker. Though, by the time I'm done with you, you'll wish you hadn't." The smile widened until it seemed like his face would split in half. Flames began to rise behind him, though they didn't seem to burn the house, and Linus couldn't feel the heat that should have been pouring off of them. "I'm going to enjoy this far more than you could ever—"

"That's enough, Lucy."

And just like that, everything switched off.

Lucy groaned, and the red disappeared from his eyes. The fire subsided. The blackness winked out, and the remains of the sunset appeared on the horizon. The stars were bright, and Linus could see the main house across the way.

"I was just having some fun," Lucy muttered, scuffing his shoe against the porch. "I'm hellfire. I am the darkest parts of—"

"You still need to have a bath after supper," the voice said, and Linus felt his heart skip a beat. "Perhaps we could save the hellfire and the darkest parts for tomorrow."

Lucy shrugged. "Okay." And then he ran past Linus into the house, shouting for Talia and Chauncey. "Did you see what I did? He was so *scared*!"

Linus looked off the porch.

There, standing in the grass, was a man.

He was unlike anyone Linus had ever seen before. He was spindly. His light hair was a mess, sticking up at odd angles. It was starting to gray around his temple. His dark eyes were bright and glittering in the near-dark. His aquiline nose had a bump in the center, as if it'd been broken once long ago and never set right. He was smiling, hands clasped in front of him. His fingers were long and elegant as he twiddled his thumbs. He wore a green peacoat, the collar pulled up around his neck against the sea breeze. His slacks appeared too short for his long legs, the hems coming up above his ankles, revealing red socks. He wore black-and-white wing tip shoes.

"Hello, Mr. Baker," Arthur Parnassus said, sounding amused. "Welcome to Marsyas Island." His voice was lighter than Linus expected, almost as if there were musical notes behind each word. "I do hope your trip was most pleasant. The ocean can sometimes be rough in the crossing. Merle is . . . Merle. He's from the village, after all."

Linus was flabbergasted. He remembered the blurry photograph from the file. In it, Mr. Parnassus had been standing against a blue background, and he hadn't been smiling. But there had been a jovial arch to his eyebrow, and Linus had stared at it for longer than was probably proper.

He looked younger in person, far younger than his forty-five years suggested. He was as fresh-faced as the young people who came into DICOMY with their shiny degrees and ideas about how things *should* be done rather than how they actually were. They quickly learned to fall in line. Idealism had no place in government work.

Linus shook his head, trying to clear his thoughts. It wouldn't do for someone in his position to sit here gawking at the master of an orphanage. Linus Baker was nothing if not a consummate professional, and he had a job to do.

"Do you often greet your guests with threats of death and destruction, Mr. Parnassus?" he asked sternly, trying to regain control of the situation.

Mr. Parnassus chuckled. "Not usually, though it should be said we don't have many guests. Please, call me Arthur."

Linus was tense, listening to the babble of voices behind him. He felt uncomfortable having someone like Lucy behind him, out of sight. "I think Mr. Parnassus will suffice. I will be Mr. Baker during the course of this visit. From you and the children."

Mr. Parnassus nodded with barely concealed delight. Linus couldn't be sure what, exactly, about this situation necessitated such a response. He wondered if he was being mocked somehow and felt a wave of anger roll over him. He managed to push it down before it could contort his expression.

"Mr. Baker it is, then. My apologies for not welcoming you in person upon your arrival." He glanced at the house over Linus's shoulder before looking back at him. "I was otherwise detained with Lucy, though I suspect he attempted to conceal your presence from me."

Linus was gobsmacked. "He can . . . do that?"

Mr. Parnassus shrugged. "He can do many things, Mr. Baker. But I expect you'll find that out for yourself. It is the reason you're here, isn't it? Phee informed us of your arrival, and Lucy decided he'd welcome you in his own special way."

"Special," Linus said faintly. "That's what you call it."

He took a step toward the porch. "This is an unusual place,

filled with things I don't believe you've witnessed before. It would be best if you put your preconceived notions behind you, Mr. Baker. Your visit will be much more enjoyable if you do."

Linus bristled. "I'm not here for enjoyment, Mr. Parnassus. This is not a *vacation*. I'm here as ordered by the Department in Charge of Magical Youth to determine if Marsyas Orphanage should remain as is, or if other actions should be taken. You would do well to remember that. The fact that the children were running amok with no supervision isn't the best start."

Mr. Parnassus barely seemed affected. "Running amok, you say? Fascinating. And I'm aware of what it is you're here for. I just don't know if you are."

"What's that supposed to mean?"

He zigged when Linus expected him to zag. "You gave Theodore a button."

Linus blinked. "Pardon?"

Mr. Parnassus was at the bottom of the steps. Linus had barely seen him move. "A button," he repeated slowly. "Brass. You gave it to Theodore."

"Yes, well, it was the first thing I found in my pocket."

"Where did it come from?"

"What do you mean?"

"The button, Mr. Baker," he said. "Where did the button come from?"

Linus took a step back. "I don't . . . I don't quite know what you mean."

Mr. Parnassus nodded. "It's the little things. Little treasures we find without knowing their origin. And they come when we least expect them. It's beautiful, when you think about it. He loves it dearly. That was very kind of you."

"I was all but ordered to give it to him!"

"Were you? How about that." He was on the porch in front of Linus. He was taller, much taller than he had appeared on the grass in front of the house. Linus had to tilt his head back to meet his gaze. He had a freckle that nearly formed a heart below his left eye. A lock of hair had fallen on his forehead.

Linus flinched a little when Mr. Parnassus extended a hand. Linus stared at it for a moment, then remembered himself. He took the offered hand in his own. The skin was cool and dry, and as the fingers wrapped around his own, Linus felt a little curl of warmth in the back of his mind. "It's a pleasure to meet you," Mr. Parnassus said. "Regardless of the reason you're here."

Linus pulled his hand away, palm tingling. "All I ask is that you let me perform my duties without interference."

"Because of the children."

"Yes," Linus said. "Because of the children. They are the most important thing, after all."

Mr. Parnassus studied him, looking for what, Linus didn't know. Then, "Good. I'm pleased we're off to such a wonderful start. That bodes well for what will certainly be an illuminating month."

"I wouldn't call it *wonderful*—"

"Children!" Mr. Parnassus called. He bent over deftly, sweeping Sal's discarded clothing in his hand. "Come now, would you?"

There was a stampede of feet behind Linus, some heavy, some sounding as if they were squelching. Linus was jostled as they ran by him.

Sal was first, still a tiny Pomeranian. He yipped nervously, giving Linus a wide berth before jumping up on Mr. Parnassus, tail wagging. "Hello, Sal," Mr. Parnassus said, looking down. Then, remarkably, he barked, a high-pitched yip. Sal responded in kind with a series of barks before taking off toward the house. "You brought a cat?"

Linus gaped at him. "You can speak . . ."

"To Sal?" Mr. Parnassus asked. "Of course I can. He's one of mine. It's important to— Talia. Thank you for showing our guest around the grounds. That was very kind of you. And Chauncey. I doubt there has been a better bellhop in all the world."

"Really?" Chauncey warbled, eyes swaying on his stalks. "The entire *world*?" He puffed out his chest. Or, rather, he *appeared* to puff out his chest. Linus couldn't be sure he had a chest at all. "Did you hear that, Talia? The entire *world*."

Talia snorted. "I heard. You'll have your own hotel before you know it." She glanced up at Linus as she stroked her beard. "You're welcome for not braining you with the shovel when I had the chance." She winced slightly when Mr. Parnassus spoke in a low, guttural sound, almost as if he were choking.

It took a moment for Linus to realize he was speaking Gnomish.

Talia heaved a great, dramatic sigh. "Sorry, Mr. Baker. I promise I won't brain you with my shovel. Today."

And with that, she and Chauncey went down the stairs and headed toward the main house.

Linus felt a cold chill race down his spine when he heard the floor creak behind him. Lucy appeared beside them, smiling maniacally up at Linus. He didn't appear to blink.

"Yes?" Linus asked in a croak. "Erm, can I help you?"

"No," Lucy said, smile widening. "You can't. Nobody can. I am the father of snakes. The void in the—"

"That's enough of that," Mr. Parnassus said lightly. "Lucy, it's your turn to help Ms. Chapelwhite in the kitchen. You're already late. Hop to it."

Lucy sighed as he deflated. "Aw, seriously?"

"Seriously," Mr. Parnassus said, reaching down and patting him on the shoulder. "Get a move on. You know she doesn't like it when you shirk your responsibilities."

Lucy grumbled under his breath as he hopped down the stairs. He glanced back over his shoulder at Linus when he reached the bottom. Linus felt his knees wobble.

"He's bluffing," Mr. Parnassus said. "He actually loves working in the kitchen. I think he's just putting on a show for you. Quite the little entertainer, he is."

"I think I need to sit down," Linus said, feeling numb.

"Of course," Mr. Parnassus said easily. "You've had a long day." He glanced at his wrist, pulling back the sleeve of his coat to reveal a large watch. "Dinner is at half past seven, so you have a bit to get settled. Ms. Chapelwhite has prepared a feast in your honor as a welcome to Marsyas. I'm told there will be pie for dessert. I do love pie so." He took Linus's hand in his own again, squeezing gently. Linus looked up at him. "I know why you're here," he said quietly. "And I know the power you wield. All I ask is that you keep an open mind, Mr. Baker. Can you do that for me?"

Linus pulled his hand away, feeling off-kilter. "I will do what I must."

Mr. Parnassus nodded. He looked as if he were going to say something else, but instead shook his head. He turned and stepped off the porch, following his charges into the dark.

He didn't look back.

Linus barely remembered walking down the hall toward his bedroom. He felt as if he were caught in a strange dream, one he didn't know how to escape from. The sensation persisted as he passed the tiny bathroom, only to see his toiletries had been placed on a shelf underneath the mirror.

"What?" he asked no one in particular.

The bedroom at the end of the hall was small, but functional. There was a desk facing the window that opened out to the cliff overlooking the sea. A chair was pressed against it. Near what appeared to be a closet door was a small bureau. A bed with an oversize quilt sat against the opposite wall. Calliope was on the pillow, tail curled around her. She opened a single eye as he entered, tracking his movement.

He opened his mouth and was about to speak to her when the words stuck in his throat.

His suitcase sat on the bed, opened and empty.

He rushed toward it. "Where are my things?"

Calliope yawned and tucked her face in her paws, breathing deeply.

The files for the children and Mr. Parnassus were still secure in a side pocket, the zipper closed. They didn't appear to have been trifled with. But his clothes were gone, and so was—

He looked around wildly.

There, on the floor, near the desk, sat Calliope's bowls. One had been filled with water, the other with her kibble, the bag of which was placed to the side of the desk. On top of the desk was his copy of *RULES AND REGULATIONS*.

He went to the closet and threw open the doors.

His shirts and ties and slacks were hung carefully from the hangers. Next to them was the one coat he'd brought, though he hadn't been sure he'd need it.

His spare loafers were sitting on the floor.

Leaving the door open, he went to the bureau. Inside, stacked neatly, were his socks and undergarments.

The next drawer down held his pajamas and the only nonwork clothes he'd brought, pants and a polo shirt.

He backed away from the bureau slowly until his legs hit the edge of the bed. He sat down roughly, staring at the drawers and the open closet.

"I think," he said to Calliope, "that I'm in over my head."

She didn't have an opinion one way or another.

Shaking his head, he reached for his suitcase, pulling the files out and onto his lap.

"Foolish," he muttered. "Next time, know what you're walking into."

He took a deep breath before opening the file on top.

"Oh," he said rather breathlessly when he read about a wyvern named Theodore.

"What?" he choked out when he opened the file for a fourteen-year-old boy called Sal.

He didn't manage to say anything at all for Talia, though a bead of sweat trickled down his brow.

He was right about Phee. A forest sprite, and a powerful one at that.

He recoiled sharply at what he saw for a boy called Chauncey. He was ten years old, and next the word *Mother,* it read *UNKNOWN.* The same for his father. And his species. It appeared no one seemed to know, exactly, what Chauncey actually was. And now that Linus had seen him in person, he wasn't sure either.

Extremely Upper Management was right.

The children weren't like anything he'd ever seen before.

He gave very real consideration to ignoring the dinner invitation and pulling the heavy quilt up and over his head, blocking out the strange world he'd found himself in. Maybe if he slept, things would make more sense upon waking.

But then his stomach grumbled, and Linus realized he was hungry.

Ravenous, even.

He poked his not inconsiderable stomach. "Must you?"

It gurgled again.

He sighed.

Which is why he found himself standing at the front door to the main house, steeling his nerves. "It's no different than any other assignment," he muttered to himself. "You've been in this situation before. On with it, old boy. You've got this."

He reached up and banged the metal knocker against the door three times.

And waited.

A minute later, he knocked again.

Still no response.

He wiped the sweat from his brow as he stepped back, looking at the side of the house. There were lights on through the windows, but it didn't appear anyone was coming to the door.

He shook his head as he stepped again to the door. After a moment of indecision, he reached for the knob. It turned easily under his hand, and he pushed.

The door opened.

Inside was a foyer that led to a wide set of stairs to the second floor. The banisters were wooden and smooth. A large chandelier hung above the foyer, the crystals glittering in the light. He stuck his head through the doorway, listening.

He heard. . . . music? It was faint, but still. He couldn't make out the song, but it felt familiar somehow.

"Hello?" he called.

No one answered.

He stepped into the house, closing the door behind him.

To his right was a living room, a large overstuffed couch set in front of a dark fireplace. There was a painting above the fireplace, a whimsical portrait of swirling eddies. He thought he saw the ruffled skirt of the couch shift, but he couldn't be sure it wasn't just a trick of the low light.

Ahead were the stairs.

To his left was a formal dining room, though it didn't appear to be in use. The smaller chandelier above the table was dark, and the table was covered with books, old by the looks of them.

"Hello?" he tried again.

No one responded.

He did the only thing he could.

He followed the sound of the music.

The closer he got, the more the notes filled in, trumpets low and sharp, a sweet masculine voice singing that somewhere beyond the sea, she's there watching for me.

Linus had this record. He loved it so.

As Bobby Darin sang about watching ships from golden sands, Linus moved through the dream, fingers tracing along the books on the table. He barely glanced down at the titles, entranced by the telltale scratch of a record spinning.

He came to two swinging doors, portholes in their center.

He stood on his tiptoes, peering through them.

The kitchen was bright and airy. It was bigger than any kitchen he'd ever seen before. He was sure the entire guest house could fit inside, with room to spare. Lights hung from the ceiling surrounded by glass globes like fishbowls. He could see a gigantic refrigerator next to an industrial-sized oven. The granite counters were sparkling clean, and—

His jaw dropped.

Ms. Chapelwhite was moving through the kitchen, feet barely touching the floor. Her wings glittered behind her, much brighter than Phee's had been. They fluttered with every step she took.

But it was the other person in the kitchen that caught Linus's eye the most.

Lucy was standing on a stepstool in front of the counter. He had a plastic knife in his hand and was chopping a tomato, dropping the pieces into a large pink bowl to his left.

And he was bouncing along with Bobby Darin. As the orchestra swelled mid-song, drums beating, trumpets blaring, he shook his entire body in time with the music. Bobby came back in, saying he knew without a doubt, his heart would lead him there.

And Lucy was rocking his head back, bellowing the words as he danced.

Ms. Chapelwhite was singing along with him, twirling in the kitchen as she moved in and out of sight.

It was a feeling of unreality that washed over Linus then, a discordant wave that felt like it was sucking him down. He couldn't catch his breath.

"What are you doing?" a voice whispered.

Linus let out a strangled yelp and turned to find Phee and Talia standing behind him. Phee had cleaned herself up, her red hair like fire, her freckles more pronounced. Her wings were folded against her back.

Talia had changed into a different outfit, though it was remarkably similar to the one she'd been wearing before, sans cap. Her long, white hair hung down on her shoulders, the same luxuriant color as her beard.

They both stared up at him suspiciously.

Linus didn't know what to say. "I'm . . ."

"Spying?" Phee suggested.

He stiffened. "Absolutely not—"

"We don't like spies here," Talia said ominously. "The last spy who tried to infiltrate our house was never heard from again." She leaned forward, eyes narrowing. "Because we cooked him and ate him for supper."

"You did no such thing," Mr. Parnassus said, appearing out of nowhere. Linus was beginning to understand it was something he did. At some point, he'd removed his coat. He now wore a thick sweater, the ends of which fell over the backs of his hands. "Because we've never been so lucky as to have a spy. A spy suggests someone capable of infiltration without displaying their intent. Anyone that has come here has made their intentions perfectly clear. Isn't that right, Mr. Baker?"

"Yes," he said. "Quite."

Mr. Parnassus smiled. "And besides, we don't harm our guests. Certainly not to the point of murder. That would be rude."

That didn't make Linus feel any better.

"Beyond the Sea" gave way to Bobby singing about wanting a girl to call his own so he wouldn't have to dream alone.

"Shall we?" Mr. Parnassus asked.

Linus nodded.

They all stared at him.

It took him a moment to realize he was blocking the door. He stepped aside. Phee and Talia pushed through to the kitchen. Mr. Parnassus called over his shoulder, "Theodore! Supper!"

Linus heard a loud scuffling coming from the living room. He looked beyond Mr. Parnassus in time to see Theodore burst out from underneath the couch, tripping over his wings. He growled as he flipped end over end, tail smacking against the floor. He lay on his back for a moment, breathing heavily.

"Slow and steady, Theodore," Mr. Parnassus said kindly. "We'd never start without you."

Theodore sighed (possibly—Linus couldn't be sure) and righted himself. He chirped as he gingerly stood on his back legs, folding his wings behind him with great care, first the right, and then the left. He took a tentative step forward, claws sliding on the wood floor before he found a grip.

"He prefers to fly everywhere," Mr. Parnassus whispered to Linus. "But whenever it's time to eat, I ask him to walk."

"Why?"

"Because he must get used to his feet on the ground. He can't spend all his time on wings. He'll tire, especially being so young. If he ever finds himself in danger, he needs to learn to use his legs as well as his wings."

Linus was startled. "Danger, why would he—"

"How many wyverns are left in the world, Mr. Baker?"

That shut Linus up quickly. The answer, though he couldn't be exact, was not many.

Mr. Parnassus nodded. "Precisely."

Theodore took his exaggerated steps toward them, head cocked to the side. When he stood at their feet, he looked up at Mr. Parnassus, chirped, and spread his wings.

"Yes, yes," Mr. Parnassus said, leaning down to run a finger along his snout. "Very impressive. I'm proud of you, Theodore."

He folded his wings again, then looked up at Linus before leaning down and biting gently on the tip of one of his loafers.

Mr. Parnassus looked at him expectantly.

Linus wasn't sure what for.

"He's saying thank you for the button."

Linus would prefer not being gnawed on to show gratitude, but it was already too late for that. "Oh. Well. You're . . . welcome?"

Theodore chirped again and went through the door that Mr. Parnassus held open for him.

"Shall we?" he asked Linus.

Linus nodded and walked through the door into the kitchen.

There was another table set at the other end of the kitchen. This one looked more used than the one in the formal dining room. There was a slightly worn tablecloth spread out, weighted down by place settings. Three plates and sets of silverware were on one side. There were four place settings on the other side, though one didn't have a spoon or a fork. And there were settings at either end of the table. Candles were lit and flickering.

In the center, there was food stacked high. He saw scalloped potatoes and bread and some sort of meat he couldn't recognize. There were leafy greens; the tomatoes that Lucy had been chopping looked like red beetles in the candlelight.

A feast, he'd been told, in his honor.

Linus wondered if it were poisoned.

Most of the children were already sitting at the table. Chauncey sat in the middle, with Phee and Talia on either side of him. Across from them were Theodore (climbing on the chair in front of the plate with no forks or spoons) and Ms. Chapelwhite. Next to her was an empty chair, and then Sal. He glanced back at Linus, found he was being watched, and then turned around quickly, lowering his head, picking at the tablecloth.

Mr. Parnassus sat at one end of the table.

That left the other end as the only open seat, seeing as how Linus was most likely not going to sit next to Sal. The poor boy probably wouldn't eat a single bite if that were the case.

No one spoke as he approached. He pulled out the chair, the

legs of which scraped against the floor. He winced, cleared his throat, and sat. He wished Bobby were still singing to distract from the awkwardness, but he couldn't see a record player anywhere.

He unfolded his cloth napkin next to his plate and spread it over his lap.

Everyone stared at him.

He fidgeted in his chair.

Lucy was suddenly there beside him, causing Linus to jump in his seat. "Oh dear," he said.

"Mr. Baker," Lucy said sweetly. "Can I get you something to drink? Juice, perhaps? Tea?" He leaned forward and dropped his voice. "The blood of a baby born in a cemetery under a full moon?"

"Lucy," Mr. Parnassus warned.

Lucy stared at Linus. "Whatever you want, I can give you," he whispered.

Linus coughed weakly. "Water. Water is fine."

"One water coming right up!" He reached up, grabbing an empty glass set next to Linus's plate. He took it to the sink, climbing up onto his stool. He stuck his tongue out in concentration (through the gap where his two front teeth used to be) as he turned on the tap. Once the glass was full, he held it with both hands as he climbed down from his stool. He spilled nary a drop as he handed it over to Linus.

"There," he said. "You're welcome! And I'm not even thinking about banishing your soul to eternal damnation or anything!"

"Thank you," Linus managed to say. "That's very kind of you."

Lucy laughed, a sound Linus was sure would haunt him for the rest of his life, before he went to the remaining empty chair. Sal pulled it out for him. On the chair sat a booster seat. Lucy climbed up into it, and Sal pushed the chair back toward the table, keeping his gaze downcast.

Mr. Parnassus smiled at the children. "Wonderful. As you are all aware, even though *someone* decided to hide his arrival from me, we have a guest."

Lucy sank down in his booster seat just a little.

"Mr. Baker is here to make sure you're all healthy and happy," Mr. Parnassus continued. "I ask that you treat him as you would me or Ms. Chapelwhite. Which means with respect. If I find out that any of you have done anything . . . untoward, there will be a loss of privileges. Are we clear?"

The children nodded, including Theodore.

"Good," Mr. Parnassus said, smiling quietly. "Now, before we eat, one thing you learned today. Phee?"

"I learned how to make the foliage thicker," Phee said. "It took a lot of concentrating, but I did it."

"Wonderful. I knew you could do it. Chauncey?"

His eyeballs knocked together. "I can unpack suitcases all by myself! *And* I got a tip!"

"How impressive. I doubt a suitcase has ever been unpacked as well as you did. Talia, if you please."

Talia stroked her beard. "If I stand really still, strange men think I'm a statue."

Linus choked on his tongue.

"Illuminating," Mr. Parnassus said, a twinkle in his eye. "Theodore?"

He chirped and growled, head resting on the tabletop.

Everyone laughed.

Except for Linus, that is, because he wasn't sure what had happened.

"He learned that buttons are the best things in the world," Ms. Chapelwhite said to Linus, glancing fondly down at Theodore. "And I learned that I still judge people by their appearance, though I should know better."

Linus understood who *that* was intended toward. He thought that was as close to an apology as he'd ever get from her.

"Sometimes," Mr. Parnassus said, "our prejudices color our

thoughts when we least expect them to. If we can recognize that, and learn from it, we can become better people. Lucy?"

Linus felt parched. He picked up his glass of water.

Lucy looked toward the ceiling, and in a monotone voice said, "I learned that I am the bringer of death and destroyer of worlds."

Linus sprayed water on the table in front of him.

Everyone turned slowly to stare at him again.

"Apologies," he said quickly. He took the napkin from his lap and wiped down his plate. "Went down the wrong pipe."

"Indeed," Mr. Parnassus said. "Almost like it was planned that way. Lucy? Should we try one more time?"

Lucy sighed. "I learned once again that I'm not just the sum of my parts."

"Of course not. You're more. Sal?"

Sal glanced at Linus, then turned his gaze downward. His lips moved, but Linus couldn't make out what he was saying.

Neither could Mr. Parnassus, or so it seemed. "Louder, please. So we can hear you."

Sal's shoulders slumped. "I learned that I still get scared of people I don't know."

Mr. Parnassus reached out and squeezed his arm. "And that's okay. Because even the bravest of us can still be afraid sometimes, so long as we don't let our fear become all we know."

Sal nodded but didn't look back up.

Mr. Parnassus sat back in his chair, looking across the table at Linus. "As for me, I learned that gifts come in all shapes and sizes, and when we expect them the least. Mr. Baker? What is it you have learned today?"

Linus shifted in his seat. "Oh, I don't think I should—I'm here to observe—it wouldn't be proper for me to—"

"Please, Mr. Baker?" Chauncey said wetly, tentacle creeping along on the table, suckers sticking to the tablecloth and causing it to bunch up. "You just *have* to."

"Yes, Mr. Baker," Lucy said in that same dead voice. "You

absolutely have to. I'd hate to think what would happen if you didn't. Why, it might bring about a plague of locusts. You wouldn't want that, would you?"

Linus felt the blood rush from his face.

"Children," Mr. Parnassus said as Ms. Chapelwhite covered up a smile. "Let him speak. And Lucy, we talked about the locust plague. That's only to be done under direct supervision. Mr. Baker?"

They looked at him expectantly.

It seemed as if he wasn't going to get out of this. He said the first thing that came to his mind. "I . . . I learned that there are things in this world that defy the imagination."

"Things?" Talia said, eyes narrowing. "And what would these *things* be?"

"The ocean," Linus said quickly. "Yes, the *ocean*. I've never seen it before. And I've always wanted to. It's . . . it's vaster than I even realized."

"Oh," Talia said. "That's . . . so boring. Can we eat now? I'm starving."

"Yes," Mr. Parnassus said, never looking away from Linus. "Of course. You've earned it."

As strange as the situation Linus found himself in was, dinner went relatively smoothly for the first ten minutes. It was while he was picking at the salad on his plate (not responding to the call of the potatoes, no matter how loud it was), that it came to a screeching halt.

It started, of course, with Talia.

"Mr. Baker?" she asked innocently. "Wouldn't you like something more than just the salad?"

"No," he said. "Thank you. I'm quite fine."

She hummed under her breath. "You sure? A man of your size can't live on rabbit food alone."

"Talia," Mr. Parnassus said. "Leave Mr. Baker—"

"It's *because* of my size," Linus interjected, not wanting someone to speak for him again. He was in *charge* here, after all. And the sooner they knew that, the better.

"What's wrong with your size?" Talia asked.

He flushed. "There's too much of it."

She frowned. "There's nothing wrong with being round."

He stabbed a tomato. "I'm not—"

"*I'm* round."

"Well, yes. But you're a gnome. You're supposed to be round." She squinted at him. "So why can't you be?"

"It's not—it's a matter of health—I can't—"

"I want to be round," Lucy announced. And then he was. One moment, he was the skinny little thing sitting in his booster seat, and the next, he began to blow up like a balloon, his chest stretching out, bones cracking obscenely. His eyes bulged from his head, and Linus was sure they were about to pop out onto the table. "Look!" he said through pinched lips. "I'm a gnome or Mr. Baker!"

"Why have you never seen the ocean?" Phee asked as Linus stared in horror at Lucy. "It's always there. It never goes anywhere. It's too big to move."

Lucy deflated, bones rearranging themselves until he was nothing but a six-year-old boy again. "It is," he agreed, as if he hadn't just blown up to three times his size. "I tried."

"That was a weird day," Chauncey said, sliding a potato through his mouth with a tentacle. Linus watched as it slid down inside of him, perfectly clear though tinged green. It began to break down into tiny particles. "So many fish died. And then you brought them back to life. Most of them."

"I've just . . . I've never had time," Linus said, feeling dizzy. "I—too many responsibilities. I have an important job and—"

Theodore attacked the meat Ms. Chapelwhite had set on his plate, growling low in his throat.

"Arthur says that we should always make time for the things we like," Talia said. "If we don't, we might forget how to be happy. Are you not happy, Mr. Baker?"

"I'm perfectly happy."

"You're not happy being round," Phee said. "So you can't be *perfectly* happy."

"I'm not *round*—"

"What *is* your job, Mr. Baker?" Chauncey asked, eyes bouncing on his stalks. "Is it in the city?"

Linus wasn't hungry anymore. "I—yes. It's in the city."

Chauncey sighed dreamily. "I love the city. All those hotels that need bellhops. It sounds like paradise."

"You've never *been* to the city," Lucy reminded him.

"So? I can love something even if I've only seen pictures of it. Mr. Baker loves the ocean, and he only saw it for the first time today!"

"If he loves it so much, why doesn't he marry it?" Phee asked.

Theodore chirped through a mouthful of meat. The children laughed. Even Sal cracked a smile.

Before Linus could ask, Ms. Chapelwhite said, "Theodore hopes you and the ocean are very happy together."

"I'm not going to marry the *ocean*—"

"Ohhh," Talia said, eyes wide, mustache twitching. "Because you're already married, right?"

"You're *married*?" Phee demanded. "Who is your wife? Is she still in your suitcase? Why would you put her there? Is she a contortionist?"

"Is your wife your cat?" Lucy asked. "I like cats, but they don't like me." His eyes started to glow red. "They worry I'll eat them. To be fair, I've never had one before, so I don't know if they're delicious or not. Is your wife delicious, Mr. Baker?"

"We don't eat pets, Lucy," Mr. Parnassus said, wiping his mouth daintily.

The red faded from Lucy's eyes immediately. "Right. Because

pets are friends. And since Mr. Baker's cat is his wife, that's like his *best* friend."

"Exactly," Mr. Parnassus said, sounding amused.

"No," Linus said. "*Not* exactly. Why, I never—"

"I like being round," Talia announced. "It means there's more of me to love."

"I love you, Talia," Chauncey said, laying one of his eyes on her shoulder. That same eye turned slowly to look at Linus. "Can you tell me more about the city? Is it bright at night? Because of all the lights?"

Linus could barely keep up. "I—I suppose it is, but I don't like being out at night."

"Because of the things in the dark that could rip your bones from your flesh?" Lucy asked through a mouthful of bread.

"No," Linus said, feeling queasy. "Because I would rather be home than anywhere else at all." That was truer now than it'd ever been before.

"Home is where you feel like yourself," Ms. Chapelwhite said, and Linus could only agree. "It's the same for us, isn't it, children? Home is where we get to be who we are."

"My garden is here," Talia said.

"The best garden," Mr. Parnassus said.

"And my trees," Phee added.

"The most wonderful trees," Mr. Parnassus agreed.

Theodore chirped, and Ms. Chapelwhite stroked one of his wings. "Your button, yes. It is here too."

"What a lovely gift," Mr. Parnassus said, smiling at the wyvern.

"And where else can I practice being a bellhop but at home?" Chauncey asked. "You have to practice something before being good at it."

"Practice makes perfect," Mr. Parnassus said.

"And this is the only place in the world where I don't have to worry about priests trying to stick a cross on my face to cast my soul back to the pits of hell," Lucy announced. He laughed as he shoved more bread in his mouth.

"Pesky priests, to be sure," Mr. Parnassus said.

"Are you going to take our home away from us?"

The table fell quiet.

Linus blinked. He looked around for the source of the voice and was surprised to find it came from Sal. Sal, who was looking down at the table, hands curled into fists. His mouth was set into a thin line, and his shoulders were shaking.

Mr. Parnassus reached out and laid his hand on one of Sal's fists. A long finger tapped the inside of Sal's wrist. He said, "That isn't Mr. Baker's intention. I don't think he ever wishes for something like that to happen. Not to anyone."

Linus thought to disagree, but he didn't think it would do any good. Especially in the light of an obviously traumatized child. And while Mr. Parnassus wasn't *wrong* exactly, he didn't like when someone else spoke for him.

Mr. Parnassus continued. "His job is to make sure I'm doing *my* job correctly. And what is my job?"

"To keep us safe," the children intoned. Even Sal.

"Precisely," Mr. Parnassus said. "And I like to think I'm good at it."

"Because you've had practice?" Chauncey asked.

Mr. Parnassus smiled at him. "Yes. Because I've had practice. And if I have my say, you will never be separated."

That was a challenge, and Linus didn't care for it one bit. "I don't think it's right to—"

"Who's ready for dessert?" Ms. Chapelwhite asked.

The children began to cheer.

SEVEN

Mr. Parnassus led Linus down a long hallway at the top of the stairs. "The children's rooms," he said, nodding at the doors on either side of the hall. There were signs hung from each of them with the names of the children: Chauncey and Sal on the right. Phee and Talia on the left. He pointed toward a hatch in the ceiling. The outline of a wyvern had been drawn on it. "Theodore's nest is up in the turret. He has a small hoard up there, but his favorite place is under the couch."

"I'll want to inspect them," Linus said, making a mental note of the layout.

"I figured you would. We can arrange for that tomorrow, seeing as how the children will be getting ready for bed shortly. Either Ms. Chapelwhite can show you while the children are in their studies, or we can do it before, and then you can join us in the classroom."

"What about Ms. Chapelwhite?" Linus asked, staring at the etchings of trees into the wood of Phee's door as they passed it by.

"She was here long before we ever were," Mr. Parnassus said. "The island is hers. We're merely borrowing it. She lives deep in the woods on the other side of the island."

Linus had so many questions. This island. This house. This man. But another was more prominent, given the number of doors he'd counted. Near the end of the hall, four remained. One was marked as a bathroom for the girls. The other was for the boys. A third door had ARTHUR'S OFFICE written in a legend on it. "And Lucy? Where does he stay?"

Mr. Parnassus stopped in front of the office and nodded toward the remaining door. "In my room."

Linus's eyes narrowed. "You share a room with a small boy—"

"Nothing untoward, I assure you." He didn't sound offended by the implication. "There was a large walk-in closet that I had converted into a room for Lucy when he came to stay with us. It . . . it's better for him if I'm near. He used to have such terrible nightmares. He still does, sometimes, though they aren't as vicious as they used to be. I like to think his time here has helped. He doesn't like being far away from me, if he can help it, though I am trying to teach him independence. He's . . . a work in progress."

Mr. Parnassus opened the office door. It was smaller than Linus expected, and crammed full, almost uncomfortably so. There was a desk set in the middle, surrounded by stacks of books, many of which leaned precariously. There was a single window that looked out over the ocean. It appeared endless in the night. In the distance, Linus saw the flashing wink of a lonely lighthouse.

Mr. Parnassus shut the door behind them, nodding for Linus to take a seat. He did so, taking out a small notebook that he always carried in his pocket, filled with notes he kept on each of his cases. He'd been lax in his duties here so far, kept off-kilter by the very idea of this place, but that would do no longer. He'd always prided himself on the copious notes he took, and if he was to give weekly reports as Extremely Upper Management requested, he would make sure they were the best he'd ever written.

"Do you mind?" he asked, pointing at a stubby pencil on the desk.

"Of course," Mr. Parnassus said. "What's mine is yours."

Something fluttered in Linus's stomach. He thought it must

have been something he ate. He opened his notepad and licked the tip of the pencil, an old habit he'd never been able to break. "Now, if you please. Let's discuss—"

"Sal is our newest arrival," Mr. Parnassus said, as if Linus hadn't spoken at all. He sat across from Linus in the chair behind the desk, steepling his hands under his chin. "Three months ago."

"Oh? I suppose I did read that in his file. He seems nervous, though I suppose teenagers often are in the face of authority."

Mr. Parnassus snorted. "Nervous. That's one word for it. Did you also read in his file that these three months are the longest he's ever stayed in one place since he was seven years old?"

"I . . . no. I don't suppose I got that far. I was distracted by . . . well. The enormity of this assignment."

Mr. Parnassus smiled sympathetically. "They didn't tell you what you were walking into, did they? Extremely Upper Management. Not until you got here."

Linus fidgeted in his seat. "No. Only that it was classified." Also that the children were problematic, but Linus didn't know if he should say that aloud.

"Surely you can see why."

"I can," Linus agreed. "One doesn't often meet the Antichrist."

Mr. Parnassus looked at him sharply. "We don't use that word here. I understand that you have a job to do, Mr. Baker, but I am the master of this house, and you will abide by my rules. Is that clear?"

Linus nodded slowly. He hadn't expected to be rebuked so severely, especially by someone who exuded calm like the man sitting across from him. He had underestimated Mr. Parnassus. He couldn't make that mistake again. "I meant no disrespect."

Mr. Parnassus relaxed again. "No. I don't think you did. And how could you have known? You don't know him. You don't know us. You have the files, but they only tell you the basics, I'm sure. Mr. Baker, what's written in those files are nothing but bones, and we are more than just our bones, are we not?" He paused, considering. "Except for Chauncey, seeing as how he doesn't actually *have* any bones. Though my point remains the same."

"What is he?" Linus asked. Then, "Oh dear, that sounds rude. No offense intended. I've never . . . I've never *seen* something—some*one*—like him before."

"I expect not," Mr. Parnassus said. He turned his head toward a stack of books to the right, eyes darting down the titles. He seemed to find the one he wanted about halfway down. He tapped the spine, forcing the edges out. The stack swayed. He pinched the cover of the book between two fingers and pulled quickly. The book came out. The top half of the stack fell neatly in its place. He didn't seem to notice Linus gaping at him as he opened the book on his desk and began to flip through the pages. "We aren't exactly sure what Chauncey is, or even really where he came from. A mystery, though I believe— Aha! Here we go." He turned the book toward Linus and tapped on the page.

Linus leaned forward. "*Medusozoa*? That's . . . a jellyfish."

"Correct!" Mr. Parnassus said brightly. "And I think that's part of it, at least. He doesn't sting, nor does he carry any kind of poison. There's possibly some sea cucumber in there as well, though it doesn't explain his appendages."

"It doesn't explain *anything*," Linus said, feeling rather helpless. "Where did he come from?"

Mr. Parnassus pulled the book back as he closed it. "No one knows, Mr. Baker. There are mysteries that may never be solved, no matter how hard we try. And if we spend too long trying to solve them, we may miss what's right in front of us."

"That's not how things work in the real world, Mr. Parnassus," Linus said. "Everything has an explanation. There is a reason for all things. That's the opening line of *RULES AND REGULATIONS* for the Department in Charge of Magical Youth."

Mr. Parnassus arched an eyebrow. "The world is a weird and wonderful place. Why must we try and explain it all away? For our personal satisfaction?"

"Because knowledge is power."

Mr. Parnassus snorted. "Ah. Power. Spoken like a true representative of DICOMY. Why am I not surprised you have the rule book memorized? You should know there's a chance that you'll find Chauncey under your bed at one point or another."

That startled Linus. "What? Why?"

"Because for the longest time, before he came here, he was called a monster, even by people who should have known better. He was told the stories of monsters hiding under beds whose calling in life was to frighten others. He thought that was who he was supposed to be. That it was his *job* to scare people, because it'd been ingrained in his . . . head that was all he was capable of. It wasn't until he came here that he realized he could be something more."

"So he chose to be a bellhop," Linus said numbly.

"He did. He saw it in a film we watched some months back. And for whatever reason, he was entranced by the idea."

"But he'll never be able to—" Linus stopped himself before the words could come out.

But Mr. Parnassus knew exactly what he was going to say. "He'll never be able to be a bellhop because what hotel would ever hire one such as him?"

"That's not . . ." It wasn't *what,* exactly? Fair? Right? Just? None of those things? Linus couldn't be sure. There were *reasons* such laws existed, and while Linus had never understood them, not really, there was nothing he could do about that. Linus knew that people often feared (though he felt that word was coded for something else entirely) what they didn't understand. The Department in Charge of Registration was born from the need to safeguard those who were extraordinary. At the beginning, children had been ripped from their homes and put into schools, though that was something of a misnomer. They were all but prisons, and though there were no bars on the windows, DICOMY had been created as a way to placate the cries of those who protested such treatment. And when it became clear that there were many orphans, the caseworkers had been split into two groups: those who dealt with registered families in conjunction with the Department in Charge of Registration, and those who worked with the orphans in the orphanages.

No, it wasn't very fair at all.

"It's not," Mr. Parnassus said, agreeing with the unspoken words. "But I allow him to dream of such things because he's a child, and who knows what the future will bring? Change often starts with the smallest of whispers. Like-minded people building it up to a roar. Which brings me back to Sal. Can I be blunt with you, Mr. Baker?"

Linus felt as if he had whiplash. "I would hope for nothing less."

"Good," Mr. Parnassus said. "You scare him."

Linus blinked. "Me? I don't know that I've scared anyone in my life."

"I highly doubt that's true. You work for DICOMY, after all."

"What does that have to do with—"

"And it's not necessarily *you,* as in you specifically. It's what you represent. You're a caseworker, Mr. Baker. While most of the children here have a vague understanding of what that entails, Sal has firsthand experience with people exactly like you. This is his twelfth orphanage."

Linus felt his stomach twist. "*Twelfth?* That can't be possible! He would—"

"He would what?" Mr. Parnassus asked. "Be shuttled off into one of the Department-run schools that DICOMY seems to be so fond of these days? It's where the children go after you finish with them, isn't it?"

Linus started sweating. "I don't—I don't suppose I can be sure. I . . . do what is required of my position, and nothing more."

"Nothing more?" Mr. Parnassus echoed. "How unfortunate.

Have you ever been to one of the schools, Mr. Baker? Ever followed up with any of the children after you've dealt with them?"

"It's—that's the job of upper levels. The Supervisors. I'm merely a caseworker."

"I highly doubt you're merely anything. Why are you a caseworker? Why have you never gone beyond this job?"

"Because it's what I know," Linus said, a line of sweat dripping down his neck. He didn't know how the tables had gotten turned so neatly that he hadn't even noticed. He had to regain control.

"Aren't you curious?"

Linus shook his head. "I can't be curious."

Mr. Parnassus looked surprised. "Why is that?"

"It does me no good. Facts, Mr. Parnassus. I deal in facts. Curiosities lead to flights of fancy, and I can't afford to be distracted."

"I can't imagine a life lived in such a way," Mr. Parnassus said quietly. "It sounds like no life lived at all."

"It's good then that I don't need your opinion on the matter," Linus snapped.

"I meant no offense—"

"I'm here to ensure that this place is up to code. To review your procedures to see if the Marsyas Orphanage is following guidelines set by DICOMY to ensure the funding provided to you is being used properly—"

Mr. Parnassus snorted. "Funding? I didn't expect you to have a sense of humor. How delightful."

Linus struggled to keep in control of the conversation. "Just because you house children of a more . . . unusual variety, doesn't mean I'll get distracted from the reason I'm here. It's about the children, Mr. Parnassus. And nothing more."

He nodded. "I can respect that. While we may be unconventional, I expect you'll see that I will do anything to keep them safe. As I said previously, the world is a weird and wonderful place, but that doesn't mean it's not without its teeth. And it will bite you when you least expect it."

Linus didn't know what to do with that. "You don't leave the island. Or, at least, the children don't."

"How do you figure?"

"The van out front. The tires are overgrown with weeds and flowers."

Mr. Parnassus sat back in his chair again, that strange smile on his face. "Very observant. Of course, it could be Phee or Talia. They do love growing things. But I suspect you wouldn't believe that."

"No. I wouldn't. Why does it look as if it hadn't been moved in some time?"

"Surely you traveled through the village."

"I—yes. With Ms. Chapelwhite." He hesitated. What had she told him as they drove through Marsyas?

The people of Marsyas don't appreciate our kind.

Sprites?

All magical creatures, Mr. Baker.

Mr. Parnassus nodded, as if he could read Linus's thoughts. "I can't say that we're unwelcome, but it's intimated that it's best for everyone if we stay where we are. Rumors tend to run rampant, and trying to get in front of them is like trying to beat back a wall of fire upon a dry field of grass. Though, I expect it helps that the government pays the people of the village for their silence as to the existence of this place. It also doesn't hurt that with this stipend comes thinly veiled threats of prosecution. It's easier for everyone if we stay where we are. Fortunately, the island is bigger than it looks and provides what the children need. Ms. Chapelwhite travels into the village for supplies every week or so. They know her, as well as she can be known."

Linus's head was swirling. He hadn't known that people were paid to keep their mouths shut, though he supposed it made a twisted sort of sense. "You don't leave?"

Mr. Parnassus shrugged. "I'm happy where I am because they're happy where they are. I suppose we could look about traveling beyond Marsyas and the village, but it hasn't come up. At least not yet. I expect we'll have to deal with it one day."

Linus shook his head as he picked up the notepad and pencil. "Sal. He shifts into a dog."

"A Pomeranian, if we're being specific."

"And you say this has been the longest he's been in one place?"

"Indeed."

"There are children who aren't classified who aren't that different from him. I met a child who could shift into a deer. Why is he here?"

Mr. Parnassus eyed him warily. "Because he can pass on his shift with a bite."

Linus felt the air whoosh out of his lungs. "Truly?"

He nodded. "Yes. There was an . . . incident. At one of his previous orphanages. He was struck by a woman who worked in the kitchens for trying to take an apple. He retaliated in the only way he knew how. She underwent the change the following week."

Linus thought the room was spinning. "I've never . . . I didn't know that was possible. I thought it was genetic."

"I think you'll find the impossible is more accessible here than you were led to believe."

"And Talia?"

"One of my first. Her family was killed rather tragically when their garden burned. Some thought it was set ablaze on purpose, though no one seemed to care much about that."

Linus winced. He remembered the signs hanging from the buses telling everyone to SEE SOMETHING, SAY SOMETHING. "You speak Gnomish."

"I speak many languages, Mr. Baker. I like learning new things. And it helps bring me closer to my charges."

"And why is she classified?"

"Have you ever met a female gnome, Mr. Baker?"

No. He hadn't. Which was odd, seeing as how he'd never even thought about it before. Linus scribbled on his notepad quickly. "And then there's Phee."

Mr. Parnassus chuckled. "Fiercely independent, she is. She's here because there has never been a sprite so young with so much power. When they tried to rescue her from a most . . . dire situation, she managed to turn three men into trees. Another, much older sprite was able to turn them back. Eventually. Fortunately for me, Ms. Chapelwhite assists her in ways I cannot. She's taken her under her wing, both figuratively and literally. She's blossomed quite beautifully under Ms. Chapelwhite's tutelage. We're very lucky she offered to assist us."

"And why did she?" Linus asked. "This is her island. Sprites are fiercely territorial. Why did she allow you here at all?"

Mr. Parnassus shrugged again. "The greater good, I suppose."

He spoke just like a sprite, in vague little circles. Linus didn't appreciate it. "And what would that be?"

"To see children who aren't wanted by anyone be allowed to prosper. You know as well as I do that the term *orphanage* is a misnomer, Mr. Baker. No one comes here looking to adopt."

No, he supposed they didn't, seeing as how the Marsyas Orphanage was hidden from most everyone. But did that really matter? Had he known any of the children in an orphanage such as this to be adopted? He couldn't think of a single instance. How had he never noticed that before? "Theodore?"

"Isn't this all in your files, Mr. Baker?"

No. It wasn't. In fact, Linus thought Mr. Parnassus had been correct when he'd said they were nothing but bones. "It's best I hear it directly from the source. Nuances can be missed when they are merely words on paper."

"He's not just an animal," Mr. Parnassus said.

"I never said he was."

He sighed. "No, I don't suppose you did. Forgive me. I've

dealt with people like you before. I forget that you're not all the same, even though I don't know quite what to make of you yet."

Linus felt strangely bare. "What you see is what you get with me. This is all I am."

"Oh, I doubt that immensely," he said. "Theodore is . . . special. I know you know just how rare someone like him is."

"Yes."

"He's still a juvenile, though his precise age is unknown. He . . . thinks differently than the rest of us, and though we understand each other, it's more in abstract thought rather than specifics. Does that make sense?"

"Not in the slightest," Linus admitted.

"You'll see," Mr. Parnassus said. "You're here for an entire month, after all. And I believe that leaves one child left, though I think you did that on purpose. Ms. Chapelwhite says she found you fainted dead away at the mere thought."

Linus flushed as he cleared his throat. "It was . . . unexpected."

"That's a good word to use to describe Lucy, I'm sure."

"Is he . . ." Linus hesitated. Then, "Is it true? Is he the actual Anti—I mean, the son of the Devil?"

"I believe he is," Mr. Parnassus said, and Linus's breath caught in his throat. "Though the notion of what someone like him is supposed to be is more fiction than fact."

"If that's true, then he's supposed to bring about the End of Days!" Linus exclaimed.

"He's six years old."

"He proclaimed himself to be hellfire and darkness when he threatened me!"

Mr. Parnassus chuckled. "It was his way of saying hello. He's got a morbid sense of humor for one so young. It's endearing once you get used to it."

Linus gaped at him.

Mr. Parnassus sighed as he leaned forward. "Look, Mr. Baker. I know it's—a lot to swallow, but I've had Lucy for a year. There were plans to . . . well. Let's just say this was a last resort. Regardless of his parentage, he is a *child*. And I refuse to believe that a person's path is set in stone. A person is more than where they come from."

"Than the sum of their parts."

Mr. Parnassus nodded. "Yes. Exactly. Lucy might cause fear in the majority of the world, but he doesn't cause it in me. I've seen what he is capable of. Behind the eyes and the demon in his soul, he is charming and witty and terribly smart. I will fight for him as I would for any of my children."

That didn't sit right with Linus. "But they're not yours. You're the master of the house, not their father. They are your charges."

Mr. Parnassus smiled tightly. "Of course. A slip of the tongue. It's been a long day, and I expect tomorrow will bring much of the same. It's worth it, though."

"Is it?"

"Of course. I couldn't see myself doing anything different. Can you?"

"We're not here to talk about me, Mr. Parnassus," Linus pointed out.

He spread his hands. "And why is that? You seem to know everything about us. And anything you don't know can be read in what I'm sure is a meticulous file."

"Not everything," Linus said, closing his notebook. "For example, there doesn't seem to be much information about *you*. In fact, your file was rather thin. Why is that?"

Mr. Parnassus looked amused again, and Linus wondered what he was missing. "Shouldn't that be a question for Extremely Upper Management? They're the ones who sent you here."

He was right, of course. It was disconcerting how little information there was. Mr. Arthur Parnassus's file told him nothing more than his age and education. There'd been an odd statement at the end: *Mr. Parnassus will be exemplary for the more problematic of children given his capabilities.* Linus hadn't known what to make of that, and now, seeing him face to face only left him with more questions. "I have a feeling they won't tell me much more than they already have."

"In that, I suspect you'd be right."

Linus stood. "I expect full transparency and your cooperation in this investigation."

Mr. Parnassus laughed. "What happened to this being a visit?"

"That was your word, sir, not mine. We both know what this is. The only reason DICOMY would have sent me here was if there was cause for concern. And I can see why. You have a powder keg under your roof, one more powerful than should ever exist."

"And he should be found at fault for existing? What choice did he have in the matter?"

That felt like a discussion for when Linus had his wits about him. Or possibly never. The implications alone made him feel faint again. "I am here to see if further action should be taken."

"Further action," Mr. Parnassus said, frustration slipping into his voice for the first time. "They have no one, Mr. Baker. No one but me. Do you really think DICOMY would allow someone like Lucy into one of their schools? Think hard before you answer."

"That's neither here nor there," Linus said stiffly.

Mr. Parnassus looked toward the ceiling. "Of course it's not. Because that's what happens after you're done, and that's none of your concern." He shook his head. "If you only knew."

"If there isn't anything amiss, then you have nothing to worry about," Linus said. "You may think me callous, Mr. Parnassus, but I assure you I do care. I wouldn't be in this position if I didn't."

"I believe that you believe that." He looked at Linus again. "My apologies, Mr. Baker. Yes, you will do your job, one way or another. But I think if you open your eyes, you'll see what's right in front of you rather than what's listed in a file."

Linus's skin felt like it was crawling. He needed to get out of this office. It seemed as if the walls were closing in. "Thank you for your hospitality, even if you didn't have a choice. I'm going to retire for the night. It's been a rather eventful day, and I expect more of the same tomorrow."

He turned and opened the door. Before he shut it behind him, he heard, "Good night, Mr. Baker."

Calliope was waiting inside the door when he arrived back at the guest house. He hadn't come across anyone else since leaving the office, though he heard voices echoing around him behind closed doors. He'd forced himself not to run out the front door.

Calliope spared him a glance before walking through the open door to do her business. The air was cold, and while he waited, he stared up at the main house. Lights shone through the second-floor windows, and he thought he saw movement behind closed curtains. If he remembered the layout of the upper floor correctly, it would be Sal's room he was seeing.

"Twelve different orphanages," he muttered to himself. "Something like that should have been in his file. Why on earth would he not have been enrolled in a school?"

Calliope came back inside, purring as she rubbed against his legs. He closed the door and locked it for good measure, though he figured if someone *wanted* to get in, they could.

Back in the bedroom, he remembered the warning from Mr. Parnassus about how Chauncey liked to hide under beds to scare people. He couldn't quite see the dark space underneath as it was hidden by the quilt that hung nearly to the floor.

He scrubbed a hand over his face. "I'm overthinking things. Of course he's not there. That's ridiculous."

He turned to go to the bathroom to perform his nightly routine.

He was in the middle of brushing his teeth, toothpaste in a glob on his generous chin, when he turned and marched back to the room. He fell to his knees, lifted up the quilt, and peered under the bed.

No monsters (children or otherwise) were hidden underneath.

"There," he said through a mouthful of toothpaste. "See? It's fine."

He almost believed it.

By the time he'd donned his pajamas and crawled into bed, he was sure he was going to toss and turn for the remainder of the night. He didn't sleep well in strange places, and learning everything he had today wouldn't help. He tried to read *RULES AND REGULATIONS* (because no matter what Mr. Parnassus said, he absolutely did *not* have it memorized), but he found himself thinking of dark eyes above a quiet smile, and then there was nothing but white.

EIGHT

He blinked his eyes open slowly the next morning.

Warm sunlight filtered in through the window. He smelled salt in the air.

It felt like a lovely dream.

But then reality burst through, and he remembered where he was.

And what he'd seen.

"Oh dear," he muttered roughly as he sat up in the bed, rubbing a hand over his face.

Calliope lay curled at the edge of the bed near his feet, tail swishing back and forth, eyes closed.

He yawned as he pulled the comforter back, putting his feet on the floor. He stretched, popping his back. Regardless of the situation he'd found himself in, he had to admit he hadn't had such a good night's sleep since he could remember. Between that, the morning sunlight, and the distant crash of the waves, he could almost pretend that this was nothing but a well-earned holiday, and that he was—

Something cold and wet wrapped around his ankle.

Linus screamed as he jerked his legs up. In his fear, he miscalculated his own strength, and his legs went up and over his head as he somersaulted backward and off the other side of the bed. He landed on the floor on his back with a jarring crash, breath leaving his lungs in a spectacular fashion.

He turned his head toward the underside of the bed.

"Hello," Chauncey said, eyes dancing on the end of their stalks. "I'm not actually trying to scare you. It's almost time for breakfast. We're having eggs!"

Linus looked back up toward the ceiling and waited for his heartbeat to slow.

Department in Charge of Magical Youth
Case Report #1 Marsyas Orphanage
Linus Baker, Caseworker BY78941

I solemnly swear the contents of this report are accurate and true. I understand per DICOMY guidelines that any discoverable falsehoods will result in censure and could lead to termination.

This report, and the ones to follow, will contain the observations I've made throughout each week of my investigation.

Marsyas Island and the orphanage herein are not what I expected.

It should be noted that the files given to me for this assignment are woefully inadequate, leaving out pertinent facts that I believe could have prepared me for what this investigation will entail. Either parts of the files were missing or they have been redacted. If it's the former, then this is a serious breach of conduct. If it's the latter, my temporary classification level should have negated that. I would recommend a review of protocols for all classified level four assignments in the future, to make sure no other caseworker walks into a situation without the required knowledge.

My apologies if this comes across as demanding. I merely believe more should have been provided.

The Marsyas Orphanage isn't what I thought it would be. The house itself is foreboding, though it appears to be well-maintained. It is large, and the interior is cluttered, although in a way that makes it feel like a lived-in home rather than the sanctuary of a hoarder. Aside, of course, from the actual hoard that belongs to the wyvern Theodore, but I have yet to see what that consists of, exactly.

The children each have their own rooms. In these first few days, I have seen the interiors of those belonging to the gnome Talia (the walls are adorned with more flowers than appear to be in the entirety of the garden), the sprite Phee (I do believe her bed is actually a tree growing through the floorboards, though for the life of me, I can't figure how that's possible), the . . . Chauncey (there is standing saltwater on the floor that I'm assured gets swabbed out once a week), and Theodore (he has built a nest in the attic that I was only allowed to see once I gave him another button; since I didn't have a spare, I had to snip one from one of my dress shirts. I assume I will be compensated for this).

I have not seen the room belonging to Sal yet. He doesn't trust me, and actually appears to be terrified of me, though through no fault of his own. He rarely says a word in my presence, but given his history, I can understand why. A history, I might add, I was not privy to as his file mostly discusses the abilities of his shift (leaving, of course, the most important part out). While this is certainly fascinating, I would suggest that it's not enough. I'm told this is his twelfth orphanage. This information would have allowed me a better understanding upon my arrival.

I haven't seen Lucy's room. I haven't asked. He has offered many times; once, he cornered me and whispered that I wouldn't believe my eyes, but I don't think I'm ready to see it yet. I will make sure to view it before I leave. If it is the last thing I do, my last will and testament has been filed with Human Resources. If enough of my remains exist, please see that they are cremated.

It should be noted that in addition to the children, there is an island sprite called Zoe Chapelwhite. The fact that I was not made aware of her presence until arrival is most unusual. Sprites, as I'm sure you're aware, are highly territorial. I came to an island that is ostensibly hers without an invitation directly from her. It would have been well within her rights to deny me entrance, or worse. This suggests that either DICOMY wasn't aware of her, or didn't feel the need to make me aware of her existence.

Which brings me to Mr. Parnassus; his file consisted of a single page that told me nothing of the master of Marsyas Orphanage. This certainly will not do. I know that I can always ask him to tell me about himself, but I would prefer to read about him instead of engaging in conversation. I am here to observe and report. The fact that I must become a conversationalist in addition to my current duties is vexing.

There is something about him—Mr. Parnassus—that I can't quite put my finger on. He certainly seems capable. The children appear to be happy, possibly even thriving. Mr. Parnassus has the uncanny ability to know where the children are at all times and what they're doing, even if they're out of sight. He's unlike anyone else I've met before.

Perhaps speaking to him won't be such a difficult task after all. And I will need to. Because regardless of how happy the children seem to be, the house appears to be on the verge of chaos. Upon my arrival, the children were roaming the grounds of the island. I'm told they are allowed to foster their own pursuits for a time each day, but it seems . . . unwise to allow these specific children to be unsupervised for any significant amount of time. It's well documented that magical youth are not in complete control of whatever powers they possess, some less than others.

That being said, I understand the need for secrecy here, given who these children are. I must admit that it might be a bit overblown. Regardless of their backgrounds, they are just children, after all.

How problematic could they possibly be with the guidelines set forth in *RULES AND REGULATIONS*?

"Fire and ash!" Lucy bellowed as he paced back and forth. "Death and destruction! I, the harbinger of calamity, will bring pestilence and plague to the people of this world. The blood of the innocents will sustain me, and you will all fall to your knees in benediction as I am your *god*."

He bowed.

The children and Mr. Parnassus clapped politely. Theodore chirped and spun in a circle.

Linus gaped.

"That was a lovely story, Lucy," Mr. Parnassus said. "I especially liked your use of metaphors. Keep in mind that pestilence and plague are technically the same thing, so it did get a little repetitious at the end, but other than that, quite impressive. Well done."

They were in the parlor of the main house, which had been converted into a classroom. There were six small desks lined up in front of a larger one. An old green chalkboard was set near the window, looking as if it'd recently been scrubbed clean. Thick pieces of chalk were set in a box near the floor. There was a map of the Earth on one wall, and a projector sitting on a metal stand in a corner. The walls were lined with books, much like Mr. Parnassus's office was. There were encyclopedias and novels and nonfiction books about Greek gods and goddesses and the scientific names of flora and fauna and Linus thought he'd seen one with gold lettering on the spine that said *The History of Gnomes: Cultural Relevance and Their Place in Society*. It appeared to be at least a thousand pages long, and Linus was itching to get his hands on it.

Lucy took a seat at his desk, looking rather pleased with himself. He'd been the second to last to perform in what Mr. Parnassus indicated was a block in the curriculum known as Expressing Yourself. The children were invited to the front of the class in order to tell a story of their own creation, either true or made up. Talia had told a rather pointed tale of an intruder who came to an island and was never heard from again. Theodore (according to Mr. Parnassus) had spun a jaunty limerick that caused everyone (except for Linus) to laugh until they had tears in their eyes. Phee spoke of a specific tree in the woods that she was growing and her hopes for its roots. Chauncey regaled them with the history of bellhops (something, Linus gathered, that was an ongoing series).

And then there was Lucy.

Lucy who had stood atop Mr. Parnassus's desk and basically threatened the entire planet with annihilation, his little fists above his head, eyes blazing.

Expressing Yourself was, according to Mr. Parnassus, an idea that would give the children confidence. Linus knew all too well the horrors of having to speak in front of an audience. Twice a week, the children were required to speak in front of the others about whatever topic they fancied. In addition to giving them an opportunity to practice public speaking, Mr. Parnassus said he believed it to be a creative outlet. "The minds of children are wondrous things," he said to Linus as they followed the others toward the parlor. "Some of the things they come up with seem to defy the imagination."

Linus understood that wholeheartedly. He absolutely believed that Lucy was capable of everything he'd shouted.

Linus sat in a chair at the back of the parlor. He'd been offered a seat much closer, but he'd shaken his head, saying it was best if he sat out of the way to observe. He had his notepad and pencil ready, set atop his copy of *RULES AND REGULATIONS* (something he'd thought to leave in his room, but decided against; one should always be prepared should the rules need to be reviewed) when the first child had stood in front, but it'd been quickly forgotten. He reminded himself that he needed to take copious notes so his reports weren't lacking, especially since there was nothing in the *RULES AND REGULATIONS* about children expressing themselves in such a manner.

And since Lucy was finished, that meant five children had expressed themselves.

Which left—

"Sal?" Mr. Parnassus said. "If you please."

Sal slumped lower in his chair as if he were trying to make himself smaller. It was almost comical, given his size. He glanced back at Linus quickly before jerking his head forward again when he saw he was being watched. He muttered something that Linus couldn't make out.

Mr. Parnassus stood in front of his desk. He reached down and tapped a finger on Sal's shoulder. He said, "The things we fear the most are often the things we should fear the least. It's irrational, but it's what makes us human. And if we're able to conquer those fears, then there is nothing we're not capable of."

Theodore chirped from the top of his desk, wings fluttering.

"Theodore's right," Phee said, chin in her hands. "You can do it, Sal."

Chauncey's eyes bounced. "Yeah! You got this!"

"You're made of strong stuff on the inside," Talia said. "And it's what's on the inside that counts."

Lucy tilted his head back and stared at the ceiling. "My insides are rotted and festering like an infected wound leaking pus."

"See?" Mr. Parnassus said to Sal. "Everyone here believes in you. All it takes is you believing in yourself."

Sal glanced back at Linus again, who tried to give what he hoped was an encouraging smile. It must not have gone over very well, as Sal grimaced, but either he had found the courage or resigned himself that he wasn't getting out of it, because he opened the lid to his desk and pulled out a piece of paper. He stood slowly. He was stiff as he walked to the front of the class. Mr. Parnassus sat on the edge of his desk. His slacks were still too short and revealed socks that were a brightly offensive shade of orange.

Sal stood in front of the class, staring at the paper gripped tightly in his hands. The paper shook slightly. Linus sat statue-still, sure that any movement from him would send Sal running.

Sal's lips started moving, his murmur barely audible.

"A little louder," Mr. Parnassus said softly. "Everyone wants to hear you. Project, Sal. Your voice is a weapon. Never forget that."

The fingers tightened around the page in his hands. Linus thought it would rip.

Sal cleared his throat and began again.

He said, "I am but paper. Brittle and thin. I am held up to the sun, and it shines right through me. I get written on, and I can never be used again. These scratches are a history. They're a story. They tell things for others to read, but they only see the words, and not what the words are written upon. I am but paper, and though there are many like me, none are exactly the same. I am parched parchment. I have lines. I have holes. Get me wet, and I melt. Light me on fire, and I burn. Take me in hardened hands, and I crumple. I tear. I am but paper. Brittle and thin."

He hurried back to his seat.

Everyone cheered.

Linus stared.

"Wonderful," Mr. Parnassus said approvingly. "Thank you for that, Sal. I particularly liked the scratches as a history. It spoke to me, because we all have that history, I think, though none are quite the same as the others as you so deftly pointed out. Well done."

Linus could have sworn he saw Sal smile, but it was gone before he could be sure.

Mr. Parnassus clapped his hands. "Well, then. Shall we move on? Since it's Tuesday, that means we will begin the morning with maths."

Everyone groaned. Theodore thunked his head repeatedly against the surface of his desk.

"And yet, we'll still proceed," Mr. Parnassus said, sounding amused. "Phee? Would you hand out the primers? Today, we're going to return to the wild and wonderful world of algebra. Advanced for some, and an opportunity to refresh for others. How lucky are we?"

Even Linus groaned at that.

Linus left the guest house after lunch, preparing to return to the parlor for what was promising to be an exciting discussion on the Magna Carta when Ms. Chapelwhite appeared out of nowhere, startling him to the point where he almost stumbled back against the porch.

"Why would you do that?" he gasped, clutching at his chest, sure that his poor heart was about to explode. "My blood pressure is high as it is! Are you trying to kill me?"

"If I wanted to kill you, I know many other ways to go about it," she said easily. "You need to come with me."

"I shall do no such thing. I have children to observe, and a report that I've barely begun. And besides, the *RULES AND REGULATIONS* state that a caseworker mustn't let himself be distracted when on assignment and—"

"It's important."

He eyed her warily. "Why?"

Her wings fluttered behind her. Even though it was impossible, she appeared to grow until she towered above him. "I am the sprite of Marsyas. This is my island. You are here because I have allowed you to be. You would do well to remember that, Mr. Baker."

"Yes, yes, of course," he said hastily. "What I meant to say was, I will definitely come with you wherever you ask me to go." He swallowed thickly. "Within reason."

She snorted as she took a step back. "Your bravery knows no bounds."

He bristled. "Now see here, just because—"

"Do you have other shoes?"

He looked down at his loafers. "Yes? But they're pretty much the same. Why?"

She shrugged. "We'll be walking through the forest."

"Oh. Well. Perhaps we could postpone that for another day—"

But she had already turned and started walking away from him. He gave very serious consideration to ignoring her and going back to the relative safety of the main house, but then he remembered that she *could* banish him if she wanted to.

And part of him—albeit a small part—was curious about what she wanted to show him. It'd been a long time since he'd been curious about anything at all.

Besides, it was a perfectly lovely day. Perhaps it would do him some good to be outside in all this sunshine.

Ten minutes later, he wished for death.

If Talia had come to him with her shovel, he didn't think he'd have stopped her.

If Lucy had stood above him, eyes blazing, fire burning, he would have welcomed him with open arms.

Anything to keep from hiking in the woods.

"I'm thinking," he gasped, sweat pouring off his brow, "that a bit of a break is in order. How does that sound? Lovely, I believe."

Ms. Chapelwhite glanced back at him, a frown on her face. She didn't look winded in the slightest. "It's not much farther."

"Oh," Linus managed to say. "Great. Great! That's . . . great." He tripped over a tree root, but managed to keep himself upright by the grace of God. "And I hope that measurements of distance and time are the same for sprites as they are for humans, meaning *not much farther* is exactly as it sounds."

"You don't get out much, do you?"

He wiped his brow with his sleeve. "I get out as much as is required of someone of my position."

"Into nature, I mean."

"Oh. Then, no. I prefer the comfort and dare I say *safety* of my home. I would rather sit in my chair and listen to my music, thank you very much."

She held back a large tree limb for him. "You've always wanted to see the ocean."

"Dreams are merely that—dreams. They're meant to be flights of fancy. They're not necessarily supposed to come true."

"And yet, here you are by the sea, far from your chair and home." She stopped and turned her face toward the sky. "There's music everywhere, Mr. Baker. You just have to learn to listen for it."

He followed her gaze. Above them, trees swayed, the wind rustling through the leaves. Branches creaked. Birds called. He thought he heard the chatter of squirrels. And underneath it all, the song of the ocean, waves against the shore, the scent of salt heavy in the air.

"It's nice," he admitted. "Not the hiking part. I could do without that, if I'm being honest. Rather uncomfortable for someone like me."

"You're wearing a tie in the middle of the woods."

"I hadn't *planned* on being in the middle of the woods," he snapped. "In fact, I'm supposed to be in the house taking notes."

She began to move again through the trees, her feet barely touching the ground. "For your investigation."

"*Yes,* for my investigation. And if I find you're hindering me in any way—"

"Does Mr. Parnassus get to read your reports before you send them?"

Linus narrowed his eyes as he stepped over a log overgrown with moss. Ahead, he could see flashes of white sand and the ocean. "Absolutely not. That would be improper. I would *never*—"

"Good," she said.

That caused him to blink. "It is?"

"Yes."

"Why?"

She looked back at him. "Because you'll want to include this in your report, and I don't want him to know about it." And with that, she stepped out onto the beach.

He stared after her for a moment before following.

Walking on the beach in loafers was not something Linus enjoyed. He gave brief thought to removing them and his socks and letting his toes dig into the sand, but it fell away when he saw what was waiting for them on the beach.

It was hastily built, the raft. It consisted of four planks of wood tied together with thick, yellow twine. There was a small mast, upon which fluttered what appeared to be a flag.

"What is it?" Linus asked, taking a step toward it, feet sinking into the wet sand. "Is there someone else on the island? That's not big enough for a man or woman. Is it a child?"

Ms. Chapelwhite shook her head grimly. "No. It was sent here from the village. Someone launched it from their boat. I'm sure they intended it to reach the docks like the last one, but the tide brought it here."

"Like the last one?" Linus asked, perplexed. "How many have there been?"

"This is the third."

"Why on earth would anyone— Oh. Oh dear."

Ms. Chapelwhite had unfurled the parchment attached to the mast. In blocky lettering were the words: LEAVE. WE DON'T WANT YOUR KIND HERE.

"I haven't told Mr. Parnassus about them," she said quietly. "But it wouldn't surprise me if he didn't somehow know already. He's . . . observant."

"And this is directed toward whom? The children? Mr. Parnassus? You?"

"All of us, I think, though I've been here far longer than the others." She let the flag drop back against the mast. "And they would know better if it was just me."

His brow furrowed at that chilling sentiment. "Why would anyone do such a thing? They're just children. Yes, they are . . . different than most, but that shouldn't matter."

"It shouldn't," she agreed, taking a step back, wiping her hands as if they were dirty from touching the parchment. "But it does. I told you about the village, Mr. Baker. And you asked me why they are the way they are."

"And you danced around answering my question, if I recall."

Her mouth was a thin line. Her wings were sparkling in the sunlight. "You're not a stupid man. That much is clear. They are the way they are because we're different. Even you asked me if I was registered only minutes after we met."

"This is abuse," Linus said stiffly, trying to ignore the pointed jab. "Plain and simple. Maybe the people of the village don't know exactly who inhabits this island, and that's probably for the best. But regardless of that fact, no one deserves to be made to feel lesser than they are." He frowned. "Especially if the government pays them for their silence. That has to be a breach of some sort of contract."

"It's not only this village, Mr. Baker. Just because you don't experience prejudice in your everyday doesn't stop it from existing for the rest of us."

SEE SOMETHING, SAY SOMETHING, the sign on the bus had read. And everywhere, really, wasn't it? More and more lately. On buses. In newspapers. Billboards. Radio ads. Why, he'd even seen the words printed on a grocery bag of all places.

"No," he said slowly. "I don't suppose it does."

She looked at him, the flowers in her hair appearing as if they were in bloom. He thought they actually were. "And yet these children are separated from their peers."

"For the safety of others, of course—"

"Or for their own safety."

"Isn't that the same thing?"

She shook her head. "No. And I think you know that."

He didn't know what to say in response, so he said nothing at all.

Ms. Chapelwhite sighed. "I wanted you to see it for yourself. So you knew more than what was in those files of yours. The children don't know, and it's best to keep it that way."

"Do you know who sent it?"

"No."

"And Mr. Parnassus?"

She shrugged.

He glanced around, suddenly nervous. "Do you think they're in danger? Could someone come to the island and attempt to cause harm?" The very thought caused his stomach to clench. It wouldn't do. Violence against any child was wrong, no matter what they were capable of. He'd seen a master of an orphanage strike a boy in the face once, just because the boy had managed to change a piece of fruit to ice. That orphanage had been shut down almost immediately, and the master charged.

He'd gotten away with a slap on the wrist.

Linus didn't know what had happened to the boy.

The smile that grew on Ms. Chapelwhite's face held no humor. In fact, Linus thought, it looked almost feral. "They wouldn't dare," she said, showing far too many teeth. "The moment they stepped onto my island with the intention of hurting someone in that house, it would be the last thing they'd do."

He believed her. He thought hard for a moment, and then said, "Perhaps we should send a message in response."

She cocked her head at him. "Wouldn't that be against your rules and regulations?"

He couldn't meet her knowing gaze. "I don't believe there's a subparagraph for a situation like this."

"What do you have in mind?"

"You're an island sprite."

"Your observational skills are astounding."

He snorted. "Which means you control the currents around your island, correct? And the wind."

"You seem to know an awful lot about magical creatures, Mr. Baker."

"I'm very good at what I do," he said primly. He pulled his pencil from his pocket. "Hold the parchment out for me, would you?"

She hesitated briefly before doing just that.

It took him a few minutes. He had to go over each letter multiple times to make his words clear. By the time he finished, Ms. Chapelwhite's smile had softened, and it was perhaps the most sincere expression he'd seen since he'd met her.

"I didn't think you capable of such a thing, Mr. Baker," she said, sounding gleeful.

"I didn't either," he muttered, wiping the sweat from his brow. "It's best if we don't mention this again."

He helped her push the raft back into the water, though he thought she was just humoring him. She most likely didn't need his assistance. By the time the raft set sail again, parchment flapping, his loafers were wet, his socks soaked, and he was breathing heavily.

But he felt lighter somehow. Like he wasn't paint blending into the wall.

He felt real.

He felt *present*.

Almost like he could be seen.

The wind picked up, and the raft sailed away, back toward the mainland in the distance.

He didn't know if anyone would actually find it, if it would actually make it across the channel.

And even if they *did* find it, they'd probably ignore it.

That almost didn't matter.

LEAVE. WE DON'T WANT YOUR KIND HERE, one side of the parchment said.

NO, THANK YOU, the other side said.

They stood on the beach in the sand with water lapping at their feet for a long time.

NINE

On the first Friday Linus Baker spent on the island, he received an invitation. It wasn't one he expected, and upon hearing it, he wasn't sure it was one he wanted to accept. He could think of six or seven or quite possibly one hundred things he'd rather do. He had to remind himself he was on Marsyas for a reason, and it was important he see all sides of the orphanage.

The invitation had come from a knock on the door of the guest house where Linus was attempting to finish his first report from his time on Marsyas. The ferry would come tomorrow to take him to the mainland so he could send it via post back to DICOMY. He'd been deep into his writing, careful to only allow one admonition per page regarding Extremely Upper Management's lack of transparency before sending him to the island. He'd made it a game of sorts, trying to make his responses to their transgressions as subtle as possible. He'd been thankful for the interruption of a knock at the door when the last line he'd written read . . . *and furthermore, the very idea that Extremely Upper Management would employ obfuscation and outright deception with their caseworkers is most uncivilized.*

It was probably for the best if he rethought that last sentence.

He was pleasantly surprised to find Mr. Parnassus standing on the porch of the guest house, looking windswept and warm in the afternoon sunlight, something that Linus was finding himself not only getting used to seeing, but rather looking forward to. He told himself it was because Mr. Parnassus was a cheery fellow, and if this were the real world, perhaps they could have been friends, something that Linus was in short supply of. That was all it was.

It didn't matter that Mr. Parnassus didn't appear to own a pair of slacks that actually fit his long legs, given that they were always too short. Today he wore blue socks with clouds on them. Linus refused to be charmed.

He mostly succeeded.

Still, when Mr. Parnassus extended his invitation, Linus felt his throat close, and his tongue become as dry as burnt toast. "Pardon?" he managed to ask.

Mr. Parnassus smiled knowingly. "I said it might be a good idea if you were to sit in on my one-on-one with Lucy, just so you may get the full experience of Marsyas. I expect Extremely Upper Management anticipates your observations of such, don't you think?"

Linus did. In fact, he was beginning to think that perhaps Extremely Upper Management cared more about Lucy than any other person on the island. Oh, it wasn't spelled out as such in the files he'd been given, but Linus had been doing this line of work for a long time and was more perceptive than most gave him credit for.

That didn't mean he'd jump at such an invitation.

He had only made partial headway on his first few days on the island. Sal was still petrified of him, and Phee was dismissive, but Talia only threatened to bury him in her garden once or twice per day, and Chauncey seemed happy about anything and everything (especially when he got to deliver fresh towels or bedsheets to Linus, always managing to cough politely enough to ensure a tip). Theodore, of course, thought the sun rose and set because of Linus, something that shouldn't have tugged at his heartstrings as much as it did. It was only a *button* (four now, in fact; Linus had decided one of his dress shirts was ready for retirement, and he would snip a new button each morning), and that they were plastic and not brass didn't seem to matter to Theodore.

Lucy, on the other hand, was still an enigma. A terrifying enigma, to be sure, given that he was the Antichrist, but an enigma nonetheless. Just the day before, Linus had found himself in the library of the main house, an old room on the first floor filled with books from floor to ceiling. He'd been perusing the shelves when he'd caught movement in the shadows out of the corner of his eye. He'd whirled around, but there was nothing there.

Until he'd looked up to see Lucy crouched on the top of a bookshelf, staring down at him with bright eyes and a twisted smirk on his face.

Linus gasped, heart racing.

Lucy said, "Hello, Mr. Baker. You would do well to remember that human souls are cheap trinkets to one such as me." He giggled and leapt from the bookshelf, landing on his feet. He looked up at Linus and whispered, "I love cheap trinkets." And then he'd run from the library. Linus saw him only an hour later munching on an oatmeal raisin cookie in the kitchen, bopping his head along with The Coasters singing about how they were gonna find her, searchin' every which-a-way.

So, no, Linus wasn't necessarily jumping on the invitation.

But he had a job to do.

It was why he was here.

And the more he learned about Lucy, the better prepared he'd be when reporting to Extremely Upper Management.

(It had *nothing* to do with the idea of also getting to know Mr. Parnassus a little better. And even if it *did,* it was because the file on the master told him next to nothing, and he needed to be thorough. It was outlined as such in the *RULES AND REGULATIONS,* page 138, paragraph six, and he would follow it to the letter.)

"Does he know I'll be there?" Linus asked, wiping the sweat from his brow.

Mr. Parnassus chuckled. "It was his idea."

"Oh dear," Linus said faintly.

"Should I tell him to expect you?"

No. No, he shouldn't. In fact, he should tell Lucy that Linus had taken ill and would be down for the evening. And then Linus could spend his Friday night in his pajamas listening to the little radio in the living room and pretending he was at home. It wasn't a record player, but it would do in a pinch. "Yes," he said. "I will be there."

Mr. Parnassus smiled widely. Linus felt his skin flush at the sight of it. "Wonderful," he said. "I think you'll be surprised. Five o'clock sharp, Mr. Baker." He whirled on his heel and headed toward the main house, whistling a jaunty tune.

Linus closed the door and slumped against it. "Well, old boy, you've stepped into it now, haven't you?"

Calliope sat in the windowsill, blinking slowly in the sunlight.

Linus Baker had never been the religious sort. While he didn't mind if others were, it was never for him. His mother had been . . . not quite fervent but so close that there was barely a difference. She took him to church on Sundays, and he'd sit in his freshly starched shirt that itched terribly, and would stand when he was supposed to stand, and kneel when he was supposed to kneel. He liked the hymns, though he couldn't carry a tune if he'd been given a bucket, but that was about it. He thought it preposterous: the idea of fire and brimstone, that sinners went to Hell while everyone else went to Heaven. Sins seemed to be subjective. Oh, murder was bad, and harming others was too, but was that comparable to someone who'd nicked a candy bar from the corner store when they were nine years old? Because if it was, Linus was destined for Hell given the Crunchie bar he'd slipped into his pocket and consumed late at night while hiding under his comforter.

When he'd become old enough to understand the power of the word *no,* he hadn't had to go to church after that. *No,* he'd told Mother, *no, I don't think I want to go.*

She'd been upset, of course. She worried about his soul, telling him that he was going to go on a path from which he wouldn't be able to return. There would be drugs and booze and *girls,* and she would be there to pick up the pieces because that's what a mother did (and, he thought, to tell him *I told you so*).

But, as it turned out, drugs were never a problem, and while Linus did enjoy a glass of wine with dinner once a month, it never turned into more than that.

And as for *girls,* his mother needn't have worried. By then, Linus had already noticed how his skin had tingled when his seventeen-year-old neighbor, Timmy Wellington, mowed the lawn without his shirt on. No, girls weren't going to bring about Linus Baker's downfall.

So no, Linus hadn't been of the religious sort at all.

Granted, that was before he knew the Antichrist was a six-year-old on Marsyas Island. For the first time in his life, Linus wished he had a crucifix or a Bible or *something* with which to protect himself should Lucy decide he needed a sacrifice in order to come into his full powers.

It certainly didn't help when he passed Phee and Talia in the garden, both of them watching every step he took toward the main house. "Dead man walkin'," Talia intoned in a flat voice. "We got a dead man walkin' here."

Phee covered up her laughter with a cough.

"Good afternoon," he said stiffly.

"Good afternoon, Mr. Baker," Phee and Talia said sweetly, though Linus knew better.

They whispered behind him as he reached the porch to the main house. He glanced back at them, and they waved cheekily.

Oddly, he found himself struggling against a smile at the sight of them.

He scowled instead.

He walked inside the house. He heard Ms. Chapelwhite singing in the kitchen. She'd warmed up to him considerably ever since their trip to the beach. And by that, he meant she acknowledged his presence with a nod that almost seemed cordial rather than perfunctory.

He closed the door behind him and heard a chirp coming from the couch in front of the fireplace. He looked down to see a scaly tail sticking out from underneath. "Hello, Theodore," he said.

The tail disappeared, and Theodore stuck his head out, tongue flicking. He chirped again, this time a question. Linus didn't need to speak wyvern to understand what he was asking for. "I already gave you one this morning. The more you get, the less you appreciate their worth." He felt a little silly, given that plastic buttons were worth nothing at all, but it still felt important to impart such a lesson.

Theodore sighed morosely and disappeared back under the couch, grumbling to himself.

He walked up the stairs, the wood creaking ominously under his weight. The sconces on the walls appeared to flicker, and Linus told himself it was just because the house was old, and the wiring probably could use some upkeep. He made a mental note to ask in his report about the status of funding to the Marsyas Orphanage. Mr. Parnassus had seemed dismissive at the idea of *funding*, but Linus thought he had to be mistaken.

The doors to the bedrooms on the second floor were shut on either side of him, with the exception of Chauncey's. Linus was about to pass his room when he stopped, hearing Chauncey talking inside. He peeked through the slightly open door to see Chauncey standing in saltwater in front of a full-length mirror near the window, a porter's cap on his head between the stalks of his eyes. "How do you do, Mr. and Mrs. Worthington?" Chauncey asked, one of his tentacles lifting the cap as he bowed low. "Welcome back to the Everland Hotel! May I take your luggage? Oh, why thank you for noticing, Mrs. Worthington! Yes, I *did* get a new uniform. Only the best for Everland. I do hope you enjoy your stay!"

Linus left him to it.

He wondered if it would be too much to get Chauncey a coat to complete his costume. Perhaps he could see if there was something in the village—

No. That wasn't what he was here for. He was here to observe and nothing more. He couldn't influence the orphanage. It wouldn't be proper. The *RULES AND REGULATIONS* were specific about such matters.

He thought he heard movement behind Sal's door, but it was shut tight. Best not to attempt to say hello. He wouldn't want to frighten the poor boy.

In addition to having never seen inside of Sal's room, he had yet to go through the last door in the hall. Mr. Parnassus hadn't invited him before today, though Lucy had on numerous occasions, much to Linus's chagrin. He knew he'd have to inspect both before he left the island, but he'd been putting it off this first week, something he shouldn't have done.

He stood in front of the door for a long moment, before taking a deep breath and raising his shaking hand to knock.

Before he could, the door unlatched and opened just a smidge.

Linus took a step back. There didn't seem to be any light coming from inside.

He cleared his throat. "Hello?"

No response.

He steeled his nerves and pushed open the door.

The late afternoon sun had been bright when he'd walked inside the house, the sea air warm. But the interior of the room reminded him of being back in the city, dark and cold and dank. He took a step inside. And then another.

And then another.

The door slammed shut behind him.

He spun around, heart in his throat. He was reaching for the door when candles flared to life around him, spouts of fire reaching up two feet or more.

"Welcome to my domain," a child's voice rang out behind him. "You have entered here at my invitation." The voice cackled. "Bear witness to the true depth of my power! I am Lucifer! I am Beelzebub, the prince of devils! I am—"

"—going to find yourself with a loss of privileges if you should decide to continue," Linus heard Mr. Parnassus say.

The candles snuffed out.

The darkness faded.

Sunlight poured in through the window.

Linus blinked against the bright light.

Mr. Parnassus sat in a high-backed chair near the window, legs crossed, hands in his lap, an amused expression on his face. There was an empty chair across from him, undoubtedly for the boy who lay on his back on the thick rug.

"He heard you coming," Mr. Parnassus said with a shrug. "I cautioned him against it, but since this is his time to do as he wishes, I thought he shouldn't be stifled."

Lucy looked up at Linus, who was plastered against the bedroom door. "I am who I am."

"Quite," Linus said, his voice a squeak, barely able to peel himself from the door.

The room itself was large and spacious. There was a four-poster bed set against the far wall, made of dark wood, ornate vines and leaves carved into the posts. There was a desk, far older than the others in the house, covered in reams of paper and stacks of books. An unlit fireplace sat opposite the bed. If Linus hadn't just been frightened half out of his mind, he would have thought it would be perfect for cold winter nights.

"Would you like to show Mr. Baker your room?" Mr. Parnassus asked Lucy. "He'd probably like to see it very much. Wouldn't you, Mr. Baker?"

No. No, he wouldn't. Not very much at all. "Ye-es," Linus said. "That certainly seems . . . doable."

Lucy turned over on his stomach, propping his chin in his hands. "Are you sure, Mr. Baker? You don't sound so sure."

"I'm sure," Linus said firmly.

Lucy picked himself up off the ground. "Well, don't say I didn't warn you."

Mr. Parnassus sighed. "Lucy, you're going to give Mr. Baker the wrong idea."

"And what idea would that be?"

"You know what."

Lucy threw his hands up. "I'm just trying to build anticipation. Expect the unexpected! You told me that life is meant to surprise you. I'm trying to surprise him."

"I think you're setting yourself up for nothing but disappointment."

Lucy's eyes narrowed. "And whose fault is *that*? If you'd have listened to my decorating ideas, there would be no room for disappointment. There would only be joy." He glanced at Linus. "Well, for me."

Mr. Parnassus spread his hands in a placating gesture. "I don't think having severed human heads is conducive to a good night's sleep or the health and sanity of Mr. Baker, even if they were to be made of papier-mâché."

"Severed heads?" Linus asked in a strangled voice.

Lucy sighed. "Just representations of my enemies. The Pope. Evangelicals who attend megachurches. You know, like normal people have."

Linus didn't think Lucy quite had the grasp of what was *normal,* but he managed to keep that to himself. "So, no heads?"

"None," Lucy said with a scowl. "Not even the skull of an animal from the woods that I *didn't kill* and just found." He shot a glare at Mr. Parnassus.

"What did I say about animals?" Mr. Parnassus said.

Lucy stomped toward a closed door near the chairs. "I'm not supposed to kill them because only serial killers do that, and if they're already dead, I can't play with the remains because I'll smell bad."

"And?"

"*And* it's wrong."

"Let's lead with that next time," Mr. Parnassus said. "It might sound more humane."

"Stifling my creativity," Lucy muttered. He put his hand on the doorknob and looked over at Linus. His disgruntled expression disappeared, and that syrupy-sweet smile returned that caused chills to run down Linus's spine. "Are you coming, Mr. Baker?"

Linus tried to make his feet move, but they remained firmly rooted near the bedroom door. "Is Mr. Parnassus joining us?" he asked.

Mr. Parnassus shook his head. "I'll let him give you the tour, as the other children did." He paused. Then, "I'm still working on Sal."

"Great," Linus said weakly. "That's . . . that's fine."

"Why are you sweating?" Lucy asked, smile widening. "Something wrong, Mr. Baker?"

"No, no," Linus said. "Just . . . a little overwarm, is all. Temperate climate, you know. Not used to it back in the city."

"Oh, of course," Lucy said. "That must be it. Come here, Mr. Baker. I have something to show you."

Linus swallowed thickly. He told himself he was being foolish, that Mr. Parnassus was *right there,* and Lucy wouldn't dare do anything untoward in his presence.

The *problem* with that was Linus's brain chose that exact moment to wonder if there had ever been another caseworker to visit the island before, and what became of them. There *had* to have been, right? He can't have been the first. Why, the idea was preposterous.

And *if* there had been others before him, what had become of them? Had they too entered Lucy's room, only to never be seen again? Would Linus follow Lucy through the door to find the carcasses of his predecessors nailed to the ceiling above the bed? Linus certainly could be firm when he needed to be, but he did have a weak constitution, and the sight of blood tended to cause him to feel woozy. He didn't know what would happen if he had to see intestines strewn about like wet decorative garlands.

He glanced at Mr. Parnassus, who nodded encouragingly. It did not soothe Linus in the slightest. For all he knew, Mr. Parnassus was just as evil as Lucy, brightly colored socks and wonderful smile be damned.

He nearly tripped at *wonderful smile.*

He pushed it away.

He could do this.

He could *do this.*

It was just a *child.*

He fixed a pleasant look on his face (barely above a grimace) and said, "I would be delighted to see your room, Lucy. I do hope it's tidy. A disheveled room is the sign of a disheveled mind. It's best to keep things clean when possible."

Lucy's eyes danced. "Is that right, Mr. Baker? Well, let's see what my mind is like, then."

Linus was sure this was one of the stressors his physician had warned him of. There was nothing he could do about that now.

He stopped next to Lucy.

He looked down at him.

Lucy grinned. Linus thought he had more teeth than was humanly possible.

He turned the doorknob.

He pushed open the door.

It creaked on its hinges and—

Revealed a small space with a twin bed against one wall, the comforter plaid, the pillowcase white. There was room enough for a bureau, but not much else. Atop the bureau sat a collection of shiny rocks shot with veins of quartz.

On the walls were vinyl records, each hung on a pushpin through the hole in its middle. There was Little Richard, the Big Bopper, Frankie Lymon and the Teenagers, Ritchie Valens, and Buddy Holly. In fact, there were more Buddy Holly records than any other.

Linus was startled at the sight of them. He recognized most of the records, because he had them back in the city at his own home. Many nights had been spent listening to "Peggy Sue" and "That'll Be the Day" and "Chantilly Lace."

But aside from Little Richard and Frankie Lymon, they all had something else in common. It was slightly morbid, when he thought about it. But it made sense.

He hadn't even noticed Lucy had closed the door behind them. "The day the music died," Lucy said.

Linus spun around, heart tripping all over itself. Lucy stood at the door, back pressed against it. "What?"

He waved a hand toward the records. "Buddy Holly and Ritchie Valens and the Big Bopper."

"A plane crash," Linus said quietly.

Lucy nodded and pushed himself off the door. "Ritchie and Bopper weren't even supposed to be on the plane, did you know that?"

He did. He said, "I think so."

"Bopper was sick and took someone else's seat."

Waylon Jennings, though Linus kept that to himself.

"And Ritchie won his seat in a coin toss. Buddy didn't want to be stuck in a bus because it was cold, and they had to go to Montana." Lucy reached up and touched "Chantilly Lace." He looked almost reverent. "The pilot wasn't given the correct weather information, and the plane didn't have the proper instruments needed to fly. Weird, right?" He smiled at Linus. "I like music that makes me happy. And I like death. It's strange how people can mix the two. They all died by chance, and then people sang about them after. I like those songs, but not as much as the ones sung by dead people."

Linus coughed roughly. "I—I like music too. I have some of these records at my house."

Lucy perked up at that. "Dead people music?"

He shrugged. "I . . . guess? The older the music, the more likely the singer is dead."

"Yeah," Lucy breathed. His eyes begin to tinge with red. "That's true. Death is wonderful to music. It makes the singers sound like ghosts."

Linus thought it was probably a good time to change the subject to something less morbid. "I like your room."

Lucy looked around, the light fading from his eyes. "It's the best. I like having my own room. Arthur says that it's important to have independence." He glanced at Linus before looking away, and Linus could have sworn he looked almost *nervous*. "Just as long as he doesn't go too far away." His eyes widened. "But I'm not a baby! I can be fine by myself! In fact, I'm by myself all the time!"

Linus arched an eyebrow. "*All* the time? Oh, no. No, no, no. That won't do. I'll need to have a word with Mr. Parnassus, if that's the case. A child of your age should never be by himself *all* the time—"

"I didn't mean it like *that*," Lucy cried. "What I meant was is that I'm *never* by myself! Ever! Everywhere I go, he's there! He's like a shadow. It's so annoying."

"Well, if you say so."

Lucy nodded furiously. "I do. That's *exactly* what I said. So, no need to talk to Arthur about it or put it in reports and say bad things about me." His smile was positively angelic. "I swear I'm a good person." The smile faded. "And you don't need to worry about looking under my bed. And if you do, the bird skeleton under it isn't mine, and I don't know who put it there, but they should be punished because that's wrong." He smiled again.

Linus stared at him.

"Okay!" he said, stepping forward and grabbing Linus by the hand. "That's it! That's my room! No need to see anything else!" He pulled Linus toward the door and flung it open. "Arthur! He saw my room and said everything looks good and there's nothing bad in it at all and that I'm a good person. And he likes the same music as me! *Dead people music.*"

Mr. Parnassus looked up from the book in his lap. "Is that right? Dead people music?"

Lucy lifted his head up to look at Linus, still holding his hand tightly. "We like dead things, don't we, Mr. Baker?"

Linus sputtered.

Lucy let him go and collapsed on the floor at Mr. Parnassus's feet where he'd been when Linus had arrived. He folded his hands on his stomach and stared up at the ceiling. "My brain is filled with spiders burrowing their eggs in the gray matter. Soon they'll hatch and consume me."

Linus had no idea what to do with that.

Thankfully, it appeared Mr. Parnassus did. He closed the book in his lap and set it on the small table next to the chairs. He tapped one of his wing tip shoes against Lucy's shoulder. "How descriptive. We'll discuss that more in detail in just a moment. First, Mr. Baker would like to observe. Would that be all right with you?"

Lucy glanced at Linus before looking back toward the ceiling. "That's fine. He likes dead things almost as much as I do."

That wasn't even remotely true.

"Indeed," Mr. Parnassus said, motioning for Linus to sit in the vacant chair. "How fortuitous. Where did we leave off before Mr. Baker arrived?"

Linus sat. He pulled his notepad out, along with his pencil. He didn't know why his fingers were shaking.

"Categorical Imperative," Lucy said. "Kant."

"Ah, that's right," Mr. Parnassus said. "Thank you for reminding me." Linus got the idea that he didn't need to be reminded at all. "And what did Kant say about the Categorical Imperative?"

Lucy sighed. "That it's the supreme principle of morality. It's an objective. A rationally necessary and unconditional principle that we must always follow despite any natural desires or inclinations to the contrary."

"And was Kant right?"

"That to be immoral is to be irrational?"

"Yes."

Lucy scrunched up his face. "No?"

"And why not?"

"Because people aren't black and white. No matter how hard you try, you can't stay on one path without diversions. And that doesn't mean you're a bad person."

Mr. Parnassus nodded. "Even if you have spiders in your brain?"

Lucy shrugged. "Maybe. But Kant was talking about normal people. I'm not normal."

"Why is that?"

He tapped his stomach. "Because of where I came from."

"Where did you come from?"

"A vagina after it was penetrated by a penis."

"Lucy," Mr. Parnassus admonished, as Linus choked.

Lucy rolled his eyes. He shifted as if he were uncomfortable. "I came from a place where things weren't so good."

"Are they better now?"

"Mostly."

"Why do you think that is?"

Lucy squinted up at Linus before turning his head toward Mr. Parnassus. "Because I have my own room here. And my records. And you and the others, even though Theodore won't let me see his hoard."

"And the spiders?"

"Still there."

"But?"

"But I can have spiders in my head as long as I don't let them consume me and then destroy the world as we know it."

Linus could barely breathe.

Mr. Parnassus didn't seem to have that problem. He was smiling. "Exactly. To err is to be human, irrational or not. And while some mistakes are bigger than others, if we learn from them, we become better people. Even if we have spiders in our brains."

"I'm unholy."

"So some people say."

Lucy's face scrunched up as if he was thinking hard. "Arthur?"

"Yes?"

"Did you know your name is a mountain?"

Mr. Parnassus blinked, as if he'd been caught off guard. "I did. How did you know that?"

Lucy shrugged. "I know a lot of things, but I don't always know how I know them. Does that make sense?"

"Sort of."

"Mount Parnassus was sacred to Apollo."

"I know."

"And do you know Linus of Thrace?"

Mr. Parnassus shifted in his seat. "I . . . don't think so."

"Oh! Well, Apollo killed Linus with his arrows because of a musical contest. Are you going to kill Mr. Baker?" Lucy turned his head slowly to look at Linus. "If you do, can you make sure to use arrows? I don't want him to be un-holey too."

He began to cackle.

Mr. Parnassus sighed as Linus's chest hitched. "Did you just tell that entire story to be able to make a joke?"

"Yes," Lucy said, wiping his eyes. "Because you told me once that if we can't laugh at ourselves, we're doing it wrong." He frowned. "Am I doing it wrong? Nobody seems to be laughing."

"Humor is subjective, I'm afraid," Mr. Parnassus said.

"That's unfortunate," Lucy said, staring back up at the ceiling. "Humanity is so weird. If we're not laughing, we're crying or running for our lives because monsters are trying to eat us. And they don't even have to be *real* monsters. They could be the ones we make up in our heads. Don't you think that's weird?"

"I suppose. But I'd rather be that way than the alternative."

"Which is?"

"Not feeling anything at all."

Linus looked away.

Lucy was delighted when Mr. Parnassus ended the session early at a quarter after six. He was told he could head to the kitchen to see if Ms. Chapelwhite needed his help. He jumped up and spun in a little circle as he stomped his feet before heading toward the door, bellowing over his shoulder that he hoped Linus found their time together illuminating.

Linus wasn't sure *illuminating* was the right word.

They sat in silence as Lucy descended the stairs, making far too much noise for a boy his size. It sounded as if he bounced off every surface he could find on his way to the first floor.

Linus knew Mr. Parnassus was waiting on him, and he took the opportunity to gather his thoughts as best he could. His notepad was distressingly blank. He'd forgotten to take down a single observation. That wasn't good for someone in his position, but he thought he was owed a little leeway with all he'd seen and heard since arriving on the island.

"He's not what I expected," Linus finally said, staring off into nothing.

"No?"

He shook his head. "There's . . . connotations behind the name. Antichrist." He looked apologetically at Mr. Parnassus. "If I'm being honest."

"Is there?" Mr. Parnassus asked dryly. "I hadn't noticed."

"I'm not sorry for that."

"And I don't expect you to be." Mr. Parnassus looked down at his hands. "Can I tell you a secret?"

That startled Linus. He'd gathered that the master of Marsyas didn't dispense his secrets often. It was infuriating, but understandable. "Yes? Of course."

"I worried too, when I heard he was being sent to the island."

Linus stared at him. "You *worried*?"

Mr. Parnassus arched an eyebrow. Linus found that he had to remind himself that according to his file, this man was five years older than he. He looked oddly young. Linus didn't know why, but he sat a little straighter, and if he sucked in his stomach slightly, it was no one's business but his own. "Why do you sound so offended?"

"I *worry* when the bus is late. I *worry* when I sleep through my alarm. I *worry* when I go to the store on the weekends, and avocados are so expensive. Those are worries, Mr. Parnassus."

"Those are mundane," he corrected gently. "The trappings of a normal life. And there's nothing wrong with that. I say worried because it's the best way I know how to express my feelings. I worried because he was alone, but I feel that way with all these children. I worried how he would fit in with the others who were already here. I worried that I wouldn't be able to provide him what he needed."

"And him being what he is?" Linus asked. "Did you worry about that too? It seems to me that should have been at the fore-front of all your *worries*."

He shrugged. "Of course, but it didn't outweigh anything else. I understood the severity of the situation, Mr. Baker. But I couldn't let that become the focus. That's all he's ever known, people worrying about what he is, what he's capable of. Because their worry was only a thin cover for fear and revulsion. And children are far more observant than we give them credit for. If he saw the same thing in me as everyone else, what hope would there be?"

"Hope?" Linus said stupidly.

"Hope," Mr. Parnassus repeated. "Because that is what we must give him, what we must give all of them. Hope and guidance and a place to call their own, a home where they can be who they are without fear of repercussion."

"Forgive me, but I think to equate Lucy to the others is a bit shortsighted. He's *not* like anyone else."

"Neither is Talia," Mr. Parnassus snapped. "Or Theodore. Or Phee or Sal or Chauncey. They're here because they *aren't* like everyone else. But that doesn't mean that's the way it needs to stay."

"You sound naïve."

"I'm *frustrated*," Mr. Parnassus said. "These children are faced with nothing but preconceived notions about who they are. And they grow up to be adults who know only the same. You said it yourself: Lucy wasn't who you expected him to be, which means you already had decided in your head what he was. How can we fight prejudice if we do nothing to change it? If we allow it to fester, what's the point?"

"And yet you stay here on the island," Linus said defensively. "You don't leave. You don't let *them* leave."

"I am protecting them from a world that doesn't understand. One day at a time, Mr. Baker. If I can instill confidence in them, a sense of self, then hopefully it will give them the tools they need to face the real world, especially since it will be just as hard for them. It doesn't help when DICOMY sends someone like you to interfere."

"Someone like me?" Linus asked. "What's *that* supposed—"

Mr. Parnassus huffed out a breath. "I apologize. That was unfair. I know you're only doing your job." His smile was brittle. "Regardless of your employer, I think you are capable of seeing beyond a file or a particular nomenclature."

Linus wasn't sure if he'd been insulted or complimented. "Have there been others? Before me? Caseworkers."

Mr. Parnassus nodded slowly. "Once. I only had Talia and Phee then, although Zoe—Ms. Chapelwhite—had already offered her assistance. There were rumors of the others, nothing concrete. But I made this house a home for those I had, and in preparation in case more came. Your predecessor, he . . . changed. He was lovely, and I thought he was going to stay. But then he changed."

Linus heard all the things that weren't being said. He understood now why Ms. Chapelwhite had laughed at him when he'd awkwardly asked if she and Mr. Parnassus were involved. And though it was surely none of his business, he asked, "What happened to him?"

"He was promoted," Mr. Parnassus said quietly. "First to Supervision. And then, last I heard, to Extremely Upper Management. Just like he always wanted. I learned a very harsh lesson then: Sometimes wishes should never be spoken aloud as they won't come true."

Linus blinked. Surely he couldn't mean— "Not the man with jowls."

Mr. Parnassus chuckled. "No."

"Or the bespectacled man."

"No, Mr. Baker. Not the bespectacled man."

That left the handsome man with wavy hair. Mr. Werner. The one who had told Linus there were *concerns* about the capabilities of Arthur Parnassus. Linus was scandalized, though he couldn't quite be sure why. "But he is so . . . *so* . . ."

"So?" Mr. Parnassus asked.

Linus latched onto the only thing he could think of. "He serves dried-out ham at the holiday parties! It's *terrible*."

Mr. Parnassus stared at him for a moment before he burst out laughing. Linus was startled by how warm and crackly the sound was, like waves crashing over smooth rocks. "Oh, my dear Mr. Baker. I do truly marvel at you."

Linus felt oddly proud. "I try."

"So you do," he said, wiping his eyes.

They sat in silence again, and it was the most comfortable Linus had felt since arriving on the island. He didn't dare examine it much, for fear it would show him things he wasn't ready to see, but he knew it was there. But, like all things, it was temporary. His time here, much like his time in this world, was finite. It wouldn't do to think otherwise.

Then, without even thinking, he said, "Kant, Arthur? Seriously? Of all the things."

Mr. Parnassus's eyes sparkled in the failing sunlight. "He had his fallacies."

"Oh, that's an understatement if I ever heard one. Schopenhauer said—"

"*Schopenhauer?* I take back every nice thing I've ever said about you, Linus. You are banished from the island. Leave immediately."

"He had some very pointed critiques! And he did so only to further validate Kant's work!"

Mr. Parnassus scoffed. "Validation wasn't something Kant—"

"My good man, that's where you are surely wrong."

And on and on it went.

TEN

The ferry was waiting at the docks when Ms. Chapelwhite stopped her car. Linus could see Merle moving about on deck. He waved at them irritably, a scowl on his face. "Quite the impatient fellow, isn't he?" Linus mused as the gate lowered from the ferry.

"You don't know the half of it," Ms. Chapelwhite muttered. "Man acts like he has business elsewhere. Mr. Parnassus is the only one who pays him for use of that rickety old boat, and he knows it. We don't even need to use it, but we do to keep the peace."

"How would you— You know what? I don't want to know. Shall we, then?"

She sighed. "If we must."

"I fear we must," Linus said wisely.

She glanced at him as she put the car in drive and pulled forward slowly. He thought she was going to say something, but she didn't speak. He wondered if he was projecting.

The ferry listed slightly as the car boarded, and though Linus felt queasy, it wasn't as it'd been when he'd first arrived a week ago. That gave him pause. Had it really only been a week? He'd arrived on a Saturday, and . . . yes. It'd been exactly a week. He didn't know why that surprised him. He was homesick still, but it was a dull ache in the pit of his stomach.

That probably wasn't a good sign.

Ms. Chapelwhite turned off the car as the gate rose again behind them. The horn blew from somewhere above them, and they were off. Linus stuck his hand out of the car, letting the sea breeze blow between his fingers.

They had only been aboard a few minutes when Merle appeared. "You have my money?" he demanded. "And remember, the fee has doubled."

Ms. Chapelwhite snorted. "I do, you old codger." She leaned over to reach into the glove compartment.

Linus panicked. "Who's piloting the ferry?"

Merle frowned at him. "These things can mostly handle themselves. Computers, wouldn't you know."

"Oh," Linus said without thinking. "What's the point of you, then?"

Merle glared. "What did you say?"

"Your fee," Ms. Chapelwhite said sweetly, thrusting an envelope into his hands. "And Mr. Parnassus asked that I relay a message to you. He hopes the fee doesn't double yet again in the foreseeable future."

Merle's hand was shaking as he snatched the envelope from her hand. "I bet he does. Price of doing business, I'm afraid. It's a tough economy."

"Is it? I hadn't noticed."

Merle's smile was cruel. "Of course you hadn't. Your kind thinks it's better than all the rest of us—"

"You would do well to stand down," Linus advised. "And be careful not to drink that fee away. I'd hate to think how you'd survive this *tough economy* if you did."

Merle glared at him before spinning on his heels and stomping back to the wheelhouse.

"Bastard," Linus muttered. He glanced over at Ms. Chapelwhite, only to find her staring at him. "What?"

She shook her head. "You— It doesn't matter."

"Out with it, Ms. Chapelwhite."

"Call me Zoe, would you? This Ms. Chapelwhite business is getting old."

"Zoe," Linus said slowly. "I . . . suppose that's all right."

"And you'll be Linus."

"I don't know why it matters so much," he grumbled, but he didn't tell her no.

She dropped him off in front of the post office, pointing a few blocks down to the storefront for the grocer's. "Come down when you're finished. I'll try to make it quick. I want to get back to the island so we're not late."

"For what?" he asked, one hand on the door handle, a large, flat envelope in the other.

She grinned at him. "It's the second Saturday of the month."

"So?"

"We go on adventures with the children. It's a tradition."

Linus didn't like the sound of that. "What sort of adventures?"

She looked him up and down. "I'll need to get a few things for you. What you're wearing simply won't do, and I assume that's all you brought. What's your waist size?"

He balked. "I don't know that it's any of your business!"

She shoved him out of the car. "I have a good idea. Leave it to me. I'll see you at the grocer's!"

The tires screeched as she peeled off. People on the sidewalk stared at him as rubber smoke billowed. He coughed, waving his hand in front of his face. "How do you do?" he asked a couple walking arm in arm. They lifted their noses at him and hurried across the street.

He looked down at himself. He wore slacks and a dress shirt and a tie, his usual attire. He wasn't sure he wanted to know what

Ms. Chapelwhite—*Zoe*—had in mind. No matter. He would tell her as much when he met her later.

Much like the rest of the village, the interior of the post office was bright and sunny. It was painted in light pastels, lines of oversize shells along the walls. There was a bulletin board with a familiar flyer: SEE SOMETHING, SAY SOMETHING. REGISTRATION HELPS EVERYONE!

A man stood behind the counter, watching him warily. His eyes were small, and he had thick, gnarled hair sticking out of his ears. His skin was weathered and tan. "Help you?"

"I believe so," Linus said, stepping up to the counter. "I need to mail this off to the Department in Charge of Magical Youth." He handed over the envelope that held his first weekly report. It was extensive, probably more so than was necessary, but he hadn't made many revisions to its twenty-seven handwritten pages.

"DICOMY, is it?" the man asked, staring down at the envelope with barely disguised interest that made Linus nervous. "Heard a representative was here. About damn time too, if you ask me."

"I didn't," Linus said stiffly.

The man ignored him. He set the envelope on a scale before looking back at Linus. "I hope you're going to do the right thing."

Linus frowned. "And what would that be?"

"Close that place down. It's a menace."

"How so?" He was proud how even his voice was.

The man leaned forward as he dropped his voice. His breath smelled cloyingly of elderberry mints. "There's rumors, you know."

Linus struggled not to recoil. "No, I don't. What rumors?"

"Dark things," the man said. "*Evil* things. Those ain't children. They're *monsters* who do monstrous things. People go to that island and never return."

"What people?"

The man shrugged. "You know. People. They go on out there and are never heard from again. That Parnassus too. A queer fellow, if there ever was one. Lord knows what he's got them doing out there all by themselves." He paused. Then, "I've even seen some of them."

"The children?"

He snorted. "Yeah, if you can call them that."

Linus cocked his head. "Sounds like you watched them closely."

"Oh yeah," the man said. "They don't come here anymore, but when they did, you can bet I kept my eye on them."

"Interesting," Linus said. "I'm sure I can amend my report to let DICOMY know that a man of your age took an unhealthy interest in orphaned children. Would that do? Especially if they already pay you to keep quiet, which doesn't seem something you're capable of."

The man took a step back, eyes widening. "That's not what I—"

"I'm not here for your opinion, sir. I'm here to mail out that envelope. That's all that's required of you."

The man's eyes narrowed. "Three twenty-five."

"I'll need a receipt," Linus said as he paid. "To be reimbursed. Money doesn't grow on trees, after all."

The man slammed the receipt on the counter. Linus signed it, took his copy, and had turned to leave when, "You're Linus Baker?"

He glanced back. "Yes."

"Have a message for you."

"If it's anything like the message you just relayed, I don't need it."

The man shook his head. "Foolish. It ain't from me, though you would do well to listen so you aren't the next to disappear. It's all official. From DICOMY."

He wasn't expecting anything, at least so soon. He waited as the man dug around through a crate next to him before finding a small envelope and handing it over. It was from DICOMY, just as the man had said. Official seal and all.

He was about to tear into it when he felt the man's eyes on him again.

A thought struck him. "Say, you wouldn't know anything about raft building, would you?"

The man looked confused. "Raft building, Mr. Baker?"

Linus smiled tightly. "Forget I asked." He turned and left the post office.

Once out on the street, he opened the envelope. Inside was a single sheet of paper.

He unfolded it.

It read:

DEPARTMENT IN CHARGE OF MAGICAL YOUTH

MEMO FROM EXTREMELY UPPER MANGEMENT

Mr. Baker:

We are looking forward to your reports. As a reminder, we expect you to leave nothing out.

Nothing.

Sincerely,

Charles Werner

CHARLES WERNER

EXTREMELY UPPER MANAGEMENT

Linus stared down at it for a long time.

He found Zoe in the grocer's, right where she'd said she'd be. She had a full cart in front of her, and appeared to be arguing with the butcher over a large piece of meat. "All right?" he asked, coming to stand beside her.

"Fine," Zoe muttered, glaring at the butcher. "Just dickering."

"No dickering," the butcher said in a thick accent that Linus couldn't place. "No dickering. All price go up!"

Zoe's eyes narrowed. "For everyone?"

"Yes!" the butcher insisted. "For everyone!"

"I don't believe you."

"I take meat back, then."

Zoe reached out and snatched it from the countertop. "No. It's fine. But I'll remember this, Marcel. Don't you think I won't."

He flinched but didn't say another word.

She dropped the meat in the cart and began to push it away. Linus followed.

"What's all that about?"

She gave him a tight smile. "Nothing I couldn't handle. Get your report sent off?"

"I did."

"And I don't suppose you'll tell me what was in it."

He gaped at her. "Of *course* not! That is a privileged communication meant for—"

She waved him off. "Might as well try."

"—and *furthermore,* as outlined in *RULES AND REGULA-TIONS,* page 519, paragraph twelve, subparagraph—"

She sighed. "I have no one to blame but myself."

He thought about telling Zoe (odd, that, calling her by her first name; most unusual) what the man at the post office had said, but he didn't. He wasn't sure why. Perhaps it was because he felt it wasn't anything she hadn't heard before. And besides, he told himself, the sun was shining. It was such a lovely day. There was no need to put a damper on it with the words of a bigot.

There was a damper put on the day almost immediately after their return to the island.

Really. He should have expected it.

Merle hadn't said much beyond muttering how they took

longer than expected, but they ignored him. As they were ferried back to the island, Linus watched a seagull following them overhead, and he remembered his mouse pad at DICOMY, the picture of the beach asking if he wished he was here.

He was. He *was* here.

And that was dangerous thinking. Because this was not a holiday, a trip well deserved after all his hard work. He was *still* working, and regardless of where he was, he couldn't forget that. He had already gone far beyond what he was used to—this *Zoe* and *Arthur* business certainly wasn't professional—but it would only be for three weeks more. His house waited for him, as did his sunflowers. Calliope certainly wanted to go home, no matter how often she could be found lying out in the sunlight in the garden for hours without moving. And so *what* if she had meowed at him for the first time when he'd traced a finger between her ears, wondering if he was about to lose a hand? It meant nothing.

Linus had a life.

A life which, unfortunately, seemed to be bent on stretching the boundaries of his sanity.

He stood in front of the mirror in the bedroom of the guest house and stared at his reflection. "Oh dear."

Zoe had shoved a bag into his hand, telling him she'd gotten him an outfit for the adventure that afternoon. She had ignored his protests as she'd hoisted every single grocery bag out of the back of the car as if they weighed nothing. She'd left him standing in the driveway.

He planned on leaving the bag unopened in the guest house.

If he pretended it wasn't there, then he wouldn't need to look inside.

To distract himself, he put away the clothes that had been cleaned and laid out on his bed. There was a note placed on top of them that read: *Your weekly washing service is complete! Thank you for staying at Marsyas Island! Your bellhop, Chauncey.* The fact that Chauncey seemed to have washed all his clothes, including his underthings, definitely wouldn't do. Linus would have to speak to him about boundaries. No doubt he'd angle for a tip.

It was while he was straightening out his ties that he realized only three minutes had passed, and he was *still* thinking about the bag.

"Just a peek," he muttered to himself.

He peeked.

"What in the world?" he asked no one in particular. "Surely not. This is most inappropriate. Why, I never. Who does she think she is? Sprites. Useless, the lot of them."

He closed the bag and tossed it back on the floor in the corner.

He sat on the edge of the bed. Perhaps he could open his copy of *RULES AND REGULATIONS* to give himself a refresher. He obviously needed it. He was getting too . . . *familiar* with the people here. A caseworker needed to retain a degree of separation. It allowed them to be objective and not let their opinions be colored or swayed. It could be to the detriment of a child. He had to be professional.

He stood, meaning to do just that. Perhaps he could sit on the porch in the sun while he read. That sounded perfect.

He was surprised when instead of picking up the heavy tome, he lifted the bag from the floor again. He opened it, looking in. The contents hadn't changed.

"Probably wouldn't even fit," he muttered to himself. "She can't just eyeball me and figure out my size. She shouldn't be eyeballing me anyway. It's rude."

And with *that,* of course, he felt the need to prove her wrong. That way, when he saw Zoe again (later, and certainly not after going on some kind of frivolous adventure), he could tell her that she should avoid a career as a personal shopper, seeing how bad she was at it.

Yes. He would do just that.

He put on the clothes.

They fit perfectly.

He sputtered as he stared at himself in the mirror.

It looked as if he were outfitted for a safari in the wilds of the Serengeti or exploring the jungles of Brazil. He wore tan shorts and a matching tan collared shirt. The buttons toward the top of the shirt had been removed (almost as if they'd been *torn* off), so it was open at his throat, revealing smooth, pale skin. In fact, he was showing more skin than he could remember, and his legs were as white as a specter. To make matters worse, there were brown socks that rose halfway up his calves, and sturdy boots that felt uncomfortable, as if they'd never been worn.

But the most terrible thing of all was the helmet-style hat that completed the outfit. It felt strange on his head.

So there he stood, staring at his reflection, wondering why instead of looking like an explorer from the adventure stories he'd read as a child (his mother had hated them, so they had to be hidden under his bed and read late at night with a flashlight under his comforter), he looked more like a brown egg with limbs.

"No," he said, shaking his head. "Absolutely not. I won't. I really won't. This is ridiculous. All of this is—"

There was a pounding at the front door.

He frowned as he looked away from the mirror.

The pounding came again.

He sighed. Just his luck.

He went to the door, took a deep breath, and opened it.

There, standing on the porch, were five children, all of whom were dressed in similar explorer outfits. Even Theodore wore a tan vest of sorts that had been tailored to leave room for his wings. He reared back and chirped at Linus loudly before spinning excitedly in a circle.

"Whoa," Talia breathed, looking him up and down. "You *are* round. Like me!"

Phee bent over to inspect his kneecaps critically, wings fluttering behind her. "Why are you so pale? Do you not go outside? Ever? You're almost as clear as Chauncey is."

Chauncey's eyes bounced on the end of his stalks. "Hello! I hope you found your clothes properly laundered. If you notice an item missing, it's because I accidentally lost it and feel really sorry about it. Please still consider rating my service a ten." He held out a tentacle.

Linus arched an eyebrow at him.

Chauncey sighed as he pulled his tentacle back. "Aw, man."

Lucy grinned up at Linus over a fake mustache far too large for his face. He, too, wore an explorer outfit, though his was red and he had an eyepatch for reasons Linus didn't want to know. "Hello, Mr. Baker. I am the leader of this expedition to find the treasure of the island sprite. I'm glad you've decided to join up! Most likely, you'll die a horrible death at the hands and mouths of cannibals who will roast you alive on a spit and then lick the juices from your cracking skin. If you're lucky, the necrotizing fasciitis will get to you first from a terrible bug bite, and your body will rot out from underneath you until you're nothing but a pile of bones and bloody pus. It's going to be *wonderful*."

Linus gaped at him.

"Children," another voice said. "Do give Mr. Baker some room, won't you?"

Linus looked up to see Arthur standing in front of the guest house, with Sal peering nervously from behind him. Sal was similarly dressed as the other children, and he appeared to be trying to hide his bulk behind Arthur when he saw Linus looking at him. He was unsuccessful, of course, given his size and that Arthur was as thin as a whisper.

Linus felt his throat clog slightly at the sight of the dashing figure Arthur cut in his own ensemble. Instead of tan like the others, his pants and shirt were black, with a red sash across his chest. There was what appeared to be a machete in a scabbard at his waist. He had a mustache like Lucy's, though it looked far less ridiculous on him. It wiggled slightly as Arthur smiled at him.

Linus flushed and looked away. He was suddenly very warm. A warm, round egg with pale limbs.

He'd never cared much about his appearance before. He certainly didn't need to start now. This was a visit like any other he'd done in the past.

Investigation, he reminded himself.

Not a visit.

He opened his mouth to decline whatever invitation had been offered (and not because he actually believed there would be cannibals, though with Lucy, he couldn't be sure).

But before he could utter a single word, Lucy jumped from the porch and posed grandly, hands on his hips. "Let the adventure begin!" he bellowed. He began to march toward the thick trees, knees kicking up high with every step he took.

The other children followed. Theodore took flight, hovering above their heads. Sal glanced quickly at Linus and then ran after the others.

"Coming, Linus?" Arthur asked.

"Your mustache is ridiculous," Linus muttered as he stepped off the porch and stalked after the children.

He pretended he didn't hear the quiet laughter behind him.

"Okay," Lucy said, stopping at the edge of the trees. He turned back toward the group, eyes wide. "As you all know, there is an evil sprite—"

"Hey!" Phee cried.

"Lucy, we don't call people evil," Arthur reminded him as Theodore settled on his shoulder. "It isn't polite."

Lucy rolled his eyes. "Fine. I take it back. There is a *murderous* sprite . . ." He paused, as if waiting for any objections. There were none. Even Phee seemed gleeful. Linus felt the point had been missed entirely, but thought it wise to keep his mouth shut. "A murderous sprite who has a treasure hidden deep in the woods that is ours for the taking. I cannot promise your survival. In fact, most likely even if you make it to the treasure, I will betray you and feed you to the alligators and laugh as they crunch your bones—"

"Lucy," Arthur said again.

Lucy sighed. "It's my turn to be in charge." He pouted. "You said I can do this the way I want."

"I did," Arthur agreed. "But that doesn't mean betrayal."

"But I'm secretly a villain!"

"Maybe we could all be villains," Chauncey warbled.

"You don't know how to be bad," Talia told him. "You're too nice."

"No! I can be bad! Watch!" His eyes pivoted wildly until they landed on Linus. "Mr. Baker! I won't do your laundry next week! Ha ha ha!" Then, in a panicky voice, he whispered, "I'm just kidding. I will. Please let me. Don't take that away."

"I want to be a villain," Phee said. "Especially since we're facing a murderous sprite. In case you didn't know, *I'm* also a sprite, and I should be murderous too."

"I've always wanted to murder someone," Talia said, stroking her beard. "Do you think I have time to go back and get my shovel?"

Theodore bared his teeth and hissed menacingly.

"Sal?" Lucy asked morosely. "You want to be a villain too?"

Sal peeked over Arthur's shoulder. He hesitated, then nodded.

"Fine," Lucy said, throwing up his hands. "We'll *all* be bad." He grinned at them. "And maybe I can still betray you all by being secretly *good* and—" He grimaced, face twisting as he stuck out his tongue. "No, that sounds terrible. Ugh. Ick. Blech."

Linus had a very bad feeling about this.

Lucy led the way, shouting so loudly that birds squawked angrily as they took flight from their perches in trees. He asked Arthur if he could use his machete to hack through the thick vines that hung from the trees, something Linus found particularly alarming. He was relieved when Arthur declined, saying that children shouldn't handle such things until they were older.

It didn't appear to be necessary, however. Whenever they seemed to be stuck, unable to move forward due to the growth of the forest, Phee would step forward. Her wings glistened brightly, shaking as she raised her hands. The vines slithered up the trees as if alive, revealing the path ahead.

The children exclaimed in delight, as Phee looked on smugly. Linus got the idea that she'd made the path difficult to begin with so she could be called upon. Even Sal was smiling as the vines whipped up into the trees.

Linus learned rather quickly that even though he'd experienced more of the outdoors in the last week than he had in the past year, it did not mean he was in any kind of shape. Shortly, he was huffing and puffing, sweat dripping from his brow. He brought up the rear with Arthur, who seemed inclined to take a leisurely pace, something Linus was grateful for.

"Where are we going?" Linus asked after what he was sure had been hours, but in actuality had been less than one.

Arthur shrugged, looking as if he wasn't winded in the slightest. "I haven't the foggiest. Isn't it delightful?"

"I think you and I have very different definitions of delightful. Is there any kind of structure to this outing?"

Arthur laughed. Linus was uncomfortable with how much he liked that sound. "Day in and day out, they have structure. Breakfast at eight on the dot, then classes. Lunch at noon. More classes. Individual pursuits in the afternoon. Dinner at half past seven. Bed by nine. I believe that a break in routine every now and then does wonders for the soul."

"According to *RULES AND REGULATIONS*, children shouldn't have—"

Arthur stepped easily over a large log, green moss growing up the side. He turned back and held out his hand. Linus hesitated before taking it. His movements were far less graceful, but Arthur kept him from falling on his face. Arthur dropped his hand as the children shouted a little ways ahead. "You live by that book, I think."

Linus bristled. "I do *not*. And even if I did, there's nothing wrong with that. It provides the order needed to create happy and healthy children."

"Is that right?"

Linus thought he was being mocked, but it didn't seem malicious. He doubted Arthur Parnassus had a cruel bone in his entire body. "It exists for a reason, Arthur. It's a governance that guides the world of magical youth. Experts from various fields all weighed in—"

"Human experts."

Linus stopped, hand against a tree as he caught his breath. "What?"

Arthur turned his face toward the canopy of the forest. A shaft of sunlight had pierced the leaves and limbs, and illuminated his face. He looked ethereal. "Human experts," he repeated. "Not a single magical person had any say in the creation of that tome. Every word came from the hand and mind of a human."

Linus balked. "Well . . . that's . . . that certainly can't be true. Surely there was *someone* in the magical community who provided input."

Arthur lowered his head to look at Linus. "In what position? No magical being has ever been in a position of power. Not at DICOMY. Not in any role in the government. They aren't allowed. They're marginalized, no matter their age."

"But . . . there are *physicians* who are magical. And . . . lawyers! Yes, *lawyers*. Why, I know a very pleasant lawyer who is a banshee. Very respectable."

"And what sort of law does she practice?"

"She works with magical beings attempting to fight . . . their registration. . . ."

"Ah," Arthur said. "I see. And the physicians?"

Linus felt his stomach tighten. "They treat only magical beings." He shook his head, trying to clear his muddled thoughts. "There's a reason for all things, Arthur. Our predecessors knew the only way to help assimilate magical persons into our culture was to have stringent guidelines set in place to assure a smooth transition."

Arthur's gaze hardened slightly. "And who said they needed to be assimilated at all? Was any choice given?"

"Well . . . no. I don't suppose it was. But it's for the greater good!"

"For whom? What happens when they grow up, Linus? It's not as if things will change. They'll still be registered. They'll still be monitored. There will always be someone looking over their shoulder, watching every move they make. It doesn't end because they leave this place. It's always the same."

Linus sighed. "I'm not trying to argue with you on this."

Arthur nodded. "Of course not. Because if we were arguing, it would mean that we were both so set in our ways, we weren't amenable to seeing it from another side. And I know I'm not that stubborn."

"Precisely," Linus said, relieved. Then, "Hey!"

But Arthur was already walking through the trees.

Linus took a deep breath, wiped his brow, and followed.

"It goes back to Kant," Arthur said as Linus caught up with him.

"Of course it does," Linus muttered. "Bloody ridiculous, if you ask me."

Arthur chuckled. "Whether or not he was right is something else entirely, but it certainly brings about an interesting perspective on what is or isn't moral."

"The very definition of immorality is wickedness," Linus said.

"It is," Arthur agreed. "But who are we to decide what's what?"

"Millions of years of biological evolution. We don't stick our hand in fire because it would burn. We don't murder because it's wrong."

Arthur laughed as if elated. "And yet people still do both. Once, in my youth, I knew a phoenix who loved the way the fire felt against his skin. People murder other people every day."

"You can't equate the two!"

"You already did," Arthur said gently. "My point remains the same as it is in my sessions with Lucy. The world likes to see things in black and white, in moral and immoral. But there is gray in between. And just because a person *is* capable of wickedness, doesn't mean they will act upon it. And then there is the notion of *perceived* immorality. I highly doubt Chauncey would even consider laying a tentacle on another person in violence, even if it meant protecting himself. And yet people see him and decide based upon his appearance that he is something monstrous."

"That's not fair," Linus admitted. "Even if he does hide under my bed one morning out of every three."

"Only because he's still wrestling with what he was told he was supposed to be versus who he actually is."

"But he has this place," Linus said, ducking under a branch.

Arthur nodded. "He does. But he won't always. The island isn't permanent, Linus. Even if you in your infinite wisdom decide to allow us to remain as we are, one day he will go out into the world on his own. And the best thing I can do is to prepare him for that."

"But how can you prepare him if you never let him leave?"

Arthur whirled on Linus, a frown on his face. "He's not a prisoner."

Linus took a step back. "I never—that wasn't what I—I know that. I apologize if it came across any other way."

"I prepare them," Arthur said. "But I do shelter them, somewhat. They . . . for all that they are, for all that they can do, they're still fragile. They are lost, Linus. All of them. They have no one else but each other."

"And you," Linus said quietly.

"And me," Arthur agreed. "And while I understand your point, I hope you can see mine. I know how the world works. I know the teeth that it has. It can bite you when you least expect it. Is it so bad to try and keep them from that as long as possible?"

Linus wasn't sure, and he said as much. "But the longer they remain hidden, the harder it will be when the time comes. This place . . . this island. You said it yourself. It isn't forever. There's a whole wide world beyond the sea, and while it may not be a fair world, they have to know what else is out there. This can't be everything."

"I am aware," Arthur said, looking off into the trees with an inscrutable expression. "But I like to pretend it is, sometimes. There are days it certainly feels like it could be."

Linus didn't like the way he sounded. It was almost . . . morose. "For what it's worth, I never thought I'd be discussing moral philosophy while wearing tan shorts in the middle of the woods."

Arthur burst out laughing. "I find you fascinating."

Linus felt warm again. He told himself it was the exertion. He swallowed thickly. "You knew a phoenix, then?"

Arthur's gaze was knowing, but he didn't seem inclined to push. "I did. He was . . . inquisitive. Many things happened to him, but he still kept his head held high. I often think about the man he became." Arthur smiled tightly, and Linus knew the conversation was over.

They continued through the woods.

They came to a beach on the far side of the island. It was small and made of white and brown rocks rather than sand. The waves rolled through them, and they clacked together enjoyably.

"Easy, men," Lucy said, scanning the beach. "There's something foul afoot."

"We're not all *men,*" Talia said with a scowl. "Girls can be explorers too. Like Gertrude Bell."

"And Isabella Bird," Phee said.

"And Mary Kingsley."

"And Ida Laura Pfeiffer."

"And Robyn—"

"Okay, okay," Lucy grumbled. "I get it. Girls can do everything boys can. Jeez." He looked back at Linus, the devilish smile on his face. "Do you like girls, Mr. Baker? Or boys? Or both?"

The children turned their heads slowly to stare at him.

"I like everyone," Linus managed to say.

"Boring," Talia muttered.

"I'm a boy!" Chauncey exclaimed. He frowned. "I think."

"You are whoever you want to be," Arthur told him, patting him between the eyes.

"Can we please get back to the task at hand?" Lucy pleaded. "You're going to get us all viciously murdered if you keep talking."

Sal looked around nervously, Theodore perched on his shoulder, tail wrapped around his neck loosely. "By who?"

"I don't know," Lucy said, turning back to the beach. "But as I was saying, there is something foul afoot! I can smell it."

All the children sniffed the air. Even Theodore craned his neck, nostrils flaring.

"The only thing that smells foul here is Mr. Baker," Phee said. "Because he's sweating a lot."

"I'm not used to so much exertion," Linus snapped.

"Yeah," Talia said. "It's not *his* fault he's round. Right, Mr. Baker? Us round people need to stick together."

That didn't make Linus feel any better. But he said, "Exactly."

Talia preened.

Lucy rolled his eyes. "It's not something *you* can smell. Only I can. Because I'm the leader. It's coming from over there." He pointed toward a copse of trees just off the beach. It looked dark and foreboding.

"What is it, Lucy?" Chauncey asked. "Is it the cannibals?" He didn't sound very enthused at the prospect.

"Probably," Lucy said. "They could be cooking someone as we speak. So we should definitely go over there and check it out. I've always wanted to see what a person looked like while being cooked."

"Or maybe we can stay here," Talia said, reaching up and taking Linus's hand. He stared down at her, but didn't try and pull away. "That might be for the best."

Lucy shook his head. "Explorers don't back down. *Especially* the lady explorers."

"He's right," Phee said grimly. "Even if there are cannibals."

Theodore whined and stuck his head under his wing. Sal reached up and stroked his tail.

"Bravery is a virtue," Arthur said. "In the face of adversity, it separates the strong from the weak."

"Or the stupid from the smart," Talia muttered, squeezing Linus's hand. "Boys are dumb."

Linus couldn't help but agree, though he kept it to himself.

Lucy puffed out his chest. "I'm brave! And since I'm the leader, my brave order will be that Arthur goes first to make sure it's safe while the rest of us wait right here."

Everyone nodded.

Including Linus.

Arthur arched an eyebrow at him.

"He has a point," Linus said. "Bravery is a virtue, and all that."

Arthur's lips twitched. "If I must."

"You must," Lucy told him. "And if there are cannibals, yell back at us when they start to eat you so we know to run away."

"What if they eat my mouth first?"

Lucy squinted up at him. "Um. Try not to let that happen?"

Arthur squared his shoulders. He pulled out his machete and hopped up onto a large boulder, waves crashing around him. He made for a dashing figure, like a hero of old. He pointed the machete toward the copse of trees. "For the expedition!" he cried.

"For the expedition!" the children shouted in response.

Arthur winked at Linus, jumped down from the boulder, and ran for the trees. The shadows swallowed him whole . . . and then he was gone.

They waited.

Nothing happened.

They waited a little longer.

Still nothing.

"Uh-oh," Talia whispered. "I think they probably started with his mouth."

"Should we go back?" Chauncey warbled, eyes bouncing.

"I don't know," Lucy said. He looked up at Linus. "I'm glad you're here."

Linus was touched. "Thank you, Lucy—"

"If the cannibals start chasing after us, they'll see you first. We're little, and you've got all that meat on your bones, so it'll give us time to get away. Your forthcoming sacrifice is appreciated."

Linus sighed.

"What should we do?" Phee asked worriedly.

"I think we should go in after him," Sal said.

They all looked at him.

He met Linus's gaze for a moment before looking away. His mouth twisted down. He took a deep breath and let it out slowly. "He would come for us."

Theodore chirped, pressing his snout against Sal's ear.

"He's right," Lucy said. "Arthur would come after us. I'm making a decision. We shall go after Arthur, and Mr. Baker will go first."

"You know, for a leader, you seem to delegate more than actually lead," Linus said dryly.

Lucy shrugged. "I'm six years old. Well, this body is. Mostly, I'm ancient, but that's neither here nor there."

Linus felt the ground sway beneath his feet slightly, but he managed to stave it off. "If you insist."

"I do," Lucy said, sounding relieved. "So much insisting."

Talia let go of his hand and waddled behind Linus, beginning to push on the backs of his legs. "Go. Go, go, go! Arthur could be getting eaten right this second, and you're just *standing* here!"

Linus sighed again. "I'm going."

It was ridiculous, of course. There were no cannibals on the island. It was just a story Lucy had made up. It wasn't even a very *good* story.

But that didn't stop Linus from sweating profusely as he walked across the beach toward the trees. They were of a different sort than in the forest they'd walked through. They appeared far older and denser. And even though there were no cannibals, Linus could see why they would choose this copse if they did exist. It looked like the perfect place to consume human flesh.

The bravery of the children was unmatched. They followed him, but at a good fifteen paces behind him, all huddled together, eyes wide.

Linus absolutely did not feel fond at the sight of them.

He turned back toward the trees. "Hello, Arthur!" he called out. "Are you in there?"

There was no response.

Linus frowned. Surely this was a game that Arthur was taking too seriously.

He called out again.

Nothing.

"Uh-oh," he heard Lucy say behind him. "He's probably been quartered already."

"What's that mean?" Chauncey asked. "He's getting paid? I like quarters."

"It means getting chopped up," Talia said. "Into *pieces*."

"Ooh," Chauncey said. "I don't like that at all."

This was stupid. There were no cannibals. Linus stepped up to the trees, took a deep breath, and crossed into the forest.

It was . . . cooler inside the tree line. Cooler than it should have been in the shadows. The humidity seemed to have faded away, and Linus actually shivered. There was a thin path ahead, winding its way through the trees. It didn't look as if anything had been hacked (either vines *or* Arthur). Linus took that as a good sign.

He walked farther, only pausing to look back over his shoulder once more. The children stood at the entrance to the copse, apparently having decided they could go no farther.

Phee gave him a thumbs-up.

Lucy said, "You're not dead!" He sounded strangely disappointed.

"Leaders give positive reinforcement," Talia told him.

"Oh. Good job not dying!"

"That was better," Talia said.

Chauncey's stalks lowered until his eyes were sitting on top of his body. "I don't like this."

"Come on," Sal said as Theodore nibbled on his ear. "We all go together." He took a step into the trees, and the children followed, huddled around him.

It caused Linus's heart to ache sweetly.

He turned back around, schooling his face. What was *wrong* with him? This wasn't supposed to be this way. He wasn't supposed to—

The path was suddenly blocked by a large tree sprouting in front of him with a roar, dirt spraying up in a large plume.

Linus yelped as he stumbled back.

The children screamed.

A voice rang out, echoing around them as the tree groaned. "Who dares to step inside my woods?"

Linus recognized it as Zoe almost immediately. He sighed.

He was going to have so many words with both her and Arthur later.

The children rushed ahead and stood around Linus, looking up at him with wide eyes.

"Who is it?" Lucy whispered furiously. "Is it the cannibals?"

"I don't know," Linus said. "Could be. And while I might be a complete meal, they could be full after consuming Arthur and are only interested in something a little more . . . snack-sized."

Talia gasped. "But . . . but *I'm* snack-sized."

"We all are," Phee moaned.

"Oh no!" Chauncey said, trying to move between Linus's legs with varying degrees of success.

Sal was looking at the trees around them, eyes narrowed. Theodore had shoved his head inside Sal's shirt. "We need to be brave," Sal said.

"He's right," Lucy said, stepping so he stood next to Sal. "The bravest."

"I'm just going to be brave right here," Chauncey said from underneath Linus.

"I should have brought my shovel," Talia muttered. "I could have smashed the stupid cannibals in the head."

"What should we do?" Phee asked. "Should we charge?"

Lucy shook his head before bellowing, "I demand to know who resides here!"

Zoe's voice was deep, but Linus could hear the smirk. "Who are you to demand *anything* of me, child?"

"I am Commander Lucy, the leader of this expedition! Reveal yourself, and I promise to cause you no harm. Though, if you attack and are still hungry, Mr. Baker here has offered to sacrifice himself so that we may live."

"I offered *no such thing—*"

"*The* Commander Lucy?" Zoe asked, words echoing around them. "Oh my, I've heard of you."

Lucy blinked. "You have?"

"Yes, indeed. You're famous."

"I am? I mean, I am! That's me! The famous Commander Lucy!"

"What is it you seek from me, Commander Lucy?"

He looked back at the others.

"Treasure," Phee decided.

"And Arthur," Chauncey said.

"What if we can only pick one?" Talia asked. She was holding Linus's hand again.

"We pick Arthur," Sal said, sounding more sure of himself than Linus had ever heard him.

"Aw, really?" Lucy said, kicking the dirt. "But . . . but, *treasure.*"

"Arthur," Sal insisted, and Theodore chirped his agreement from underneath Sal's shirt. When Linus had begun to understand those chirps, he didn't know.

Lucy sighed. "Fine." He turned back around. "We seek Arthur Parnassus!"

"Is that it?" Zoe asked, voice booming.

"Well, I mean, I wouldn't say no to treasure—"

"Lucy!" Chauncey hissed.

Lucy groaned. "Just Arthur!"

"Then so be it!"

The tree shrank back down into the ground in a flash.

The pathway was clear.

"Would you like to lead the way, Commander Lucy?" Linus asked.

Lucy shook his head. "You were doing such a good job of it, and you look like you don't hear that often enough. I don't want to take that away from you."

Linus prayed for strength as he led the way, Talia still holding his hand. The other children gathered behind them, with Sal and Theodore bringing up the rear.

They didn't have to travel far; soon, the path led to a small clearing. And in this clearing sat a house. It was a single level, made of wood and covered with ivy. It looked ancient, grass growing thickly at its base. The door was open. Linus thought of the stories from his youth, of witches luring children inside. But the witches he knew weren't cannibals.

Well. Mostly.

It struck him, then, just who this house belonged to, and how much of an honor this would be. For an adult sprite, their dwelling was their most important possession. It was their home where all their secrets were kept. Sprites were notorious for their privacy, and he had no doubt that Phee would one day be the same, though he hoped she would remember the time spent at Marsyas in her youth. She wouldn't have to be so alone.

The fact that Zoe Chapelwhite was inviting them in was not lost on Linus. He wondered if Arthur had been here before. (Linus thought he had.) And why Zoe had allowed Linus on her island to begin with. And who the orphanage house belonged to. All questions he didn't have the answers to.

Was it his place to ask? He wasn't sure. It didn't have any bearing on the children, did it?

"Whoa," Lucy breathed. "Look at that."

Flowers were beginning to bloom along the vines amongst the ivy. It looked as if they were growing from the house itself. Bright colors—pink and gold and red and blue like the sky and ocean—raced along vines. It took only moments for the entire house to be covered in them, even stretching up and over the roof.

Phee sighed dreamily. "So pretty."

Linus couldn't help agreeing. He'd never seen anything like it. He thought how muted his sunflowers must seem in comparison. He didn't know how he'd ever thought they were bright.

Going home was going to be quite the shock.

A figure appeared in the doorway.

The children moved closer to Linus.

Zoe stepped into the sunlight. She wore a white dress that

contrasted beautifully with her dark skin. The flowers in her hair matched the ones that grew along her house. Her wings were spread wide. She smiled at them. "Explorers! I'm pleased to see you've found your way."

"I *knew* it!" Lucy crowed, throwing his hands up. "There were no cannibals. It was Zoe the whole time!" He shook his head. "*I* wasn't scared, but everyone else was. Big babies."

The other children, it would seem, disagreed with this vehemently, if their indignant cries were any indication.

"Is Arthur alive?" Chauncey asked. "Nobody ate him or anything?"

"Nobody ate him," Zoe said. She stepped out of the doorway. "He's inside, waiting for all of you. Perhaps there is lunch. Maybe even a pie. But you'll have to find out for yourself."

Any lingering fear they might have had apparently disappeared immediately with the promise of food, as they all charged through the doorway, even Sal. Theodore squawked, but managed to hold on to the bigger boy.

Linus stayed right where he was, unsure of what he should do next. Zoe had offered an invitation, but it'd been to the children. He didn't know if that extended to him.

Zoe pushed away from the house. With every step she took, the grass grew under her feet. She stopped in front of him, eyeing him curiously.

"Zoe," he said with a nod.

She was amused. "Linus. I heard you had quite the adventure."

"Indeed. A bit out of my comfort zone."

"I expect that's how most explorers feel when they step out of the only world they know for the first time."

"You often say one thing while meaning another, don't you?"

She grinned. "I have no idea what you're talking about."

He didn't believe her at all. "Arthur all right?"

Her eyes narrowed slightly. "*Arthur* is fine."

Linus nodded slowly. "Because he's been here before, I take it."

"Is there a question you'd like to ask, Linus?"

There were so many. "No. Just . . . making conversation."

"You're not very good at it."

"That's not the first time I've heard that, if I'm being honest."

Her expression softened. "No, I don't believe it is. Yes. He's been here before."

"But not the children?"

She shook her head. "No. This is the first time."

"Why now?"

She stared at him, eyes alight with something he couldn't quite place. "This island is theirs just as much as it's mine. It was time."

He frowned. "Not for my benefit, I hope."

"No, Linus. Not for your benefit. It would have happened whether you were here or not. Would you like to come inside?"

He tried to cover his surprise, but failed miserably. "This island isn't mine."

She hesitated. "No. But I wouldn't leave you out here by yourself. There might be cannibals, after all."

"Could be," he agreed. Then, "Thank you."

"For?"

He wasn't quite sure. "Most things, I suspect."

"That's all-encompassing."

"I find it's best to be that way, lest I forget one thing in particular."

She laughed. The flowers along her hair and house grew brighter with the sound. "You're very dear, Linus Baker. There's a surface to you that's hard but cracked. Dig a little deeper, and there is all this life teeming wildly. It's a conundrum."

He flushed. "I don't know about all that."

"I heard you philosophized in the woods. I think Arthur rather enjoyed himself."

Linus began to sputter. "It's not—I suppose we—it wasn't anything much."

"I think it was quite a lot, actually." And with that, she turned and headed inside the house, leaving Linus to stare after her.

The interior of the house appeared to be an extension of what could be found outside. Instead of a floor, there was exposed earth, the grass forming a thick carpet. Pots filled with flowers hung from the ceiling. Tiny blue crabs and snails with shells of green and gold clung to the walls. The windows were open, and Linus could hear the ocean in the distance. It was a sound he had grown accustomed to. He would miss it when it was time for him to leave.

Food had been spread out for them on a wooden counter. The children held what appeared to be large shells, stacking food high on them. There were sandwiches and potato salad and strawberries so red Linus thought they had to be fake until Theodore bit into one, eyes rolling back in his head in ecstasy.

Arthur Parnassus sat in an old chair, hands folded in his lap as he watched with amusement as the children began to gorge themselves, even as Zoe warned them to slow down. Expeditions were hungry work; Linus's stomach was growling too.

"I'm glad to see you survived," Linus said, shifting awkwardly as he stood next to the chair.

Arthur tilted his head back to look up at him. "Quite brave of me, I know."

Linus snorted. "Indeed. They'll write epic poems about you."

"I should like that, I think."

"Of course you would."

The corners of Arthur's eyes crinkled. "Before they descended upon their bounty, I was told you were a good caretaker in my absence."

Linus shook his head. "Lucy was probably having one over on you—"

"It came from Sal."

Linus blinked. "Come again?"

"Sal said you held Talia's hand without her needing to ask. And that you listened to all of them, letting them make their own decisions."

Linus was flustered. "It wasn't—I was just going along."

"Well, thank you, regardless. As I'm sure you know, that's quite high praise coming from him."

Linus did know. "He's getting used to me, I guess."

Arthur shook his head. "It's not that. It's . . . He sees things. Perhaps more than the rest of us. The good in people. The bad. He's come across all kinds in his short life. He can see what others cannot."

"I'm just me," Linus said, unsure of where this was going. "I don't know how to be anyone but who I already am. This is how I've always been. It's not much, but I do the best I can with what I have."

Arthur looked at him sadly. He reached out and squeezed Linus's hand briefly before letting go. "I suppose the best is all one could ask for." He stood, smiling, though his smile wasn't as bright as it usually was. "How is the bounty, explorers?"

"Good!" Chauncey said, swallowing an entire sandwich in one bite. It sank down inside of him and began to break apart.

"It would be better if there were actual treasure," Lucy muttered.

"And what if the treasure was the friendships we solidified along the way?" Arthur asked.

Lucy pulled a face. "That's the worst treasure in the world. They already *were* my friends. I want rubies."

Theodore perked up and chirped a question.

"No," Talia said through a mouthful of potato salad. Bits of egg and mustard dotted her beard. "No rubies."

His wings drooped.

"But there is pie," Zoe said. "Baked especially for you."

Lucy sighed. "If I must."

"You must," Arthur said. "And I do believe you will enjoy it as much as any rubies." He glanced back at Linus. "Are you hungry, dear explorer?"

Linus nodded and joined the others.

It was in the din of food (Chauncey facedown in his pie) and laughter (Chauncey spraying bits of pie when Lucy told a rather ribald joke that was highly inappropriate for someone his age) when Linus noticed Zoe and Phee slipping out the door. Arthur and the other children were distracted ("Chauncey!" Lucy cried happily. "You got pie in my *nose*!") and Linus felt the strange and sudden urge to see what the sprites were up to.

He found them just inside the tree line beyond the house. Zoe had her hand on Phee's shoulder, their wings glistening in the shafts of light that pierced the canopy.

"And what did you feel?" Zoe was asking. They didn't glance in his direction, though he thought they knew he was there. The days where Linus could move quietly were far behind him.

"The earth," Phee said promptly, her hair like fire. "The trees. Their root system beneath the sand and dirt. It was like . . . it was like it was waiting for me. Listening."

Zoe looked pleased. "Precisely. There is a world hidden underneath what we can see. Most won't understand it for what it is. We're lucky, I think. We can feel what others cannot."

Phee looked off into the forest, her wings fluttering. "I like the trees. Better than I like most people."

Linus snorted, unable to stop himself. He tried to cover it up, but it was too late. They turned their heads to look at him slowly. "Sorry," he said hastily. "So sorry. I didn't mean—I shouldn't have interrupted."

"Something you'd like to say?" Zoe asked, and though there was no heat to her words, it still felt pointed.

He started to shake his head, but stopped himself. "It's just that . . . I have sunflowers. At my home in the city." He felt a sharp pang in his chest, but he rubbed it away. "Gangly things that don't always do what I want them to, but I planted them myself, and cared for them as they grew. I tend to like them more than I like most people."

Phee narrowed her eyes. "Sunflowers."

Linus wiped his brow. "Yes. They're not . . . Well. They're nothing so grand as what's in Talia's garden, nor as the trees here, but it's a bit of color in all the gray of steel and rain."

Phee considered him. "And you like the color?"

"I do," Linus said. "It's something small, but I think the smaller things can be just as important."

"Everything has to start somewhere," Zoe said, patting the top of Phee's head. "And as long as we nurture them, they can grow beyond anything we thought possible. Isn't that right, Linus?"

"Of course," Linus said, knowing both of them would be listening to his every word. The least he could do was be truthful about it. "I admit I miss them more than I expected to. It's funny, isn't it?"

"No," Phee said. "I would miss this place if I ever had to leave."

Oh dear. That wasn't what he was going for. He'd stepped in it now. "Yes, I can see that." He looked up into the trees. "Certainly has its charms, I'll give you that."

"*Populus tremuloides,*" Phee said.

Linus squinted at her. "I beg your pardon?"

Zoe covered up a laugh with the back of her hand.

"*Populus tremuloides,*" Phee said again. "I read about them in a book. Quaking aspens. If you ever see them, you'll find them in large groves. Their trunks are mostly white, but their leaves are a brilliant shade of yellow, almost gold. Like the sun." She looked off into the forest again. "Almost like sunflowers."

"They sound lovely," Linus said, unsure of what else to say.

"They are," Phee said. "But it's what's underneath that's most important. The groves can be made up of thousands of trees, sometimes even in the tens of thousands. Each of them is different, but the secret is that they're all the same."

Linus blinked. "How so?"

Phee crouched down to the ground, her fingers leaving trails in the loose soil. "They're clones of each other, a single organism managed by an extensive root system underneath the earth. All the trees are genetically the same, though they each have their own personality, as trees often do. But before they grow, their roots can lay dormant for decades, waiting until the conditions are right. It simply takes time. There's one clone that's said to be almost eighty thousand years old, and is possibly the oldest living organism in existence."

Linus nodded slowly. "I see."

"Do you?" Phee asked. "Because even if you wiped out the grove, if you tear down all the trees, unless you get to the roots, they'll just be reborn again, and grow as they had before. Maybe not quite the same, but eventually, their trunks will be white, and their leaves will turn gold. I would like to see them one day. I think they'd have much to tell me."

"They would," Zoe said. "More than you can even possibly know. They have a long, long memory."

"Have you seen them?" Linus asked.

"Perhaps."

"Sprites," Linus muttered to himself. Then, "If they're all the same, how can you tell them apart?"

"You have to see what's underneath it all," Phee said. She dug her hands into the earth. "You have to put in the time to learn what the differences are. It's slow going, but that's what patience is for. The roots can go on forever, waiting for the right time." She frowned at the ground. "I wonder if I can . . ."

Linus took a step forward when she grunted as if wounded.

Zoe shook her head in warning, and he stopped in his tracks. There was a subtle shift in the air, as if it'd become slightly heavier. Phee's wings began to flutter rapidly, light refracting off them in little rainbows. She pushed her hands into the soil until they were covered completely. Sweat dripped from the tip of her nose onto the ground. Her brow furrowed. She sighed as she pulled her hands from the ground.

Linus was speechless when a green stalk grew from the earth. Leaves unfurled, long and thin. The stalk swayed back and forth underneath Phee's palms, her fingers twitching. He was stunned when a yellow flower bloomed, the petals bright. It grew a few more inches before Phee lowered her hands.

"It's not a sunflower," she said quietly. "I don't think they'd survive here for long, even with the best of intentions. It's called a bush daisy."

Linus struggled to find his voice. "Did you . . . was that . . . did you just *grow* that?"

She shuffled her bare feet. "It isn't much, I know. Talia is better with the flowers. I prefer trees. They live longer."

"Isn't much?" Linus said incredulously. "Phee, it's wonderful."

She looked startled as she glanced between Linus and Zoe. "It is?"

He rushed forward, crouching down near the flower. His hand was shaking when he reached out to touch it gently, half convinced it wasn't real, just a trick of the eye. He gasped quietly when he rubbed the silky smooth petal between his fingers. It was such a little thing, yet it was there when only moments before there had been nothing at all. He looked up at Phee, who was staring down at him, gnawing on her bottom lip. "It is," he said firmly. "Absolutely wonderful. I've never seen such a thing. Why, I'd even say it's better than the sunflowers."

"Let's not go *that* far," Phee grumbled, though it looked as if she were fighting a smile.

"How did you do it?" he asked, the petal still between his fingers.

She shrugged. "I listened to the earth. It sings. Most people don't realize that. You have to listen for it with all your might. Some will never hear it, no matter how hard they try. But I can hear it as well as I can hear you. It sang to me, and I promised it in return that I would care for it if it should give me what I asked for." She glanced down at the flower. "Do you really like it?"

"Yes," Linus whispered. "Very much."

She grinned at him. "Good. You should know I've named it Linus. You should feel honored."

"I am," Linus said, absurdly touched.

"It's a perfect name for it," she continued. "It's a little flimsy, and honestly isn't much to look at and will probably die if someone doesn't take care of it regularly."

Linus sighed. "Ah. I see."

"Good," she said, her smile widening. She sobered slightly as she looked down at the flower. "But it's still nice, if you think about it. It wasn't there, and now it is. That's all that really matters in the long run."

"You can make something out of nothing," Linus said. "That's impressive."

"Not something out of nothing," she said, not unkindly. "It was just . . . hidden away. I knew what to look for because I listened for it. As long as you listen, you can hear all manner of things you never thought were there to begin with. Now, if you'll excuse me, I'm going to go put so much pie in my mouth, I'll probably choke. And then I'll eat some more. I swear, if Lucy didn't leave any for me, I'm going to grow a tree out of his ears."

And with that, she headed toward the small house, wings fluttering behind her.

Linus stared after her. "That . . . was an effective threat."

Zoe laughed. "It was, wasn't it?"

"She's capable."

"They all are, if only one can see past the flourish above to the roots beneath."

"A little on the nose, that," he said.

"I suppose it is," Zoe said. "But something tells me that subtlety is lost on you." She turned toward the house, stepping into Phee's footprints in the soil. "Coming, Linus? I do believe you deserve another piece of pie after your lesson."

"In a moment," he said. He looked to the flower again as Zoe went inside. He pressed a finger against the center as lightly as he could. He pulled it away, the tip yellowed with pollen. Without thinking, he stuck his finger against his tongue. The pollen was wild and bitter and oh so alive.

He closed his eyes and breathed.

ELEVEN

Department in Charge of Magical Youth
Case Report #2 Marsyas Orphanage
Linus Baker, Caseworker BY78941

I solemnly swear the contents of this report are accurate and true. I understand per DICOMY guidelines that any discoverable falsehoods will result in censure and could lead to termination.

My second week at the Marsyas Orphanage has brought new insights into its inhabitants. Where once there seemed to be chaos, I now see a strange yet definitive order. It has nothing to do with hastily brought changes at my arrival (of which I assume there were a few; such things usually occur before a caseworker walks through the door), but more so with me growing accustomed to how things are run.

Ms. Chapelwhite, though she isn't on any kind of DICOMY payroll, cares for these children as if they were her own. Given that she's a sprite, it's a little surprising, as her kind are known for their solitary existences and being extraordinarily protective of the lands that they tend to. In fact, I don't know that I've ever met a sprite who wasn't fiercely protective of their privacy. And while Ms. Chapelwhite isn't exactly forthcoming, she does work in tandem with the master of the house to ensure the children are well provided for. She is often found in the kitchen preparing meals, and even takes to handling study groups for the lessons Mr. Parnassus has taught. She is well-versed on a variety of subjects, and her tutelage enhances what the children have learned. It appears to be free of any sort of propaganda, though that might be for my benefit.

I've now seen Lucy's room, and sat in on one of his sessions with Mr. Parnassus. If you take away what is known about the boy—who he is supposed to be—you are left with an inquisitive youth who tends to say things for shock value rather than with any sincerity. He is intelligent, almost frighteningly so, and well-spoken. If DICOMY weren't sure he was the Antichrist—a word that's not to be uttered at the Marsyas Orphanage—I would think he was nothing more than a boy capable of conjuring images meant to scare. However, I expect this is what he wants me to think. I would do well to keep my guard up. Just because he appears as a child doesn't mean he isn't capable of great calamity.

His room is small, converted from a walk-in closet in Mr. Parnassus's own room. He was somewhat shy in showing me where he resides, but his love for music allowed me to form a connection with him. I believe—under proper guidance—that he will be capable of becoming a productive member of society. So long, that is, as he doesn't give in to his true nature. It does beg the question of nature versus nurture, if there is inherent evil in the world that can be overcome by a normalized upbringing. Can he be rehabilitated? Assimilated? That remains to be seen.

I haven't seen Sal's room, though I think I am slowly gaining his trust. I have to be careful with him. He reminds me of a skittish foal. That being said, I have heard him speak more in the last day than I have in the entirety of my stay on the island thus far. Granted, he wasn't speaking to me but around me, but I don't know that it matters. He's like a sunflower, I think. He needs to be coaxed with proper care to show his true colors.

Theodore—the wyvern—has a hoard that I haven't seen yet, though it has to be filled with at least a dozen of my buttons. I may not ever see it, but as of yet, it doesn't cause me any great concern. They're only buttons, after all. I plan on keeping a sharp eye out in case there are hints at anything more nefarious.

The biggest issue I see to date is what appears to be isolation. The children don't leave the island, large as it is. There is a reason for it, and one I am bothered by. It would have been helpful to know before my arrival that the villagers are paid by the government for their silence. Little details like this are important, and the fact that I was unaware makes me look unprofessional. It does raise the question, too, of the source of these payments. Do they come from the funding that's earmarked for this specific orphanage? I would expect an auditor would take issue if that's the case.

The village nearby seems to be somewhat hostile to the inhabitants of the orphanage. I believe DICOMY isn't doing itself any favors with its campaigns in conjunction with the Department in Charge of Registration. There are signs of SEE SOMETHING, SAY SOMETHING in every corner of the village, and it's reminiscent of those in the city, though they seem more cluttered here. If the children don't feel welcome in the real world, how can we ever hope to integrate them into society?

I'm thinking of a day trip, perhaps. To test the waters. I'll need to bring it up to Mr. Parnassus, of course. I think it would do the children good, and hopefully allow the villagers to see their fears are unfounded. If Arthur says no, I suppose I'll have to abide by it.

Such a strange fellow Arthur is. He cares for the children.

That much is clear. While he doesn't follow *RULES AND REGULATIONS* to the letter (possibly not at all), I think there is merit to what he does. The children all care about each other immensely, and I believe that is in no small part due to Arthur.

Still, he is an enigma. For all that I've learned about this place, I feel as if I know him the least. I will need to rectify that, I think.

For the children, of course.

Talia showed me more of her garden today. Gnomes are quite proficient in horticulture, but she seems to outshine even the very best and . . .

It was a Tuesday in Linus's second week at on Marsyas when Calliope decided she needed to be chased, after committing theft.

It certainly wasn't something Linus wanted to do; it was after lunch and he was sitting on the porch in the sun, dozing quite peacefully. He still had a few moments before he needed to return to the main house to sit in on the children's studies, and he was using that time wisely.

And then there was the idea of chasing a cat at all. Linus, for all that he was capable of, didn't like to chase *anything*. Chasing implied running, and Linus had decided long ago that running wasn't something he liked very much. He never understood those who woke up even before the sun had risen, donned their fancy expensive sneakers, and went running on *purpose*. It was most unusual.

But then Calliope burst out of the guest house, hackles raised and eyes wide, as felines sometimes did for mysterious reasons. She looked at him wildly, tail up in a rigid line, claws digging into the floorboards.

And she had one of his ties in her mouth.

Linus frowned. "What are you—"

Calliope bolted off the porch toward the garden.

Linus almost toppled over as he stood from his chair, managing to stay upright by the grace of God. He watched as Calliope ran, the black tie trailing behind her. "Hey!" he shouted. "Damn cat, what are you doing? Stop this instant!"

She didn't stop. She disappeared behind a hedge.

For a moment, Linus thought about letting her go. It was just a tie, after all. He actually hadn't worn a tie this week. It was much too warm, and Phee had asked why he always wore one. When he told her it was proper for someone in his position to wear a tie, she'd stared at him before walking away, shaking her head.

But it absolutely *wasn't* because of Phee that he'd forgone his tie on Sunday for the first time. And then when Monday had come around again, he'd decided it certainly wasn't necessary, at least for the time being. Once he returned to the city, he'd have to wear one, of course, but now?

It wasn't like he was being supervised.

Who would know?

(Phee did, apparently, if her smirk was any indication.)

But still. That tie had cost him more than he cared to think about, and just because he wasn't wearing it *now* didn't give Calliope the right to take it from him. He'd need it when he went back home.

And so he chased after his cat.

He was sweating by the time he made it to the garden. A man of his size and shape meeting with wind resistance made running that much more difficult. And sure, maybe he wasn't *running* exactly, but jogging was just as bad.

He entered the garden, calling after Calliope, demanding that she show herself. She didn't, of course, because she was a cat and therefore didn't listen to anything anyone told her. He looked under hedges and in flowerbeds, sure he'd find her crouching, tail twitching as she gnawed on his tie.

"I don't know why island life has made you this way," he said loudly as he pushed himself up from the ground, "but I promise you things will change when we get back home. This is unacceptable."

He made his way farther into the garden, reaching a part he hadn't yet seen before. It wrapped around the side of the house and was much denser than what Talia had shown him so far. Here, the flowers looked wilder, their blooms bright, almost shocking. The sun was on the other side of the house, and the shadows were plentiful. There were many places for a cat to hide.

He stepped around an old tree, the limbs gnarled, the leaves folded and saw—

"There you are," he said with a sigh. "What on earth has gotten into you?"

Calliope sat on her haunches, tie lying on the ground at her feet. She looked up at him with knowing eyes. She meowed again, a sound he still wasn't used to.

"I don't care," he replied. "You can't steal my things. It's impolite, and I don't like having to chase . . . after . . . you . . ."

He blinked.

There, behind Calliope, was what appeared to be a cellar door at the base of the house. The foundation was made of stone, and the doors were thick and wooden. He stepped forward with a frown, seeing what appeared to be scorch marks upon the doors, as if there had been a fire behind them once upon a time. He thought for a moment, trying to remember if he'd ever been told there was a basement to the house. He didn't think he had, and aside from Sal's room, he'd seen what he thought was almost every inch of the house. If this was a basement, there was no entrance to it inside.

There was a rusted padlock on the door. Whatever was down there—if anything at all—would remain hidden. For a moment, Linus thought about getting one of Talia's shovels and using it to pry open the door, but dismissed it immediately. It was locked for a reason. Most likely to keep the children out. If there had once been a fire down there, it was unsafe. Arthur had probably put the padlock there himself. It didn't look as if anyone had been here in ages; the path to the cellar door was overgrown with weeds, which seemed at odds with the rest of Talia's garden.

"Most likely a coal cellar," Linus muttered. "Would explain the scorching. And since coal isn't used as much anymore, better to be safe than sorry."

He bent over and scooped up his tie.

Calliope watched him with bright eyes.

"This is mine," he told her. "Stealing is wrong."

She licked her paw and rubbed it over her face.

"Yes, well, regardless."

He glanced once more at the cellar door before turning back the way he'd come.

He would have to remember to ask Arthur about the cellar door when they had a moment alone.

Which, much to his growing consternation, didn't happen. *Why* he would feel any sort of consternation over such a thing was beyond him, but there it was. Linus was learning that whatever feelings Arthur Parnassus evoked in him were temporary and the result of proximity. Linus didn't have many friends (perhaps, if he was being honest with himself, none at all), and considering Arthur Parnassus a friend was a nice idea, however impractical it might be. They couldn't be friends. Linus was here as a caseworker for DICOMY. Arthur was a master of an orphanage. This was an *investigation*, and getting too familiar with one of the subjects of said investigation wasn't proper. The *RULES AND REGULATIONS* were clear on that: *A caseworker*, it read, *must remain objective. Objectivity is of the utmost importance for the health and well-being of the magical youth. They cannot look to depend upon a caseworker, as the caseworker is NOT THEIR FRIEND.*

Linus had a job to do, which meant he couldn't sit around hoping to speak to Arthur without little ears around. And while Linus believed the sessions between Arthur and Lucy were fascinating, his time couldn't be spent with *just* them. There were five other children to consider, and he needed to make sure it didn't look as if he were playing any favorites.

He went with Talia to her garden, listening as she extolled the virtues (the many, *many* virtues) of working in the dirt.

He followed Phee and Zoe into the woods, while Zoe talked about the importance of *listening* to the earth around them, to the trees and the grass and the birds.

He listened as Chauncey regaled him with tales of famous bellhops (most of whom Linus believed were fictional) who opened doors and carried luggage and solved crimes such as jewelry theft or brought up trays for room service. He brought out a thick tome (almost the length of the *RULES AND REGULATIONS*) from underneath his bed, wrapped in plastic to keep it from getting wet. He grunted as he lifted it above his head to show Linus the title, the plastic crinkling: *The History of Bellhops Through the Ages.*

"I've read it four and a half times," he announced proudly.

"Have you?" Linus asked.

"Oh yes. I have to make sure I know what I'm doing."

"Why?"

Chauncey blinked slowly, first his right eye, and then the left. "Why what?"

"Why do you wish to become a bellhop?"

Chauncey grinned. "Because they get to help people."

"And that's what you want to do?"

His smile faded slightly. "More than anything. I know I'm . . ." He clacked his black teeth. "Different."

Linus startled. "No, that's not what I—there's not a single thing wrong with you."

"I know," Chauncey said. "Different doesn't mean bad. Arthur says being different is sometimes better than being the same as everyone else." He looked at the book clutched in his tentacles. "When people come to hotels, they're usually tired. They want someone to help them carry their bags. And I'm really good at it. Talia asks me to lift heavy things for her all the time so I can practice." He frowned, looking down at the book. "Just because I look the way I do doesn't mean I can't help people. I know some people think I'm scary, but I promise I'm really not."

"Of course you aren't," Linus said quietly. He nodded toward the book. "Go on, then. Let's hear about these bellhops through-out the ages. I believe it will be positively riveting."

Chauncey's eyes bounced excitedly. "Oh, it *is*. Did you know that the first use of the word *bellhop* was in 1897? They're also called porters or bellmen. Isn't that amazing?"

"It is," Linus said. "Perhaps the most amazing thing I've ever heard."

He sat with Theodore near his nest (never *in*, because he didn't want to be bitten), listening to the wyvern chirp as he showed Linus each of his little treasures: a button, a silver coin, another button, a folded up piece of paper with what looked like Sal's handwriting on it (what it said, Linus couldn't tell), yet another button.

And he asked them, each of them, if they were happy. If they had any concerns. If anything scared them here on the island.

He'd asked similar questions before at other orphanages, and he could always tell when the children had been coached to say what they thought he needed to hear. There was always a note of artifice to their bright words of happiness and joy and *No, Mr. Baker, absolutely* nothing *is wrong, and I am filled with joy.*

It wasn't like that here. Here, Talia would stare at him suspi-ciously and demand to know why he was asking and did she need to get her shovel? Here, Phee would laugh and tell him she didn't want to be anywhere else, because these were *her* trees and *her* people. Here, Lucy grinned at him and said, *Oh yes, Mr. Baker, I* would *like to go somewhere else, one day,* but only if all the others came with him and agreed on his ideas of world domination. Here, Chauncey's eyes would bounce and he'd say he loved the island, but that he did wish there was a hotel here so he could carry luggage. Here, Theodore would stumble over his wings in his excitement at seeing Arthur, even if Arthur had only been gone for a few minutes.

And it was here, on the Thursday near the end of the second week, that Sal appeared at a quarter past five on the porch of the guest house, gnawing on his bottom lip.

Linus opened the door after hearing a knock, surprised to find Sal by himself. He leaned out, sure that one of the other children would be there hiding, but no.

It was just Sal.

Linus quickly schooled his face, not wanting to scare the boy. "Hello, Sal."

Sal's eyes widened, and he took a step back. He glanced over his shoulder, and even though Linus couldn't see him, he was sure Arthur was watching from somewhere. He didn't know *how* he knew, but Linus was under the impression that not much happened on the island without Arthur knowing.

Sal turned back toward Linus and lowered his gaze to the floor. His hands were in fists at his sides, and he was breathing heavily. Linus was getting worried that something was wrong, but then Calliope walked through Linus's legs and began to rub against Sal. She meowed loudly at him, arching her back, ears twitching.

Sal smiled softly down at her and seemed to relax.

"She's a good cat," Linus said quietly. "Gives me a bit of trouble every now and then, but nothing I can't handle."

"I like cats," Sal said, voice barely above a whisper. "Most times, they don't like me. Because of the dog thing."

"Calliope's a little different. She likes you."

Sal looked up at him. "Really?"

stopped looking nervous most days, put a shaking hand on the doorknob.

Linus said, "If you're not ready, then you're not ready. I won't push you on this, Sal. Please don't do this on my account."

Sal frowned as he glanced back at Linus. "But this *is* on your account."

Linus was flummoxed. "Well . . . yes, I suppose it is. But we have all the time in the world." They didn't, of course. Linus was almost halfway through his stay on Marsyas. The realization startled him.

Sal shook his head. "I—I would rather we do this now."

"If you wish. I won't touch anything of yours, if that makes you feel better. And if there's anything you want to show me, I will gladly look at it. I'm not here to judge you, Sal. Not at all."

"Then why are you here if not to judge?"

Linus balked. "I—well. I'm here to make sure this home is exactly that. A home. One that I can trust to keep all of you safe and sound."

Sal dropped his hand from the doorknob. He turned fully toward Linus. Calliope sat near his feet, looking up at him. This was as close as Linus had ever been to Sal. He was as tall as Linus was, and though Linus was thicker, Sal had a heft to him, a strength that belied how small he tried to make himself seem at times.

"Are you going to make me leave?" Sal asked, that frown deepening.

Linus hesitated. He had never lied to any child in his life. If the truth needed to be stretched, he would rather say nothing at all. "I don't want to make you do anything you don't want to," Linus said slowly. "And I don't think anyone should."

Sal studied him carefully. "You're not like the others."

"Others?"

"Caseworkers."

"Oh. I suppose not. I'm Linus Baker. You've never met a Linus Baker before."

Sal stared at him for a moment longer before turning back to the door. He pushed it open and then stepped back. He began to gnaw on his lip again, and Linus wanted to tell him he was going to hurt himself, but he asked, "May I?"

Sal nodded jerkily.

The room was nothing fancy. In fact, it seemed to be devoid of almost anything that Linus would associate with Sal. The other children had made their spaces their own, for better or worse. Here, the walls were blank. The bed was neatly made. There was a rug on the wooden floor, but it was muted and gray. There was a door to a closet and . . . that was it.

Mostly.

In one corner, there was a pile of books that reminded Linus of Arthur's office. He looked at a few of the titles and saw they were fictional classics—Shakespeare and Poe, Dumas and Sartre. That last caused Linus to arch an eyebrow. He had never quite understood existentialism.

But other than that, the room was a blank canvas, as if waiting for an artist to bring it to life. It saddened Linus, because he suspected he knew the reason why it was the way it was.

"It's lovely," he said, making a production of looking around. Out of the corner of his eye, he saw Sal peeking through the doorway, tracking his every movement. "Quite spacious. And just look out the window! Why, I think I can almost see the village from here. A wonderful view."

"You can see the lights from the village at night," Sal said from the doorway. "They sparkle. I like to pretend they're ships at sea."

"A pretty thought," Linus said. He stepped away from the window and went to the closet. "Is it all right if I look in here?"

There was a brief hesitation. Then, "Okay."

The closet was bigger than Linus expected. And there, next to a chest of drawers, was a small desk with a rolling chair tucked in underneath. Atop the desk sat a typewriter, an old Underwood. There was a blank sheet of paper already threaded through. "What's this, then?" Linus asked lightly.

He didn't hear a response. He looked back over his shoulder to see Sal standing next to the bed, looking like a lost little boy. Calliope hopped up onto the bed and rubbed against his hand. He spread his fingers into the hair on her back.

"Sal?"

"It's where I write," Sal blurted, eyes wide. "I—like to write. I'm not—it's not very good, and I probably shouldn't—"

"Ah. I seem to remember something about that. Last week in your class, you read something for everyone. You wrote it?"

Sal nodded.

"It was very good. Far better than I could ever write, I'm afraid. If you need a report filled out, I'm your man. But that's as far as my creativity extends with the written word. No computer?"

"The light hurts my eyes. And I like the sound of the typewriter better."

Linus smiled. "I understand. There's something magical about the clack of the keys that a computer can't emulate. I should know. Most days, I sit in front of one at work. It can hurt my eyes too, after a time, though I believe your vision is a little sharper than mine."

"I don't want to talk about what I write," Sal said quickly.

"Of course," Linus said easily. "It's private. I would never ask you to share something you aren't ready to."

That seemed to appease Sal slightly. "It's just—it doesn't make sense, sometimes. My thoughts. And I try to write them all down to find an order, but—" He looked as if he were struggling to find the right words.

"It's personal," Linus said. "And you'll find the order when you're ready. If it's anything like what you read previously,

I'm sure it's going to be quite moving. How long have you been writing?"

"Two months. Maybe a little less."

So only since he'd been at Marsyas. "Not before?"

Sal shook his head. "I never—no one let me before. Until I came here."

"Arthur?"

Sal scuffed a shoe against the rug. "He asked me what I wanted more than anything. For the first month, he asked me once a week, telling me when I was ready to answer, he'd do whatever he could within reason."

"And you said a typewriter?"

"No." He looked down at Calliope. "I told him I didn't want to have to move again. That I wanted to stay here."

Linus blinked against the sudden and unexpected burn in his eyes. He cleared his throat. "And what did he say?"

"That he'd do whatever he could to make sure that happened. And *then* I asked for a typewriter. Zoe brought it the next day. And the others found the desk in the attic and cleaned it up. Talia said she polished it until she thought her beard was going to fall out from all the chemicals. And then they surprised me with it." His lips curved up. "It was a good day. Almost like it was my birthday."

Linus crossed his arms to keep his hands from shaking. "And you put it in the closet? I should think it would look nice in front of the window."

Sal shrugged. "It—the closet helped me feel small. I wasn't ready to be bigger yet."

"I wonder if you're ready now," Linus mused aloud. "Your room is a little bigger than the closet, but not so big that it feels like all the walls have fallen away. It's like the village at night. You can see them, but they can't see you, though there is all that space between you. A little perspective, I think."

Sal looked down. "I never—I hadn't thought of it that way."

"Just an idea. The desk is perfect where it is, if that's what you want. It doesn't need to be moved until you're ready, or even at all. For all I know, the window might prove to be a distraction."

"Do you have a window where you work?"

Linus shook his head. He thought this was dangerously personal, but did it really hurt anyone? "I don't. DICOMY isn't . . . well. They're not fond of windows, I think."

"DICOMY," Sal spat, and Linus cursed inwardly. "They—they're—I don't—"

"It is where I work," Linus said. "But you knew that. And you said yourself that I wasn't like the others."

Sal's hands were curled into fists again. "You could be."

"Perhaps," Linus admitted. "And I can see why you'd think that with all that you've been through. But I want you to remember that you have nothing to prove to me. I have to prove myself to you, that I have your best interests in mind."

"Arthur is good," Sal said. "He doesn't—he's not like the others were. The masters. He's not—he's not *mean*."

"I know that."

"But you said you were investigating him."

Linus frowned. "I don't think I've ever said that aside from a private conversation. How did you—"

"I'm a dog," Sal snapped at him. "My hearing is better. I could hear you. You said it wasn't a visit. It was an *investigation*. I didn't—I wasn't trying to listen in, but that's what the others said too. That they were *investigating*. It's why I never get to put things up in my room like Talia or Lucy. Because it's always temporary. Anytime I've ever thought I was going to finally have a place to stay, it was taken from me."

He cursed inwardly. "That wasn't for you to hear." Sal began to shrink away from him like Linus had raised a hand to him. "No," Linus said quickly. "That's not—what I meant was, I should have been more aware of what I said. I should have been more careful with my words."

"So you're not investigating Arthur?"

Linus started to shake his head but stopped. He sighed. "It's not Arthur, Sal. Or, at least it's not *just* Arthur. It's the orphanage as a whole. I know you've had . . . less than desirable experiences in the past, but I swear to you this is different." He didn't know if he believed his own words or not.

Sal eyed him warily. "And what happens if you decide to make us leave? Won't you be the same, then?"

"I don't know," Linus said quietly. "I hope if there is a reason for such an action, you would be aware it."

Sal was quiet.

Linus thought he had overstayed his welcome. He stepped away from the closet door. Calliope glared at him. He didn't blame her. He didn't think this had gone as well as he'd hoped. And while he'd told Sal earlier that they had all the time in the world, that wasn't true. Time, as always, moved more quickly than expected. In two weeks, he'd have to make his recommendation as he left the island behind.

He gave Sal a wide berth (or as wide a berth as the room allowed for two large people). He smiled at him and was about to walk through the doorway when Sal said, "Could you help me?"

"Yes," Linus said immediately. Then, "With what?"

Sal looked down at Calliope, who wasn't quite done receiving attention, purring as he scratched her ears. His lips twitched again. He glanced up at Linus. "Moving my desk. I could probably do it on my own, but I don't want to scratch the walls or floor in my room."

Linus kept a neutral expression on his face. "If that's what you want."

Sal shrugged as if indifferent, but Linus was good at what he did. He saw through the facade.

Linus unbuttoned the sleeves of his shirt, rolling them up to his elbows. "I assume it fits through the closet doorway since you got it in there in the first place."

Sal nodded. "Barely. We just have to be careful. Chauncey got too excited and chipped the corner of the desk. He felt really bad about it, but I told him it was okay. Sometimes, things get chipped and broken, but there's still good in them."

"Adds character, I think," Linus said. "And allows for a reminder of a memory. Ready?"

Sal was. He walked into the closet first, pulling out the chair and setting the typewriter carefully on the seat. He pushed it back near the chest of drawers. He stood on one end of the desk and waited for Linus to reach the other. The desk was small, but old. Linus expected it to be heavier than it looked.

After they bent over and Sal counted to three, he was proven right. It *was* heavy, and Linus remembered his mother saying, *Lift with your knees, Linus, honestly!* The small twinge in his back reminded him he wasn't getting any younger, and he almost grinned ruefully at how little effort Sal appeared to exert. He probably *could* have moved it out by himself.

They were careful as they carried the desk through the closet doorway. Linus could see the chip on the far corner of the desk courtesy of Chauncey, and he shuffled back slowly. The desk fit through the doorway with an inch to spare on either side.

"There," Linus huffed and puffed. "Right there. In front of the window."

They set it down carefully, avoiding pinching fingers. Linus groaned rather theatrically as he stood upright, hands going to the small of his back. He heard Sal chuckle, but he didn't acknowledge it outwardly. He wanted to hear such a sound again.

Linus stepped back, eyeing their work critically. He put his hands on his hips and cocked his head. "It's missing something."

Sal frowned. "It is?"

"Yes." He went back to the closet and pushed the chair out. He lifted the typewriter and set it in the middle of the desk in front of the window. He tucked the chair back underneath the desk. "There. Now it's finished. Well? What do you think?"

Sal reached out and traced a finger along the keys almost lovingly. "It's perfect."

"I think so too. I expect your creativity to flourish even more with the muse through the window. Though, if it proves to be a distraction, we can always move it back to where it was. There's nothing wrong with that, so long as you remember that there is a big, wide world out there."

Sal looked at him. "Do you know about the woman? In the kitchen?"

There was an . . . incident. At one of his previous orphanages. He was struck by a woman who worked in the kitchens for trying to take an apple. He retaliated in the only way he knew how. She underwent the change the following week.

Linus trod carefully. "Yes."

Sal nodded and stared back down at the typewriter. "I didn't mean to."

"I know."

"I didn't . . . I didn't know that would happen."

"I know that too."

Sal's chest hitched. "I haven't done it since. And I won't do it again. I promise."

Linus put a hand on his shoulder and squeezed, much like he'd seen Arthur do. He shouldn't have done it, but for once, he didn't care what the *RULES AND REGULATIONS* said. "I believe you."

And though it trembled, Sal's smile was warm and bright.

TWELVE

There was a knock at the door to the guest house later that night. Linus frowned and glanced up from his report to look at the clock. It was almost ten, and he was about to call it a night. He was nearly finished, but his eyes were crossing, and the last yawn had been jaw-cracking. He'd decided to finish tomorrow, before having to mail off the report the day after.

He stood from his chair. Calliope barely acknowledged him from her perch in the windowsill. She blinked slowly before curling her face back under her paws.

Linus scrubbed a hand over his tired face as he went to the door. He was thankful he hadn't yet put on his pajamas. He didn't think it was proper to greet a late-night guest in sleep clothes, unless said guest was staying the night.

He opened the door to find Arthur standing on the porch, peacoat pulled tightly around him. The nights were growing cooler, the wind off the sea carrying a bite to it. Arthur's hair was ruffled on his head, and Linus wondered what it felt like.

"Good evening," Arthur said quietly.

Linus nodded. "Arthur. Is something wrong?"

"Quite the opposite."

"Oh? What is it—"

"Do you mind?" Arthur asked, nodding toward the house. "I've brought you something."

Linus squinted. "You have? I didn't ask for anything."

"I know. You wouldn't."

Before Linus could even begin to ask what *that* meant, Arthur bent over and picked up a wooden box that lay at his feet on the porch. Linus took a step back, and Arthur entered the guest house.

Linus closed the door behind him as Arthur went into the living room. He glanced down at the report sitting in the chair, but didn't appear to try and read what was written upon it. "Working late?"

"I am," Linus said slowly. "Finishing up, in fact. I hope you didn't come here to ask me what I've written. You know I can't tell you. The reports will be made available to you upon completion of the investigation as outlined in—"

"I didn't come here to ask about your reports."

That threw Linus off-kilter. "You didn't? Then why are you here?"

"As I've said, I brought you something. A gift. Here. Let me show you." He set the box he carried down on the little table next to Linus's chair. He lifted the lid with his graceful fingers.

Linus was intrigued. He couldn't remember the last time he'd been given a gift. Back at the office, birthday cards were passed around each year for the caseworkers, each signing their name with an inauthentic *Best Wishes!* for whoever's birthday it was. The cards were cheap and impersonal, but Linus supposed it was the thought that counted. And aside from the holiday luncheon that Extremely Upper Management put on—which was no gift at all—Linus hadn't received anything from anyone in a long time. His mother had long since passed, and even then, she'd only given him socks or a wool hat or trousers that she told him he would have to grow into because they were dear, *and money didn't grow on trees, honestly, Linus.*

"What is it?" he asked, more eager than he would have expected. He coughed. "What I meant to say was, I don't need anything from you."

Arthur arched an eyebrow. "It's not about *need*, Linus. That's not what gift giving is for. It's about the joy that someone is thinking of you."

Linus felt his skin warm. "You were . . . thinking about me?"

"Constantly. Though I can't claim credit for this. No, this was Lucy's idea."

"Oh my," Linus breathed. "I don't know if I want a dead animal or some such thing."

Arthur chuckled as he looked down at the opened box. "That's good. If you should have wanted a dead animal, I am certainly going about this the wrong way. I'm thrilled to say that this isn't something that used to be alive, though it can sound like it is."

Linus wasn't sure if he wanted to see what was in the box, exactly. Arthur was blocking it with his thin frame, and while Linus couldn't smell anything off-putting, or hear anything squeaking such as an overgrown rat with beady eyes, he was still hesitant. "Well, then. What is it?"

"Why don't you come over here and see?"

Linus took a deep breath and walked slowly toward Arthur. He cursed that the man was so tall. He would have to stand right next to him in order to be able to see what was inside.

He chided himself. He doubted Arthur would allow Lucy to do anything untoward. At dinner, Lucy had been grinning at Linus the whole time, and though it had the same devilish tinge to it, Linus didn't think it was nefarious. Granted, Lucy was literally the son of the Devil and had probably perfected innocence long ago.

He hoped it wouldn't explode. He didn't like explosions, especially if he had to stand so close to one.

But it wasn't a bomb. It wasn't a rat, or a dead, rotting carcass. It was a vintage portable record player. Across the inside of the lid of the box was the word *ZENITH*, the *Z* in the shape of a lightning bolt.

Linus gasped. "Look at this! It's wonderful. Why, I don't think I've seen such a thing in a very long time, and even then, it was only through store windows! The Victrola I have at home is much too large. And I know the sound isn't as grand from these little portables, but I've always wondered what it would be like to take music with you wherever you went. Like perhaps on a picnic or something." He was babbling, and he didn't know why. He closed his mouth with an audible snap of his teeth.

Arthur smiled. "Lucy hoped you would react as such. He wanted to be here to give it to you himself, but decided it would be best coming from me."

Linus shook his head. "It's thoughtful. Please tell him thank you for— No. I can do it myself tomorrow. First thing. At break-fast!" Then another thought struck him. "Oh, but I don't have any records to play. I didn't even think to bring any from home. And even if I had, I probably wouldn't have run the risk. They're flimsy, and I wouldn't like to see them break."

"Ah," Arthur said. "Lucy thought of that too." He pressed his thumb against a latch on the underside of the lid, and a little compartment opened. Inside was a blank white sleeve with a black record inside.

"What a marvel," Linus said, itching to reach out and touch the box. "Where did this come from? It looks brand new."

"I assure you it's not. Quite old, actually. I'm sure you saw the many boxes in the attic when you went to see Theodore's nest."

He had. They were stacked off in the corners in the shadows. He'd wondered at them, but figured they were just evidence of a life of an old house. Material possessions tended to grow un-abated when you least expected it. "I did."

Arthur nodded. "It sat in a box near the back for the longest time. We haven't had need for it, seeing as how we already have three record players in the house in use. Lucy, as he's wont to do, discovered it while snooping. It was dusty and in need of a polish, but he was careful. Sal helped." He looked down at it. "To be honest, we probably should have tested it before I brought it over. I'm not even sure if this old thing works."

"And the record?"

Arthur shrugged. "Lucy wouldn't let me see what it was. Said it was a surprise, but that he thought you would like it."

That set Linus a little on edge, but less so than it would have when he first arrived on the island. "Well, I suppose we should find out if he's right."

Arthur took a step back. "Would you like to do the honors?"

"Of course." He took Arthur's place and took the sleeve from the compartment. He slid the record out carefully. It too was blank, with no picture in the center frame. He set the sleeve aside as he placed the record on the platter, the small stacking spindle sticking up in the middle. He flipped the switch on the side of the player and was delighted when the record began to spin, crackling quietly. "I think we're in business," he murmured.

"It would appear so," Arthur replied.

He lowered the needle. The speakers crackled a little louder. And then—

A man began to sing, saying darling, you send me, I know you send me.

"Sam Cooke," Linus whispered. He dropped his hand back to his side. "Oh. Oh. That's wonderful."

He looked up to find Arthur staring at him just as Sam sang about how he thought it was infatuation, but that it had lasted so long.

Linus took a step back.

Arthur smiled. "Can we sit?"

Linus nodded, suddenly unsure of himself, which wasn't anything new. The room felt stuffy, and he was light-headed. He was probably just tired. It'd been a long day.

He picked his report off the chair before sitting down. He

set it on the table next to the record player as Sam continued on woo-wooing. Arthur sat in the remaining chair. Their feet were so close, Linus noticed, that if he extended his leg a little, the toes of their shoes would touch.

"I heard the strangest thing tonight," Arthur said.

Linus looked up at him, hoping Arthur couldn't read his thoughts on his face. "What would that be?"

"I was telling the children good night. I start in order, you know. From one end of the hall to the other. Lucy is always last, given that his room is in mine. But Sal is second to last. And before I knocked on his door, I heard some new, happy sounds that I did not expect."

Linus fidgeted in his seat. "I'm sure it's normal. He is a teenage boy, after all. They like to . . . explore. So long as you remind him that—"

"Oh my, no," Arthur said, fighting a smile. "No, it wasn't that."

Linus's eyes bulged. "Oh dear. That's not—I didn't mean—good heavens, what on earth is wrong with me?"

Arthur covered an obvious laugh with a cough. "I'm pleased to hear you're so open-minded."

Linus was sure he was terribly red. "I can't believe I just said that."

"I can't either, to be honest. Who knew Linus Baker could be so . . . you."

"Yes, well, I would appreciate if it never left this house. Not to Zoe. And *especially* not to the children. Sal, of course, is old enough to understand such things, but I think it would destroy Chauncey's innocence." He frowned. "Not that I'm sure how he could ever do—does he even—oh no. No, no, no."

Arthur snorted. "Lucy is younger than Chauncey. Don't you think we should worry about his innocence too?"

Linus rolled his eyes. "We both know that isn't a problem for him."

"Too right. But, as I'm sure you're now aware, I wasn't speaking about . . . *that*." The last word came out delightfully low, as if it curled around his tongue and teeth before exiting between his lips. Linus was instantly sweating. "I was talking about the clack of typewriter keys."

Linus blinked. "Oh. That . . . makes sense, now that I think about it."

"I bet it does. It was surprising, but not because it existed at all, but because it was much louder than usual. Most nights, it's faintly muffled because he's writing in his closet, the door shut."

Linus understood now. "I didn't—if I overstepped, I apologize."

Arthur held up a hand as he shook his head. "Not at all. It was . . . more than I could have hoped for. I like to think it means he's healing. And you played a part in that."

Linus looked down at his hands. "Oh, I don't think that's true. He merely needed—"

"He needed to hear it spoken aloud," Arthur said. "And I can imagine it coming from no better person."

Linus jerked his head up. "That's certainly not true. It should have come from you." He winced. "That wasn't an admonishment. I meant that it wasn't my place to suggest such things."

Arthur cocked his head. "And why not?"

"Because I'm not—I shouldn't interact. At least not on such a personal level."

"It's against your *RULES AND REGULATIONS*."

Linus nodded as Sam Cooke gave way to The Penguins, singing about their Earth Angel. It caused his heart to stumble in his chest. "It is."

"Why is that, do you think?"

"It's what's required of someone in my position. Because it allows me to remain impartial. Unbiased."

Arthur shook his head. "These children aren't animals. You aren't on a safari with binoculars, watching them from a distance.

How are you supposed to evaluate the children if you don't even take the time to know them? They're people, Linus. Even if some of them look different."

Linus bristled. "I never suggested such a thing."

Arthur sighed. "That—I apologize. That was . . . an oversimplification. I've dealt with prejudice for a long time. I have to remind myself that not everyone thinks that way. My point is you did something remarkable for a boy who came to us only used to derision. He listened to you, Linus. He learned from you, and it was a lesson he needed to be taught. I don't think he could have asked for a better teacher in that regard."

"I don't know about all that," Linus said stiffly. "I only did what I thought was right. I can only imagine what he's gone through, and you as well, as the master of this house. Especially with wards so unique."

"Yes," Arthur said. There was something in his voice that Linus couldn't quite place. "As master of this house, of course. It's why I—how did you put it shortly after your arrival?—don't let them leave."

"I could have worded that better," Linus admitted. "Especially knowing what I do now."

"No, I don't think you could have. It struck to the heart of the matter quite cleanly. I prefer bluntness to obfuscation. Things get lost in translation. Which is why when I tell you that I believe you helped Sal, I mean every word. I didn't ask him why he moved the desk. I only asked if he'd had help. He told me he had. And that it was you. It wasn't hard to fill in the blanks after that."

"It was merely a suggestion," Linus said, uncomfortable with the praise. "I told him that while it was okay to want to feel small, he shouldn't forget that he can be big when he wants to. I hope it wasn't too out of line."

"I don't think it was. I think it was the right words at the right time. As I said before, he's healing. And with that healing comes trust, though it needs to be well-earned. I think you're on your way."

"Then I would feel honored."

"Would you? That doesn't sound like it's proper. I'm sure the *RULES AND REGULATIONS* would—"

Linus scoffed. "Yeah, yeah. I hear you."

Arthur smiled. "You do? I like that very much. Thank you."

"For?"

He shrugged. "Whatever it is you're doing."

"That's . . . vague. For all you know, I could be writing in my reports that this place isn't suitable, and neither are you."

"Is that what you're writing?"

Linus hesitated. "No. But that doesn't mean I don't still have concerns, or that my mind is made up."

"Of course not."

"But it does bring me to a certain point. If you still prefer my bluntness."

Arthur folded his hands on his lap. "I cherish it, in fact."

"You don't even know what I'm going to say."

"No. I don't. But you do, and I don't think you'd say it without having thought through it. Let's have it."

Linus glanced at the record as it switched over to Buddy Holly, singing about why you and I by and by will know true love ways. The fact that it was yet another love song barely crossed Linus's mind; he was focused more on the fact that all these different singers were on the same record. He'd never heard of such a collection before.

"I think we should take the children on an outing off the island."

Buddy Holly sang in the silence.

Then, "We?"

Linus shrugged awkwardly. "You and Zoe and the children. I could come as well, to keep an eye on things. I think it would do them good. Just so they aren't so . . ." He glanced at his report. "Isolated."

"And where would we take them?"

Linus decided to play along, even though Arthur would know the village better than he. "I saw an ice cream parlor when I was in town last week. Perhaps a treat is in order. Or there was the movie theater, though I don't know if Sal would like it with how sensitive his hearing is. Being this close to the sea, I'm sure the village is a tourist destination. But given that it's off-season, there won't be as many people around. Maybe we could take them to a museum, if one exists there. Give them a bit of culture."

Arthur stared at him.

Linus didn't like it. "What?"

"Culture," he repeated.

"Just an idea." He was feeling defensive again. He liked museums. He tried to go to the history museum near his house at least a few times a year on the weekends. He always found something new in everything so old.

For the first time since he'd known him, Arthur looked uncertain. "I don't want anything to happen to them."

"I don't either," Linus said. "And if you'll allow it, I'll be there too. I can be quite protective when I need to be." He patted his stomach. "There's a lot of me to try and take down."

Arthur's gaze trailed down Linus's front, watching his fingers. Linus dropped his hand back to his lap.

Arthur looked back up at him. "I know about the raft."

Linus blinked. "You . . . do? How? Zoe said—"

"It's neither here nor there. Your message in response was appreciated. More than you could probably know. I will speak with the children. Perhaps the Saturday after next. It'll be the last full Saturday you're here. There won't be time, after. You'll be gone."

No. There wouldn't be. Time never stopped, though it often felt elastic. "I suppose I will."

Arthur stood. "Thank you."

Linus stood too. "You keep saying that, and I don't know if it's deserved."

Now the tips of their shoes did touch. Their knees bumped together. And yet, Linus didn't take a step back. Neither did Arthur.

"I know you don't believe you do," Arthur said quietly. "But I don't say things I don't mean. Life is too short for it. Do you like to dance?"

Linus exhaled heavily as he looked up at Arthur. The Moonglows began to sing about the ten commandments of love.

"I don't . . . know. I think I might have two left feet, honestly."

"I highly doubt that." Arthur nodded. He reached up as if he were going to touch the side of Linus's face, but curled his hand into a fist and stepped back. He smiled tightly. "Good night, Linus."

Then he was gone as if he'd never been there at all. Linus barely heard the door shut behind him.

He stood in the empty house as the record spun slowly, singing songs of love and longing.

Just as he was about to turn and shut it off, there was a bright flash of orange light through the window.

He rushed forward, peering out into the dark.

He could see the outline of the trees. Of the main house. Of the garden.

But nothing else.

He decided he was tired. That his eyes were playing tricks on him.

As he switched off the record player and began to turn in for the night, it never crossed his mind he'd forgotten to ask about the cellar door.

He was still distracted two days later as Zoe drove them to the village. Merle hadn't been very talkative today, which Linus was grateful for. He didn't think he could deal with the ferryman's snide remarks.

But that also allowed Linus to become lost in his own thoughts. *What* he was thinking about, exactly, he couldn't be sure; his mind felt like it was swirling, caught up in a water spout rising from the surface of the sea.

"You're quiet."

He jumped slightly, turning to look at Zoe. The flowers in her hair were uniformly gold. She wore a white sundress, though she was still barefoot. "Pardon me. I'm . . . thinking."

She snorted. "About?"

"To tell you the truth, I'm not quite sure."

"Why don't I believe that?"

He glared at her. "It's not for you to believe or not believe. It's simply the way it is."

She hummed under her breath. "Men are stupid creatures."

"Hey!"

"They are. I don't know why. Stubborn, obstinate, and stupid. It would be endearing if it wasn't so frustrating."

"I have absolutely no idea what you're talking about."

"Now *that* I believe. Unfortunately."

"Just drive, Zoe," he muttered as the gate lowered in front of them. Merle sullenly waved them off. He didn't even shout at them to hurry back.

The man in the post office was still as churlish as he'd been the week previous. He grunted when Linus handed over the report sealed within the envelope. Linus paid the fee and asked if there was any correspondence for him.

"There is," the man muttered. "Been here for a couple of days. If you weren't all the way on that island, perhaps you could have gotten it sooner."

"Maybe if you delivered to the island as I'm sure you deliver everywhere else, we wouldn't be having this discussion," Linus snapped.

The man mumbled under his breath, but handed over a thin envelope addressed to Linus.

Linus didn't even bother thanking him, suddenly feeling daringly vindictive. Why, he didn't even say *goodbye* as he left the post office. It was positively scandalous.

"That'll show him," he said to himself as he stepped out onto the sidewalk. He almost turned around and went back inside to apologize, but somehow managed to stop himself. Instead, he tore open the envelope carefully, pulling out the single sheet of paper.

DEPARTMENT IN CHARGE OF MAGICAL YOUTH
MEMO FROM EXTREMELY UPPER MANGEMENT

Mr. Baker:

Thank you for your initial report. It was most illuminating about the workings of the Marsyas Orphanage. As always, you were very thorough about the subjects you're investigating.

We would caution you, however, against editorializing. While we can certainly appreciate your frustration in what you perceive to be a lack of information, we would remind you that we are not dealing with ordinary children here. And that someone in your position shouldn't necessarily be questioning the decisions made by Extremely Upper Management.

In addition, we do have some concerns regarding Zoe Chapelwhite. While we were aware of her presence on the island (tut-tut, Mr. Baker), we didn't know she was so intertwined in the lives of the children. Is she involved with Mr. Parnassus romantically? Does she spend alone time with the children? While the child sprite Phee could certainly learn from an elder of her kind, we would urge caution if Ms. Chapelwhite is doing anything other than that. She is not registered. While she appears to be currently outside of our reach, the orphanage is not, and even a single misstep could prove to be disastrous. If there is anything untoward occurring in the house, it must be documented. For the safety of the children, of course.

Also, a request: Your report included many details on the children of the house. However, when it came to Mr. Parnassus, we found it to be quite lacking. If your secondary report doesn't include more details on the master of the house, we ask that your third report provide more information while remaining completely objective. Be vigilant, Mr. Baker. Arthur Parnassus has a long history with Marsyas, and he'll know the island backward and forward. Do keep on your toes. Even the most charming of individuals have secrets.

We look forward to your further reports.

Sincerely,

CHARLES WERNER
EXTREMELY UPPER MANAGEMENT

Linus stared down at the letter in the autumn sun for a long time.

So long, in fact, that he was startled later by a horn honking. He looked up to see Zoe parked in front of him, squinting through the windshield. There were groceries already in sacks in the back seat. She had done her shopping and returned, and Linus hadn't moved from the front of the post office.

"Everything all right?" she asked as he approached the car.

"Fine," he said. Before he opened the door, he folded the memo and put it back inside the envelope. "Everything is fine." He climbed inside her car. It was so fine, in fact, that he couldn't look at her. Instead, he stared straight ahead.

"Doesn't seem like it is."

"Nothing to worry about," he said, over-bright. "Let's go home, shall we?"

"Home," she agreed quietly. She pulled away from the curb, and they left the village behind.

Suddenly, he said, "Arthur."

"What about him?"

"He's . . . different."

He felt Zoe glance at him, but he stared resolutely ahead. "Is he?"

"I think so. And I think you know it."

"He isn't like anyone else," she agreed.

"Have you known him long?"

"Long enough."

"Sprites," he muttered. Then, "He knew about the raft."

Out of the corner of his eye, he saw her hands tighten on the steering wheel. "Of course he did."

"You don't sound surprised."

"No," she said slowly. "I don't suppose I do."

He waited for her to elaborate.

She didn't.

Linus clutched the envelope in his hands. "What's on the agenda today?" he asked, trying to dispel the thick tension in the car. "Another adventure like last Saturday? I suppose I could be convinced to put on the costume again. While it wasn't my favorite, I didn't mind it as much as I expected."

"No," Zoe said, hair bouncing in the wind. "This is the third Saturday of the month."

"Which means?"

Zoe grinned at him, though her smile wasn't as bright as it normally was. "Which means a picnic in the garden."

Linus blinked. "Oh, that doesn't sound so—"

"It's Chauncey's turn to choose the menu. He prefers raw fish. Has some new experimental recipes he's going to try."

Linus sighed. "Of course he is." But he found himself fighting a smile, and once they were back on the ferry heading toward the island, even Merle couldn't lower his spirits. The letter from Extremely Upper Management was the furthest thing from his mind. He hoped there would be no blowfish. He heard they were poisonous.

THIRTEEN

Department in Charge of Magical Youth
Case Report #3 Marsyas Orphanage
Linus Baker, Caseworker BY78941

I solemnly swear the contents of this report are accurate and true. I understand per DICOMY guidelines that any discoverable falsehoods will result in censure and could lead to termination.

This report will cover my observations of my third week on the island.

In thinking about the contents of my previous report, I addressed a specific issue with Mr. Parnassus: that of the perceived isolation of the children of Marsyas. I understand his hesitance; as I indicated in report #2, there is a strange aura of prejudice over the village. And while it does appear to be more concentrated than, say, in the city, I assume it's just because of the proximity of the village to the island.

I try to put myself in the shoes of the villagers; they live near an old house on an island inhabited by magical youth. But since the children are kept away, it allows rumors to run rampant. While some of the children are certainly atypical, that doesn't mean they shouldn't be allowed to enter the village whenever they wish.

Mr. Parnassus seems to be reluctant, though he did promise to think about it. I find it fascinating, the bond he's created with the children. They care for him greatly, and I believe they see him as a father figure. Never having been a master of an orphanage myself, I cannot attest to the strength one must have in order to run such a household. While it's certainly unusual, I think it works for them.

However, it could also potentially work against them. Since they will need to leave the island one day, they can't always depend upon Mr. Parnassus. In my previous dealings with other masters in different orphanages, I have seen everything from bland indifference to outright cruelty. While I can respect the RULES AND REGULATIONS, I think it should be said they are *guidelines* rather than actual law. And even then, the guidelines were written decades ago, and have never been updated. How are we supposed to enforce something that hasn't been changed with the times?

I was asked to add more detail about Mr. Parnassus. Here is what I learned:

Phee is a forest sprite, under the occasional tutelage of Zoe Chapelwhite. And I believe because of this, it has enabled her to have more control, possibly greater than any other child sprite I've ever encountered, few though they may be. And while it does take her time, she is able to grow trees and flowers unlike anything I've ever seen before. I believe that Ms. Chapelwhite has helped her in this regard.

Theodore is a wyvern, yes, and when we typically think of one such as him, while considering he is rare, we (yes, *we*) tend to think them nothing but animals. I can assure Extremely Upper Management that isn't the case. Theodore is capable of complex thought and feelings, just as any human. He is intelligent and resourceful. Yesterday, after I'd recovered from a bout of food poisoning brought upon by ingesting raw fish, he came alone to the guest house where I reside and asked if he could show me part of his hoard. Notice my use of the word *ask*. Because he does have language, though it might not be what we're used to hearing. And even in my short time here, I've been able to pick up on the cadences of his chirps.

Talia is a rather grumpy child, but I have attributed that to her being a gnome. At least initially, given that's what I was taught about her species. I find our perception is colored by what we're taught. Even as children, we're told the world is a certain way, and these are the rules. This is the way things are, and one of those things is that gnomes are bad-tempered and will brain you upside the head with a shovel as much as look at you. And while this might describe Talia on a surface level, one could argue that would be the case with most preteen girls. It's not a species trait. It's hormones. One only needs to spend the time with her to dive beneath the surface of those waves of bravado to see that she is fiercely protective of those she cares about. Gnomes, as we know, live in what's referred to as a donsy. At least they did when their numbers were greater. Talia has made her donsy here.

Chauncey is here simply because of what he is. And given that we don't know what that is exactly, DICOMY needed a place to put him. I believe—and this is not editorializing as much as it is based upon experience—he is considered classified level four simply because of the way he looks. He was told repeatedly he was a monster—by children, by masters, by people in positions who should have known better. The more you beat down on a dog, the more it cowers when a hand is raised. And yet, even though Chauncey had been beaten verbally before Marsyas (I don't think physically, though words can deliver just as much of a lashing), he is a bright and loving child. He dreams. Is that understood, I wonder? He dreams of a future that he may never have. And while his dreams may seem small, they are still his and his alone.

Sal is the most reticent of the group. He *had* been physically abused before his arrival on the island. That much has been clearly documented, though it wasn't provided in the files I was given. Mr. Parnassus showed me the incident reports signed off by DICOMY on the specific instances. The fact that this happened at all was a travesty. The fact that it happened to a boy who is shy and demure is unacceptable. Sal has been here the shortest amount of time and still has a long way to go before I believe he will be fully recovered. But I think he will, because even though he's sure to be startled at the smallest of sounds, he is blossoming right before my very eyes. He loves to write, and I've been fortunate enough to read some of his work. I expect we'll see great things from him, given the opportunity. Though it brings me no joy to make the comparison again, a dog will cower until they can cower no more. He needs to be encouraged, not feared.

You might be wondering, as I'm sure you are, what this has to do with Mr. Parnassus. It has nothing to do *with* him. It is *because* of him that these things are possible. This isn't simply an orphanage. It is a house of healing, and one that I think is necessary. There was a poet, Emma Lazarus, who wrote, "Give me your tired, your poor, your huddled masses yearning to breathe free."

You'll notice, I'm sure, that I haven't yet mentioned Lucy.

It's been two days since I started this report. I have taken my time, given that finding the right words seems to be of the utmost importance. Last night, there was an event. I was awoken from a deep slumber by the strangest of incidents. . . .

That might have been an understatement.

Linus gasped awake, shooting up in his bed, hand clutched to his chest, his heart beating rapidly. He was disoriented, unsure of what was happening. His eyes adjusted to the darkness, and it took him a moment to understand what he was seeing.

The house appeared to be shrinking.

The ceiling overhead was much closer than it'd been when he'd gone to sleep.

"What on earth?" he exclaimed.

He heard a meow come from somewhere below him. He looked over the side of the bed, only to see that it wasn't the house that was shrinking. No, the reason the ceiling looked so much closer was because the bed was floating five feet off the ground.

"Oh dear," Linus said, clutching the comforter as Calliope stared up at him, eyes bright in the dark, tail twitching.

Linus had never been in a floating bed before. He pinched himself quite hard to make sure he wasn't dreaming.

He wasn't.

"Oh dear," he said again.

And then he heard a low, rumbling roar come from outside the house.

He pulled the comforter up to his chin as the bed swayed gently. It seemed like the safest option.

Calliope called up to him again.

"I know," he managed to say, voice muffled by the heavy blanket. "It's probably nothing, right? I should just go back to sleep. That would be best thing for everyone. For all I know, this is something that happens all the time."

The bed tilted sharply to the right, and Linus barely managed to shout before he hit the floor, pillows and blankets raining down around him.

He groaned as he rolled over onto his back.

Calliope licked his thinning hair. He never understood why cats did that.

"Well, obviously I'm up now," he said, staring up at the bed above him. "Might as well see what this is all about. Perhaps it's just . . . an earthquake. Yes. An earthquake, and it's almost over."

He pushed himself up from the floor, knocking his head against the bottom of the bed. He rubbed his forehead as he muttered to himself. He managed to find his shoes, which thankfully still appeared to be anchored to the floor. He slipped them on and exited the bedroom, Calliope following close behind him.

The chair in the living room was floating, spinning lazily in the air. The portable record player flipped on and off. The lights flickered.

"I can deal with most things," he whispered to Calliope. "But I believe I'll draw the line at ghosts. I don't think I much like the idea of being haunted."

That rumbling sound happened again, and he felt it vibrate up through the floors. But it appeared to be coming from outside the house, and though he was loath to do so, he opened the front door.

The lights were flashing in the main house. He was reminded of the bright orange light he'd seen after Mr. Parnassus had left a few nights before, but it wasn't the same. It looked as if something was happening inside the main house. And though he wanted nothing more than to shut the door against it and pretend none of this was happening, he stepped off the porch onto the grass.

And promptly screamed when a hand fell on his shoulder.

He whirled around to see Zoe standing behind him, a worried look on her face.

"Why would you *do* that?" he growled at her. "Are you *trying* to send me to an early grave? It's like you get enjoyment out of frightening me!"

"It's Lucy," she said quietly, wings glistening behind her in the moonlight. She looked ethereal. "He's having a nightmare. You must come at once."

The children were downstairs in the main house, standing together, staring up at the ceiling. They were huddled around Sal, who had a frown on his face. They all appeared relieved when they saw Linus and Zoe.

"Everyone all right?" Linus asked. "Anybody hurt?"

They shook their heads.

"It happens sometimes," Phee said, folding her arms across her thin frame. "We know what to do when it does, though it hasn't happened in months."

"That doesn't mean he's bad!" Chauncey warbled, eyes darting around. "He just . . . shakes things. Like our rooms. And the entire house."

"And just because he can shake the entire house doesn't mean he wants to hurt us," Talia said, eyes narrowed.

Theodore chirped his agreement from his position on Sal's shoulder.

"We know he wouldn't do anything to us," Sal said quietly. "And it might seem scary, but it's not his fault. He can't help who he is."

It took Linus a moment to realize what they were doing: They thought he was going to use this against Lucy. Against *them*. That stung more than Linus expected it would, though he understood. While they might slowly have begun to trust him, he was still a caseworker from DICOMY. He was still here investigating. And this, no matter what it was, wouldn't look good.

"I'm glad you're safe," Linus said, ignoring the pang in his chest. "That's what's important."

Phee looked troubled. "Of course we're safe. Lucy wouldn't do anything to us."

"I know that," Linus said.

They didn't seem to believe him.

There came another roar from up the stairs. It sounded as if something monstrous had awoken.

Linus sighed. He didn't know why he decided now was a perfect time to test his mettle. "Stay here with them?" he asked Zoe.

She looked like she was about to object, but then nodded instead. "If that's what you want."

What Linus *wanted* was to still be asleep in his bed, but that was out of the question. He said, "It is. Do you think you need to take them out of the house?" He eyed the furniture floating around them warily.

"No. He won't harm them."

And for reasons Linus couldn't quite explain, he trusted her. Trusted *them*.

He smiled at the children weakly before turning toward the stairs.

"Mr. Baker!"

He glanced over his shoulder.

Chauncey waved at him. "I like your pajamas!"

"Um. Thank you, that's very— Would you put your arm away? You don't get tips for paying compliments!"

Chauncey sighed and dropped his tentacle.

Talia stroked her beard. "Remember, if you see anything . . . strange, it's only a hallucination."

He swallowed thickly. "Oh. That's . . . wonderful advice. Much appreciated."

She preened.

The banister on the stairs felt like it was vibrating under his hand as he took step after step. The pictures and paintings on the walls spun in lazy circles. He heard sharp blasts of music—bits and pieces of a dozen different songs that he recognized. There was big band and jazz and rock 'n' roll and echoes of the day the music died, the Big Bopper and Buddy Holly and Ritchie Valens singing around him in ghostly voices.

He reached the top of the stairs. All the doors aside from the one at the very end were open. He took another step, and they all slammed shut at once. He gasped, taking a step back as the hallway began to *twist,* the wood creaking. He closed his eyes, counted to three, and opened them again.

The hallway was as it always was.

"Okay, old boy," he muttered to himself. "You can do this."

The doors stayed closed as he passed them by, though lights flickered behind them, illuminating the floor in quick bursts. The music was louder as he approached the door at the end, and it was as if every record ever made was being played at the same time, a screeching cacophony of sound that caused Linus's teeth to rattle in their sockets.

He had the ridiculous notion of knocking as he reached the last door, but shook his head. He took a deep breath as he put his hand on the knob and twisted it.

The music died as the door opened.

Linus thought he caught a flash of orange light out of the corner of his eye, but it faded before he could figure out where it'd come from.

Lucy's bedroom door was wide open, hanging slightly off its hinges.

Lucy himself stood in the center of the room, hands outstretched away from him like wings, digits straining. The records that had adorned his walls circled around him slowly. Some had cracked and splintered. His head had fallen back and his eyes were open, but they were blank and unseeing. His mouth was open, and the cords stuck out from his neck.

Arthur was kneeling before him, a hand cupped around the back of Lucy's neck. He glanced at Linus, eyes widening slightly, before he turned back to Lucy. He began to whisper something that Linus couldn't quite make out, but the tone was soft and soothing. He squeezed Lucy's neck slightly.

Linus took a step closer.

"—and I know you're scared," Arthur was saying. "And I know sometimes you see things when you close your eyes that no one should ever see. But there is good in you, Lucifer, overwhelmingly so. I know there is. You are special. You are important. Not just to the others. But to me. There has never been anyone like you before, and I see you for all that you are, and all the things you aren't. Come home. All I want you to do is come home."

Lucy arched his back as if electrified. His mouth opened wider, almost impossibly so. That roaring sound came again, crawling out from his throat. It was dark and twisted, and Lucy's eyes flashed red, a deep and ancient thing that caused Linus's skin to crawl.

But Arthur never let him go.

Lucy relaxed, slumping forward. Arthur caught him.

The sashes in the windows stopped fluttering.

The records fell to the floor, some of them breaking into small pieces that scattered along the floor.

"Arthur?" Lucy asked, voice breaking. "Arthur? What happened? Where am— Oh. Oh, Arthur."

"I'm here," Arthur said, pulling him into a hug. Lucy buried his face in Arthur's neck and began to sob, his little body shaking. "I'm here."

"It was so bad," Lucy cried. "I was lost, and there were *spiders*. I couldn't find you. Their webs were so big, and I was lost."

"But you did find me," Arthur said lightly. "Because you're here. And Mr. Baker is here too."

"He is?" Lucy sniffled. He turned his face to look over toward the door. His face was blotchy and streaked with tears. "Hello, Mr. Baker. I'm sorry if I woke you. I didn't mean to."

Linus shook his head, struggling to find the right words. "No need for apologies, dear boy. I'm a light sleeper as is." He was anything but. His mother always said a stampede of wild horses wouldn't be able to wake him. "I'm just pleased you're all right. That's the most important thing of all."

Lucy nodded. "I get bad dreams, sometimes."

"I do too."

"You do?"

Linus shrugged. "It's part of being alive, I think. But even if you have bad dreams, you must remember they're only that:

dreams. You will always wake from them. And they will fade, eventually. I've found that waking from a bad dream brings a sense of relief unlike anything else in the world. It means what you were seeing wasn't real."

"I broke my records," Lucy said bitterly. He stepped away from Arthur, wiping an arm across his face. "I loved them so much, and now they're broken." He stared pathetically down at the shards of shiny black plastic on the floor.

"None of that," Linus admonished. "These were only the ones on your wall, correct?" He walked farther into the room and crouched down next to Lucy, picking up a piece of broken record.

"Not all of them," Lucy said. "Some of them were ones I listened to. They were even my *favorites*."

"Can I tell you something?"

Lucy nodded, staring down at his records.

Linus picked up another piece. It looked as if it fit with the piece he already had. He pushed them together in front of Lucy. They went together perfectly, making a whole. "When something is broken, you can put it back together. It may not fit quite the same, or work like it did once before, but that doesn't mean it's no longer useful. Look, see? A bit of glue and a bit of luck, and it'll be right as rain. Why, hanging on your wall, you wouldn't even be able to tell the difference."

"But what about the ones I listen to?" Lucy asked with a sniffle. "The ones on the walls were scratched already."

Linus hesitated. But before he could think of anything to say, Arthur beat him to it.

"There is a record store in the village."

Linus and Lucy looked up at him. "There is?" Lucy asked.

Arthur nodded slowly. He had a strange expression on his face. "There is. We could go there, if you'd like."

Lucy wiped his eyes again. "Really? You think that'd be okay?"

"I do," Arthur said. He stood slowly. "I think that'd be just fine. Perhaps we could make a day of it. All of us."

"Even Mr. Baker?"

"If he's amenable," Arthur said, sounding amused. "Perhaps he'd like to pick out records with you, since you both have an affinity for music. Your tastes far exceed my own."

Lucy whirled around, face brightening. Linus marveled at the resilience. "Will you go with us, Mr. Baker? We could look at music together!"

Linus was taken aback. He finally managed to say, "Ye-es, that . . . that would certainly be doable."

"Why don't you go tell the others they can go back to bed?" Arthur asked. "I'm sure they'll want to see that you're okay before they do."

Lucy grinned at him, a dazzling thing that caused Linus's heart to ache. "Okay!" He ran out the door, shouting down the hallway that he wasn't dead, and that nothing got lit on fire this time, and wasn't that *grand*?

Linus stood back up, knees popping. "Getting old," he muttered, strangely embarrassed. "Though, I suppose it happens to the best of—"

"He doesn't hurt anyone," Arthur said, voice hard.

Linus looked up in surprise. Arthur was frowning at him, and that strange expression was back. Linus couldn't read it at all. And why he was distracted by Arthur's pajamas, he didn't know. Arthur wore a pair of shorts, his knees pale and knobby. His shirt was ruffled. He looked younger than ever. And almost lost. "That's good to hear."

"And I know you'll probably need to put this in your report," Arthur continued, as if Linus hadn't spoken at all. "I can't blame you for that, nor will I try and stop you. But I do ask that you remember that Lucy has never hurt anyone. He's . . . I meant what I said. He's good. There is so much good in him. But I don't think he would survive away from here. If this place were to close, or if he were to be removed, I don't know that he'll—"

Linus didn't think before he reached out and took Arthur by

the hand. Their palms slid together, fingers intertwining. Arthur held on tightly. "I understand what you're saying."

Arthur looked relieved.

But before he could speak, Linus had to finish. "However, even if he's not a danger to anyone else, what about to himself?"

Arthur shook his head. "That's not—"

"That's why you keep him here with you, though. Correct? So he's always within reach should the need arise."

"Yes."

"Has he ever hurt himself?"

Arthur sighed. "Not—not physically. But he's an expert in self-flagellation after. If something is broken, no matter who it belongs to, he always carries the guilt upon his shoulders."

"Something tells me you know a little about that."

Arthur's lips quirked. "A little."

"He seems well enough now."

"Regardless of who he is, he's still a child. They bounce back remarkably. He'll be fine, I think. At least until the next one." Arthur narrowed his eyes slightly. "And I'll be there for that one too."

It was a challenge, and one Linus couldn't meet. Whatever his recommendation would be, it was still up to DICOMY. "You said they didn't happen often. At least not anymore. And I think I would have noticed something like this during my time here."

"I thought—I *hoped* he was moving past them." Arthur sounded frustrated.

"What brought this on, then? Do you know? Did something happen today?"

Arthur shook his head. "Not that I'm aware of. I think . . . however grotesque it may be, I think there's something to it when he says he has spiders on the brain. There is much we don't know about what it means to be the Anti—"

"Ah," Linus chided, squeezing Arthur's hand. "We don't say that word around here."

Arthur smiled quietly. "No, I don't suppose we do. Thank you for reminding me. The spiders, while certainly not *actual* spiders, are a representation of what's going on in his head. Little threads of darkness woven into his light."

"Parts of a whole," Linus said. "We all have our issues. I have a spare tire around my middle. His father is Satan. Nothing that can't be worked out if we try hard enough."

Arthur tilted his head back toward the ceiling, closing his eyes as his smile widened. "I rather like you just the way you are."

Linus felt overwarm again. He was sure his palm was sweating heavily, but couldn't find the strength to pull it away. "I—well. That's . . . I suppose that's good."

"I suppose."

He was desperate to change the subject before he said something he'd regret. It was a battle he was losing, but he had to fight.

He let go of Arthur's hand as he said, "So, to the village, then? I see you've made up your mind."

Arthur opened his eyes and sighed. He looked at Linus. "You were right. It's probably time. I worry, but then I always will."

"I'm sure everything will be fine," Linus said, taking a step back. "And if it's not, I assure you I'll speak my mind. I don't have the time nor the patience for any rudeness." He felt strangely untethered, as if he were floating outside his own body. He wondered if this would all seem like a dream tomorrow. "Time for bed, I think. The morning will be here before we know it."

He turned, sure his face was bright red. He was almost to the door when Arthur said his name.

He stopped, but didn't turn around.

"I meant what I said." Arthur's voice was hushed.

"About?"

"Liking you the way you are. I don't know that I've ever thought that more about anyone I've ever met."

Linus gripped the door knob. "That's . . . thank you. That's very kind of you to say. Good night, Arthur."

Arthur chuckled. "Good night, Linus."

And with that, Linus fled the bedroom.

He didn't sleep the rest of the night.

Once he'd pushed his bed back to its rightful place in the guest house bedroom, he'd collapsed on top of it, sure he'd pass out after the night he'd had.

He didn't.

Instead, he lay awake, thinking of the way Arthur's hand had felt in his, the way they'd fit together. It was foolish, and most likely dangerous, but in the quiet darkness, there was no one who could take it away from him.

FOURTEEN

Merle stood on the ferry, gaping.

Linus leaned out the open window from the front passenger seat. "Are you going to lower the gate?"

Merle didn't move.

"Useless man," Linus muttered. "I don't know why we're supposed to trust him in charge of a large boat. I'm surprised he hasn't killed anyone yet."

"Are we going to crash and sink in the ocean and maybe die?" Chauncey asked. "That would be neat."

Linus sighed. He really needed to learn to censor himself better. He turned around to look in the back of the van. Six children stared at him with varying degrees of interest at the idea of sinking in the ocean and dying, Lucy and Chauncey more so than the others.

Zoe, sitting in the third row, arched an eyebrow at him, indicating without so much as a single word that this was his mess and he might as well own up to it.

He hoped he wouldn't live to regret this.

Chances were pretty high he would.

"We're not going to sink into the ocean and die," Linus said, as patiently as possible. "It's merely an expression used by adults, and therefore, children such as yourselves shouldn't say anything like it."

Arthur snorted from the driver's seat, but Linus ignored him. He was on very strange ground with Arthur since the night in his bedroom. Where once he'd had no problem in speaking his mind to the master of the house, he now found himself blushing and sputtering as if he were a school boy. It was ridiculous.

"Do adults think about death a lot?" Lucy asked. He cocked his head at an odd angle. "That must mean I'm an adult too, because I think about it all the time. I like dead things. I would still like you if you were dead, Mr. Baker. Maybe even more."

Zoe smothered a laugh with the back of her hand and turned to look out the window.

Useless. Her and Arthur both.

"Adults don't think about death a lot," Linus said sternly. "In fact, they barely think about it at all. Why, it doesn't even cross my mind."

"Then why are so many books written by adults about mortality?" Phee asked.

"I don't—it's because—that's neither here nor there! What I'm *trying* to say is that there is to be no more talk about death or dying!"

Talia nodded sagely as she stroked her beard. "Exactly. Because it's better not to know if we're about to die. That way, we don't start screaming right now. It'll be a surprise. We can always scream then."

Theodore chirped worriedly, hiding his head under his wing as he sat on Sal's lap. Sal reached down and stroked his back.

"I can tell you when you're going to die," Lucy said. He leaned his head back and stared at the ceiling of the van. "I think I could see the future if I tried hard enough. Mr. Baker? Do you want me to see when you're going to die? Ooh, yes, it's coming to me now. I can see it! You're going to perish in a terrible—"

"I *don't*," Linus snapped. "And I will tell you *again*, while we're in the village, you can't go around offering to tell people about what fate awaits them!"

Lucy sighed. "How am I supposed to make new friends if I can't tell them about how they'll die? What's the point?"

"Ice cream and records," Arthur said.

"Oh. Okay!"

This was a very bad idea.

"Do you think I look good?" Chauncey asked for what had to be the hundredth time. "I don't know if I got my outfit quite right."

He wore a tiny trench coat, and a top hat was set between his eyes. He said it was his disguise, but it did little. It'd been his idea, and Linus hadn't felt like arguing, especially when Chauncey had exclaimed quite loudly that he couldn't go to the village *nude,* even though that was how he spent most of his time on the island. Linus had never thought about it that way. And now he couldn't *not.*

"You look fine," Linus said. "Dashing, even."

"Like a spy hidden in the shadows about to reveal a big secret," Sal told him.

"Or like he's going to open his coat and flash us," Talia muttered.

"Hey! I wouldn't do that! Only if you asked!"

Zoe was no longer trying to hide her laughter.

Linus turned back around in the seat, staring out the windshield. Merle was still gaping at them.

"Second thoughts?" Arthur asked. Linus didn't have to look at him to know he was smiling.

"No," Linus said. "Of course not. This is going to be fine. This is going to— Good *God*, man! Lower the damn gate!"

"Ooooh," the children said.

"Mr. Baker cursed," Talia whispered in awe.

It was going to be fine.

"We'll be back later this afternoon," Arthur said to Merle as they exited the ferry. "I do hope that won't be a problem. I'll make sure there's something a little extra in it for you."

Merle nodded, still slack-jawed. "That's . . . that's fine, Mr. Parnassus."

"I assumed it would be. It's good to see you again."

Merle fled back to the ferry.

"Odd fellow, isn't he?" Arthur asked. He drove toward the village.

As it was toward the end of September and therefore the beginning of the off-season, the village of Marsyas wasn't as bustling as it normally was. Even when Linus had arrived three weeks prior, there were still crowds on the sidewalks, peering into the shops, or children in swimsuits, following their parents who wore flip-flops on their pasty feet, carrying umbrellas and towels and coolers as they headed toward the beach.

The town wasn't dead, exactly, but quiet, which put Linus at ease. He wanted this to go as smoothly as possible, so they could do it again after he left. The fact that he was thinking in terms of the orphanage remaining as it was never really crossed his mind. That would come later.

But those who *were* on the street didn't do much to hide the fact that they were gawking.

Talia, nearest to the window, waved as they drove by a woman and her two children.

The children waved back.

The mother grabbed them and held them close as if she thought they were about to be snatched.

Chauncey, who sat on the opposite end of the bench, plastered his face against the window, eyes darting around. "There's the hotel! I see it! Look at it! Look at— Oh. My. *God*. There's a *bellhop*. A real, live bellhop! Look! *Look*."

And there was, a thin man helping an elderly woman wearing an inordinate amount of fur from an expensive car. They heard Chauncey's unholy screech, and Linus looked back in time to see Chauncey press his mouth against the glass and blow out a large puff of air, causing his head to expand.

The old woman staggered, hand going to her throat. The bell-hop managed to catch her before she fell.

"Wow," Chauncey breathed as he peeled his face from the glass. "Bellhops can do *everything*."

It was going to be fine.

It *was*.

Arthur pulled into a car lot reserved for those headed to the beach. Since it was the off-season, it was mostly empty, and there was no one in the pay booth, which had been shuttered. He pulled into the first free space and turned off the van. "Children," he said mildly. "Please exit the vehicle and buddy up."

A herd of charging, heavily pregnant rhinoceroses would have been quieter than the children were at that moment.

Linus gripped the report in his lap as the van rocked back and forth. The third report was sealed in the envelope as it always was, stamped and addressed to Extremely Upper Management, care of the Department in Charge of Magical Youth. He thought about going to the post office first, but figured it would be best to wait until they were finished. No need for distractions. He set it on the dashboard.

"All right?" Arthur asked quietly.

Linus glanced at him before remembering how their hands felt together, and looked away again. Such frivolous thoughts. "I'm fine," he said gruffly. "Everything is fine."

"I believe that's your mantra for today. You've said it enough."

"Yes, well, the more I say it, perhaps the more it will be true."

Arthur reached out and touched his shoulder briefly. "The children will be on their best behavior."

"It's not them I'm worried about," Linus admitted.

"I distinctly remember a man who proclaimed he wouldn't stand for rudeness. Quite the fierce sight he made. I was impressed."

"You should probably get out more if that impressed you."

Arthur laughed. "You are delightful. And just look! I am out here. Now. Let's see what we see, shall we? We can't stay in the van forever."

No, they couldn't, even if Linus wanted to. He was being silly, but he couldn't curb the strange twist of dread in the pit of his stomach. This had been his idea, one he'd pushed for, but now that they were here?

He looked out the windshield. On the side of the building in front of them, under an advertisement for Chunky Cola—*We Have All the Chunks!*—there was a banner, reminding people to SEE SOMETHING, SAY SOMETHING.

"You have their identification papers?" Linus asked quietly.

"I do."

"Okay."

Linus opened the door and stepped out of the van.

The children had lined up in pairs at the rear. Lucy and Talia. Sal and Theodore. Phee and Chauncey. They had come up with their buddies on their own, and while Linus had figured Sal and Theodore would be together, the idea of Lucy and Talia was enough to send shivers down his spine. They tended to feed off each other. He'd had to tell Talia in no uncertain terms that she could not bring her shovel, much to her displeasure.

Which was why he was startled when Arthur said, "Phee and Chauncey, you're with Ms. Chapelwhite. Sal and Theodore, you're with me. Lucy and Talia, you are assigned to Mr. Baker."

Lucy and Talia turned their heads slowly in unison, matching smiles on their faces that sent a cold chill down Linus's spine.

He sputtered. "Perhaps we should—I mean, there's really no need for—I think we should—oh dear."

"What's the matter, Mr. Baker?" Lucy asked sweetly.

"Yes, Mr. Baker," Talia asked. "What's the matter?"

"I'm *fine*," he said. "Everything is *fine*. Though, I think it would be a good idea if we all stick together."

"As much as we can," Arthur said easily. His slacks were too short for his legs again. His socks were purple. Linus was doomed. "Though, I think most of them will get bored inside the record store, and who better to help Lucy choose music than you? Children, did you remember your allowances?"

All of them nodded, except for Chauncey, who wailed, "No! I forgot! I was too busy getting dressed! Now I'm broke, and I have *nothing*."

"Luckily for you, I figured that to be the case," Arthur said. "Which is why I gave yours to Zoe."

Chauncey immediately calmed, looking up at Arthur in adoration.

Arthur looked down at his watch. "If we end up going our separate ways, plan on meeting up at the ice cream parlor at half past two. Agreed?"

Everyone agreed.

"Then let's go!" Arthur said cheerfully.

Lucy and Talia immediately reached up and took Linus's hands.

"Do you think there's a graveyard here, Mr. Baker?" Lucy asked. "I would like to see it, if there is."

"I told you I should have brought my shovel," Talia muttered. "How am I supposed to dig up dead bodies without my shovel?"

Perhaps Linus was going to live to regret this after all.

As much as Linus tried to avoid it, they managed to separate from the group after approximately three minutes and twenty-six seconds. Linus wasn't quite sure how it happened. One moment, they were all together, and the next, Talia grunted something in Gnomish that seemed to express extreme happiness, and they were pulled into a store, a bell chiming overhead as the door closed behind them.

"What?" Linus asked, glancing over his shoulder to see the others continuing down the street. Arthur winked at him before continuing on. "Wait, maybe we should—"

But Talia wasn't to be deterred. She pulled from Linus's grasp and marched forward, muttering to herself in Gnomish.

"Oh no," Lucy moaned. "Of all the places we could have gone into, she picked the worst."

Linus blinked.

They were in a hardware store.

And Talia was pacing in front of a display of gardening equipment, stroking her beard and inspecting each trowel and spade and fork hoe. She stopped and gasped. "These are the new B.L. Macks! I didn't even know they were out yet!" She reached out and pulled a queerly shaped spade from the display, the handle adorned with imprints of flowers. She turned and showed it to Linus. "These are the top-rated spades in *Garden Tools Monthly*! I didn't think they were going to be released until next spring! Do you know what this means?"

Linus had no idea. "Ye-es?"

Talia nodded furiously. "Exactly! Just think! I can buy this, and we can go to the graveyard like Lucy wanted! I can dig up *so many things* with this!"

"Don't say that so loudly!" Linus hissed at her, but she ignored him, proceeding to mime digging as if getting used to the grip and heft of the spade.

Even Lucy seemed interested. "It's a little small," he said doubtfully. "How are you going to dig up an entire grave with that little thing?"

"It's not about the size," Talia scoffed. "But what you do with it. Isn't that right, Mr. Baker?"

Linus coughed. "I—that's quite right, I suppose."

"And I'm a *gnome,* Lucy. You know how well I can dig."

Lucy nodded, looking relieved. "Good. Because we might have to dig up at least three or four bodies—"

"We're not digging up *any* bodies," Linus snapped. "So get that idea out of your heads *right* now."

"We're not?" Talia asked, looking down at the spade. "But then what's the point?"

"The point? The point of *what*?"

"Going to the graveyard," Lucy said, tugging on his hand.

"We're not *going* to the graveyard!"

Talia squinted up at him. "But you said we could."

"Oh no," Lucy moaned. "Is he going senile? He's so old, he's losing his mind! Help! Please, someone help us! This man who is supposed to be watching us is going senile and I worry what he might do!"

A squat woman appeared down one of the aisles looking worried, a smudge of dirt on her forehead, gardening gloves on her hands. She held a pair of pruning shears. "My goodness, what's going on? Are you all . . . right . . . ?"

She stopped when she saw Talia with the spade. She looked slowly over to Lucy, who grinned at her, showing many teeth.

She took a step back. "You're from the island."

"Yes," Talia said in a no-nonsense voice. "And I'd like to talk to you about the B.L. Macks. When did they come in? Are they as good as their rating suggests? They seem to be lighter than I expected."

"We're going to the graveyard," Lucy added in an ominous monotone. "Do a lot of people die here? I hope so."

The woman's eyes widened.

"We're *not*," Linus said hastily. "Talia here has the most beautiful garden that is well cared for. Why, I don't know that I've ever seen something so immaculate."

It didn't appear to do much to calm the woman, though Talia preened. "Thank you, Mr. Baker!" She looked back at the woman. "You can't tell by the way he dresses, but sometimes, Mr. Baker has good taste."

The woman nodded, head jerking up and down. "That's . . . nice." She cleared her throat. "A garden you say? On the island? I thought it was . . ." She blanched.

Talia cocked her head. "You thought it was what?"

"It . . . uh. Doesn't matter." She glanced quickly at Linus before very obviously forcing a smile on her face. "Tell me about your garden, and I'll see if I can figure what would be right for you."

"Oh no," Lucy groaned. "Now she'll never stop talking."

Talia ignored him as she launched into a very thorough explanation of her garden. In fact, it was so thorough, Linus thought she was going over it inch by inch. And while he secretly agreed with Lucy, he remained focused on the shopkeeper, watching for any sign that she was just humoring Talia in order to get them to leave.

Though that certainly seemed to be the case at the beginning, the woman began to relax and interrupted Talia, asking questions about pH levels in the soil, and what kinds of flowers and plants she grew. The woman seemed impressed with Talia's knowledge and what she had created.

Eventually, she said, "While the B.L. Macks are considered top end, I've found they tend to wear down quicker. Someone like you"—she coughed—"who knows what they're doing, might do better with the Foxfaires. They're sturdier and don't cost quite as much. It's what I use here in the shop and at home."

Talia put the spade back on the shelf almost reverently. "Foxfaires? *Garden Tools Monthly* said they—"

"*Garden Tools Monthly*?" the woman scoffed. "Oh, my dear child, *Garden Tools Monthly* is now the *Garden Tools Weekly* of the garden tool world. It's all about the *Garden Tools Bi-Monthly*. It's what all serious gardeners read."

Talia gasped. "It *is*?" She glared up at Linus. "Why didn't I know this? What else has been kept from me?"

Linus shrugged helplessly. "I have no idea what's going on."

The woman squinted at him. "Are you all right, sir? Are you senile?"

Linus sighed as Lucy cackled.

The total, after being rung up, was astounding. Linus had never spent so much on gardening tools in his life.

Talia smiled up at the woman. "Can you excuse me for a moment?"

The woman nodded.

Talia turned away from her, smile disappearing. She looked frantic. She grabbed Linus's hand and tugged on it, pulling him down. "I don't have enough," she whispered. "And we can't push her down and steal it, right? Because that's wrong."

"We absolutely cannot push her down and steal it," Linus said.

Lucy rolled his eyes. "I knew you were going to say that." He frowned and then reached into his pocket. He pulled out a handful of crumpled bills. He held it out to Talia. "Is that enough, you think?"

Talia shook her head. "No, Lucy. You can't. Those are for your records."

Lucy shrugged. "I know. But not all of them are broken. And the ones that did break were my fault anyway. You can have it."

"Put your money away," Linus said quietly. "Both of you."

"But, my *tools*—"

He stepped forward to the counter, dropping their hands as he pulled out his own wallet. He smiled weakly at the woman as he handed her his Diners Club Card, something he only used in emergencies. She placed it on top of the imprinter and snapped the handle over for the receipt.

He heard whispering behind him and glanced back, wanting to make sure that they weren't actually planning on robbing the garden store. Instead, he found Talia smiling, her eyes wet as Lucy wrapped an arm around her shoulders.

The woman cleared her throat, and Linus turned back around. She handed him his card and started to bag up the tools. Linus felt Talia step beside him, reaching up to the counter, waving her hands as she couldn't quite see over it. The woman handed her the bags.

She hesitated. Then, "This garden of yours. It sounds lovely."

"It is," Talia replied without a trace of ego.

"Would it—I like to take pictures of the gardens here in Marsyas." She pointed toward a cork board on the wall with photographs of different gardens. "From the people who shop here. Every garden is different, I think. They reflect the personalities of those who care for them."

"There are no dead bodies in our garden," Lucy said helpfully. "But other than that, it's pretty much exactly like Talia."

"That's good to hear," the woman said faintly. She shook her head. "Perhaps—if it's all right with your Mr. Baker here—perhaps I could come out and see your garden one day? In the spring, when things are blooming? Or sooner, if that would be all right."

"Yes," Talia said, eyes sparkling. "Oh *yes*. Except, it wouldn't be Mr. Baker. You'll need to ask Arthur. But I'm sure he'll be okay with it. Mr. Baker is here to make sure we aren't starving or getting beaten or being kept in cages. He goes home soon."

Linus turned his head toward the ceiling, asking silently for guidance.

"Oh," the woman said. "That's . . . good?"

Lucy nodded. "So good. But Mr. Baker isn't all bad. I mean, sure, I tried to scare him off the island when he first arrived, but now, I like that he's alive and not . . . the other way."

Linus sighed.

"Wonderful," the woman said weakly. "Lovely to hear. I'll send word to Arthur when I can make the trip."

Talia gave her a dazzling smile. "I hope you're prepared to be amazed. My garden makes all those ones on your picture wall look like crap."

It was time to go. "Thank you," Linus said stiffly as he grabbed the children by the arms and began to pull them from the store.

"Bye, plant lady!" Lucy screeched. "See you *real* soon!"

They were outside back in the sunlight when Linus was able to breathe again. But before he could speak his mind, he was surprised when his right leg was wrapped tightly in a hug. He looked down to find Talia holding on to him. "Thank you, Mr. Baker," she said quietly. "That was very nice of you."

He hesitated, but then reached down and patted the top of her head through her cap, something he wouldn't have dared to do even a few days ago. "Think nothing of it."

"He's so wonderful and generous," Lucy said, spinning in a circle on the sidewalk, arms outstretched for reasons Linus didn't understand. "And I hope he remembers to do the same for me, so I don't have to spend my own money and feel left out and have to open a pit to hell and watch this village be swallowed whole. Because that would just be *so easy.*"

Linus barely had time to wonder why Lucy's threats didn't scare him as much as they once had before they were on their way.

"Far out," the man in the record store breathed, eyes glazed and bloodshot. He had long hair that fell on his shoulders and he looked as if he could use a bath.

Which meant, of course, that Lucy was entranced. "Far out," he agreed. He'd managed to climb onto the countertop, and was sitting in front of the man—"Call me J-Bone, can ya dig?"—on his knees. There was another man in the back of the store, watching them warily.

"You're, like . . ." J-Bone made an explosion noise, spreading his hands wide.

"Yes," Lucy said. "That's me. Boom."

J-Bone—Linus distrusted him immediately for having such a name, honestly—looked down at Talia, who was sitting on the floor of the record store, humming as she inspected each of her new tools. "Little dude's got a beard. And she's a *lady*-dude."

"It's very soft," Lucy said. "She has all these soaps for it. They smell like flowers and girly stuff."

"Righteous," J-Bone said. "Respect, lady-dude."

"This is a trowel," Talia said. "It's mine."

"Cool." He turned back to Lucy, who was only inches from his face. "What can I get you, little dude?"

"I require records," Lucy announced. "My others were broken after I had a bad dream about getting eaten by spiders, and I need to replace them. Mr. Baker is going to pay for it, so we can spare no expense."

J-Bone nodded. "I don't know what you just said, but I heard records, and records I can do." He nodded toward the man standing in the back. "Me and Marty can hook you up."

"You smell funny," Lucy said, leaning forward and sniffing deeply. "Like . . . plants, but not like any that Talia has in her garden."

"Oh, yeah," J-Bone said. "I grow and smoke my own—"

"That's quite enough of that," Linus said. "We don't need to know anything about your extracurricular activities."

"Who's the square?" J-Bone whispered.

"Mr. Baker," Lucy whispered back. "He's here to make sure I don't burn anyone alive with the power of my mind and then consume their souls from their smoking carcass."

"Rock on, little dude," J-Bone said, offering a high five which Lucy gladly accepted. "I mean, I hope that doesn't happen to me, but you do you." He tossed his hair back over his shoulder. "What are you looking for?"

"The Big Bopper. Ritchie Valens. Buddy Holly."

"Whoa. Old school."

"It keeps the spiders in my head away."

"I can dig it. You like the King?"

Lucy scoffed as he bounced on his knees. "Do I like the King? Of *course* I like the King. I think my real dad met him once."

Linus chose not to ask a follow-up question to that one.

"Real dad, huh?" J-Bone asked, leaning forward on the counter.

"Yeah." Lucy's eyes shifted side to side. "He's . . . not around."

"Deadbeat?"

"You could say that. He's got a lot going on."

"Oh, man, I get that. My dad doesn't think I'm doing anything with my life, you know? Thinks that I should be doing more than the record store."

Lucy was scandalized. "But—but the record store is the best place *ever*!"

"Right? He wants me to be a personal injury attorney like him."

Lucy pulled a face. "My real dad knows a *lot* of personal injury attorneys. Trust me when I say, you'll be better off here."

"That's what I think. Ever heard of Santo and Johnny?"

"'Sleep Walk' is my *jam,* man!" Lucy exclaimed. "But I don't have *that* record."

"You're in luck. Because I think I got one copy left in the back. Let's see if we can find it."

Lucy jumped off the counter as J-Bone came around. They began to walk toward the back of the store. "Yo, Marty!" J-Bone said. "Got a little dude looking for some golden oldies. Let's see if we can help him out."

"Righteous," Lucy exclaimed, staring adoringly up at J-Bone. "Goldie oldies!"

Marty didn't speak. He just nodded and turned to walk farther into the store.

Linus didn't like how far away they were getting from him.

He glanced down at Talia. "I'm going to make sure they're okay. You all right staying here by yourself?"

She rolled her eyes. "I *am* two hundred and sixty-three years old. I'm sure I'll be fine."

"Don't leave the store."

She ignored him, going back to lovingly tracing her new tools with a finger.

Lucy, J-Bone, and Marty were out of sight. Linus followed where they'd gone. Around the corner near the back of the store was a door that had been shut. Linus tried to open it, but found it locked. He frowned and pressed against it again.

It didn't budge.

From inside came a cry and a loud crash.

Linus didn't hesitate. He threw his weight against the door. He heard it crack in its frame. He stepped back and rushed forward, crashing into it with his shoulder.

The door burst off its hinges, falling onto the ground.

Linus almost stumbled but managed to catch himself at the last minute.

Inside, he found Marty slumped against the far wall. J-Bone stood above him, a disgusted look on his face.

Lucy was flipping through records stacked in a crate.

"What happened?" Linus demanded.

Lucy looked up at him and shrugged. "Oh, he started talking about Jesus and God and that I was an abomination or something." He nodded toward the unconscious Marty. Around his neck hanging on a chain was an ornate silver cross. "He tried to shove that in my face." Lucy laughed as he shook his head. "What does he think I am, a vampire? That's silly. I *like* crosses. They're just two sticks put together, but they mean so much to so many. I tried making a symbol out of Popsicle sticks that I could sell and get rich, but Arthur said it wasn't right. Look, Linus! Chuck Berry! Righteous!" He crowed in excitement as he pulled a record up from the crate.

"So not cool, man," J-Bone scolded the unconscious Marty. "Like, for real. Music is for everyone." He nudged Marty's leg. "Whoa. Total knockout. Little dude, you are hardcore."

"So hardcore," Lucy agreed.

Linus glanced down at Marty again. He was breathing. He'd probably wake up with a headache and nothing more. Linus thought about giving him *another* bump on the head with a well-placed kick, but his shoulder hurt, and he had exerted enough energy for the time being. "Did he hurt you?"

Lucy looked up from the Chuck Berry record. "Why do you sound like that?"

"Like what?"

"Like you're mad. Are you mad at me?" Lucy frowned. "I didn't do anything, really."

"He didn't," J-Bone said. "Marty is so fired, you don't even know."

Linus shook his head. "I could never be mad at you. Not for this. If I sound angry, it's at this . . . this *man,* not you."

"Oh. Because you like me, huh?"

Yes. God help him, yes. Very much so. All of them, really. "Something like that."

Lucy nodded and went back to the crate. "I found six I wanted. Can I get six?"

"Six it is."

He walked over to Lucy to help him carry the records he'd found before he dropped them. They left Marty on the floor and went back to the front of the shop—

Only to find Talia's bag of tools on the floor. But no Talia.

Linus's heart was in his throat. He had turned his back for just a *second* and—

He saw her standing at the front of the store, looking out the window. There was a little girl outside on the sidewalk, no more than five or six years old. She was smiling, her dark hair in twin braids on her shoulders. She put her hand against the window.

Talia did the same. Their hands were the same size and matched perfectly. Talia laughed, and the girl smiled.

She smiled, that is, until a woman came running up the sidewalk, snatching her away, a horrified look on her face. She held the girl against her, turning the girl's head against her shoulder. She glared at Talia through the glass. "How *dare* you?" she snapped. "You leave my daughter alone, you freak!"

Linus stepped forward angrily. "Now, see here—"

But the woman spat wetly at the window and then turned and hurried away, the little girl held tightly against her chest.

"That lady was mean," Lucy whispered to Linus. "You want me to throw her against the wall like I did Marty? Would that be righteous?"

"No," Linus said, pulling Lucy along. "That would *not* be righteous. The only time you should do that is if you need to defend yourself or others. She was vicious, but she only used words."

"Words can hurt too," Lucy told him.

"I know. But we must pick and choose our fights. Just because someone else acts a certain way, doesn't mean we should respond in kind. It's what makes us different. It's what makes us good."

"Big man is right," J-Bone said, coming up behind them. "People suck, but sometimes, they should just drown in their own suckage without our help."

Linus was positive that wasn't what he meant at all. He wasn't very happy with his new nickname either.

Talia was still standing at the window. The woman's spittle dripped down the glass. Talia didn't seem too upset, but he couldn't be sure. She looked surprised when Lucy and Linus appeared beside her.

"That was weird, huh?" she said. She shook her head. "People are strange."

"Are you all right?"

She shrugged. "The girl was nice. She said she liked my beard. It was just the old lady who was a jerk."

"She—the woman wasn't—"

"I know what she was or wasn't," Talia said lightly. "I've seen it before. It's awful, but it's not anything I've haven't dealt with. But it's funny, right?"

Linus didn't find anything about this to be humorous. "What is?"

"That there's so much hope even when it doesn't seem like it."

He was gobsmacked. "How do you mean?"

"The little girl. She wasn't scared of me. She was nice. She didn't care what I looked like. That means she can make up her own mind. Maybe that woman will tell her I'm bad. And maybe she'll believe it. Or maybe she won't believe it at all. Arthur told me that in order to change the minds of many, you have to first start with the minds of few. She's just one person. But so is the lady." Talia grinned. "Can we go to the graveyard now? I want to try out my spade. What did you get, Lucy?"

"Chuck Berry," Lucy said proudly. "I also threw Marty against the wall!"

"Cracked the plaster and everything!" J-Bone said with a laugh. "It was gnarly."

"Wow," Talia said, suitably impressed. "Is he dead? Do we need to bury him? Let me go get my tools, and we can—"

"Nah, he's not dead. I didn't think that would make Mr. Baker too happy, so I let him keep his insides on his inside."

Talia sighed. "Probably for the best. I really like Chuck Berry. I can't wait to listen to that one."

"Right? It's so righteous!" He looked up at Linus. "Can we pay for these now? We can't steal them because J-Bone isn't a square. Right?" He sounded as if he would still be okay with stealing them regardless.

"That's right, he's not a square," Linus said, vowing silently to never repeat those words again. "We can pay—"

"Nah," J-Bone said. "Your money's not good here. You get

those for free, little dude. Sorry about the whole Marty-trying-to-exorcise-you thing. Give me some skin."

Lucy did and gladly. "Linus! I get them for free! That's even better than stealing!"

Linus sighed. "That's not . . . I don't know why I even bother."

"Such a square, big man," Lucy muttered, but he knocked his shoulder against Linus's hip, as if to show he didn't mean it.

At half past two, they met the others in front of the ice cream parlor. People were giving them a wide berth and staring openly, but none of the children seemed to notice. They were listening to Chauncey, who appeared to be wearing a different hat than he'd been before. He was flailing excitedly while Zoe and Arthur watched him, looking amused.

"*There* they are!" Chauncey exclaimed. "Lucy! Talia! You'll never believe what happened! *Look what I got.*" He lifted the hat off his head, stalks stretching excitedly as his eyes rose. In his tentacles, he held a familiar cap that looked like—

"He *gave* it to me," Chauncey cried. "I didn't have to ask! All I did was tell the bellhop I thought he was the greatest man who ever lived and that when I grew up, I wanted to be just like him, and he *gave it to me.* Can you believe that?" He set it back on his head. "How does it look?"

"Quite dashing," Linus said. "I almost wish I had a suitcase so I could hand it off to you to carry for me."

Chauncey squealed. "You mean it? You really think so?"

"It looks good," Lucy said, patting the top of the hat. "Maybe we can figure out how to make a matching coat for it. I think I like it better than your other hat, though that one is good too."

"Thanks, Lucy! Always at your service!"

"And just what do you have?" Arthur asked, squatting down as Talia and Lucy showed him their treasures. "Ah! What a lovely spade. And those records! We'll have to listen to them as soon as we get back to the island."

"Everything all right?" Zoe asked quietly, while the children were distracted.

"If you're asking if any felonies were committed . . . sort of. But nothing I couldn't handle."

"Anything we need to worry about?"

Linus shook his head. "We'll talk about it more once there aren't so many little ears around. I don't think they need to know what Lucy—"

"I threw a square named Marty against a wall after he tried to exorcise me in a small locked room! And then I got the records for free from J-Bone! Isn't that *righteous?*"

"Oooh," the rest of the children said.

Linus sighed.

"I think it's time for ice cream," Arthur said.

The ice cream parlor was cheerfully old-fashioned. There were red plastic swivel seats lining the front of the counter, and Little Richard was wailing overhead about a girl named Sue, tutti frutti, oh Rudy. It was brightly lit, the walls painted candy red and pink. A bell tinkled as they walked through the door.

A man was facing away from them, bent over a counter behind rows of tubs of ice cream in various colors and consistencies. He turned, a smile already growing on his face and said, "Welcome! What can I—" The smile faded. His eyes widened.

The children pressed their hands against the glass, looking down at the ice cream. "Whoa," Phee said. "I'm going to get every kind at once. I'm going to get absolutely *sick* of ice cream."

"You can pick out two flavors," Arthur told her. "Nothing more. You don't want to spoil your appetite for dinner."

"Yes, I do," she assured him. "I want to spoil it so bad."

"You're—you—" the man behind the counter sputtered.

"Yes," Linus said. "I am me. Thank you for noticing. Children, please form a line. One at a time, so the gentleman isn't overwhelmed—"

"No," the man said, shaking his head furiously. "Absolutely not. You need to leave."

The children fell quiet.

Before Linus could speak, dread beginning to flood through him, Arthur beat him to it. "Come again?"

The man was turning red. A vein throbbed in his forehead. "I don't serve your kind here."

Zoe blinked. "Excuse me?"

The man pointed at a wall. There, ever present, was a familiar poster. SEE SOMETHING, SAY SOMETHING!

"I reserve the right to refuse service," the man said. "To *anyone* I choose. I see something, I say something. And I'm saying there is no way you're getting anything from me." He glared at Theodore, sitting on Sal's shoulder. "You aren't welcome in my shop. You aren't welcome in this *village*. I don't care how much we're paid to keep quiet. Go back to your damn island."

"You shut your flapping mouth!" Linus snapped. "You don't get to—"

"I *do*," the man retorted, slamming his hands on top of the counter. It echoed loudly around them and—

Theodore squawked angrily as his perch suddenly vanished. The clothes Sal had been in suddenly collapsed as he shifted into a Pomeranian. Linus remembered the first time he'd done that, when Linus had first arrived on the island. It had been done out of *fear.*

This man had scared Sal so much, he'd turned into a dog.

There were pitiful yips coming from the pile of clothes as Sal struggled to get free. Phee and Talia bent over to help him as Theodore flew over to Zoe. Chauncey moved to hide behind Linus, peeking out from around his legs, his new cap almost falling to the ground.

Lucy looked down at Sal, whose front paws were caught in his shirt. Phee and Talia were whispering quietly to him, telling him it was all right, to stop moving so they could get him free. Lucy turned back toward the man behind the counter. "You shouldn't have scared my brother," he said in a flat voice. "I can make you do things. *Bad* things."

The man opened his mouth to snarl, but was interrupted when Arthur Parnassus said, "Lucy."

Linus had never heard Arthur sound the way he did right then. It was cold and harsh, and though it was just a single word, it felt like it was *grating* against Linus's skin. He looked over to see Arthur staring at the man behind the counter, eyes narrowed, hands flexing at his sides.

The man behind the counter didn't seem to be afraid of the children.

But he was afraid of Arthur.

"How dare you?" Arthur said quietly, and Linus thought of a tiger hunting. "How dare you speak to them that way? They're *children.*"

"I don't care," the man said, taking a step back. "They're *abominations.* I know what their kind is capable of—"

Arthur took a step forward. "You should be more worried about what *I'm* capable of."

The room felt warmer than it'd been just moments before.

Much warmer.

"Arthur, no," Zoe said. "Not here. Not in front of the children. You need to think this through."

Arthur ignored her. "All they wanted was ice cream. That's *it.* We would've paid and they would have been happy, and then we would have *left.* How dare you, sir!"

Linus stepped forward in front of Arthur. He turned away from the man behind the counter to look up. He took Arthur's face in his hands. He felt like he was burning from the inside out. "This isn't the right way to go about this."

Arthur tried to jerk his face away, but Linus held on. "He can't—"

"He can," Linus said quietly. "And it's not fair. At all. But you need to remember your position. You need to remember who looks up to you. Who you care for. And what they'll think. Because what you do here, now, will stay with them forever."

Arthur's eyes flashed again before he slumped. He tried for a smile, and mostly made it. "You're right, of course. It's not—"

The bell above the door tinkled again. "What's going on here?"

Linus dropped his hands and stepped back.

"Helen!" the man behind the counter cried. "These—these *things* won't leave!"

"Well. They don't appear to have gotten their ice cream yet, Norman, so I should expect not."

It was the squat woman from the hardware store. She still had the smudge of dirt on her forehead, though she'd divested herself of her gardening gloves. She didn't look pleased. Linus hoped they weren't going to have more trouble.

"I'm not serving them," Norman growled. "I *won't*."

The woman—Helen—sniffed daintily. "That's not up to you to decide. I would hate to bring up at the next council meeting how you're turning away potential customers. Your lease is coming up for review after the new year, isn't it? It'd be a shame if it wasn't renewed."

Linus thought the vein in Norman's forehead was about to burst. "You wouldn't do that."

Helen arched an eyebrow. "Do you really want to find out?"

"I won't do it!"

"Then go into the back and I'll handle it."

"But—"

"Norman."

Linus thought Norman was going to argue further. Instead, he glared at the children and Arthur again before he spun on his heels and stomped through a swinging door. It slammed against the wall.

Helen sighed. "What a daft little bitch."

"I want to be just like you when I grow up," Talia breathed in awe. Phee stood next to her, nodding in agreement. She held Sal in her arms, his face pressed against her neck.

Helen winced. "Oh. Ignore me. I shouldn't have said that. Never curse, children. Understood?"

They nodded, but Linus could already see Lucy mouthing *daft little bitch* in glee.

"Who are you?" Zoe asked suspiciously.

She smiled at her. "I own the hardware store. I had the most delightful discussion with Talia here about gardens earlier today. She was most knowledgeable."

"Helen is also the mayor of Marsyas," Arthur said. Whatever had been burning within him appeared to have subsided. He had his composure back and once again looked calm.

"There is that," Helen agreed. "Arthur, it's nice to see you again."

"The mayor?" Talia asked. "Do you do *everything*?"

Linus had to agree. He hadn't expected that.

"You would think so," Helen said. She glanced at the door, still swinging on its hinges. "And apparently that includes cleaning up after men throwing their snits. Honestly. For all their bluster, I've noticed that men melt so very easily. Little snowflakes, they are."

"I don't," Lucy told her seriously. "I was going to make him think his skin was boiling off before you got here. But I'm still a man."

Helen looked astonished, but recovered quickly. "Well, I'm glad I showed up when I did. And I think you have a ways still yet to go before you're a man. But I have hopes you will be a better man. You're certainly in good company."

Lucy grinned up at her.

She clapped her hands. "Ice cream! Isn't that why you're here?"

"You can serve ice cream too?" Talia asked.

Helen nodded as she walked around the counter where Norman had been standing. "It was my first job. I was seventeen. It was a different parlor back then, but I expect I still know how to work a scoop. It's how I know Arthur here. He would come in here when he was a child."

That got Linus's attention.

"Arthur was a *child*?" Phee asked, astonished.

"Why would you think otherwise?" Arthur asked, taking Sal from her.

"I don't know. I . . . guess, I always thought you looked like you do now."

"Oh, that's almost certainly true," Helen said. "He dressed the same, at least. Like the world's smallest adult. Always polite. He liked cherry flavor the most, if memory serves."

Everyone turned slowly to stare at Arthur. Even Linus.

Arthur shrugged. "I liked how pink it was. Children, in a line. Linus, would you help Sal, please? I think he'd like that."

Linus could do nothing but nod dumbly. His mind was racing, and he had so many questions he could barely think straight. Chauncey handed him Sal's clothes. He carried them under his arm as Arthur handed Sal over.

Sal was shaking, but he curled against Linus.

"There's a restroom behind you," Helen said as Lucy began to ask her if the pistachio flavor had any bugs in it. "For some privacy."

"Thank you," Arthur whispered as he stroked a finger down Sal's back.

"For what?" Linus asked.

Arthur met his gaze. "You know what. I shouldn't have let that man get to me the way he did."

Linus shook his head. "It wasn't—I didn't do anything."

"You did," Arthur said. "Even if you don't believe it, I'll believe it enough for the both of us. You're a good man, Linus Baker. I'm so very pleased to know you."

Linus swallowed thickly before he turned toward the restroom.

It was unisex and efficient, with a sink and a toilet. He set Sal's clothes down and leaned his back against the wall.

"It's okay," he said to the trembling dog in his arms. "I know it can be scary, sometimes. But I also know that Arthur and Zoe would never let any harm come to you. Neither would Talia or Phee. Or Theodore or Chauncey or Lucy. In fact, I think they would do just about anything to keep you safe. Did you hear when Lucy called you his brother? I think all the other children feel the same."

Sal whined softly, his nose cold against Linus's neck.

"It's not fair," Linus said, staring off into nothing. "The way some people can be. But as long as you remember to be just and kind like I know you are, what those people think won't matter in the long run. Hate is loud, but I think you'll learn it's because it's only a few people shouting, desperate to be heard. You might not ever be able to change their minds, but so long as you remember you're not alone, you will overcome."

Sal barked.

"Yes, he was a daft little bitch, wasn't he? Now, I'll stand outside the door and wait for you to change back and get dressed. And then we'll go out and get some ice cream. Though I probably shouldn't—not good for the waistline, after all—I've got my eye on the mint chocolate chip. I've earned a little treat; I think you have too. How about it?"

Sal wiggled in his arms.

"Good. That's better. And if you ever feel scared like this again, there is no shame in changing as you have, so long as you remember to find your way back." He set Sal down. Sal wagged his little tail at him. "I'll be right outside."

He walked out the door, shutting it behind him. He heard

what appeared to be the snap and pop of bone, followed by a heavy sigh. Out in the shop, Lucy, Talia, and Phee were sitting in a booth. Lucy somehow already had ice cream in his hair. Chauncey was carrying his paper bowl toward them, bellhop cap sitting jauntily on his head. Zoe was standing next to the table, holding up a spoon to Theodore, his tongue flicking out, eyes rolling back in ecstasy.

Arthur was standing at the counter, speaking quietly to Helen. Linus watched as she reached over and put her hand on his.

"Okay," a voice said through the door. "I'm ready."

"Good," Linus said. "Let's see, then."

The door opened. Sal looked a little sheepish, hand rubbing against the back of his neck.

"There we go," Linus said. "Right as rain."

Sal nodded, averting his gaze. "Linus?"

"Yes?"

Sal's hands tightened into fists. "What did he mean?"

"About?"

Sal glanced up at him before looking away. "He said . . . he said he doesn't care how much he gets paid to keep quiet. What did that mean?"

Of course Sal had picked up on that. Linus hesitated, trying to find the right words. "He . . . It's foolish, really. But you're special, the lot of you. And if the world knew how special, they might not understand. It's for your safety."

Sal nodded, though he looked troubled. "Hush money."

Linus sighed. "It would appear so. But it's not important. You let me deal with it, won't you? Let's get you fed."

Helen was startled at the sight of him. She squinted at him, then back at the bathroom, then at Sal again. "That was *you*?"

Sal's shoulder tightened.

"That's so *wonderful*," Helen said. "Just when I thought I'd seen everything. You get three scoops, I think. A growing boy of your size deserves it. What flavors would you like?"

Sal looked surprised. He glanced at Linus. "Go ahead," Linus said. "Three scoops for you."

He picked out his flavors carefully, voice barely above a mumble. Helen cooed over him, causing him to smile at his shoes. When she handed over the bowl, he thanked her quietly before heading toward the table. The others cheered at the sight of him, scooting over to make room. He sat next to Lucy, putting an arm over his shoulders and pulling him close. Lucy laughed and looked up at him, eyes bright. Sal's arm stayed right where it was as they ate.

"I was just asking Arthur here about coming to see Talia's garden," Helen told him. "I hear it's quite the sight."

"It's very beautiful," Linus agreed. "She worked hard at it. I'm sure she would like to show it off. She already thinks you walk on water."

Helen laughed. "I suppose."

"But I do have to ask. Why now?"

She looked taken aback. "Pardon?"

"Linus," Arthur warned.

Linus shook his head. "No. It's a fair question. It's not as if the orphanage is anything new. Some of the children have been there for some time. *You've* apparently been here for some time." He looked at Helen. "Why now? Why haven't you gone there before? Why did it take seeing the children here before you came to that decision?"

Arthur said, "I'm sorry. He's very protective—"

Helen held up a hand. "He's right, Arthur. It's a fair question." She took a deep breath. "And I have no excuse. Perhaps I allowed my perception to become . . . colored. Or perhaps it was out of sight, out of mind."

"See something, say something," Linus muttered.

Helen frowned as she glanced at the poster on the wall. "Yes. That. It's—unfortunate. We get trapped in our own little bubbles, and even though the world is a wide and mysterious place, our bubbles keep us safe from that. To our detriment." She sighed. "But it's so easy because there's something soothing about routine. Day in and day out, it's always the same. When we're shaken from that, when that bubble bursts, it can be hard to understand all that we've missed. We might even fear it. Some of us even fight to try and get it back. I don't know that I would fight for it, but I did exist in a bubble." She smiled ruefully. "Thank goodness you popped it."

"I shouldn't have had to do that," Linus said. "*They* shouldn't have had to do that."

"No, they shouldn't have. And though I'm just one person, I ask for forgiveness for that. I promise that I won't allow it to happen again." She glanced over her shoulder at the door Norman had disappeared through. "I'll do my best to make sure that everyone in the village understands that all of the children from the orphanage are welcome at any point. I don't know how well that'll go over, but I can be very loud when I need to be." Her eyes were twinkling when she added, "I wouldn't want to be thrown against a wall."

Linus winced. "Marty?"

"Martin," Helen said, rolling her eyes. "Came and told me all about it. My nephew is an idiot. J-Bone fired him as soon as he regained consciousness. I would have done the same."

"I won't disagree with you there." He hesitated. Then, "Do you think he's going to be a problem?" At the very least, if word got out, he could see Extremely Upper Management wanting to get involved. Perhaps they'd even summon Lucy before them. It wasn't unheard of. Linus wasn't sure if he feared for Lucy or Extremely Upper Management more. Most likely the latter if he was being honest with himself.

"Oh," she said. "Don't worry about Martin. I'll deal with him myself."

He wasn't sure he wanted to know what that would entail. "Will he listen?"

She snorted. "I oversee his trust from his parents, may they rest in peace. He'll listen."

"Why?" he asked. "Why would you do anything at all?"

She reached out and took his hand in hers. "Change comes when people want it enough, Mr. Baker. And I do. I promise you that. It may take some time, but you'll see. Today has been a swift kick in the seat of my trousers." She squeezed his hand and let go. "Now. What flavor would you like?"

"Cherry," Linus said without thinking.

She laughed. "Of course you do. Two scoops, I think." She sang a quiet song as she went to give him just that.

Linus looked up to find Arthur staring at him. "What?"

Arthur shook his head slowly. "I don't know why you can't see it."

"See what?"

"You. Everything you are."

Linus shifted uncomfortably. "It's not much, but I try with what I have." Then, "I—I shouldn't have pushed. Making you all come here like I did. I should have listened to you."

Arthur looked amused again. "I think it all worked out. Some bumps in the road, but it's nothing we couldn't handle. Lucy didn't actually kill anyone, so I call that a win."

"Two scoops of cherry," Helen announced. "For each of you." It was bright pink with little bits of red fruit. "On me."

"Oh, you don't have to—" Arthur started.

She waved him off. "Think nothing of it. It's the least I can do. All I ask is that you let me come to the island to see that garden."

"Gladly," Arthur said. "Whenever you'd like. You can stay for lunch."

She smiled. "Sounds perfect. Perhaps the week after next? I have an employee, but he's on vacation this week, so it's just me. I'm sure that you and Mr. Baker here will be consummate hosts—"

"I'm afraid it'll just be me and the children," Arthur said, picking up his ice cream. His voice had taken on a strange lilt. "Linus will be leaving us a week from today. Thank you for the ice cream, Helen. And for being so kind." He turned and walked to the table.

Linus frowned. He'd never seen Arthur be so dismissive before.

"You're leaving?" Helen asked, sounding baffled. "Why?"

Linus sighed. "It's an assignment for DICOMY. My stay here was always going to be temporary."

"But you'll come back, won't you?"

Linus looked away. "Why would I? After I make my recommendation, there'd be no need. My job will be done."

"Your job," she repeated. "That's all this is to you? A job?"

"What else would it—"

She reached out and took his hand again. This time, her grip was firm. "Don't. You can lie to yourself all you want, Mr. Baker, but don't you try to lie to me. I won't stand for it. You project yourself in a certain light, but even in my shop, I could see right through the facade. The way you stood up for the children only cemented that. You *know* what else."

"It's not my home," Linus admitted quietly. "I live in the city."

Helen scoffed. "A home isn't always the house we live in. It's also the people we choose to surround ourselves with. You may not live on the island, but you can't tell me it's not your home. Your bubble, Mr. Baker. It's been popped. Why would you allow it to grow around you again?"

She turned and hollered for Norman, disappearing through the swinging door, leaving Linus staring after her. His ice cream was beginning to melt.

The man in the post office barely acknowledged his presence. He only grunted while Linus paid to have the report mailed off.

"Anything for me?" Linus asked, tired of this display.

The man glared at him before turning and digging through a plastic box, riffling through envelopes. He pulled out a large one this time. It was much thicker than any other mail Linus had received while on the island. He frowned when the man handed it over.

It was from DICOMY.

"Thank you," Linus said, distracted. The envelope was heavy and stiff when he picked it up. He left the post office.

He was in the bright sunshine. He took a deep breath. The others were back at the van waiting for him. He shouldn't open it now, but . . . he had to know what was inside.

He tore the top of the envelope carefully.

There was a file inside, much like the ones he'd been given when he'd been sent to the island. The file didn't have a name on the tab. It was blank.

The first page was a cover letter.

He pulled it out, and blinked when something fell onto the sidewalk, bouncing onto his loafer.

He looked down.

It was an old metal key.

He bent down and picked it up. It was lighter than he expected.

The cover letter said:

DEPARTMENT IN CHARGE OF MAGICAL YOUTH
MEMO FROM EXTREMELY UPPER MANGEMENT

Mr. Baker:

Thank you for your second report. It was thorough, as always, and quite enlightening. The descriptions of the daily lives of the children gave us plenty to consider.

However.

We do have some concerns.

As you'll recall, we asked previously for a more in-depth look at Arthur Parnassus. And while you did provide that to us, we couldn't help but notice that it appeared to be less . . . objective than we expected. In fact, the entire report is unlike any other you've written. You were chosen for this assignment, in part, because of your impartiality. You were able, even in the face of adversity, to maintain a degree of separation from the children and people you were investigating.

That doesn't seem to be the case here.

We would caution you against this, Mr. Baker. People will say and do anything they can in order to appease those in power. It's a weapon, and one that is wielded quite deftly. Those who aren't immune to such things might find themselves thinking in ways they shouldn't. Your time on Marsyas will end shortly. You will return to the city. You will be given another assignment, and this will occur all over again. Shield your heart, Mr. Baker, because that is what they go for first. You cannot allow yourself to lose sight of what is real here. You must remain objective. As we're sure you're aware, the RULES AND REGULATIONS dictate that any and all relationships formed must remain completely professional. You cannot be seen as being compromised, especially if there is evidence that an orphanage needs to be closed in order to protect the children.

We can, admittedly, say that we may have underestimated how susceptible you might have been to such attentions from someone like Mr. Parnassus. Seeing as how you're unmarried, we can understand how you might be feeling confused or conflicted. To that end, we want to remind you that DICOMY and Extremely Upper Management are here for you. We care about you. Upon your return from the island, we'll require you to attend a psychological evaluation. For your own peace of mind, of course. The well-being of our caseworkers is of the utmost importance. You are the lifeblood of DICOMY, and without you, there would be no us. There would be no hope for the children. You matter, Mr. Baker.

To assist you in making sure your thoughts are in order and in an effort to be fully transparent, we have enclosed a semi-complete file on Arthur Parnassus. He is, as you'll soon see, not who you think he is. The Marsyas Orphanage is an experiment of sorts. To see if someone of his . . . demeanor could be in charge of a group of unusual children. To keep them all in one place in order to protect our way of life. The island is well-known to him, seeing as how he grew up there in an orphanage that was once closed down because of him. This report is for your eyes only. It is not to be discussed with anyone else, including Mr. Parnassus. Consider it classified level four.

In addition, you will find enclosed a key. If the locks haven't been changed, this should open the cellar door hidden in the garden. It will give you insight as to what Arthur Parnassus is truly capable of.

Soon, Mr. Baker. You will be coming home soon.

We look forward to your next report and your final debrief upon your return.

Sincerely,

CHARLES WERNER
EXTREMELY UPPER MANAGEMENT

FIFTEEN

Though the curiosity was begging to kill the cat, Linus ignored it.

He ignored it as he walked back to the van.

He ignored it as he climbed inside.

He ignored it as Arthur smiled at him, asking him if he was ready to go home.

"Yes," he said evenly. "I'm ready."

The children were high on sugar and the day's outing, and babbled most of the way to the ferry. Merle scowled at them when he opened the gate, but they ignored him. By the time they were halfway across the channel to the island, the children were asleep, with the exception of Sal. Theodore was curled in his lap, wing over his head to block out the sunlight.

"Did you have a good time?" Linus heard Zoe ask him.

"I think I did," Sal replied. "Mr. Baker helped me. He told me I can be scared, but to remember there's more to me than that." He sighed. "People can be rude, and they can think dumb things about me, but I have all of you, and that's what's most important. Right, Mr. Baker?"

Linus thought it was far too late to shield his heart.

The children blinked slowly as they woke when Arthur switched off the van in front of the house. Lucy yawned and stretched, accidentally hitting Talia in the face with his elbow. She shoved his arm away. "Sorry," he said.

"Perhaps we'll have dinner a little earlier tonight," Arthur announced. "I don't think some of us will last much longer after. Let's go inside, and take your things. Make sure they're put away safely. Talia, you may go to the gazebo if that's where you'd like to store your new tools."

She shook her head as Zoe slid the van door open. "I'm going to keep them with me tonight. It's a Gnomish thing. The tools must be in my bed the first night so they know they'll belong to me."

Arthur flashed a smile. "Funny, I've never heard that before."

"Very ancient gnomish tradition. Very secretive. You're lucky I'm even telling you about it."

"Is that right? I'll remember that from this point on." And with that, he opened his door and exited the van.

It took Linus a moment to realize he was the only one left. He startled when his door was jerked open. He looked out to find Zoe watching him. "Coming?"

He nodded, gripping the folder in his hands. He noticed she glanced down at it, and her brow furrowed slightly.

He got out of the van.

She closed the door behind him. "You were awfully quiet on the ride home."

"Long day," he said.

"Is that all?"

He nodded. "Not as young as I used to be."

"No," she said slowly. "I don't suppose you are. Coming inside?"

He smiled weakly. "I should check on Calliope. Make sure she's fed and watered. Give me a bit of peace and quiet before dinner."

"Of course. I'll send one of the children to fetch you when it's time to eat." She reached out and squeezed his arm. "You did well today, Linus. I don't know that we could have done this without you. Thank you."

For the first time since he arrived on the island, he wondered if he was being used.

It hurt more than he expected.

He smiled. "I don't know if that's true."

She watched him for a moment. Then, "Are you sure you're all right?"

"Just tired," he said. "All that sunlight. I'm used to only rain."

She looked as if she were going to say something more, but Phee called out to her, telling her it was her night to help with dinner, and she had some ideas.

Zoe left him standing by the van.

He watched them disappear in the house.

Arthur was the last. He looked back over his shoulder. "See you soon?"

Linus could only nod.

He paced in front of the bed, glancing every now and then at the file he'd placed there.

"It's nothing, right?" he asked Calliope, who watched him from her perch on the windowsill. "Absolute rubbish, most likely. Why wouldn't they have given me this information before, if it were so necessary? And they accused me of losing objectivity. Me, of all people! I've never heard of such a ridiculous notion. The nerve of those people, sitting all high and mighty."

Calliope meowed at him.

"I *know*!" he exclaimed. "It's preposterous. And even if it *wasn't*, I can still appreciate the qualities of the people here. It doesn't have to mean anything. It *doesn't* mean anything."

Calliope's tail twitched.

"Precisely! And obviously Arthur has secrets. Everyone does! *I* have secrets." He stopped pacing and frowned. "Well, that's probably not true. Just because I haven't said something doesn't make it a secret. But I *could* have one! And it would be the *most* secret!"

Calliope yawned.

"You're right," Linus decided. "Why does it matter at all? It's probably nothing. A scare tactic. And even if it's *not*, it won't change anything. I don't have any untoward feelings about anyone, and in a week, we'll leave this place, and in time, we'll think back fondly about our stay here, and nothing more. We certainly won't regret not saying anything to anyone about feelings that don't exist!"

Calliope put her head on her paws and closed her eyes.

She had a good idea. Maybe Linus should sleep on it. A nap, perhaps. Or even ignore it until tomorrow. He hadn't lied when he'd said it'd been a long day. He *was* tired. Many things had happened, and while not all of them had been good, it certainly hadn't been a disaster that ended up with Lucy causing someone to explode or Talia braining another person with her new spade.

"Yes," he said to himself. "A shower and then a nap. I might not even wake up until tomorrow. I can certainly miss a meal, especially after having cherry ice cream." He paused, considering. "Which I didn't even like!"

That was a lie. It'd been delicious. It'd tasted like childhood.

He turned to walk toward the bathroom.

Instead, his feet led him to the edge of the bed.

He looked down at the file. The key sat next to it.

He told himself to leave it alone.

That if there was anything to know, he could just ask.

He remembered the flash in Arthur's eyes.

The way his skin had felt so hot.

He remembered the way Arthur smiled, the way he laughed, the way he existed here on this island as if he had everything in the world he could ever want. It pulled at him, and he thought of how his world had been cold and wet and gray until he'd come here. It felt like he was seeing in color for the first time.

"Don't you wish you were here?" he whispered.

Oh yes. He thought he might wish that more than anything.

He had to stop it. Because he didn't think he could take it if it all turned out to be a lie.

He opened the file. It began just as the previous one had.

NAME: ARTHUR PARNASSUS
AGE: FORTY-FIVE YEARS OLD
HAIR: BLOND
EYE COLOR: DARK BROWN

This was the same as the first file. The rest had been an outline of Arthur Parnassus, giving a vague idea of who he was and how long he'd been master of the Marsyas Orphanage.

This file, however, continued as the others had.

MOTHER: UNKNOWN (BELIEVED DECEASED)
FATHER: UNKNOWN (BELIEVED DECEASED)

What had Helen said?

It was my first job. I was seventeen. It was a different parlor back then, but I expect I still know how to work a scoop. It's how I know Arthur here. He would come in here when he was a child.

And then he read the next line, the one that said SPECIES OF MAGICAL BEING, and everything changed.

Dinner was, in a word, *awkward*.

"Aren't you hungry, Mr. Baker?" Talia asked. "You're not eating."

Linus choked on his tongue.

Everyone stared at him.

He wiped his mouth with a napkin. "I seem to be quite full from the ice cream."

Lucy frowned. "Really? But you have so much room. I ate all my ice cream, and I'm *still* hungry." As if to prove a point, Lucy attempted to stick an entire pork chop in his mouth. He wasn't very successful.

Linus smiled tightly. "It is as it is. I may have . . . so much room, as you say, but that doesn't mean I need to fill it."

Theodore peered over at him, a bit of fat hanging from his mouth.

"You're being awfully quiet too," Phee said, chasing a small tomato with her fork. "Is it because Lucy almost killed a man today?"

"I didn't almost kill him! I wasn't even trying very hard. If I wanted to, I could have exploded him with the power of my mind."

That certainly didn't make Linus feel any better, though it didn't frighten him as much as it would have a couple of weeks ago. He wondered if this was what Extremely Upper Management meant in their letter. Against his better judgment, he was almost *charmed*. That wasn't a good sign.

"You shouldn't kill people," Chauncey said. He had yet to remove his bellhop cap. Arthur had told him he could wear it to dinner just this once. "Killing people is bad. You could go to jail."

Lucy attacked his pork chop viciously. "No jail could hold me. I would escape and come back here. No one would dare come after me because I could make their organs melt."

"We don't melt people's organs," Zoe reminded him patiently. "It's not polite."

Lucy sighed through a mouthful of meat, cheeks bulging.

"You should eat," Sal told Linus quietly. "Everyone needs to eat."

And how could he refute that coming from Sal? Linus made a show of taking a big bite of the salad on his plate.

That seemed to appease everyone. Almost everyone. Arthur was watching him from across the table. Linus was doing his best not to meet his gaze. It seemed safer that way.

He didn't know what Arthur was capable of.

Linus begged off after dinner, saying he was more exhausted than he expected. Lucy looked a little disappointed that Linus wouldn't be listening to the new records he'd purchased, but Linus promised him that tomorrow was a new day.

"You do look a little flushed," Zoe said. "I hope you're not coming down with something." She had a strange glint in her eyes. "Especially seeing as how it's your last week here and all."

Linus nodded. "I'm sure it's nothing."

She took his plate from him, still nearly full. "Well, get some rest, Linus. We'd hate to see you sick. We need you, you know."

Ah. Did they? Did they really?

Linus was almost to the door when Arthur said his name.

He closed his eyes, hand on the doorknob. "Yes? What is it?"

"If you need anything, all you have to do is ask."

He thought the knob would crack under his fingers. "That's very kind of you, but there's nothing I need."

Arthur placed a hand on his shoulder. "Are you sure?"

Oh, how easy would it be to turn around? To look upon the man who had twisted his heart so? The man who, in not so many words, had kept so much from him?

"I'm sure," Linus whispered.

The hand fell away. "Be well, Linus."

He was out the door and into the night as quick as he coul d go.

He stared at the ceiling in the dark, the comforter pulled up to his chin. Sleep was impossible. That blasted file had made sure of

that. Even now, he could feel its presence underneath the mattress where he'd shoved it earlier. He didn't want Chauncey finding it if he came in to take Linus's laundry.

Which brought another wave crashing over him.

Did they know? Did the children know about who Arthur
was? About *what* he was?

He could see it clearly in his mind, though he didn't want
to. Arthur in the classroom, telling the children that a man was
coming from the mainland. A man who would be there to evaluate them, to *investigate* them. A man from the Department in
Charge of Magical Youth who had the power to take this all away
from them. Lucy, of course, would offer to make the intruder's
skin crack from his bones. Theodore could eat what remained
and then regurgitate it into a hole Talia had dug. The hole would
be filled in, and Phee would grow a tree on top of it. When someone came to ask after this interloper, Chauncey would offer to
take their luggage, and Sal would say earnestly that they had no
idea who Linus Baker was.

Arthur, of course, would tell them in no uncertain terms that
murder wasn't the answer. Instead, he whispered in Linus's head,
you must make him care about you. You must make him think
for perhaps the first time in his life that he has found a place to
belong.

It was ridiculous, these thoughts. All of them. But thoughts
late at night when sleep is nothing but a fleeting notion usually
were. In the dark, all of it seemed as if it could be real.

It was after midnight when he sat up in the bed. Calliope
yawned from her spot near his feet.

"What if it's all a lie?" he asked her in the dark. "How did I
get to the place where I wouldn't be able to stand that?"

She didn't answer.

Life before had been mundane and ordinary. He had known
his place in the world, though every now and then, the dark

clouds parted with a ray of sunshine in the form of a question he barely allowed himself to ponder.

Don't you wish you were here?

More than anything.

And then another thought struck him, one so foreign that he was barely able to grasp onto it. It was so outside the realm of what he thought possible that it boggled the mind.

What if, he thought, it's not Arthur who is lying? What if it's not the children?

What if it's DICOMY?

There would be a way to prove that.

One way.

"No," he said, lying back down on the bed. "Absolutely not."

Calliope purred.

"I'll just go to sleep, and in six days, we'll go home, and all of this won't matter. What did the letter call me? *Susceptible?* Bah. Why, the very idea is ridiculous."

He felt better.

He closed his eyes.

And saw how Chauncey had hid under his bed the first morning, how Talia had looked sitting on the floor of a record shop with her tools, how Theodore took the buttons as if they were the greatest gift, how Phee had lifted a trembling Sal from a pile of clothes, how Lucy had cried after breaking his music, how Zoe had welcomed him into her home.

And, of course, Arthur's smile. That quiet, beautiful smile that felt like seeing the ocean for the first time.

Linus Baker opened his eyes.

"Oh dear," he whispered.

The night air was cold, much colder than it'd been since he arrived. The stars were like ice in the black sky above. The moon was barely a sliver. He shivered as he pulled his coat tighter over his pajamas. He reached down to his pocket, making sure the key was still there.

It was.

He stepped off the porch.

The main house was dark, as it should have been at this late hour. The children would be asleep in their beds.

He barely made a sound as he walked toward the garden. For a man his size, he could be light on his feet when he needed to be. The air smelled of salt and felt heavy against his skin.

He followed the path through the garden. He wondered what Helen would think when she came. He thought she'd be impressed. He hoped so. Talia deserved it. She'd worked hard.

He rounded the back of the house. He stumbled over a thick root, but managed to stay upright.

There, in front of him, was the cellar door.

The scorch marks made a terrible amount of sense now.

His throat clicked as he swallowed. He could, Linus knew, turn around right now and forget about all of this. He could go back to his bed, and for the next six days, keep a professional distance and do what he'd been sent here to do. Then he would board the ferry for the last time, and a train would be waiting to take him home. The sunlight would fade behind dark clouds, and eventually, it would start to rain. He *knew* that life. That was the life for a man like Linus. It was dreary and gray, but it was the life he'd led for many, many years. This last month, this bright flash of color, would be nothing but a memory.

He took the key from his pocket.

"It probably won't even fit the lock," he muttered. "It's most likely been changed."

It hadn't. The key slid into the rusted padlock perfectly.

He turned it.

The lock popped open with the smallest of sounds.

It fell to the weeds.

"Last chance," he told himself. "Last chance to forget all this foolishness."

The door was heavier than he expected, so much so that he could barely lift it. He grunted as he pulled it open, arms straining at the weight. It took him a moment to figure out why. Though the outside of the cellar doors were wooden, the *inside* was a sheet of thick metal, as if it'd been reinforced.

And in the starlight, he could see shallow grooves carved into the metal.

He raised his hand and pressed his fingers against the grooves. There were five of them, close together. As if someone with small hands had scraped them from the inside.

That caused a cold chill to run down Linus's spine.

Before him, disappearing into a thick darkness, were a set of stone stairs. He took a moment to let his eyes adjust, wishing he'd remembered to bring a flashlight. Or he could wait for daylight.

He entered the cellar.

Linus kept a hand pressed against the wall to keep his balance. The wall was made of smooth stone. He counted each step he took. He was at thirteen when the stairs ended. He couldn't see a thing. He felt along the wall, hoping to find a light switch. He bumped into something, a bright snarl of pain rolling up his shin and into his thigh. He grimaced and felt for—

There.

A switch.

He flicked it up.

A single bulb flared to life in the middle of the room.

Linus blinked against the dull light.

The cellar was smaller than he expected. The room in the guest house where he'd spent the last three weeks was bigger, though not by much. The walls and ceiling were made of stone, and almost every inch of them were covered in what appeared to be soot. He looked down at his hands and saw they were black. He rubbed his fingers together, and the soot fell away to the floor.

He'd bumped his knee into a desk set against the wall near the light switch. It had been partially burned, the wood blackened and cracked. There was a twin bed, the metal frame broken. There was no mattress, though Linus supposed that made sense. It would be too easy to burn. Instead, there were thick tarps that Linus expected to be flame retardant.

And that was it.

That was everything in the cellar.

"Oh no," he whispered. "No, no, no."

Something in the corner caught his eyes. The single bulb in the room wasn't strong, and there were more shadows than not. He approached the far wall, and as he got closer, he felt his knees turn to jelly.

Tick marks.

Tick marks scratched into the wall.

Four lines in a row. Crossed with a fifth.

"Five," he said. "Ten. Fifteen. Twenty. Twenty-five."

He stopped counting when he reached sixty. It was too much for him to handle. He thought they were meant to keep track of days, and the idea caused his heart to ache.

He swallowed past the lump in his throat. The unfairness of it all threatened to overwhelm him.

DICOMY hadn't been lying.

The file had been true.

"I haven't been down here in years," a voice said from behind him.

Linus closed his eyes. "No. I don't expect you have."

"I thought you seemed a little . . . off," Arthur said quietly. "After you returned to us from the post office, something had changed. I didn't know what, but it had. I chose to believe you when you said you were tired, but then at dinner, you looked as if you'd seen a ghost."

"I tried to hide it," Linus admitted. "It doesn't appear I did a very good job of it."

Arthur chuckled, though it sounded sad. "You're much more expressive than you think. It's one of the things I— No matter. That's neither here nor there. For the moment, at least."

Linus curled his hands into fists to keep them from shaking. "So it's true, then?"

"What is?"

"What I read. In the file DICOMY sent to me."

"I don't know. I've never read my file. For all I know, it's full of half-truths and outright lies. Or, perhaps, everything is correct. One can never tell with DICOMY."

Linus turned around slowly as he opened his eyes.

Arthur stood at the foot of the stairs. He was dressed for bed, meaning he wore his shorts and a thin T-shirt. Irrationally, Linus wanted to offer his coat. It was much too cold for Arthur to be out in what he was wearing. He didn't even have socks on. Or shoes. His feet looked strangely vulnerable.

He was watching Linus, though there didn't appear to be any anger in his gaze. If anything, he looked slightly stricken, though Linus couldn't be sure.

"He gave you a key," Arthur said. It wasn't a question.

Linus nodded. "There was a key, yes. I— Wait. What do you mean *he*?"

"Charles Werner."

"How do you—" He stopped and took a deep breath.

But I made this house a home for those I had, and in preparation in case more came. Your predecessor, he . . . changed. He was lovely, and I thought he was going to stay. But then he changed.

What happened to him?

He was promoted. First to Supervision. And then, last I heard, to Extremely Upper Management. Just like he always wanted. I learned a very harsh lesson then: Sometimes wishes should never be spoken aloud as they won't come true.

"I'm sorry," Linus said rather helplessly.

"For what?"

Linus wasn't sure exactly. "I don't—" He shook his head. "I don't know what he intended."

"Oh, I think I do." Arthur stepped away from the bottom of the stairs. He traced a finger over the burnt surface of the desk. "I suspect he read something in your reports that caused him concern. This was his way of intervening."

"Why?"

"Because that's who he is. People can present themselves as being one way, and once you're sure you know them, once you're sure you've found what you're looking for, they reveal themselves for who they really are. He used me, I think. To get him what he wanted. *Where* he wanted." Arthur rubbed his hands together. "I was younger, then. Enamored. Foolish, though you wouldn't have been able to convince me. I thought it was love. I can see now it wasn't."

"He said this was an experiment," Linus blurted. "To see if— if someone like you could—"

Arthur arched an eyebrow. "Someone like me?"

"You know what I mean."

"Then why can't you say it?"

Linus's chest hitched. "A magical creature."

"Yes."

"Perhaps the rarest of them all."

"So it would seem."

"You're. . . ."

"Say it. Please. Let me hear you say it. I want to hear it from you."

You knew a phoenix, then?

I did. He was . . . inquisitive. Many things happened to him, but he still kept his head held high. I often think about the man he became.

Linus Baker said, "You're a phoenix."

"I am," Arthur said simply. "And I believe I'm the last of my kind. I never knew my parents. I've never met anyone else like me."

Linus could barely breathe.

"I couldn't control it," Arthur said, looking down at his hands. "Not when I was a child. The master then wasn't someone I like to think about if I can help it. He was cruel and harsh, more likely to beat you than look at you. He hated us for what we were. I never knew why. Perhaps something had happened to him or his family before he came to this place. Or maybe he had just listened to the words of the people of the world, and let it fill him like poison. Things were different, then, if you can believe it. Worse for people like us. There are certain laws in place now that didn't exist back then that are meant to prevent . . . well. The village wasn't so bad, but . . . it was only a tiny place in the big, wide world. It was cherry ice cream from a pretty girl. It made me think that perhaps this island wasn't the be-all and end-all. And so I made a grave mistake."

"You asked for help."

Arthur nodded. "I sent a letter to DICOMY, or at least I tried to. I told them how horribly we were being treated. The abuse we suffered at the hands of this man. There were other children here, though he seemed to have a specific vendetta against me, and I took the brunt of it. But I was okay with that, because the more he focused on me, the less he concerned himself with the others. But even I had a breaking point. I knew that if I didn't do something, and soon, I was going to hurt someone."

The more you beat down on a dog, the more it cowers when a hand is raised. If pushed hard enough, a dog might bite and snap, if only to protect itself.

"I thought I was being clever with my letter. I smuggled it out, folded into the top waistband of my pants. But somehow, he found out about it while we were in the village. I snuck off, trying to make it to the post office, but he found me. He took the letter from me." Arthur looked away. "That night was the first night I spent in here. I burned after that. I burned brightly."

Linus thought he was going to be sick. "That's not—that's not fair. He should have never been in a position to do that to you. He should have never been allowed to lay a hand on you."

"Oh, I know that *now*. But then? I was a child." Arthur held out his hand, palm up. His fingers flexed slightly, and fire bloomed like a flower. Linus, who had seen so many strange and wonderful things in his lifetime, was entranced. "Back then, I thought it was what I deserved for being what I was. He beat that into me enough until I had no choice but to believe him." The fire began to move then, crawling up his wrist. It wound its way around his arm. When it reached his shirt, Linus was sure it would start to burn.

It didn't.

Instead, the fire grew until it began to snap and crackle. It rose in the air behind him, spreading out until Linus couldn't deny what he was seeing.

Wings.

Arthur Parnassus had wings of fire.

They were beautiful. Linus could see burning feathers in the red and orange, and he remembered the night he'd seen the flash outside the guest house after Arthur had left. The wings stretched as much as they could in the small room, and Linus thought they were at least ten feet long from tip to tip. And though he could feel the heat from them, it didn't feel scorching. The wings fluttered, leaving trails of golden fire. Above his head, Linus thought he could make out the outline of a bird's head, the beak sharp and pointed.

Arthur closed his hand.

The phoenix curled back down toward the top of his head, wings folding in. The fire snuffed out, leaving thick wisps of smoke, the afterimages of a great bird dancing in Linus's eyes.

"I tried to burn my way out," Arthur whispered. "But the master had prepared for that. The metal slats against the door. The walls made of stone. Stone, I learned, can withstand intense heat. It became obvious rather quickly I would choke on the smoke before I ever escaped. So I did the only thing I could. I stayed. He was smart. He himself never brought me food or changed the bucket I used as a toilet. He made one of the other children do it, knowing I would never harm them."

Though Linus didn't want to know, he asked, "How long were you down here?" He couldn't bear to look at the tick marks scratched into the wall.

Arthur looked pained. "By the time I left, I had thought it'd been a few weeks. It turned out to be six months. When you're constantly in the dark, time gets . . . slippery."

Linus hung his head.

"Eventually, someone came. Either because they suspected something was off, or because they decided an inspection was necessary. I was told the master tried to explain away my absence, but one of the other children was brave enough to speak up. I was found, and the orphanage was shut down. I was sent to one of DICOMY's schools which was better, though not by much. At least there, I could go outside and spread my wings."

"I don't understand," Linus admitted. "Why would you ever return to this place? After everything that happened to you?"

Arthur closed his eyes. "Because this was my hell. And I couldn't allow it to stay that way. This house had never been a home, and I thought I could change that. When I went to DICOMY with the idea of reopening the Marsyas Orphanage, I could see the greed in their eyes. Here, they could keep track of me. Here, they could send others who they thought were the most dangerous. They assigned Charles to me, telling me he would help get things in order. He did, but to his own end. Zoe tried to warn me, though I chose not to believe her."

Anger swelled within Linus. "And where was she? How in God's name did she not help you?"

He shrugged. "She didn't know. She hid herself away, fearing reprisal. She was the great secret of this island, and one they would have tried to harness back then. I only met her once before I went into the cellar. I stumbled upon her in the woods, and she nearly killed me until she saw me for what I was. She fled instead. After I returned to the island, she came to me and told me that she was sorry for all that I had endured. That she would allow me to stay, and that she would help if needed."

"That's not—"

"She isn't to be blamed," Arthur said sharply as his eyes flashed open. "I certainly don't. There was nothing she could have done that wouldn't have put herself in danger."

"They know about her now," Linus admitted. "I included her in my report."

"We know. We made the decision after we received notice that DICOMY was sending a caseworker. She was tired of hiding. She accepted the risk because of how important the children are to her. She needed you to see that she was wasn't going to let them go without a fight."

Linus shook his head. "I can't—why on earth would DICOMY allow you this place at all? Why would they agree to put children in your care?" He blanched and added quickly, "You're quite capable, of course, it's just that—"

"Guilt is a powerful tool," Arthur said. "For all I endured here, it would fall back on DICOMY if word ever got out. They thought they could use it as leverage. For my silence, they would allow me this house. To keep track of me, yes, but in the end, they saw the island as a solitary and desolate place where the only village nearby could be easily bought off. One where they could send who they considered to be the most . . . extreme. This was their grand experiment. They thought I was a pawn."

"But you were playing them," Linus whispered. "Give me your tired, your poor, your huddled masses yearning to breathe free."

Arthur smiled. "Oh yes. I took their huddled masses and gave them a home where they could breathe without fear of retaliation." His smile faded. "I thought I had everything planned. And maybe I made mistakes. Keeping the children on the island for one. That was born out of fear. I told myself they had enough. That the island and Zoe and I could provide everything they could ever need. I love them more than anything in this world. And I convinced myself that love would be enough to sustain them. But I didn't account for one thing."

"What?"

Arthur looked at him. "You. You were the most unexpected thing of all."

Linus gaped at him. "Me? But *why*?"

"Because of who you are. I know you don't see it, Linus. But I see it enough for the both of us. You make me feel like I'm burning up from the inside out."

Linus couldn't find a way to believe him. "I'm just one person. I'm just me."

"I know. And what a lovely person you are."

This couldn't be real. "You played them. DICOMY. To get what you wanted."

Arthur's eyes narrowed. "Yes."

Linus had to fight to get the words out. "You could be doing the same to me. To get what you want. To have me—to have me *say* what you want in my reports."

Arthur sucked in a sharp breath. "Oh. Oh, Linus. Do you really think so little of me?"

"I don't know *what* to think," Linus snapped. "You're not who I thought you were! You've lied to me!"

"I withheld the truth," Arthur said gently.

"Is there a difference?"

"I think—"

"Do they know about you? The children?"

Arthur shook his head slowly. "I learned rather quickly how to hide myself from most everyone."

"Why?"

"Because I wanted them to think there was still good in this world. They were sent to me shattered into the tiniest of pieces. The less they knew about me the better. They needed to focus on their own healing. And I was—"

"They could have found solidarity with you," Linus argued. "They could have—"

"And I was instructed by DICOMY never to reveal myself to them."

Linus took a step back. He hit the wall. "What?"

"It was part of the deal," Arthur said. "One of their conditions before they agreed to allow me to return here. I could reopen Marsyas, but who I am—*what* I am—would remain a secret."

"Why?"

"You know why, Linus. Phoenixes are . . . we—*I* can burn brightly, and I don't know if there's a limit. I believe I could burn the very sky if I pushed myself hard enough. If they couldn't figure out a way to harness that power, then at the very least, they'd put a muzzle on it. Fear and hatred comes from not being able to understand what—"

"That's no excuse," Linus snapped. "Just because you can do things others cannot doesn't make you something to be reviled."

He shrugged awkwardly. "It was their way of showing that regardless of what I was getting in return, they still had a hold over me. It was a reminder that all of this could be taken away whenever they wanted. When Charles left, shortly after Talia and Phee arrived, he told me to remember that. And if he ever got word I had reneged on my promise, or that he even *thought* I had, he would send someone to investigate. And if need be, shut us down. I'm sure the thought crossed their mind at one point or another that instead of me living quietly on this island with their castoffs, I would instead amass an army. Preposterous, of course. I never wanted anything more than a home I could call my own."

"It's not fair."

"No. It's not. Life rarely is. But we deal with it the best we can. And we allow ourselves to hope for the best. Because a life without hope isn't a life lived at all."

"You have to tell them. They need to know who you are."

"Why?"

"Because they have to see they aren't alone!" Linus cried, slamming his palms back against the wall. "That magic exists where we least expect it to. That they can grow up to be whoever they choose to be!"

"Can they?"

"Yes! And though it may not seem like it now, things can change. Talia said that you told her in order to change the minds of many, you have to first start with the minds of a few."

He smiled. "She said that?"

"Yes."

"I didn't think she was even listening."

"Of *course* they listen," Linus said, exasperated. "They listen to every single thing you say. They look to you because you are their *family*. You are their—" He stopped, breathing heavily. He shouldn't say it. It wasn't right. None of this was. It wasn't—"You are their father, Arthur. You said you love them more than life itself. You have to know they feel the same about you. Of course they do. How can they not? Look at you. Look at what you've made here. You are a fire, and they need to know how you burn. Not only because of who you are, but because of what they have made you into."

Arthur's expression stuttered and broke. He lowered his head. His shoulders shook.

Linus wanted to console him, wanted to take Arthur in his arms and hold him tight, but he couldn't get his feet to move. He was confused, all his thoughts swirling in a storm in his head. He latched on to the only thing he could. "And when—when I go back, when I leave this place, I will do my best to make sure Extremely Upper Management knows this. That the island—"

Arthur's head snapped up. "When you go back?"

Linus looked away. "My time here was always going to be short. There was always an end date. And while it came much quicker than I anticipated, I have a home. A life. A job. One that is now more important than ever, I think. You have opened my eyes, Arthur. All of you. I will be forever grateful."

"Grateful," Arthur said dully. "Of course. Forgive me. I don't know what I was thinking." Linus looked up to see him smile, though it seemed to tremble. "Anything you can do to assist us will be more than wonderful. You . . . you are a good man, Linus Baker. I am honored to have known you. We'll have to make sure your last week here on the island is one you'll never forget." He started to turn, but then paused. "And I promise you, the thought of using you for anything has never crossed my mind. You're too precious to put into words. I think . . . it's like one of Theodore's buttons. If you asked him why he cared about them so, he would tell you it's because they exist at all."

And then he was up the stairs and into the night.

Linus stood in the cellar, staring at the space Arthur had left behind. The air was still warm, and Linus swore he could hear the crackling of fire.

SIXTEEN

If Linus's life were a drama, the last week of his stay on Marsyas would have been cold and rainy, the gray clouds shifting overhead to match his mood.

But it was sunny, of course. The sky and the sea were cerulean.

On Monday, Linus sat in on the children's classes, listening as they discussed the Magna Carta in the morning and *The Canterbury Tales* in the afternoon. Sal was quite vexed the stories were unfinished, which led Arthur to bring up the *The Mystery of Edwin Drood*. Sal vowed to read it and come up with his own ending. Linus thought it would be marvelous and wondered if he would ever get to read it.

On Tuesday from the hours of five in the afternoon to seven, he sat with Talia in her garden. She was fretting slightly over what Helen would think when she visited next week. She worried that Helen wouldn't like what she'd grown. "What if it's not good enough?" Talia muttered in Gnomish, and the fact that Linus understood her barely crossed his mind.

"I think you'll find that it's more than adequate," he replied.

She scowled at him. "More than adequate. Gee, Linus. Thank you for that. I feel so much better already."

He patted her on the top of the head. "We do need to keep the ego in check. You have nothing to fear."

She looked around her garden doubtfully. "Really?"

"Really. It's the most beautiful garden I've ever seen."

She blushed under her beard.

On Wednesday, he sat with Phee and Zoe in the woods. He'd forgone a tie, and his shirt was open at his throat. He was bare-foot, the grass soft underneath his feet. Sunlight filtered through the trees, and Zoe was telling Phee that it wasn't just about what she *could* grow, but about cultivating what was already there. "It's not always about creation," Zoe said quietly as flowers bloomed underneath her hands. "It's about the love and care you put into the earth. It's intent. It'll know your intentions, and, if they're good and pure, there is nothing you won't be able to do."

That afternoon, he was in Chauncey's room, and Chauncey was saying, "Welcome to the Everland Hotel, sir! May I take your luggage?" and Linus replied, "Thank you, my good man, that would be wonderful." He handed over an empty satchel. Chauncey hefted it over his shoulder, his bellhop cap sitting crooked on his head. After, he made sure to tip Chauncey hand-somely. It was what one did after having received first-rate ser-vice, after all. The saltwater on the floor was warm.

It was late afternoon on Wednesday, and Linus was starting to panic, a feeling settling over his shoulders like a heavy cloak that this wasn't right, that he was making a mistake.

He had put his luggage on his bed with the intention of be-ginning to pack. He was leaving the day after tomorrow, and he told himself he might as well get started. But he stood in his room staring down at his bag. His copy of the *RULES AND REGULA-TIONS* lay on the floor near the bed. He couldn't remember the last time he'd picked it up. He asked himself why it'd been so important in the first place.

He didn't know how much longer he would have stood there if he hadn't heard the tapping on the bedroom window.

He looked up.

Theodore was perched outside, wings folded at his sides, head cocked. He tapped his snout against the glass again.

Linus went to the window, sliding it open. "Hello, Theodore."

Theodore chattered in response, greeting Linus as he hopped inside. His wings opened and he half jumped, half flew to the bed, landing near Calliope. His eyes narrowed at her, and he snapped his jaws. She stood slowly, arching her back as she stretched. And then she walked to Theodore and lifted her paw to smack him across the face before yawning and jumping down from the bed.

Theodore shook his head, a little dazed.

"You deserved that," Linus chided him gently. "I've told you not to antagonize her."

Theodore grumbled at him. Then, he chirped a question.

Linus blinked. "Come with you? Where?"

Theodore chirped again.

"A surprise? I don't think I like surprises."

Theodore wasn't having any of it. He flew up to Linus's shoulder, landing and nipping at Linus's ear until he had no choice but to obey. "Cheeky little git," Linus muttered. "You can't just bite until people do what you— *Ow*! I'm *going*!"

The afternoon sun felt warm on Linus's face as they left the guest house. He listened as Theodore babbled in his ear. As the seagulls called overhead. As the waves crashed against the cliffs below. The ache in his heart was sharp and bittersweet.

They entered the main house. It was quiet, which meant that either everyone was out doing their own thing, or Lucy was up to something terrible that would end in death.

Theodore jumped down from Linus's shoulder, wings out as he landed on the ground. He stumbled over them as he hurried toward the couch, tumbling end over end. He landed on his back, blinking up at Linus.

Linus fought a smile. "You'll grow into them yet. Quite a lot, I think."

Theodore turned over and found his footing. He shook

himself from his head to the tip of his tail. He looked back up at Linus, chirped again, and disappeared under the couch.

Linus stared after him, disbelieving what he'd just heard. He'd seen part of Theodore's hoard—the one he kept in the turret—but this was more important.

Another chirp came out from underneath the couch.

"Are you sure?" he asked quietly.

Theodore said he was sure.

Linus slowly went to his hands and knees and crawled toward the couch. Obviously he wouldn't be able to fit underneath, but if he lifted up the skirt, he'd be able to see just fine.

So that was what he did.

He lay flat on his stomach and peered underneath the couch into Theodore's lair, cheek pressed against the floor.

Off to his right, there was a soft blanket that had been fashioned into a nest. A small pillow—the size of Linus's hand—sat atop it. Spread out around it were Theodore's treasures. There were coins and rocks shot with quartz (much like the ones in Lucy's room) and a pretty red-and-white shell with a crack through the middle.

But that wasn't all.

There was a piece of paper that Linus could make out a few words: *Brittle and thin. I am held—*

There was a dried flower that looked like the ones Linus had seen in the garden.

There was a leaf so green that only a sprite could have grown it.

There was a piece of a broken record.

There was a picture that looked as if it'd been torn from a magazine, of a smiling bellhop, helping a woman with her bags.

There was a picture of Arthur as a younger man, the edges curled with age.

And next to it, piled lovingly, were buttons.

So many buttons.

It's the little things, I expect. Little treasures we find without knowing their origin. And they come when we least expect them. It's beautiful, when you think about it.

Linus blinked against the sudden burn in his eyes.

"It's wonderful," he whispered.

Theodore chirped that of course it was. He went to the buttons and nudged his nose into the pile as if searching for something. His tail thumped against the floor as he lifted his head.

In his mouth was a familiar brass button.

He turned and walked toward Linus.

Linus watched as his jaw clenched. Theodore bit down onto the button before dropping it to the floor.

Linus could see the impressions of Theodore's fangs in the brass.

Theodore nudged it toward him. He looked up at Linus and chirped.

"For me?" Linus asked. "You want me to take it?"

Theodore nodded.

"But that's—" Linus sighed. "It's yours."

Theodore nudged it toward him again.

Linus did the only thing he could—he took it.

He sat up from the floor, pressing his back against the couch. He stared down at the button in his hand, tracing a finger over the grooves from Theodore's fangs. The wyvern poked his head out from underneath the couch and chirped up at him.

"Thank you," Linus said quietly. "It's the nicest thing anyone has ever given me. I'll keep it for always."

Theodore lay his head against Linus's thigh.

They stayed there as the evening sunlight drifted along the wall.

It was Thursday morning when the anger of men came to a head.

Linus was in the kitchen with Zoe and Lucy, who was bellowing at the top of his lungs along with Bobby Darin's sweet, sweet voice. Linus was smiling, and he was laughing, though his heart felt like shards in his chest. Sticky buns were in the oven, and if he listened hard enough (though Lucy was doing his very best to make sure he couldn't), he would hear the sounds of the others moving throughout the house.

"So many leftover pecans," Zoe said. "I'm not sure we needed to—"

Linus startled when she dropped the bowl she was washing back into the sink, soapy water splashing onto the floor.

She stood stiffly. Her fingers twitched, her wings unfurling, moving hummingbird-fast.

"Zoe?" Linus asked. "Are you all right? What's happened?"

"No," she whispered as Lucy continued to sing, unaware. "No, not now. They can't. They *can't.*"

Lucy said, "What? Who are you—"

Zoe turned around, little soap bubbles falling from her fingers and floating to the floor. Her eyes were brighter than Linus had ever seen before, filled with an otherworldly light, irises glittering like shattered glass. Not since Linus had known her had he been afraid of her, and this was still true. But he would be foolish to think that she was anything but an old and powerful sprite, or forget that he was merely a guest on her island.

He started toward her slowly, not wanting to surprise her in case she'd become unaware of his presence. Before he could reach her, Arthur burst into the kitchen, eyes narrowed. The room grew warmer, and for a moment, Linus thought he saw the flash of fire, though it might have just been a trick of the morning light.

"What is it?" he demanded. "What's happened?"

"The village," Zoe said, her voice soft and dreamy, her words almost like musical notes. "They're gathering at the shore of the mainland."

"What?" Lucy asked. "Why? Do they want to come here?" He frowned down at the pecans on the countertop. "They can't have my sticky buns. I made them just the way I like them. I know sharing is a nice thing to do, but I don't feel very nice today." He looked to Linus. "Do I have to share my sticky buns?"

"Of course not," Linus said evenly. "If that's what they want, they'll have to make their own."

Lucy grinned, though it seemed nervous. "I made two for you, Mr. Baker. I don't want you wasting away."

"Lucy," Arthur said. "Would you please gather the others in the classroom? It's almost time to begin your lessons."

Lucy sighed. "But—"

"Lucy."

He grumbled under his breath as he hopped down from his stool. He paused at the kitchen doorway, glancing back at the three of them. "Is something wrong?"

"Of course not," Arthur said. "Everything is perfectly fine. If you please, Lucy."

He hesitated only a moment longer before leaving the kitchen, calling for the others, telling them that apparently sticky buns wouldn't get them out of their lessons as he'd thought they would.

Arthur went to Zoe, gripping her by the shoulders. Her eyes cleared, and she blinked rapidly. "You felt it too."

Arthur nodded. "Have they started to cross?"

"No. They're . . . stopped. At the docks. I don't know why. But the ferry hasn't left the village." Her voice hardened. "They would be foolish to try."

A chill arced down Linus's spine. "Who?"

"I don't know," she said. "But there are a few of them." She looked past Arthur into nothing. "They're angry. It's like a storm."

Arthur dropped his hands and took a step back. "You will stay here with the children. Go on as normal. Tell them nothing is amiss. I'll deal with this myself. I'll return as soon as I'm able."

She reached for him, hands circling his wrist. "You shouldn't have to do this, Arthur, not after what . . . let me go. I will—"

Arthur backed away from her slowly. "No. On the chance they still come to the island, the children will need you more. You can protect them better than I could. If it comes down to it, take them to your house. Close the forest behind you so that nothing gets through. Cover the whole island if you have to. We've talked about this, Zoe. We always knew this was a possibility."

She looked as if she were about to argue, but subsided at the expression on Arthur's face. "I don't want you going alone."

"He won't be," Linus said.

They turned to him in surprise, as if they'd forgotten he was there at all.

He sucked in his stomach and puffed out his chest, hands on his hips. "I don't know what's going on, exactly, but I have a good idea. And if it has anything to do with the people in the village, then it's high time I gave them a piece of my mind." He thought he probably looked ridiculous, and his words didn't have the weight to them he'd hoped, but he didn't break their gazes.

Arthur said, "I won't have you in any danger, Linus. It would be best if you—"

"I can handle myself," Linus said with a sniff. "I may not look like much, but I assure you I'm more than I appear. I can be quite stern when I need to be. And I'm a representative of the government. In my experience, people listen to authority." This was only somewhat true, but Linus kept that little detail to himself.

Arthur sagged. "You silly, brave man. I know what you are. But if you would just—"

"Then it's settled," Linus said. "Let's go. I don't like cold sticky buns, so the sooner we deal with this and can return, the better." He started for the doorway, but stopped when a thought crossed his mind. "How are we to cross if the ferry is on the other side?"

"Catch."

He turned in time to see Zoe toss a set of keys toward him. He fumbled with them, but managed to keep them from falling to the floor. He frowned when he saw it was the keys to her ridiculous car. "While I appreciate the effort, I don't see how this will help us. There is quite a bit of water between us and the village, and unless your car is a submersible, then I don't know how this will be of any use."

"It's better if I don't tell you," she said. "It'll only make you worry."

"Oh dear," Linus said faintly. "I don't know if I like the sound of that."

She stood on her tiptoes, kissing Arthur on the cheek. "If they see you . . ."

Arthur shook his head. "Then they do. It's time to step from the shadows and into the light. Past time, I think." He glanced at Linus. "Someone wise taught me that."

They left her standing in the sunlit kitchen, sticky buns warming in the oven.

The car bounced down the road, Linus's foot pressing as hard on the gas pedal as he dared. His heart was racing, and his mouth was dry, but there was a sharp clarity to his vision. The trees seemed greener, the flowers that lined the road more brilliant. He glanced in the side mirror in time to see the forest closing off behind them with a low groan, covering the road with thick branches. If one didn't know what to look for, there appeared to be no way through.

Arthur sat in the passenger seat, hands folded in his lap. His eyes were closed. He was breathing slowly in through his nose and out through his mouth.

They reached the dock at the edge of the island without incident. The sea was calm, the whitecapped waves small as they fell upon the shore. In the distance, across the channel, Linus could see the ferry still docked at the village. He brought the car to a stop, the brakes squeaking.

Arthur opened his eyes.

"What now?" Linus asked nervously, sweaty hands flexing on the steering wheel. "Unless this car *is* a submersible, I don't see how we can cross. And if it is, I must tell you I have no experience piloting such a vehicle, and we'll most likely drown at the bottom of the sea."

Arthur chuckled. "I don't think we'll have to worry about that. Do you trust me?"

"Yes," Linus said. "Of course I do. How could I not?"

Arthur looked over at him. "Then drive, my dear Linus. Drive and see what that trust has gotten you."

Linus looked ahead through the windshield.

He took a deep breath.

He lifted his foot off the brake.

The car began to roll forward.

He pressed his foot down on the gas.

The car picked up speed.

His knuckles turned white as they left the last bit of road and hit the white sand of the beach. His throat closed as the ocean filled the windshield. "*Arthur*—"

Arthur said, "Have faith. I would never let anything happen to you." He reached over and put his hand on Linus's leg, squeezing tightly.

Linus didn't slow.

He didn't stop.

The roar of the ocean filled his ears as the dry sand turned wet and the first spray of saltwater misted against his face. Before he could shout in warning, the sea crackled in front of them, the water vibrating and shifting as if something just underneath the surface was rising. He closed his eyes tightly, sure they were about to have wave after wave rush over them, pulling them under.

The car rattled around them, the steering wheel jerking in his hand. He prayed to whoever was listening for guidance.

"Open your eyes," Arthur whispered.

"I would really rather not," he said through gritted teeth. "Staring death in the face is vastly overrated."

"Good thing we're not dying, then. At least not today."

Linus opened his eyes.

He was stunned when he saw they were on the sea. He twisted his head to look back, only to see the shore shrinking behind them. He gasped, struggling to breathe. "What on *earth*?"

He turned forward again. A white crystalline road lay before them, materializing from the ocean. He peered over the side of his door, looking down. The road beneath them was almost double the width of the car, snapping and crackling, but holding.

"Salt," Arthur said, and Linus could hear the amusement in his voice. "It's the salt from the ocean. It'll hold."

"How is this possible?" Linus asked in wonder. Then, "Zoe."

Arthur nodded. "She is capable of a great many things, more than even I know. I've only ever seen her do this once before. We decided long ago to make use of the ferry, to keep the people of the village at ease. It's better to deal with Merle when we have to, instead of inciting fear by a car crossing the water."

Linus choked on a hysterical laugh. "Oh, of course. Just a road made from the salt of the ocean. Why didn't I think of that?"

"You didn't know it was a possibility," Arthur said quietly. "But those of us who dream of impossible things know just how far we can go when pushed to do so."

"Well, then," Linus said faintly. "Let's see how they like us being pushed, shall we?"

He pressed the gas pedal as hard as he could.

The car roared forward along the salt road.

They could see a group of people standing on the docks near the ferry. Some had their arms raised in the air, hands curled into fists. Their shouts were drowned out by the sounds of the car and sea, but their mouths were twisted, their eyes narrowed. Some carried signs that looked hastily made, bearing such legends as I SAW SOMETHING, I AM SAYING SOMETHING and

I AM ANTI-ANTICHRIST and, absurdly, I DIDN'T HAVE ANYTHING CLEVER TO WRITE.

Their shouts died down when they saw the car approaching. Linus couldn't fault them for the looks of shock on their faces. He was sure that if he were standing on the shore, watching a car driving along the surface of the ocean, he'd probably wear the same expression.

The salt road ended at the beach near the docks. He brought the car to a halt on the sand, turning it off. The engine ticked.

Silence fell.

Then, at the front, the man from the ice cream shop (*Norman,* Linus thought with mild disdain) shouted, "They're using *magic!*"

The crowd began to roar in earnest once more.

Helen was standing at the front of the crowd on the dock as if to block them from gaining access to the ferry. She looked furious, her face smudged with dirt. Merle stood next to her, arms across his chest, a scowl on his face.

Linus and Arthur exited the vehicle, slamming the doors shut behind them. Linus was relieved to see the crowd wasn't as large as it first appeared. There were perhaps a dozen people, including Helen and Merle. He wasn't surprised to see Marty from the record shop in the crowd, wearing a neck brace. He held a sign that said YES, I WAS INJURED BY THE SCION OF THE DEVIL. ASK ME HOW! Next to him was the man from the post office. Linus wasn't surprised. He never liked that fellow all that much to begin with.

The shouts died once more as Linus and Arthur climbed the steps next to the dock, though they didn't die out completely.

"What is the *meaning* of this?" Linus demanded as he reached the dock. "My name is Linus Baker, and I am in the employ of the Department in Charge of Magical Youth. Yes, that's correct. A *government official.* And when a government official wants answers, said answers had best be given as quickly as possible."

"They tried to swarm my ferry," Merle said, eyeing the crowd and Arthur with distaste in equal measure. "Said they wanted to get to the island. I wouldn't let them."

"Thank you, Merle," Linus said, surprised at the ferryman's thoughtfulness. "I wouldn't have expected—"

"They refused to pay me," Merle snapped. "I don't do nothin' for free."

Linus bit his tongue.

"You shouldn't have come," Helen told Arthur. "I have this under control. I wouldn't let anything happen to you or the children." She glared at her nephew, who tried to slink back farther into the crowd. "*Some* people don't know when to keep their mouths shut. Oh, you can try and hide, Martin Smythe, but I see you. I see you very well. I see all of you. And I have a long, *long* memory."

"I'm sure you have this well in hand," Arthur said, voice even. "But it always helps to have people by your side."

Linus stepped forward. The sun was bright, causing him to sweat profusely. He glared at the group of people before him. He'd never been the intimidating sort, much to his consternation, but he wasn't about to allow these people to do whatever had gotten stuck in their heads. "What is the meaning of this?"

He felt a savage glee when the crowd took a step back as one.

"Well? You seemed to have a voice just fine until we arrived. Anyone? Surely someone is willing to speak."

It was Norman who did. Linus wasn't surprised. "We want them gone," he growled. "The children. The orphanage. The island. All of it."

Linus stared at him. "And how do you expect to rid yourselves of an entire island?"

Norman flushed with anger. "That's—you see—that's not the *point*."

Linus threw up his hands. "Then what, pray tell, *is* the point?"

Norman spluttered before saying, "The Antichrist child. He almost *killed* Marty!"

The crowd rumbled behind him in agreement.

Norman nodded furiously. "Yes, that's right. There Marty was, minding his own business when that—that *thing* came into town and threatened his life! Threw the poor sod against the wall like it was nothing. He's permanently injured. The fact that he's even walking is a miracle!"

Helen scoffed. "Permanently injured, my arse."

"Look at his neck brace!" the postmaster cried. "No one wears a neck brace unless they've been seriously hurt!"

"Really," Helen said. "Because that neck brace seems to be the *exact* one I had in my closet at home that I was given after a car accident years ago."

"It's not!" Marty exclaimed. "I went to the doctor, and he gave it to me after telling me that my spine was mostly powder and I was lucky to be alive!"

"That I believe," Linus muttered. "You would be spineless."

Helen rolled her eyes. "Martin, there's a tag on the back. It has my initials on it. You forgot to tear it off. We can all see it."

"Oh," Martin said. "Well, that's . . . merely a coincidence?"

"It doesn't matter," Norman said hotly. "We have all decided the children are a menace. They represent a danger to us all. We've abided long enough with their wickedness. What happens if they come for the rest of us, just as they did Marty?"

"Did he tell you that he tried to take a small child into a locked room by himself in an attempt to exorcise him?" Linus asked. "Because I'm positive there are laws against kidnapping and attempted assault, regardless of who the child may be."

The crowd turned slowly to look at Marty.

Marty found something awfully curious at the ground beneath his feet.

Norman shook his head. "His actions were misguided, but the point remains the same. Are we not allowed to protect ourselves? You say they're children. Fine. But we have our *own* children to worry about."

"Strange," Helen said, coming to stand next to Linus. "Because not a single one of you is a parent."

Norman was getting worked up again. "That's because they were too afraid to be here!"

"Name one," Helen said.

Norman said, "I won't have you trying to trick me. I know you don't see it, Helen, and that's on you. But we won't allow our lives to be threatened when—"

Linus laughed bitterly. "Threatened? By *whom*? Who in the world has threatened you aside from me?"

"They have!" a woman cried in the back of the crowed. "By simply existing, they're a threat!"

"I don't believe you," Linus said. "I have been by their side for a month, and I have heard nary a *whisper* of a threat. In fact, the only time I've *ever* thought there was danger, aside from Marty's ill-advised attempt against a child, was from you lot here. Say you crossed to the island. What would you do? Would you lay your hands upon them? Would you strike them? Hurt them? Kill them?"

Norman paled. "That's not what we—"

"Then what *are* you doing? Because surely you have some idea. You have gathered yourselves in a crowd, working yourselves up in a tizzy. Your groupthink has poisoned you, and I hate to wonder what would have happened had you gained access to the island. I never thought I'd say this, but thank Christ Merle was here to refuse you passage on his ferry."

"Yeah," Merle said. "I told you payment was required, but you refused!"

"Honestly, Merle," Helen said. "Learn to keep your mouth shut when you're receiving soft praise, why don't you?"

"Disperse," Linus said. "Or I will do everything in my power to make sure—"

He couldn't see who it came from. Someone in the middle of the crowd. He didn't think it was Marty, but it happened quickly. A hand raised, and clutched in its fingers was a large rock. The hand pulled back before jerking forward, the rock flying toward them. Linus didn't have time to consider who it had been aimed for, but Helen was in its path. He moved in front of her, his back to the crowd, shielding her. He closed his eyes and waited for impact.

It never came.

Instead, it was as if the sun had crashed to the Earth. The air grew warmer and warmer until it felt like it was on fire. He opened his eyes, his face inches from Helen's. But she wasn't looking at him. She was staring up above him in wonder, her eyes reflecting waves of fire.

He turned slowly.

Standing between them and the crowd was Arthur Parnassus, though not as he'd been.

The phoenix had risen.

His arms were spread wide away from him. The wings Linus had glimpsed briefly in the darkened cellar were stretched at least ten feet on either side of Arthur. Fire crawled up and down his arms and shoulders. Above him, the head of the phoenix pulled back, the rock held in its beak. It bit down, shattering the rock into tiny pieces that rained down in front of Arthur.

There was fear in the people before them, yes, fear that wouldn't be cured by such a display, even one as magnificent as this. But it was tempered by the same wonder he'd seen in Helen, the same wonder he was sure was on his own face.

The wings fluttered, fire crackling.

The phoenix tilted its head back and cried out, a piercing shriek that warmed Linus to his core.

Linus left Helen standing on the dock.

He circled Arthur slowly, ducking under one of the wings, feeling the heat of them on his back.

Arthur was staring straight ahead, his eyes burning. The phoenix flapped its wings, little tendrils of fire spinning off. It cocked its head as it stared down at Linus, eyes blinking slowly.

Without a second thought, Linus reached up and cupped Arthur's face. His skin was hot, but Linus wasn't afraid of being singed and blackened. Arthur would never allow it.

The fire tickled against the backs of his hands. "There, there," Linus said quietly. "That's enough of that, I think. You've made your point quite well."

The fire faded from Arthur's eyes.

The wings pulled back.

The phoenix lowered its head toward them. Linus looked up at it and gasped when the great bird pressed its beak against his forehead momentarily before it too was gone in a thick plume of black smoke.

"You've gone and done it now," Linus whispered.

"It was time," Arthur said. Sweat dripped down his forehead, and his face was pale. "All right?"

"Quite. I'd like to avoid a rock upside the head if at all possible, so it's much appreciated." He dropped his hands, aware that they still had an audience. He was angry, angrier than he'd been in a long time. He started to turn to give them a piece of his mind, to threaten them within an inch of their lives, but stopped when Arthur shook his head. "You've had your say. Let me."

Linus nodded tightly, though he didn't leave Arthur's side. He glared at the crowd, daring any of them to throw another rock.

Whatever fight had been in them was gone. Their eyes were wide, their faces pale. Their signs lay forgotten on the ground. Marty had removed his neck brace, probably because he'd wanted to look up and see the phoenix unleashed.

Arthur said, "I don't know you as well as I'd like. And you don't know me. If you did, you would have known that attempting to harm me and mine is never a good idea."

Linus grew warm again, though the phoenix was gone.

The crowd took another step back.

Arthur sighed, shoulders slumping. "I don't . . . I don't know what to do here. I don't know what to say. I'm under no impression that words alone will change hearts and minds, especially when those words come from me. You fear what you don't understand. You see us as chaos to the ordered world you know. And I haven't done much to fight that, given how isolated I've kept the children on the island. Perhaps if I'd . . ." He shook his head. "We make mistakes. Constantly. It's what makes us human, even if we're different from one another. You see us as something to be feared. And for the longest time, I've seen you as nothing but living ghosts from a past I'd give anything to forget. But this is our home, and one we share. I won't beg. I won't plead. And if push comes to shove, I will do what I must to ensure the safety of my wards. But I hope to avoid that if at all possible. Instead, I'll ask for you to listen instead of judging that which you don't understand." He looked to Marty, who shrank back. "Lucy meant you no real harm," he said, not unkindly. "If he had, your insides would be on your outside."

"Perhaps a little less," Linus muttered as the crowd gasped in unison.

"Too right," Arthur said. Then, louder, "Not that he'd ever do that. All he wanted was his records. He does love them so. Regardless of what else he is, he is still a child, as they all are. And don't all children deserve to be protected? To be loved and nurtured so that they may grow and shape the world to make it a better place? In that way, they are no different than any other child in the village, or beyond. But they're told they are, by people such as yourselves, and people who govern them and our world. People who put rules and restrictions in place to keep them separated and isolated. I don't know what it will take to change that, if anything. But it won't start at the top. It'll start with us."

The crowd watched him warily.

Arthur sighed. "I don't know what else to say."

"I do," Helen said, stepping forward. She was furious, her hands balled into fists. "You have the right to assemble peacefully. You have the right to express your opinions. But the moment it crosses the line into violence, it becomes a matter of legality. Magical youth are protected by laws, as all children are. Any harm that comes to them will be met with the swiftest of consequences. I'll make sure of it. I'll do my level best to make sure *anyone* who lays a hand on a child, magical or not, will wish they hadn't. You may think you can shrug off anything Linus or Arthur says, but mark my words, if I even catch a *whiff* of further discord, I will show you why I'm not to be trifled with."

Norman was the first to react.

He stormed off, pushing his way through the crowd, muttering to himself.

The postmaster followed, though he glanced back over his shoulder, a stunned expression on his face.

A few more walked after them. Marty tried to leave too, but Helen said, "Martin Smythe! You stay *right* where you are. You and I are going to have a very long conversation about proper etiquette in group settings and the penalties of lying. And if it was you who threw that rock, I'm going to drain your trust fund and donate it all to charity."

"You *can't*!" Marty wailed.

"I can," Helen said primly. "I'm the trustee. And it would be very, very easy."

The crowd dispersed. Linus was startled when a few people muttered apologies toward Arthur, though they kept their distance. He expected news of what they'd seen to spread through the village rapidly. He wouldn't be surprised if the story would eventually end up as Arthur having turned into a monstrous bird and threatening to burn their skin from their bones and destroy the village.

Merle said, "I'll take you back to the island, if you want. Half price."

Linus snorted. "I think we'll be fine, Merle. But thank you for your generosity." He paused, considering. "And I really mean that."

Merle grumbled under his breath about a salt road putting him out of business as he walked down the dock toward his ferry.

Arthur was watching the people walk away toward the village. "Do you think they'll listen?" he asked Helen.

Helen frowned. "I don't know. I hope so, but then I hope for many things that don't always come to be." She looked at him almost shyly. "Your feathers were very pretty."

He smiled. "Thank you, Helen. For all that you've done."

She shook her head. "Give me time, Arthur. Give all of us time. I'll do what I can." She squeezed his hand before turning to Linus. "Off, then? Saturday, right?"

He blinked. In all the excitement, he'd forgotten his journey was almost at an end. "Yes," he said. "Saturday."

"I see." She looked between Arthur and Linus. "I do hope you find yourself back here again one day, Mr. Baker. It's certainly . . . eventful, when you're around. Safe travels."

And with that, she moved down the dock, grabbing Martin by the ear and pulling him away, much to his righteous indignation.

Linus moved next to Arthur. The backs of their hands brushed together. "How did it feel?" he asked.

"What?"

"Stretching your wings."

Arthur turned his face toward the sun, lips quirking slightly. "Like I was free for the first time in a very long time. Come, my dear Linus. Let's go home. I'm sure Zoe has her hands full. I'll drive."

"Home," Linus echoed, wondering just where that could actually be.

They headed back toward the car. Moments later, they were on the salt road, the wind in their hair, the cerulean sea lapping at the tires.

SEVENTEEN

On Friday afternoon, there was a knock at the door of the guest house.

Linus looked up from his final report. He'd been working on it most of the day. He'd only written a single sentence after the customary introduction.

He stood from his chair and went to the door.

He was surprised to find the children of Marsyas Orphanage standing on the porch. They were dressed as if ready for an adventure.

"I have returned!" Commander Lucy crowed. "For one last expedition. Mr. Baker, I am asking you to join us. The perils will be great, and I cannot promise you'll get out of this alive. I have received word there are man-eating snakes and insects that will burrow under your skin and chomp your eyeballs from the inside out. But the reward—should you survive!—will be more than even your wildest dreams. Do you accept?"

"I don't know," Linus said slowly. "Man-eating snakes, you say? Sounds dangerous."

Lucy glanced back at the others before he leaned forward and whispered, "They're not real. I'm just playing. But don't tell the others."

"Ah," Linus said. "I see. Well, it just so happens that I am an expert in man-eating snakes, especially in ways to avoid them.

I suppose I should come along to make sure nothing happens to you."

"Oh thank God," Chauncey sighed. "I didn't want to get eaten today."

"Go change!" Talia said, shoving Linus back inside the house. "You can't go dressed like that!"

"I can't? What's wrong with—" He stiffened and slumped. "Oh no! I don't think I can take another step! Is it the flesh-burrowing insects?"

"Why are you *like* this?" Talia growled. "Phee! Help me!"

Phee bellowed and ran forward, throwing her negligible weight against Linus. He snorted as he took another step toward the bedroom. "Much better, thank you. I'll be out in a flash."

He listened to the children chatter excitedly about the up-coming adventure as he went into the bedroom. He shut the door behind him and leaned against it, tilting his head back and closing his eyes.

"You can do this," he whispered. "Come on, old boy. One last adventure."

He pushed himself away from the door and went to the closet.

He found the adventurer clothes.

He put them on.

He still looked absolutely ridiculous.

And for once, he found he didn't care at all.

The adventurers traipsed their way through the jungle. They fended off cannibals that attacked with spears and arrows and thinly veiled threats to eat their spleens. They snuck by man-eating snakes hanging like thick vines from the trees. Commander Lucy was overtaken by insects that were going to burrow behind his eyes. He gasped and gagged and flailed around, finally collapsing against a tree, his tongue hanging from his mouth. It was only thanks to his troops that he was able to be revived at the last possible moment, living to fight another day.

They eventually made their way to familiar ground, and in the distance Linus could see a copse of trees that hid the house of an island sprite. They came out of the tree line and onto the beach just as her voice boomed around them. "I see you have returned! You truly are foolish. You barely escaped with your lives the last time."

"Hark!" Commander Lucy cried. "You won't get the best of us! We demand that you relinquish your treasures. We won't take no for an answer!"

"You won't?"

"No!" the children shouted.

"No," Linus echoed quietly.

"Oh. Well, then. I suppose I might as well give up now. You're far too strong for the likes of me."

"I *knew* it," Lucy breathed fervently. He raised his hands above his head. "Men!" He glanced back at Talia and Phee. "And also women. Follow me to your just reward!"

They did. Of course they did. They would follow him anywhere.

Linus would too.

They charged across the beach and into the trees.

Linus sighed. He wasn't going to charge anywhere. His charging days were pretty much over with. He wiped his brow and trudged toward the trees.

He frowned once he reached the tree line. It had grown strangely silent. Six children should have been making much more noise. Especially *these* six children. He hesitated but then stepped into the trees.

Paper lanterns had been hung from the branches. They were the same ones that had been hung in the gazebo. He reached up and pressed a hand against one of them. The light inside was bright, and he didn't think it came from a bulb or a candle.

They were waiting for him as he reached the house in the middle of the trees. Talia and Phee. Sal, Theodore, Chauncey, and Lucy. Zoe, the flowers in her hair green and gold.

And Arthur, of course. Always Arthur.

They held a sign out in front of them, a long roll of paper with painted words that read: WE'LL MISS YOU, MR. BAKER!!! There were handprints on it. Little ones for Talia and Phee and Lucy. A bigger one for Sal. A line that he thought came from Chauncey's tentacles. And a drip of paint that looked like claws from Theodore.

Linus took in a shuddering breath. "I . . . I didn't expect this. What a wonderful thing you've all done. Look at it. Look at you."

"It was my idea," Lucy said.

Talia stomped on his foot.

He winced. "Well, mostly all my idea. The others helped, though. A little." He brightened. "But guess what?"

"What?"

"There was no treasure after all! It was a lie to get you here for your party!"

"Oh. I see. So the real treasure was the friendships we made along the way?"

"You guys are the worst," Lucy muttered. "The literal worst."

And what a party it was. There was food—so much so that Linus thought the table would collapse under the weight of it. There was roast and hot rolls and salad with cucumbers that crunched between their teeth. There was cake and pie and bowls of tart raspberries they could dip in cream.

And music! All kinds of music. There was a record player sitting on the counter, and the day the music died was bright and loud with Ritchie and Buddy and the Big Bopper singing from beyond. Lucy was in charge, and he never failed to disappoint.

They laughed on this day. Oh, how they laughed. Even though Linus thought his heart was breaking, he laughed until there were tears in his eyes, until he was sure his sides would split. As the sun began to set and the lanterns grew brighter, they laughed and laughed and laughed.

Linus was wiping tears away (from amusement, he told himself) when the music changed yet again.

He recognized it even before Nat King Cole began to sing.

He looked up to see Arthur Parnassus standing before him, hand outstretched.

Thank you.

You keep saying that, and I don't know if it's deserved.

I know you don't believe you do. But I don't say things I don't mean. Life is too short for it. Do you like to dance?

I don't . . . know. I think I might have two left feet, honestly.

I highly doubt that.

And Linus Baker allowed himself to be selfish. Just this once.

He took Arthur's hand and stood slowly as Nat told him to smile even though his heart was breaking.

Arthur pulled him close, and they began to sway back and forth.

"Smile and maybe tomorrow," Arthur whispered in his ear. "You'll see the sun come shining through for you."

Linus lay his head against Arthur's chest. He could feel the heat from him burning from the inside out.

They danced.

It stretched on for what felt like ages, though Linus knew the song didn't last long. He heard Arthur whispering the words to him. He surprised even himself. Apparently, he didn't have two left feet after all.

But, like all things magical, the song eventually came to an end.

The house around them was quiet. Linus blinked as if waking from a dream. He lifted his head. Arthur looked down at him, eyes glittering like fire. Linus stepped back.

Zoe sat with Phee and Talia in her lap. Theodore was perched on Sal's shoulder. Lucy and Chauncey lay pressed against his legs. All of them looked tired. Happy, but tired. Lucy smiled at him, but it broke when he yawned. "Did you like your treasure, Mr. Baker?"

Linus looked up at Arthur again. "I did," he whispered. "I liked it more than anything."

Zoe carried Phee and Talia as they walked back toward the main house. Talia was snoring loudly.

Sal had put Theodore in his shirt, and the wyvern's head lay against his throat.

Arthur held Chauncey by his tentacle.

Linus brought up the rear, Lucy sleepy in his arms.

He wished it could last forever.

It was over in what seemed like an instant.

He said good night to Talia. To Phee. To Sal and Theodore. He shifted Lucy to one arm and reached down and patted Chauncey on the top of his head.

Arthur asked a question with his eyes.

Linus shook his head. "I've got him."

Arthur nodded and turned to remind the others it was time to brush their teeth.

He took Lucy into Arthur's bedroom and set him down. "Go get your pajamas on," he said quietly.

Lucy nodded and turned toward the closet door. He shut it behind him.

Linus stood in the middle of the room, unsure of everything. He thought he knew the way of things. How the world worked. His place in it.

Now, he wasn't so sure.

Lucy returned in pajama pants and a white shirt. His hair was sticking up as if he'd run his hand through it. His bare feet were so small.

"Go brush your teeth," Linus instructed gently.

Lucy looked up at him suspiciously. "You'll be here when I get back?"

Linus nodded. "I promise."

Lucy went back out into the hall. He heard Chauncey yell that Theodore was eating the toothpaste again, and Theodore chirping in response that he was *not*.

Linus put his face into his hands.

He'd composed himself by the time Lucy came back into the room, face freshly scrubbed. He yawned again. "I'm so tired," he said.

"Adventuring is hard work, I suspect."

"Good adventure, though."

"The best," Linus agreed.

He took Lucy by the hand and led him to his room. The records they'd glued meticulously back together were hung on the wall (though, from the Buddy Holly record, a piece they hadn't been able to find was still missing; Theodore had moved quickly, it would seem). Linus pulled the covers down on the bed, and Lucy crawled up and underneath, snuggling down onto his pillow.

Linus pulled the covers back up to his shoulders. Lucy turned on his side, looking up at Linus. "I don't want you to go."

Linus swallowed thickly as he crouched down next to the bed. "I know. And I'm sorry about that. But my time here is just about finished."

"Why?"

"Because I have responsibilities."

"Why?"

"Because I'm an adult. And adults have jobs."

Lucy grimaced. "I never want to be an adult. It sounds boring."

He reached out and brushed a lock of Lucy's hair from his brow. "I think you'll make a fine adult, though it won't happen for a long time to come."

"You're not going to let them take us away, are you?"

Linus shook his head. "No. I'm going to do everything I can to make sure that doesn't happen."

"You will?"

"Yes, Lucy."

"Oh. That's nice of you." Then, "You're going to be gone when I wake up."

Linus looked away but didn't answer.

He felt Lucy's hand brush against his face. "The others don't know, but I do. I can see things, sometimes. I don't know why. You. Arthur. He burns. Did you know that?"

Linus inhaled sharply. "Did he tell you that?"

"No. I don't think he's allowed. But we know. We all know. Just like we know what you both did when you left the other day. He's one of us. Just like you."

"I'm afraid I don't have magic."

"You do, Mr. Baker. Arthur told me that there can be magic in the ordinary."

He looked back at Lucy.

His eyes were closed.

He breathed deeply.

Linus stood.

"Thank you," he whispered.

He made sure to leave the door open a little when he left, so that a sliver of light shone in to chase away the nightmares should they try and find the sleeping boy.

The other doors were all closed. He touched each of them as he wandered slowly down the hall.

The only light that was on came from under Sal's door.

He thought about knocking.

He didn't.

He paused at the top of the stairs.

Took a breath.

And then descended.

There was a whispered argument occurring on the first floor. He hesitated, unsure if he should make his presence known. He couldn't hear what was being said, but he knew it wasn't for him.

Zoe stood at the front door, jabbing Arthur in the chest, her brow furrowed, her eyes narrowed. She looked unhappy. Not quite angry but . . . something. She stopped when the last step creaked under Linus.

They looked over at him.

"Lucy's asleep," he said, scratching the back of his neck.

"Men," Zoe growled. "Useless, the lot of you." She stepped away from Arthur, her expression tight as she glared at Linus. "Bright and early, then?"

Linus nodded. "Train leaves at seven sharp. Merle is expecting us at a quarter after six."

"And you just have to be on it, don't you?"

He said nothing.

"Fine," she muttered. "I'll be here. Don't keep me waiting." She whirled on her heels and left without saying anything else. She left the door wide open.

Arthur stared after her, jaw clenched.

"Everything all right?"

"No, I don't think it is."

His head hurt. "If you're both worried about my final report, let me assure you that—"

"It's not the damn report."

"Okay," Linus said slowly. He wasn't sure he'd ever heard Arthur curse before. "Then what is it?"

Arthur shook his head.

"Stubborn," Linus muttered, and he couldn't help how fond he sounded. He didn't know what else to do, so he did the only thing he could.

He walked toward the door.

He thought something would happen the moment he was shoulder to shoulder with Arthur. What, he didn't know. But it didn't. He was a coward.

"Good night, then," he managed to say. He continued on to the door.

And then Arthur said, "Stay."

He stopped as he closed his eyes. His voice was shaky when he asked, "What?"

"Stay. Here. With us. Stay here with me."

Linus shook his head. "You know I can't."

"No, I don't. I *don't* know that."

Linus turned and opened his eyes.

Arthur was pale, his mouth in a thin line. Linus thought he could see the faint outline of burning wings behind him, but it might have just been a trick of the low light. "It was always temporary," Linus said. "I don't belong here."

"If you can't belong here, then where *can* you belong?"

"I have a life," Linus said. "I have a home. I have—"

A home isn't always the house we live in. It's also the people we choose to surround ourselves with. You may not live on the island, but you can't tell me it's not your home. Your bubble, Mr. Baker. It's been popped. Why would you allow it to grow around you again?

"I have a job to do," he finished lamely. "People are counting on me. Not just—not just here. There are other children who could need me. Who could be in the same position you were in once. Shouldn't I do everything I can to help them?"

Arthur nodded tightly as he glanced away. "Of course. Of course that's what's important. Forgive me. I didn't mean to make it sound like it wasn't." When he looked at Linus again, his expression was smooth, almost . . . blank. He bowed slightly. "Thank you, Linus. For everything. For seeing us for who we really are. You will always be welcome on the island. I know the children will miss you." The expression stuttered slightly. "I know I will miss you."

Linus opened his mouth, but nothing came out. And he *despised* himself for it. Here was this man, this wonderful man, exposing his heart. Linus had to give him something, no matter how small.

He tried again. He said, "If things were—if this were different, I . . . you have to know, Arthur. You have to. This place. These children. *You.* If only I could . . ."

Arthur smiled quietly. "I know. Good night, Linus. And safe travels. Do take care of yourself."

He shut the door, leaving Linus standing on the porch in the dark.

Linus sat on the porch. There was a faint light in the east. The stars were bright. His luggage was beside him. Calliope too, in her crate, though she wasn't amused at the early hour. Linus could commiserate, especially since he hadn't slept a wink.

He took a deep breath. It came out in a mist. "I think it's time."

He stood. He grabbed his luggage and the crate, and stepped off the porch.

As promised, Zoe was waiting by her little car. She took his suitcase from him and set it in the trunk without a word.

He climbed into the passenger seat, settling Calliope's crate on his lap.

Zoe hopped in and started the car.

Then they were off.

Linus watched the house in the side mirror as it slowly shrank behind them.

Merle was waiting at the docks. The headlights from the car illuminated his scowl. He lowered the gate. "Rates for this early hour are doubled," he said.

Linus surprised himself. "Shut up, Merle."

Merle's eyes widened.

Linus didn't look away.

Merle broke first. He grumbled as he walked back to the wheelhouse.

The crossing was smooth. The ocean was nearly flat. The sky grew brighter. Zoe didn't speak. When they reached the village, Merle didn't even look at them as he lowered the gate. "I expect you to come right back," Merle said as they exited the ferry. "I have a busy day and—"

Zoe gunned the engine, and whatever else Merle had to say was lost.

The train hadn't yet arrived when they reached the platform. The stars were disappearing as the sun started to rise. Linus could hear the distant crashing of the waves as Zoe turned off the car. He flexed his hands on his knees.

"Zoe, I—"

She got out of the car and walked around to the back. He heard her open the trunk. He sighed as he pushed the door open. He fumbled with Calliope's crate but managed to climb out without dropping her. Zoe set his luggage next to the platform before going back to the trunk and slamming it closed.

"I get it," he said.

She laughed, though without humor. "Do you? Because I wonder."

"I don't expect you to understand."

She shook her head. "Good. Because I don't."

"I can't just *stay* here. There are rules to follow. Regulations that must be—"

"To hell with your rules and regulations!"

He gaped at her. Then, he said the only thing he could, "Life, it—it doesn't work that way."

"Why doesn't it?" she snapped. "Why can't life work whatever way we want it to? What's the point of living if you only do it how others want you to?"

"It's the best we can do."

She scoffed. "And this is your best? *This?*"

He said nothing as the whistle of a coming train came from down the tracks.

"Let me tell you something, Linus Baker," she said, hands clenched on the top of the driver's door. "There are moments in your life, moments when chances have to be taken. It's scary because there is always the possibility of failure. I know that. I *know* that. Because once upon a time, I took a chance on a man that I had failed before. I was *scared.* I was *terrified.* I thought I might lose everything. But I wasn't living, then. The life I had before wasn't *living.* It was getting by. And I will never regret the chances I took. Because it brought me to them. To all of them. I made my choice. And you're making yours." She opened the door and got in the car. The engine turned over. She looked back at him just once when she said, "Don't you wish things could be different?"

"Don't you wish you were here?" he whispered, but she wouldn't have heard him. By the time he finished speaking, she was away, sand kicking up from the tires.

He stared at the orange phone on the platform while he waited for the train, thinking how easy it would be if he picked it up and made a call. To tell whoever answered he wanted to come back home.

"Just you, then?" the attendant asked cheerily as he stepped off the train. "Don't usually see people leaving this late in the season."

"Going home," Linus muttered as he handed over his ticket.

"Ah," the attendant said. "No place like home, or so I'm told. Me, I like riding the rails. All the wondrous things I see, you know?" He glanced down at the ticket. "Back to the city! I hear there's quite the storm there. Hasn't stopped raining in a dog's age!". He grinned as he handed back the ticket. "Help you with your luggage, sir?"

Linus blinked against the burn. "Yes. Fine. Thank you. I'll take the crate. She doesn't like most other people."

The attendant peered down. "Ah, I see. Yes. I'll take your luggage. The car you're in is right this way, sir. And luckily for you, it's empty. Not another soul in sight. Could get some sleep, if you need it."

He whistled as he lifted the suitcase and carried it onto the train.

Linus looked down at the crate. "Ready to go home?"

Calliope turned around and presented him with her backside.

Linus sighed.

Two hours later, the first drops of rain began to fall.

EIGHTEEN

It was raining heavily back in the city when he stepped off the train.

He pulled his coat tightly around him, squinting up at the metal-gray sky.

Calliope hissed as water began to drip through the slats on the top of her crate.

He picked up his suitcase and walked toward the bus stop.

The bus was late.

Of course it was.

He took off his coat and put it on top of Calliope's crate.

It did the job. For now.

He sneezed.

He hoped he wasn't getting sick. That would be just his luck, wouldn't it?

Twenty minutes later, the bus came, tires sluicing water.

The doors slid open.

Linus was soaked as he stepped onto the bus.

"Hello," he said to the driver.

The driver grunted in response as Linus struggled to swipe his pass.

The bus was mostly empty. There was a man in the back, head pressed against the window, and a woman who eyed Linus suspiciously.

He took a seat away from them.

"Almost home," he whispered to Calliope.

She didn't respond.

He looked out the window as the bus pulled away from the train station.

A sign next to the train station caught his eye.

On it, a family was at a picnic in the park. The sun was shining. They sat on a checkered blanket, and the wicker basket sitting between them was open and overflowing with cheeses and grapes and sandwiches with the crusts cut off. The mother was laughing. The father was smiling. The boy and the girl were staring adoringly up at their parents.

Above them, the sign read: KEEP YOUR FAMILY SAFE! SEE SOMETHING, SAY SOMETHING!

Linus looked away.

He had to change buses once, and by the time he stepped off the second bus it was almost five in the afternoon. The wind had picked up, and it was cold and miserable. He was three blocks from home. He expected to feel relief at this moment.

He didn't. Not really.

He huffed as he lifted the crate and suitcase.

He was almost there.

His street was quiet as he turned onto it.

The streetlights were lit, beads of water clinging against the panes of glass.

86 Hermes Way was dark. Oh, the brick pathway to the house was the same, and the lawn was the same, but it still felt . . . dark.

It took him a moment to realize what little splash of color there'd once been—his sunflowers—was gone.

He stared at the front of his house for a moment.

He shook his head.

He'd worry about it tomorrow.

He walked up the path and reached the porch. He set down his suitcase as he fumbled for his keys. They fell to the floor, and he grumbled as he bent over to pick them up.

Through the rain, he heard, "That you, Mr. Baker?"

He sighed as he stood upright. "It is, Mrs. Klapper. I have returned. How are you?"

"Your flowers died. Drowned, if you can believe that. I had a boy come pull them. They were rotting. Hurts the resale value of a neighborhood when a house looks so rundown. I have the receipt for what I paid the boy. I expect to be reimbursed."

"Of course, Mrs. Klapper. Thank you."

She wore the same terry cloth robe and was smoking out of the same pipe. Her hair was in the same bouffant. It was all the same. Every little piece of it.

He started to put the key in the lock when she spoke again. "You back for good?"

Linus felt like screaming. "Yes, Mrs. Klapper."

She squinted at him from across the way. "You look as if you've gotten some sun. You don't seem as pale as you once did. Lost some weight too. Quite a vacation you had."

His clothes *were* a little looser on him than they'd once been, but for the first time in a long time, he found himself not caring about that at all. "It wasn't a vacation. I told you I left for work."

"Uh-huh. So you said. Though, I suppose there's nothing wrong with snapping at the office, threatening to murder everyone, and then getting sent away to a rehab facility."

"That's not what happened!"

She waved a hand at him. "None of my business if it was. Though, you should know it's already the talk of the neighborhood." She frowned at him. "Hurts the resale value."

He gripped the doorknob tightly. "Are you planning on selling your home?"

She blinked at him as smoke curled around her craggy face. "No. Of course not. Where would I go?"

"Then why on God's green earth do you care about the damn resale value?"

She stared at him.

He glared back at her.

She took a puff on her pipe. "I got your mail. Most of it was ads. You don't seem to get much personal mail. I used the coupons. I was sure you wouldn't mind."

"I'll get it tomorrow."

He was sure that was the end of it, but of course she continued on. "You should know you missed your opportunity! My grandson met a nice man while you were gone. He's a pediatrician. I expect there to be a spring wedding. It will be in a church, of course, because they are both godly men."

"Good for them."

She nodded as she stuck the stem of her pipe back between her teeth. "Welcome home, Mr. Baker. Keep that filthy animal out of my yard. The squirrels have known a month of peace. I'd like to keep it that way."

He didn't bother saying goodbye. It was rude, but he was tired. He went inside the house and slammed the door behind him for good measure.

It was stale inside his house, the smell of a home that hadn't been lived in for a while thick in the air. He set down his suitcase and the crate before switching on the light.

It was the same. Perhaps a bit dusty.

There was his chair. His Victrola. His books.

It was all the same.

He bent down and opened the gate for Calliope.

She shot out, tail standing straight up behind her. She was damp and didn't appear to be amused. She disappeared down the hall to the laundry room where her litter box was.

"It's good to be home," he whispered.

He wondered how many times he would need to say that before he believed it.

He set his suitcase at the foot of the bed.

He changed out of his wet clothes.

He donned his spare pajamas.

He fed Calliope.

He tried to eat himself, but he wasn't very hungry.

He sat in his chair.

He got up from his chair.

"Some music," he decided. "Perhaps I should listen to some music."

He selected Ol' Blue Eyes. Frank always made him happy.

He slid the record from the sleeve and lifted the lid to the Victrola. He set the record on the spinner. He switched the player on, and the speakers crackled. He lowered the arm and closed his eyes.

But what came from the Victrola wasn't Frank Sinatra.

He must have switched up the sleeves before he left.

Trumpets flared brightly.

A sweet masculine voice began to sing.

Bobby Darin, grooving about somewhere beyond the sea.

He remembered the way Lucy had bounced in the kitchen, bellowing the words at the top of his lungs.

He put his face in his hands.

As Bobby sang, Linus's shoulders shook.

He went to bed.

The blankets and pillow were slightly musty, but he was too tired to worry about that now.

He stared at the ceiling for a long time.

Eventually, he slept.

He dreamed of an island in the ocean.

On Sunday, he cleaned. He opened the windows to air out the house, even though it was raining. He scrubbed the floors. He wiped the walls. He washed the counters. He changed the sheets on the bed. He took a toothbrush to the grout on the tile in the bathroom. He swept. He mopped.

His back was aching by the time he finished. It was early afternoon, and he thought about lunch, but his stomach was a lead weight.

Laundry. He needed to do laundry.

And he still needed to complete his final report.

He went to the suitcase at the end of the bed. He lay it on its side and unlatched the buckles. He lifted the lid and froze.

There. On the top of his folded clothes, on top of files, on top of *RULES AND REGULATIONS*, was a brown envelope.

He hadn't put it in there.

At least he didn't think he had.

He lifted the envelope. It felt stiff in his hands.

On the top were two words, written in black, blocky letters: DON'T FORGET.

He slid the envelope open.

Inside was a photograph.

His eyes stung as he looked down at it.

Zoe must have taken the picture. He didn't even remember seeing her with a camera. It was the first adventure they'd taken through the woods to her house. In it, Lucy and Talia were laughing. Sal sat with Theodore in his lap. Chauncey and Phee were wrestling over the last roll. Arthur and Linus sat together. Linus was watching the children with amusement.

And Arthur was watching Linus, that quiet smile on his face.

It was grief, then, that Linus felt in his little house on Hermes Way. Grief bright and glassy, unlike anything he'd ever experienced before. He was but paper, brittle and thin, and he clutched the photograph to his chest, hugging it close.

Later, much later, he sat in his chair, the final report in his lap. It still only had one sentence written on it after the introduction.

He thought it was enough.

He set it aside.

He listened to the Big Bopper bopping along. He drifted, eventually, and disappeared onto an ocean, the waves lapping beneath him, and it felt like home.

Outside, the rain fell steadily.

His alarm went off bright and early Monday morning.

He got up.

He fed the cat.

He took a shower.

He dressed in a suit and tie.

He picked up his briefcase.

He remembered his umbrella.

The bus was full. There was barely room to stand, much less to sit.

People didn't look up at him except to scowl when he

accidentally bumped into them. They returned to their newspapers as he apologized.

No one greeted him as he walked into DICOMY.

He walked through the desks, and no one said, "Welcome back, Linus. We missed you."

There were no streamers on Row L, Desk Seven. No balloons. No paper lanterns.

He sat down, setting his briefcase beside him.

Mr. Tremblay glanced over at him from Row L, Desk Six. "I thought you'd been sacked."

"No," Linus said as evenly as he could. "I was on assignment."

Mr. Tremblay frowned. "Are you sure? I could have sworn that you'd been sacked."

"I'm sure."

"Oh!" He looked relieved, and Linus started to feel a bit better. Maybe he'd been missed after all. "That means you can have all your cases back. Thank God. I didn't have time for them in the slightest, so you'll have a lot of catching up to do. I'll dig them up for you first thing."

"That's very kind of you," Linus said tightly.

"I know, Mr. Barkly."

He said, "It's Mr. Baker, you git. Don't make me correct you again."

Mr. Tremblay gaped at him.

He opened his briefcase. He lifted out the files he'd been given and his final report. He hesitated before taking out the only thing that remained.

He set the framed photograph on the desk near the computer.

"What is that?" Mr. Tremblay asked, craning his neck. "Is that a *personal* thing? You know you can't have that!"

"Maybe you should consider minding your own business for once," Linus snapped without looking at him.

"On your head, then," Mr. Tremblay muttered. "See if I'm ever nice to you again."

Linus ignored him. He straightened out the photograph until he had it just right.

He turned on his computer and got to work.

"Mr. *Baker!*"

He groaned to himself. Today had been going . . . Well, it'd been going. He didn't look up as he heard the sounds of heels clicking against the floor, getting closer and closer.

A shadow fell on his desk.

The typing around him stopped as his coworkers listened in. It was probably the most exciting thing that had happened in the last month.

Ms. Jenkins stood above him, the same dour expression on her face. Gunther, of course, stood slightly behind her, his clipboard ever present. He smiled sickly sweet down at Linus.

"Hello, Ms. Jenkins," Linus said dutifully. "It's nice to see you."

"Yes, I expect it is," she said with a sniff. "You've returned."

"Your observational skills remain unparalleled."

Her gaze narrowed. "Excuse me?"

He coughed and cleared his throat. "I said, yes, I have returned."

"From your assignment."

"Yes."

"Your *secret* assignment."

"I suppose."

The skin under her left eye twitched. "Just because Extremely Upper Management did us all a favor and got rid of you for a month doesn't mean things have changed around here."

"I can see that."

"I expect you to be caught up with all of your work by the end of the week."

Impossible, of course, but she knew that. "Yes, Ms. Jenkins."

"Your caseload will be returned to you by lunchtime."

"Yes, Ms. Jenkins."

She leaned forward, putting her hands flat on his desk. Her nails were painted black. "Gunning for a promotion, are you? Think you have what it takes to be a Supervisor?"

He laughed. He didn't mean to, but he did.

Ms. Jenkins looked scandalized.

Gunther's smile fell from his face. He looked shocked.

"No," Linus managed to say. "I'm not trying for a promotion. I don't think I'm quite cut out for Supervision."

"For once we agree," Ms. Jenkins said nastily. "I couldn't think of anyone more ill-suited than you. You are lucky you still have a desk to return to. If I had my way, you would . . . have . . . had . . . Mr. *Baker*! What is *that*?"

She pointed a black fingernail at the photograph.

"It's mine," he said. "It's mine, and I like it."

"It is *prohibited*," she said shrilly. "Per *RULES AND REGU-LATIONS*, caseworkers are *not* allowed personal effects unless sanctioned by Supervision!"

Linus looked up at her. "Then sanction it."

She took a step back, hand going to her throat. Gunther scribbled furiously onto his clipboard.

"What did you say?" she asked dangerously.

"Sanction it," Linus repeated.

"I will *not*. This will go into your permanent file! How dare you speak to me this— Gunther! Demerits! Demerits for Mr. Baker!"

Gunther's smile returned. "Of course. How many?"

"Five! No, *ten*. *Ten* demerits!"

The caseworkers around them began to whisper fervently.

"Ten demerits," Gunther said, sounding rather gleeful. "Yes. So wise, Ms. Jenkins. So knowing."

"That . . . that *thing* will be gone by the end of the day," Ms. Jenkins said. "Mark my words, Mr. Baker. If it's not, I will see to it you don't have a job to return to."

Linus said nothing.

That didn't sit well with her. "Do you understand me?"

"Yes," he said through gritted teeth.

"Yes *what*?"

"Yes, Ms. Jenkins."

She sniffed again. "That's better. Insolence will not be tolerated. I know you've been . . . wherever for the last month, but the rules have not changed. You would do well to remember that."

"Of course, Ms. Jenkins. Is there anything else I can help you with?"

Her words seemed to drip poison when she said, "Yes. There is. You have been summoned. By Extremely Upper Management. *Again*. Tomorrow. Eight o'clock on the dot. Do not be late. Or do, and save me the trouble."

She whirled around. "What are you all staring at? Get back to work!"

The caseworkers began to type immediately.

Ms. Jenkins glared at Linus over her shoulder once more before stalking away, Gunther trailing after her.

"I wonder who my new desk neighbor will be?" Mr. Tremblay asked.

Linus ignored him.

He stared down at the photograph.

Right below it was a mouse pad with a faded picture of a white sandy beach and the bluest ocean in all the world.

It said, of course, DON'T YOU WISH YOU WERE HERE?

By lunchtime, files had been piled on his desk. Dozens of them. He opened the top one. The last notes were his own.

They hadn't been touched in the last month. He sighed and closed it.

The office was empty by the time he left, a little before nine that night. He put the photograph in his briefcase and headed for home.

It was raining.
The bus was late.

On his porch sat a plastic bag filled with his mail. It was all bills. There was a note on the top. It was a receipt from Mrs. Klapper seeking reimbursement for gutting his flower bed.

He took the photograph out of his suitcase and set it on the night-stand next to his bed.
He watched it until he fell asleep.

At a quarter till eight the next morning, Linus pressed the gold number five in the elevator.
Everyone inside the car stared at him.
He stared back.
They looked away first.
The elevator slowly emptied until he was the only one left.

EXTREMELY UPPER MANAGEMENT
BY APPOINTMENT ONLY

He pressed the button next to the metal grate.
It slid open, rattling on its tracks.

Ms. Bubblegum blew a pink bubble. It popped prettily as she sucked it back in between her teeth. "Help you?"

"I have an appointment."

"With who?"

She had to know. "Extremely Upper Management. I'm Linus Baker."

She squinted at him. "I remember you."

"O-kay?"

"I thought you died or something."

"No. Not yet."

She tapped a couple of keys on her computer before looking back at him. "Do you have the final report?"

He opened his briefcase. Inside, his fingers brushed against the frame of a photograph before he found what he was looking for. He pulled the folder out and slid it underneath the glass.

She frowned as she picked it up. "This is it?"

"It is."

"Hold one moment."

The metal grate slammed back down.

"You can do this, old boy," he whispered.

It took longer this time for Ms. Bubblegum to return. So long, in fact, that Linus was sure he'd been forgotten about. He wondered if he should leave, but couldn't figure out how to make his feet move. They seemed rooted in place.

Minutes went by. At least twenty of them.

He was about to give in to temptation and peek inside his briefcase at the photograph when the metal gate rattled open.

Ms. Bubblegum was frowning. "They're ready to see you now."

Linus nodded.

"They're . . . not happy."

"No, I don't expect they would be."

She blew a bubble. It popped loudly. "You're a strange, strange man."

A buzzer sounded, and the wooden doors opened.

Ms. Bubblegum didn't speak as she led him past the fountain toward the black door with the gold plate on it. She opened it and stepped aside.

He didn't look at her as he walked through the door. It shut behind him. The lights lit up on the floor, showing him the way. He followed them until they spread into a circle. There was a podium in the center of the circle. On it sat his report. He swallowed thickly.

Lights burst to life above him.

And there, staring down from atop the stone wall, was Extremely Upper Management.

The woman. Jowls. The bespectacled man.

And Charles Werner.

"Mr. Baker," he said, voice smooth as silk. "Welcome back."

"Thank you," Linus said, shifting nervously.

"Your reports have been . . . well. They've been quite the topic of conversation."

"Have they?"

Jowls coughed wetly. "That's one way to put it."

"You know how I feel about euphemisms," the bespectacled man said with a frown.

"Mr. Baker," the woman said. "Is what you see before you the final report?"

"Yes."

"Truly?"

"Yes."

She sat back in her chair. "Baffling. I find it to be lacking, compared to your other reports. Very lacking, indeed."

"I believe I got straight to the point," Linus countered. "Which is, after all, what you asked of me. I made my recommendation after a month of observation. Isn't that why I'm here?"

"Careful, Mr. Baker," Jowls said, squinting down at him. "I don't like your tone."

Linus bit back a retort, something even a couple of weeks ago he would never have had to do. "My apologies. I simply—I believe I've done what was required of me."

Charles leaned forward. "Why don't you read it for us? Perhaps hearing it spoken aloud will impress upon us any meaning lost in translation."

Fine. He would play their games. He'd done it for years, ever the obedient employee. He opened the folder and looked down. "I solemnly swear the contents of this report are accurate and—"

"We know that, Mr. Baker," the bespectacled man said rather impatiently. "All the reports start the same. It never changes for anyone. It's the next part we're most interested in."

He looked up at them. "You know what it says."

Charles grinned at him. "Read it, Mr. Baker."

Linus did. "It is my recommendation that the Marsyas Orphanage remain open, and that the children therein continue under the tutelage of Arthur Parnassus."

That was it. That was all he'd written.

He closed the folder.

"Hmm," Charles said. "I didn't get anything new from that. Anyone else have further insights?"

Jowls shook his head.

The bespectacled man sat back in his chair.

The woman folded her hands in front of her.

"I thought not," Charles said. "Mr. Baker, perhaps you could expound. What is it that brought you to this conclusion?"

"My observation of the children and the way they interacted with each other and Arthur Parnassus."

"Vague," Jowls said. "I demand more."

"Why?" Linus asked. "What is it you're looking for?"

"We aren't here to answer your questions, Mr. Baker," the woman said sharply. "You are here to answer ours. Do not forget your—"

"My place?" Linus shook his head. "How can I, when I'm reminded of it constantly? I have done this job for seventeen years. I have never asked for more. I have never *wished* for more. I have done everything that has been asked of me without complaint. And here I stand before you, and you are demanding *more* from me. What more could I possibly have to give?"

"The truth," the bespectacled man said. "The truth about what you—"

He slammed his hands on the podium. The sound was sharp and flat as it echoed through the room. "I *have* given you the truth. In each of my weekly reports, you've read nothing *but* the truth. With every assignment I've been sent on, I've only ever been honest, even if it hurt me to do so."

"Objectivity," Jowls said. "As written in the *RULES AND REGULATIONS,* a caseworker must be object—"

"I know that. And I have been. I remember them. All of them. All of their names. The *hundreds* of them that I've observed. And I've maintained my distance. I've put up that wall. Can you say the same? What are the names of the children on the island? Without looking down at whatever notes you have, what are their names?"

Jowls coughed. "This is ridiculous. Of course we know their names. There's the Antichrist child—"

"Don't call him that," Linus growled. "That's not who he is."

Charles had a smug grin on his face. "It's Lucy. A rather ridiculous nickname for what he is."

"And?" Linus asked. "The other five?"

Silence.

"Talia," Linus spat. "A gnome who loves to garden. She is fierce and funny and brave. She is prickly, but once you get past it, there is a loyalty underneath that will take your breath away.

And after all that she has been through, after all that was taken from her, she still finds joy in the smallest of things."

The woman said, "Mr. Baker, you should—"

"Phee! The forest sprite. She acts tough and distant, but all she ever wanted was a home. She was found in *squalor* because her kind had been sectioned off without aid. Did you know that? Did you even read her report? Because I did. Her mother starved to death in front of her. And Phee herself nearly died, and yet when men came to the camp to try and take her from her mother's body, she managed to turn them into trees with the last of her strength. The forests on the island are thick because of her, and she would do anything to protect those she loves. She taught me about roots, and how they can be hidden away, waiting for the right moment to burst through the earth and change the landscape."

Extremely Upper Management remained silent as Linus began to pace.

"Theodore! A wyvern, one of the few that remain. Did you know he can talk? Do any of you know that? Because *I* didn't. I'd never been told. None of us had. But he can. Oh, he doesn't speak in English, but he talks just the same. And if you listen long enough, if you give him the time, you will begin to understand him. He is not an animal. He is not a predator. He has complex thoughts and feelings and *buttons*. So many buttons!" Linus reached down to his coat pocket and felt the brass button inside, indented from sharp teeth.

"Chauncey! A . . . well, no one knows what he is, but it doesn't matter! It doesn't matter because he might be more human than any of us. He's been told his whole life that he is a monster. That he is the thing that hides under beds. That he is a *nightmare*. That can't be further from the truth. He is a curious little boy who has a dream. And my God, how simple it is. How breathtakingly *lovely*. He wants to be a bellhop. He wants to work at a hotel and greet people and carry their luggage. That is *it*. But would any of you allow it? Would any of you give him the opportunity?"

They didn't respond.

"Sal," Linus growled. "Abused and neglected. Shuffled around without a care for his well-being because of what he is capable of. He bit a woman, yes, and turned her, but she hit him. She *struck a child.* If you raise your hand enough, they will cower. But every now and then, they will strike back because that's all they have left. He is shy. And quiet. And worries about everyone more than he worries about himself. And he writes. Oh Lord, he writes the most beautiful words. They are *poetry.* They are a *symphony.* They moved me more than anything else I've ever heard."

"And what of the Anti—what of the last child?" the woman asked quietly.

"Lucy," Linus said. "His name is Lucy. And he has spiders in his brain. He dreams of death and fire and destruction, and it tears at him. But do you know what I found? I found a boy, a six-year-old boy who loves going on adventures. Who has the wildest imagination. He dances. He *sings.* He lives for music, and it moves through him like the blood in his veins."

"Regardless of whether or not you like to hear it," Jowls said, "he is still what he is. That can never change."

"It can't?" Linus retorted. "I refuse to believe that. We are who we are not because of our birthright, but because of what we choose to do in this life. It cannot be boiled down to black and white. Not when there is so much in between. You cannot say something is moral or immoral without understanding the nuances behind it."

"He's immoral," the bespectacled man said. "Maybe he never asked for it, but it is what he is. His lineage demands it. There is a wickedness in him. That is the very definition of immorality."

"And who are you to decide that?" Linus asked through gritted teeth. "Who are you? You've never met him. Morality is relative. Just because you find something abhorrent, doesn't mean it actually is."

The woman frowned. "Many things are widely accepted as

abhorrent. What was it you said he dreams of? Death and fire and destruction? If I recall from your last report, his nightmares were capable of manifesting themselves. Someone could have been hurt."

"They could have," Linus agreed. "But they weren't. And it wasn't because *he* wanted to hurt anyone. He's a child who came from darkness. That doesn't have to be who he becomes. And it won't be. Not with who he has around him."

"Would you leave the other children with him?" Jowls asked. "In a locked room with no supervision."

"Yes," Linus said immediately. "Without hesitation. *I* would stay in a locked room with him. Because I trust him. Because I know that no matter where he came from, he is more than a title you've given him."

"And what happens when he grows up?" Charles asked. "What happens when he becomes a man? What if he decides this world isn't what he wants it to be? You know who his father is."

"I do," Linus said. "His father is Arthur Parnassus. And he's the best damn father Lucy has, and as far as I'm concerned, the only one."

Extremely Upper Management gasped in unison.

Linus ignored them. He was just getting started. "And what of Arthur? Because I think that's why I'm really here, isn't it? Because of what he is. You have classified these children as a level four threat when by all rights they are just like every other child in the world, magical or not. But it was never about them, was it? It was always about Arthur."

"Careful, Mr. Baker," Charles warned. "I told you once I don't like being disappointed, and you are very close to disappointing me."

"No," Linus said. "I will *not* be careful. It may not have been by your hand that he suffered, but it was by your ideals. The ideals of DICOMY. Of a registration. Of the prejudice against them. You allow it to fester, you and all the people before you who sat where you do now. You keep them segregated from everyone else because they're different than the rest of us. People *fear* them because they're taught to. See something, say something. It inspires hatred." He narrowed his eyes as he stared up at Charles Werner. "You think you can control them. You think you can control *him*. To use him to get what you want. To keep him hidden away with your other dirty little secrets. But you are wrong. All of you are *wrong*."

"That's quite enough," the bespectacled man snapped. "You are treading on very thin ice, Mr. Baker, and you don't seem to hear it cracking beneath your feet."

"Indeed," the woman said. "And it certainly doesn't help that we received a report from a concerned citizen about a confrontation between Arthur Parnassus and—"

Linus ground his teeth together. "Oh, concerned, were they? Tell me. In relaying their *concern*, did they explain what exactly they were doing at the dock to begin with? What their plans were? Because from what I could see, they were the aggressors. If Arthur Parnassus hadn't intervened, I don't even want to imagine what would've happened. Regardless of what he and the children are or what they can do, *no* one has the right to bring harm upon them. Unless anyone here thinks otherwise?"

He was met with silence.

"That's what I thought," Linus said, putting a hand on top of his final report. "My recommendation stands. The orphanage *must* remain open. For their sakes. And for yours. I promise you that I will do everything within my power to ensure this happens. You can fire me. You can try and have me censured. But I will not stop. Change starts with the voices of the few. I will be one of those few because they taught me how. And I know that I'm not alone." He paused, sucking in a breath. Then, "Also, speaking of euphemisms, for the love of all that is holy, stop calling them orphanages. That implies something that has never been the case. These are *homes*. They have always been homes. And some of them haven't been good, which is why I recommended they be closed. But not this one. Never this one. These children don't need a home, because they already have one, whether you like it or not."

"Ah," Charles said. "There it is. The disappointment. How sharp. How profound."

Linus shook his head. "You told me once you had a vested interest in what I would find. I believed you, then, though I expect it was out of fear more than anything else. I don't believe you now, because you only want to hear what you *think* you want to hear. Anything else is unsatisfactory in your eyes. I cannot help that. The only thing I can do is show you that the path you've helped set this world upon has gone off course, and hope that you one day come around to seeing it for what it truly is." He stared defiantly up at Charles. "Just because it's not what you expected doesn't mean it's wrong. Things have changed, Mr. Werner, and I know it's for the better. *I've* changed. And it has nothing to do with you. Whatever you hoped to find in the rubble you left behind on that island makes no difference to me. I know what they've become. I've seen the heart of all of them, and it beats tremendously despite everything they've gone through, either by your hand, or others." He was panting by the time he finished, but his head was clear.

"I think we're done here, Mr. Baker," Charles said coolly. "I believe we have a clear understanding of where you stand. You were right; your report said it all."

Linus felt cold, though he was sweating profusely. All the fight seemed to rush out of him, and all that remained was exhaustion. "I—I just—"

"No more," the woman said. "You've . . . no more. We will consider your recommendation and have a final decision in the coming weeks. Leave, Mr. Baker. Now."

364 ~ TJ KLUNE

He picked up his briefcase. He heard the picture frame rattle inside. He glanced back up at Extremely Upper Management before he turned and fled.

Ms. Bubblegum was waiting for him outside the chambers. Her eyes were wide, and her mouth hung open.

"What?" Linus asked irritably.

"Nothing," she managed to say. "Absolutely nothing at all. You were very . . . um. Loud."

"Yes, well, sometimes volume is needed to get through thick skulls."

"Wow," she whispered. "I need to go call—never mind who I need to call. You can find your way out, can't you?"

She hurried away and disappeared behind the door that led to her booth.

He walked slowly away. As he passed out of the offices of Extremely Upper Management, he heard her talking excitedly, but he couldn't make out the words.

He thought about leaving. About just . . . leaving it all behind.

He didn't.

He went back down to his desk.

Furious whispers ceased as soon as he walked into the room.

Everyone stared at him.

He ignored them, making his way to Row L, Desk Seven. He didn't even apologize when his wide hips bumped into things.

He felt the gazes of dozens of people tracking every step he took, but he kept his head held high. After all he'd been through, after everything he'd seen and done, what his colleagues thought of him didn't matter in the slightest.

When he made it to his desk, he sat down and opened his

briefcase. He took out the photograph and propped it up on his desk.

No one said a word.

Ms. Jenkins stood in front of her office, scowling at him. Gunther scribbled furiously on his clipboard. Linus thought he could shove his demerits up his ass.

He took a folder off the top of a pile and got back to work.

NINETEEN

Three weeks later, nothing much had changed.

Oh, yes, he dreamed of the ocean, of an island with white sandy beaches. He dreamed of a garden and a copse of trees that hid a little house. He dreamed of a burnt cellar door, and the day the music died, and of the way Lucy laughed. The way Talia muttered in Gnomish. The way Sal could be so big but felt so little in his arms. The way Chauncey stood in front of his mirror, saying *Hello, sir, welcome, welcome, welcome,* as he tipped his bellhop cap. The way Phee's wings sparkled in the sunlight. Of buttons, and wyverns named Theodore. Of Zoe, her hair bouncing in the wind as she tore down sandy roads in her car.

And of Arthur, of course. Always Arthur. Of fire burning, of wings spread in orange and gold. Of a quiet smile, the amused tilt of his head.

Oh, how he dreamed.

Every morning it was getting harder and harder to pull himself out of bed. It was always raining. The sky was always metal gray. He felt like paper. Brittle and thin. He dressed. He rode the bus to work. He sat at his desk, going through one file after another. He ate wilted lettuce for lunch. He went back to work. He rode the bus home. He sat in his chair, listening to Bobby Darin singing about somewhere beyond the sea, somewhere waiting for me.

He thought of the life he had. How he could have ever thought it'd be enough.

His thoughts were all cerulean.

Every day he went to work, he took time to touch the photograph on his desk, the photograph that no one dared say anything about. Ms. Jenkins had even kept to herself, and though Linus received demerit after demerit (Gunther gleefully scratching on his clipboard), she didn't say a word. In fact, he was ignored. Linus was just fine with that. He suspected Ms. Bubblegum had something to do with that, the gossipy thing that she was.

It wasn't all rain and clouds. He took his time, going back through his old files, reviewing the reports he'd written for all the orphanages he'd visited, making notes, preparing for a shimmery future he wasn't even sure was in his grasp. He winced at some of what he'd written (most of it, if he was being honest with himself), but he thought it important. Change, he reminded himself, started with the voices of the few. Perhaps it would amount to nothing, but he wouldn't know unless he tried. At the very least, he could follow up with some of the children he'd met before and find out where they were now. And, if all went as he hoped, he wouldn't let them be left behind or forgotten.

Which was why he began to smuggle out the reports. Every day, he would take a few more. He was a sweaty mess each time he put another in his briefcase, sure that at any moment, someone would shout his name, demanding to know what he was doing, especially when he started after the files belonging to *other* caseworkers.

But no one ever did.

He shouldn't have felt as giddy as he did, breaking the law. It should have caused his stomach to twist, his heart to burn, and perhaps it did, to an extent. But it was no match for his determination. His eyes were open, and the brief moments of exhilaration he felt did much to temper his lawlessness the more the days dragged on.

On the twenty-third day after his return from the island, the clacking of computer keys and murmur of voices once again fell silent as a figure appeared in the doorway to the offices of the caseworkers.

Ms. Bubblegum, snapping her gum, clutching a file to her chest.

She glanced over the rows of desks in front of her.

Linus slumped low in his chair. He was about to be sacked, he knew.

He watched as she walked toward Ms. Jenkins's office. Ms. Jenkins didn't seem pleased to see her, and her scowl only deepened at whatever question Ms. Bubblegum asked. She responded and pointed out toward the desks.

Ms. Bubblegum turned and made her way through the rows of desks, hips swaying delightfully. Men stared after her. Some of the women did too. She ignored them all.

Linus thought about crawling under his desk.

He didn't, but it was close.

"Mr. Baker," she said coolly. "There you are."

"Hello," he said, hands in his lap so she wouldn't see them shaking.

She frowned. "Have I ever told you my name?"

He shook his head.

"It's Doreen."

"A pleasure, Doreen."

She snapped her gum. "I almost believe you. I have something for you, Mr. Baker."

"Do you?"

She set the file down on his desk, sliding it over in front of him. "Just came down this morning."

Linus stared down at it.

Doreen leaned over, her lips near his ear. She smelled like cinnamon. She tapped a fingernail on his mouse pad. "Don't you wish you were here?" He watched as her finger rose to the photograph and traced along the frame. "Huh. How about that?" She kissed his cheek, sticky-sweet and warm.

And then she walked away.

Linus could barely breathe.

He opened the folder.

There was his final report.

And across the bottom were four signatures.

CHARLES WERNER

AGNES GEORGE

JASPER PLUMB

MARTIN ROGERS

And below that was a red stamp.

RECOMMENDATION APPROVED.

He read it again.

Approved.

Approved.

Approved.

This was—

He could—

Did he have enough to see his plan through?

He thought he did.

He stood from his desk, the chair scraping loudly against the cold cement floor.

Everyone turned to look at him.

Ms. Jenkins walked out from her office again, Gunther trailing after.

Approved.

The orphanage would stay as is.

He heard the ocean.

Don't you wish you were here? it whispered.

Yes.

Yes, he did.

But that was the funny thing about wishes. Sometimes all it took to make them come true was a first step.

He lifted his head.

He looked around.

"What are we doing?" he asked, his voice echoing loudly around the room.

No one answered, but that was okay. He didn't expect them to.

"Why are we doing this? What's the point?"

Silence.

"We're doing it wrong," he said, raising his voice. "All of this. It's wrong. We're feeding a machine that will eat us all. I can't be the only one who sees that."

Apparently, he was.

If he were a braver man, maybe he would have said more. Maybe he would have picked up his copy of the *RULES AND REGULATIONS* and thrown it in the trash, announcing grandly that it was time to toss out all the rules. Literally, but also figuratively.

By then, Ms. Jenkins would be demanding his silence. And, if he were a much braver man, he would have told her no. He would have shouted for all to hear that he'd seen what a world looks like with color in it. With happiness. With joy. This world they lived in here wasn't it, and they were all fools if they thought otherwise.

If he were a braver man, he would climb up on the desks and crow that he was Commander Linus, and it was time to go on an adventure.

They would come for him, but he'd hop from desk to desk, Gunther squawking as he tried to reach for Linus's legs but missing.

He would land near the door, this brave man. Ms. Jenkins would scream at him that he was fired, but he'd laugh at her and shout that he couldn't be fired because he *quit*.

But Linus Baker was a soft man with a heart longing for home. And so he went as quietly as he'd arrived.

He picked up his briefcase, opening it on his desk. He placed the photograph inside lovingly before closing it. There were no more files to smuggle out of DICOMY. He had everything he needed.

He took a deep breath.

And began to walk through the aisles toward the exit.

The other caseworkers began to whisper feverishly.

He ignored them, head held high. He barely bumped into any desks.

And just as he reached the exit, Ms. Jenkins shouted his name.

He stopped and looked over his shoulder.

The expression on her face was thunderous. "And where do you think *you're* going?"

"Home," he said simply. "I'm going home."

And then he left the Department in Charge of Magical Youth for the last time.

It was raining.

He'd forgotten his umbrella inside.

He turned his face toward the gray sky and laughed and laughed and laughed.

Calliope looked surprised to see him when he burst through the front door. It made sense; it wasn't even noon.

"I may have lost my mind," he told her. "Isn't it wonderful?"

She meowed a question, the first time she'd spoken since they'd left the island.

"Yes," he said. "Yes. Yes."

Life, Linus Baker knew, came down to what we made from it. It was about the choices, both big and small.

Bright and early the next morning—a Wednesday, as it turned out—Linus closed the door to one life in pursuit of another.

"Another trip?" Ms. Klapper asked from across the way.

"Another trip," Linus agreed.

"How long this time?"

"I hope forever. If they'll have me."

Her eyes widened. "Come again?"

"I'm leaving," he said, and he'd never been so sure of anything in all his years.

"But—but," she spluttered. "What about your house? What about your *job*?"

He grinned at her. "I quit my job. As for the house, well. Perhaps your grandson and his lovely fiancé would like to live next door to you. Consider it a wedding gift. But it doesn't matter right now. I'll figure that all out later. I have to go home."

"You *are* home, you fool!"

He shook his head as he lifted Calliope's crate and his suitcase. "Not yet. But I will be soon."

"Of all the—have you lost your mind? And what on earth are you *wearing*?"

He looked down at himself. Tan button-up shirt, tan shorts, brown socks. Atop his head sat a helmet-style hat. He laughed again. "It's what you're supposed to wear when you're going on an adventure. Looks ridiculous, doesn't it? But there might be cannibals and man-eating snakes and bugs that burrow their way under my skin and eat my eyes from the inside out. When faced with such things, you have to dress the part. Toodles, Mrs. Klapper. I don't know if we'll see each other again. Your squirrels will know only peace from this point on. I forgive you for the sunflowers."

He stepped off the porch into the rain, leaving 86 Hermes Way behind.

"Going on a trip?" the train attendant asked, looking down at his ticket. "All the way to the end of the line, I see. A bit out of season, isn't it?"

Linus looked out the train car window, rain dripping down the glass. "No," he said. "I'm going back to where I belong."

Four hours later, the rain stopped.

An hour after that, he saw the first blue through the clouds.

In two more hours, he thought he smelled salt in the air.

He was the only one to get off the train. Which made sense, seeing as how he was the only one left.

"Oh dear," he said, looking at the empty stretch of road next to the platform. "I might not have thought this through." He shook his head. "No matter. Time waits for no man."

He picked up the suitcase and the crate, and began to walk toward the village as the train pulled away.

He was drenched with sweat by the time he saw the first buildings. His face was red, and his suitcase felt as if he'd packed nothing but rocks.

He was sure he was about to collapse when he reached the sidewalk on the main street of the village. He thought about having a lie-down (perhaps permanently) when he heard someone gasp his name.

He squinted up.

Standing in front of her shop, a watering can in her hand, was Helen.

"Hello," he managed to say. "How nice it is to see you again."

She dropped the watering can, and it spilled its contents onto the concrete. She rushed toward him as he sat heavily on his suitcase.

"Did you *walk* here?" she demanded, grimacing as her hands came away damp after she put them on his shoulders.

"Spontaneity isn't exactly my forte," he admitted.

"You stupid man," she said. "You wonderfully stupid man. Came to your senses, did you?"

He nodded. "I think so. Either that or they've left me entirely. I'm not sure which yet."

"They don't know you're coming?"

"No. Hence the spontaneity. I'm not very good at it yet, but I hope I will become so with practice." He wheezed as she patted his back with the tips of her fingers.

"I think you've got a good start, at least. Though I suppose that means Merle also doesn't know you're here."

He winced. "Oh. Right. The ferry. That's important, isn't it? Island and all."

She rolled her eyes. "How you've made it this far, I'll never know."

"I popped my bubble," he told her, needing her to understand. "It kept me safe, but it also kept me from living. I shouldn't have left in the first place."

Her expression softened. "I know." She squared her shoulders. "But you're here now, and that's all that matters. Luckily for you, I'm the mayor. Which means when I want something done, it gets done. You stay right here. I have a phone call to make."

She hurried back to her shop.

Linus closed his eyes for what he thought was only a moment, but was startled out of a doze when a horn honked in front of him.

He opened his eyes.

An old green truck sat idling on the curb. It was flecked with rust, and the whitewall tires looked as if they barely had any tread left. Helen sat behind the steering wheel. "Well?" she asked through the open window. "Are you just going to stay there for the rest of the night?"

No. No, he wasn't.

He lifted his suitcase into the back of the truck. Calliope

purred as he set her inside the cab on the bench seat. The door creaked behind him as he closed it.

"This is very kind of you."

She snorted. "I believe I owed you a favor or two. Consider us even."

The truck groaned as she pulled away from the curb. Doris Day was on the radio, singing to dream a little dream of me.

Merle was waiting at the docks, looking as unpleasant as usual. "I can't just drop everything when you demand it," he said with a scowl. "I have— Mr. *Baker*?"

"Hello, Merle. It's nice to see you." It was almost true, surprisingly.

Merle's mouth hung open.

"Don't just stand there," Helen said. "Open the gate."

Merle recovered. "I'll have you know my rates have *quadrupled*—"

Helen smiled. "Oh, I don't think they have. That would be preposterous. Open the gate before I crash through it."

"You wouldn't dare."

She gunned the engine.

Merle ran for the ferry.

"Awful man," she said. "I wouldn't mind if he fell off his boat one day and drifted away into the sea."

"That's terrible," Linus said. Then, "We could make it happen."

She laughed, sounding surprised. "Why, Mr. Baker, I never would have thought to hear such a thing from you. I like it. Let's get you home, shall we? I expect you have some things you need to say."

He slunk lower in his seat.

The island looked the same as it had when he left it. It'd been only weeks. It felt like a lifetime.

Merle muttered something about Helen hurrying back, and she told him they would take all the time they needed and she wouldn't hear another word from him. He stared at her, but nodded slowly.

She drove along the familiar dirt road, winding toward the back of the island as the sun began to set. "I've been here a couple of times since you departed."

He looked over at her. "For the garden?"

She shrugged. "And to see what you left behind."

He turned back toward the window. "How . . . how was it?"

She reached over the crate between them and squeezed his arm. "They were okay. Sad, of course. But okay. I stayed for dinner the first time. There was music. It was lovely. They talked about you quite a bit."

He swallowed past the lump in his throat. "Oh."

"You made quite the impression on the people of this island in the time you were here."

"They did the same for me."

"Funny how that works out, isn't it? That we can find the most unexpected things when we aren't even looking for them."

He could only nod.

There were lights on upstairs in the main house.

The paper lanterns in the gazebo in the garden were lit.

It was half past five, which meant the children would be involved in their personal pursuits. Sal, he thought, would be writing in his room. Chauncey would be practicing in front of the mirror. Phee would be with Zoe in the trees. Theodore was most likely underneath the couch, and Talia in her garden. Lucy and Arthur would be upstairs, talking about philosophy and spiders on the brain.

He could breathe for the first time in weeks.

Helen stopped in front of the house. She smiled at him. "I think this is where we part ways for now. You tell Arthur I'll still be here on Saturday. Apparently, there's to be some sort of adventure."

"There always is on Saturdays," Linus whispered.

"Don't forget your suitcase."

He looked at her. "I—thank you."

She nodded. "It should be me thanking you. You've changed things, Mr. Baker, whether you intended to or not. It's a small beginning, but I think it'll grow. And I won't forget it. Go on. I think there are some people here who would like to see you."

Linus fidgeted nervously. "Maybe we should—"

She laughed. "Get out of my truck, Mr. Baker."

"It's Linus. Just call me Linus."

She smiled sweetly. "Get the hell out of my truck, Linus."

He did, pulling Calliope out with him. He reached into the bed of the truck and lifted his suitcase out. The gravel crunched under the truck's tires as Helen pulled away with a wave.

He stared after her until the taillights disappeared into the trees.

"Okay, old boy," he muttered. "You can do this."

Calliope meowed from the crate.

He bent over and opened it. "Now, don't go far—"

She shot out toward the garden.

He sighed. "Of course."

He followed her.

The flowers were in bloom, and they seemed brighter than he remembered. He walked along the path until he heard muttering in a strange tongue. He rounded a hedge to see a little bearded gnome digging in the dirt.

He stopped.

"Hello," he said quietly.

Her shoulders stiffened before she continued digging, Calliope sitting at her side.

He took another step toward her. "New tools working out well, then?"

She didn't respond, but the dirt was flying out around her.

"Helen told me she was impressed with your garden. Said it was one of the best she's ever seen."

"Yes, well," Talia said irritably, "I *am* a gnome. I'm supposed to be good at it."

He chuckled. "Of course you are."

"Why are you here?"

He hesitated, but only briefly. "Because this is where I belong. And I never should have left to begin with. I only did so in order to make sure you would be safe. All of you. And now . . ."

She sighed as she set her spade down before turning to look at him.

She was crying.

Linus didn't hesitate as he scooped her up in his arms.

She buried her face in his neck, beard tickling his throat. "I am going to bury you right here," she sobbed. "I'm digging your grave, just so you know."

"I know," he said, rubbing a hand over her back. "I would expect nothing less."

"No one would ever be able to find you! And even if they *did*, it would be too late and you'd be only bones!"

"Perhaps we can hold off on that, for at least a little while. I have something important to say to all of you."

She sniffled. "Perhaps. But if I don't like what I hear, we come right back and you will climb inside the hole without arguing."

He laughed, wild and bright. "Deal."

She ran ahead, Calliope chasing after her. Linus took a moment to breathe in the scents of the garden around him. He listened to the waves. If he had any doubts before this moment, they were gone now. He just hoped the others would feel the same.

It was time.

He left the garden, rounding the side of the house. He stopped when he saw what waited for him.

They had gathered in the front of the house. Zoe looked exasperated at the sight of him, shaking her head fondly. Phee was glaring at him. He hoped she wouldn't turn him into a tree. Or, if she did, at least that it wouldn't be an apple tree. He didn't like the idea of them eating him when he blossomed.

Chauncey was fidgeting nervously, as if he wanted to hurry toward Linus, but knew his loyalties lay with those around him. Sal stood with his arms across his chest. Theodore was sitting on his shoulder, head cocked.

Talia was wiping her eyes and muttering in Gnomish. Linus thought he heard her say that she'd have to widen his grave seeing as how he was still rotund.

And Lucy, of course. Lucy, who stood in front of them all, a strange expression on his face. Linus wondered if he was about to be hugged, or if his blood was going to start to boil, causing his organs to cook within him. It could really go either way.

Arthur stood behind them, and though his face was blank and his hands were clasped behind his back, Linus knew he was wary, he could see it in the stiff set of his shoulders. The fact that Linus had played a part in this made him feel ill. Arthur should never be so unsure. Not about this.

Linus kept his distance, though Calliope seemed to have no such problem. She was meowing quite loudly as she rubbed against Sal's legs, as talkative as she'd been since they'd left the island.

How could he have been so foolish? How could he have ever thought he could leave this place? It was color, bright and warm, and his heart felt like it was finally beating again. He hadn't realized he'd left it behind. He should have known. He should have realized.

"Hello," he said quietly. "It's nice to see you all again."

They didn't speak, though Chauncey twitched, eyes bouncing excitedly.

Linus cleared his throat. "I don't expect you to understand. I don't know that I do. I've made mistakes, some bigger than others. But I . . ." He took a deep breath. "I heard something once. Something important, though I don't think I knew just *how* important it actually was. A very wise person stood up in front of others, and though he was very nervous, he said the most profoundly beautiful thing I've ever heard." Linus tried to smile, and it cracked right down the middle. He said, "I am but paper. Brittle and thin. I am held up to the sun, and it shines right through me. I get written on, and I can never be used again. These scratches are a history. They're a story. They tell things for others to read, but they only see the words, and not what the words are written upon. I am but paper, and though there are many like me, none are exactly the same. I am parched parchment. I have lines. I have holes. Get me wet, and I melt. Light me on fire, and I burn. Take me in hardened hands, and I crumple. I tear. I am but paper. Brittle and thin."

Sal's eyes widened.

"It stuck with me," Linus continued. "Because of how important it is. How important all of you are." His voice broke, and he shook his head. "There is nothing to fear from the Department in Charge of Magical Youth. This place is your home, and your home it shall remain. You can stay here, as long as you wish. And if I have my way, others like you will know the same peace."

Talia and Phee gasped. Chauncey's mouth dropped open. Lucy grinned as Theodore spread his wings and gave a little roar of excitement. Sal dropped his arms, sagging in relief.

Zoe tilted her head.

Arthur stayed as he was.

It wasn't enough. Linus knew that.

So he gave everything he had left. "I think you're lovely. All of you. And though I've lived in a world where you didn't exist for most of my life, I don't believe that's a world I can be in any longer. It started with the sun, and it was warm. And then came the sea, and it was unlike anything I'd ever seen before. It was followed by this place, this island so mysterious and wonderful. But it was you who gave me peace and joy like I've never had before. You gave me a voice and a purpose. Nothing would have changed if it hadn't been for all of you. I believe they've listened to me, but the only reason I knew what to say at all was because of what you taught me. We're not alone. We never have been. We have each other. If I were to leave again, I would wish I were here. I don't want to wish anymore. If you'll have me, I would like to stay. For always."

Silence.

He rubbed the back of his neck nervously, wondering if he should say more.

"Excuse us for a moment, Mr. Baker," Lucy said. He turned toward the others and beckoned them close. The children bowed their heads as they began to whisper furiously. Zoe covered a laugh with the back of her hand.

Arthur never looked away from Linus.

Linus knew it was impolite to try and listen in on a meeting he was not part of. That, however, didn't stop him from trying. Unfortunately, the children didn't seem to care that he was most likely about to have a heart attack. He watched as they held their congress. At one point, Lucy drew a finger across his neck, eyes rolling back in his head, tongue hanging out. Talia nodded in agreement. Linus thought Chauncey said something about feeding the cannibals, but he might have misheard. Theodore snapped his jaws. Phee glared at Linus over her shoulder before turning back to the others. Sal muttered something under his breath, and the children gazed up at him adoringly.

"So, we're in agreement, then?" Lucy asked.

The children nodded.

They turned back toward him.

It was Lucy who spoke for them. "Does anyone else know you're here?"

Linus shook his head.

"So we could kill you, and no one would be the wiser."

"Yes, though I would like to avoid that if at all possible."

"Of course you would," Lucy said. "We have conditions."

"I would expect nothing less."

Talia said, "You have to help me in the spring in my garden and do exactly what I say."

There was no hesitation. "Yes."

Phee said, "You have to spend one day a month with me and Zoe in the woods."

"Yes."

Chauncey said, "You have to let me do your laundry!"

Oh, how his heart felt like it would burst. "If that's what you want."

"And you have to tip me!"

"Of course."

Theodore chirped and clicked, head bouncing up and down.

"Every single button I can find," Linus agreed.

Sal said, "You have to let us call you Linus."

His eyes stung. "I would love nothing more."

Lucy grinned devilishly. "And you have to dance with me, and when I have bad dreams, you have to come and tell me everything will be okay."

"Yes. Yes. Yes to all of it. To any of it. For you, I would do anything."

Lucy's smile faded. He looked so young. "Why did you leave in the first place?"

Linus hung his head. "Sometimes, you don't know what you

have until it's no longer there. And I needed to be your voice. So those far away would hear you for all that you are."

"Children," Arthur said, speaking for the first time. "Would you please go inside and help Zoe with dinner? I need to have a word with Mr. Baker."

They complained immediately.

"Now."

Lucy threw up his hands. "I don't know why you don't just kiss him and get it over with. Adults are so dumb."

Zoe choked on a laugh. "Come on. Let's leave the dumb adults to it. We absolutely will go inside and start dinner and not watch them through the windows."

"Ooh," Talia said. "I get it. Yes, let's go watch—I mean, make dinner."

They hurried up the steps to the house. Sal glanced back at them before closing the door behind him.

And immediately appeared in the window with the others, though they tried unsuccessfully to hide behind the drapes. Even Zoe.

Linus loved them very much.

The stars were beginning to appear overhead. The sky was streaked in orange and pinks and blue, blue, blue. The sea birds called. The waves crashed against the rocks.

But the only thing that mattered at this moment was the man before him. This exquisite man.

Linus waited.

"Why now?" Arthur finally asked. He sounded tired.

"It was time," Linus said. "I—I went back, thinking it was the right thing to do. I presented the results of my investigation to Extremely Upper Management." He paused, considering. "*Presented* might be a euphemism. I was quite stern, if I'm being honest."

Arthur's lips twitched. "Were you?"

"I didn't know I had it in me."

"Why did you?"

Linus spread his hands out in front of him. "Because I . . . I've seen things. Here. Learned things I didn't know before. It changed me. I didn't know how much until I no longer had it. When I could no longer wake up and walk to the house for breakfast. Or listen to you teach them. Or discuss your ludicrous thoughts on philosophy with you. Or go on adventures on Saturdays wearing ridiculous outfits while being threatened with a grisly death."

"I don't know," Arthur said. "You don't seem to have a problem wearing them now."

Linus pulled on his shirt. "They're growing on me. My point is that I left because I was scared of what could be, not of what already was. I'm not scared anymore."

Arthur nodded and looked away, jaw tight. "And the orphanage?"

Linus shook his head. "It's not . . . you know, you told me once that the word orphanage is a misnomer. That no one comes looking here to adopt."

"I did say that, didn't I?"

"You did. And as I told Extremely Upper Management, this isn't an orphanage. It's a home. And that's what it will remain."

"Truly?"

"Truly."

"And what of the others? You said you thought you could help all the others."

Linus scratched the back of his neck. "I might have done something . . . illegal? Stole a few files. Maybe more than a few. I have an idea, though it will take time."

"Why, Linus Baker. I'm utterly surprised at you. Stealing, of all things. It's not proper."

"Yes, well," he muttered. "I put the entirety of the blame on you lot here. You've corrupted me."

Linus thought he saw a flicker of fire in Arthur's eyes. "You really did all that?"

"Yes. I was frightened, but it was the right thing to do." He hesitated. Then, "I also quit."

Arthur looked surprised. "Why?"

Linus shrugged. "Because it wasn't where I belonged."

"Where do you belong, Linus?"

And with the last of his courage, Linus Baker said, "Here. With you. If you'll have me. Ask me again. Please, I beg you. Ask me to stay again."

Arthur nodded tightly. He cleared his throat. He was hoarse when he said, "Linus."

"Yes, Arthur?"

"Stay. Here. With us. With me."

Linus could barely breathe. "Yes. Always. Yes. For them. For you. For—"

He was being kissed. He hadn't even seen Arthur move. One moment, he thought he was about to break, and the next, his face was cupped in warm hands, and lips were pressed against his own. He felt as if he were on fire, burning from the inside out. He reached up, putting his hands atop Arthur's, holding them in place. He never wanted this moment to end. For all the love songs he'd ever listened to in his life, he hadn't been prepared for how a moment like this could feel.

Arthur pulled away, and began to laugh as Linus frantically kissed his chin and cheeks, his nose and forehead. Arthur dropped his hands and wrapped his arms around Linus, holding him close. Linus could hear the children cheering in the house as they began to sway in the light from a setting sun.

"I'm sorry," Linus whispered into Arthur's throat, never wanting this moment to end.

Arthur held him tighter. "You silly, delightful man. There is nothing to be sorry for. You fought for us. I could never be angry with you for that. How I cherish you."

Linus felt his heart settle in his chest.

As they continued to sway to a song only they could hear, the sun finally sank below the horizon, and all was right in this tiny little corner of the world.

Don't you wish you were here?

EPILOGUE

On a warm spring Thursday afternoon, the sound of an old truck coming up the road to the house filled the air.

Linus looked up from where he was pulling weeds, wiping a hand across his brow, leaving behind a smudge of dirt.

"Sounds like Helen," he said. "Was she coming to see you?"

Talia didn't look up as she lovingly patted the soil around a bed of petunias. "Not that I heard. She was talking about another magazine wanting to see my flowers, but she said that wouldn't be until next month. She didn't say anything when we were in the village last weekend."

Linus stood with a groan. "Better see what she wants."

"If it's my adoring public, tell them I'm not prepared for company at the moment and that it's rude to come with so little notice."

He snorted. "I'll make sure they understand."

Talia looked at him, eyes narrowing. "Don't think this gets you out of weed duty."

He patted the top of her cap. "I wouldn't dream of it. Keep at it. I won't be long."

Talia muttered under her breath in Gnomish.

He shook his head, smiling to himself. She was getting more creative with her threats. He blamed that entirely on Lucy.

He wiped his hands on his shirt and walked out of the garden toward the front of the house. The Linus from a year ago wouldn't recognize the man that existed today. His skin had burned and peeled and burned and peeled until he had what could be described as a minor tan. He wore shorts (by choice!) and his knees were dirty from kneeling in the garden for the last hour. He was still rotund, and had begrudgingly accepted it when Arthur had made his appreciation known. His hair was even thinner than it'd once been, but he had little time for such trivial things. He was comfortable in his own skin for the first time in his life. Perhaps his blood pressure was still a tad high, but life was so much more than worrying about a spare tire or hair on a pillow.

He was humming Buddy Holly when the truck pulled up and stopped with a lurch, the engine coughing and stuttering as it turned off.

"Sounds like it's about to give up," Linus observed as Helen climbed out of the truck. She wore a pair of grass-stained overalls.

"Eh. It gets the job done." She grinned at him. "You're dirty. Talia holding you to your end of the bargain, is she?"

Linus sighed. "I've got her down to three days a week now. I don't dare try to go any lower. She has yet to fill in the hole that's supposed to be my grave. It's a rather effective threat from one so small."

"It looks good on you," she said, patting his shoulder. "Arthur inside? I need to speak to both of you. And J-Bone wanted me to remind Lucy the records he ordered came in."

"Everything all right?"

Her smile faded. "I think so. But it's best I tell both of you at the same time."

He didn't like the sound of that. "Is it something from the village? I thought things were getting better. Last weekend when we were there, we only got a few glares."

She shook her head. "Not—it's nothing about the village. And who was giving you a hard time?"

He shrugged. "The usual suspects. But it's getting easier to ignore them. Children are remarkably resilient when they need to be."

She frowned. "They shouldn't *have* to be. I promised I would do my best to make sure nothing like that happened again."

"You've done wonders," he assured her. "But these things take time."

And not everyone *wanted* things to change, though he didn't think he needed to tell her that. Since she'd come to the island to see things for herself, Helen had made it her mission to make the village a welcoming place for all. First came down the SEE SOME-THING, SAY SOMETHING posters around town. That had been met with minimal resistance. But there had been greater grumblings when she'd announced her intention to position the village of Marsyas as a vacation spot for all, humans and magical beings alike. It wasn't until she'd reminded the business owners that more people meant more money for the village that the grumblings began to lessen. Linus was grimly amused by how prejudice didn't seem to be a match for profit, especially seeing as how the payments the village had been receiving for their silence regarding the island had been cut off. He took it as a victory when the village council had voted in favor, however hollow it could be.

It was a start.

And then, after Christmas, came the surprising announcement from the Department in Charge of Magical Youth about how Extremely Upper Management had all resigned after an external investigation revealed the schools they'd run had been deemed discriminatory. The investigation had been sparked by an anonymous report that outlined unsavory practices involving magical youth, citing specific examples of children under the guidance of DICOMY who had been treated as second-class citizens. A new governing board had been appointed, and while they spoke of grand and sweeping changes, the wheels of bureaucracy did indeed grind slowly, especially when met with vocal resistance. Overhauling decades of preconceptions would take time.

But if they could start with DICOMY, it could lead to other departments that dealt with magical beings beginning to change with the times.

They had to start somewhere.

A reporter had come to the island in February, apparently having tracked down Linus after hearing of his dramatic exit from DICOMY. She'd asked if he'd known anything about the anonymous report that had sent shock waves through the government. "A whistleblower," she said. "Someone with insider knowledge about the workings of the Department in Charge of Magical Youth."

He laughed nervously. "Do I look like the type to cause a ruckus?"

She wasn't fooled. "I've learned never to judge what a person is capable of based upon appearances alone. And I would protect your anonymity."

"Would you?"

"You have my word. I guard my sources fiercely."

He thought of all the other children out there in the world in places just like Marsyas. The ones he'd met, and the thousands he'd never had the pleasure of meeting, though he'd read about many of them in the files he'd stolen away. Perhaps this would help the fire to continue to burn as brightly as it could. A quiet man, yes, with a quiet heart, but he thought of the phoenix, wings spread in a darkened cellar and then on a dock for all the world to see. If this reporter could find him, chances are others could as well. But Linus thought he was done hiding in the shadows. "Then listen well, for the story I have to tell you will be unlike anything else you've heard."

She smiled.

When she left five hours later, her eyes were sparkling, and she looked hungry. She said she had enough for an entire series and would let them know when it was set to be published. She believed she would be ready as soon as the summer. "Do you know what this will do?" she asked them, standing in front of the house. "Do you have any idea what this will mean?"

"More than you know," Arthur said.

She watched him for a long moment before nodding. She turned toward her car, but stopped with her hand on the door handle. She glanced back at them. "One last question."

"Bloody reporters," Linus muttered.

She ignored him, only having eyes for Arthur. "I heard from a source that a man unlike any other has agreed to testify about his own experiences of being under the purview of the Department in Charge of Magical Youth. Would you know anything about that?"

"A man unlike any other," Arthur said. "How curious."

"Is it true?"

"I expect time will tell."

She shook her head. Something crossed her face that Linus couldn't quite parse. She said, "I must remain objective. My job is to report the facts, and nothing more."

"But?" Arthur asked.

"But as a human being, and someone who has seen glimpses of light in all the darkness, I would hope this man knows that there are many, many people who believe that what he has to say will bring about the change this world so desperately needs. Good day."

She left then, heading back toward the ferry.

They stood on the porch as her car disappeared down the dirt road, hands joined between them.

Linus said, "I told you."

Arthur smiled. "You did, didn't you? Perhaps you were right, after all. Do you really think they'll listen?"

Linus wasn't a fool; he knew that DICOMY was most likely watching him as much as they were the other residents of the island. While he wasn't magical in the slightest, he had left DICOMY and come to a place still technically considered classified, though it was something of a joke now. The children didn't hide who they were. And while they were still met with some conflict, they were welcome in the village whenever they wished. Helen made sure of that.

Oh, he wasn't naïve enough to think it would be like this everywhere. He still saw the anger and the vitriol magical beings received in the bigger cities. There were rallies and marches in favor of registration, but what made him hope that things were changing were the *counterprotesters* who gathered in greater numbers. They were mostly young people, a mixture of the magical and humans alike, and Linus knew the old guard would soon be standing on their last legs.

It was simply a matter of time.

"Yes," he said. "Eventually."

Arthur nodded. "You believe in me."

Linus blinked. "Of course I do. I believe in all of you. But you're a phoenix, Arthur. You know fire. It's time to burn it all down and see what can grow from the ashes."

"A ruckus," Arthur said, and he chuckled quietly. "If only they knew what we're capable of."

Linus smiled. "They will."

He was waiting to see if DICOMY would send a new caseworker to the island, especially after the petition Arthur had recently submitted. So far, there hadn't been word of such a thing, though Helen was here now. Maybe she'd learned something and had come to warn them.

"I'll keep working on it," she told him.

He smiled softly at her. "We know. And we're grateful for it."

He led her into the house. He could hear the sounds of a home filled with happiness around them. It creaked and groaned as a house does when it's old and well lived-in. He saw the tip of a tail thumping happily from underneath the couch. As they climbed the stairs, there came the sound of typewriter keys clacking furiously, of a cheerful "How do you do?" coming from Chauncey's room. He was practicing more and more these days, especially after he'd been asked by the manager of the hotel if he'd like to spend one day a month working with their bellhop. It seemed the man who'd given Chauncey his cap was getting on in years and would soon be looking to retire. Chauncey had collapsed in a quivering puddle, something Linus and Arthur hadn't known he was capable of. Eventually, when he pulled himself together, he tearfully accepted. He had his first day on Saturday.

Linus heard Lucy exclaiming loudly as they reached the bedroom door. He glanced back at Helen, who arched an eyebrow at him. "Lucy was the first to say something to Arthur about what he was," Linus explained. "Everyone else pretty much already knew, but Lucy decided to be more forthcoming about it. He's been asking Arthur to light things on fire for a few weeks now."

"Oh boy," Helen said.

He pushed open the door.

"—and just *think* about it, Arthur! Think about all the things that burn! Paper! Cardboard! Trees! Wait. No. Not trees. Phee will kill me if we burn trees. But we *could* if we wanted to. Between the two of us, we can light *so many things on fire*— Hi, Linus!"

Linus shook his head. "Lucy. We've talked about this."

Lucy scowled. "I know. But you also told me the only way we can learn new things is if we ask about them."

Arthur smiled. "You did say that, didn't you?"

"I regret everything," Linus muttered.

"You're fibbing," Lucy said. "You *love* me." That smile took on a sinister curve. "Just like you *loooove* Arthur."

Linus felt himself turning red, but he didn't try and argue. Everyone in the room would know he was lying. "Be that as it may, I think there's a plate of biscuits with your name on it in the kitchen. Why don't you see if Sal and Chauncey want to join you?"

Lucy stared up at him suspiciously. "Are you kicking me out to talk about me? Because if you are, I didn't do whatever you think I did."

Linus's eyes narrowed. "Did you do something I should be aware of?"

"Biscuits!" Lucy crowed, running from the room. "Hi, Helen! Bye, Helen!" He hollered for his brothers as he slammed the door shut behind him. A painting on the wall—that of a lemur in a confoundingly salacious pose that Arthur found inexplicable delight in—was knocked crooked.

"A little devil, isn't he?" Helen asked, staring at the closed door in wonder.

"Quite literally," Arthur replied. "Helen, I don't think we were expecting you."

"Sorry about that," she said. "I—it couldn't wait. I needed to see you." She glanced at Linus. "Both of you. It's important."

"By all means," Arthur said, nodding to the chair Lucy had vacated. She sat while Linus moved to stand next to Arthur. He turned redder when Arthur reached up and took his hand, kissing the back of it. He didn't pull away.

"Getting on then, are you?" Helen asked, a spark in her eyes that Linus didn't like.

"We're taking it one day at a time," Linus said stiffly.

"Oh, sure. I understand that. Talia told me last weekend that you haven't slept in the guest house since Christmas. And that they've had quite a few sleepovers with Zoe, though I don't think she quite understands why."

Arthur laughed as Linus groaned. "Meddling little things."

"It's a good look on you," she said quietly. "The both of you. I'm happy you found each other." She sobered. "I've waited to come to you with this. I wanted to make sure, but I think it's almost time."

Linus was confused. He glanced down at Arthur before looking back at Helen. "What are you talking about?"

"A child," Arthur said. "Isn't it? You've found a new child."

Linus felt goose bumps on the back of his neck.

Helen nodded. "He's undocumented. But he has no one else. He's staying with . . . some friends. People I trust, but they don't have enough room, and it was always meant to be temporary. And given . . . what he is, he'll need more than they could ever provide." She smiled, though it trembled. "I know it's asking a lot, and it might bring down more attention on you than you want, but he has nowhere else to go. They've looked for relatives, but haven't been successful. I think he's alone. He's shy, and scared, and doesn't talk much. Reminds me a little of Sal, in fact. Or, rather, how he used to be. I don't think I've ever heard that boy talk as much as he has in the last few months."

"Regular chatterbox," Linus said faintly. "What's his name?"

"And that's how I know this could be the place for him," Helen said, her smile growing. "Because you didn't ask me what he was, just who he is. I don't know that anyone has ever done that for him." She reached inside a pocket on her overalls and pulled out a photograph. She glanced down at it before handing it over. "His name is David. He's eleven years old. And he's a—"

"A yeti," Linus said in awe. He stared at the photo in Arthur's hand. In it, there was a smiling boy covered in thick, white hair. But it was his eyes that Linus noticed more than anything.

They were cerulean.

"We'll take him," Linus said immediately. "Whenever he's ready. Can we get him today? Where is he? Does he have much? Oh, we'll have to figure out where he should sleep. The guest house might work but—wait. Will he be all right here? Won't he like the cold more than anything? I suppose we can work something out. Anything we can do to make him comfortable—"

He felt Arthur squeeze his hand.

He looked down. "Gone off, have I?"

And Arthur said, "You dear, dear man. How I adore you."

Linus coughed. "Uh. Yes. You too. The same."

Helen was grinning at them. "I knew it. I knew I was doing the right thing. And yes, he likes cold, though he's survived more without having it."

"He shouldn't just be *surviving*," Linus said irritably. "He should be *living*."

"The cellar," Arthur said, and Linus gaped at him. "We could convert the cellar into a cold room. Just for him."

"Are you sure?"

Arthur nodded. "Yes. It's time, I think. To let the past rest. Take something filled with anger and sadness and make it better."

Linus Baker loved Arthur Parnassus more than he could ever put into words.

"Will it cause problems with your petition for adopting the others?" Helen asked, sounding worried. "I don't want that to be put into jeopardy."

Arthur shook his head. "I don't see why it would. This place is still considered an orphanage, though DICOMY is reviewing their guidelines, or so they say. And he is . . . unusual, just like the rest of us. If he finds that he likes it here, and wants to stay, we'll do what we can to go through the proper channels. And if he doesn't, we'll find him a place to belong."

Helen looked relieved. "There's more, you know. So many more."

"We know," Linus said. "And while we may not be able to help them all, we'll do as much as we can for all those put in our path."

She left them a little later with a promise of getting in touch soon. There were plans to be made, and she thought it would be best if Arthur and Linus were to go to David first so as not to overwhelm him with all the others.

They agreed.

Linus watched the truck through the bedroom window. Helen was speaking with Zoe through the open window. They were both smiling. Linus hadn't seen their relationship blossoming, though he seemed to be the only one. It wasn't until he'd stumbled upon them kissing that he figured out why Helen seemed to be at the island more and more.

Zoe kissed the back of Helen's hand before stepping away. The truck turned over, the engine rumbling as she began to drive down the road back toward the dock. Linus startled when arms wrapped around his waist. He turned his head slightly to brush his nose against Arthur's cheek.

"You can do this," he whispered. "Bring him here. Make him happy."

"*We* can do this," Arthur corrected gently. "Because he'll need you just as much as he needs me. He'll need all of us, I think. And we'll be ready."

Linus turned. He kissed the tip of Arthur's nose. "Thank you."

"For what?"

"This. Everything. All this color."

Arthur knew what he meant. "It was his eyes, wasn't it? That's what you saw first."

Linus nodded. "They reminded me of the sea. It's a sign. He belongs here. And we'll do everything we can to make sure he knows that."

"Do you think we should tell the children?"

"About David? Of course. They need to—"

He shook his head. "About the petition of adoption. About how your name is on it too."

Linus hesitated. "Not yet. Not until we're sure it'll go through with the both of us on there. I'd hate to say something only to have it need to be amended to just you if DICOMY rejects it because we're . . ." He coughed roughly. "You know." Linus wished he could sink into the floor. He hoped Arthur would ignore him.

Arthur didn't. "Because we're unmarried."

"Yes. That." And no, Linus absolutely had not been thinking about that at all. Not in the slightest. Why, the very idea was preposterous. Not only was it far too soon, there was—

"We may have to change that, then."

Linus gaped at him as Arthur stepped away toward the door. "Excuse me?"

Arthur glanced back at him over his shoulder. "Coming, dear Linus?"

"Now, see here! You shouldn't—you can't just *say* something like—what on *earth*—"

Arthur opened the bedroom door. He held out his hand for Linus.

Linus, still sputtering of course, took what was offered.

It turned out they needn't have worried. By the time they reached the bottom of the stairs, the children and Zoe had gathered in the kitchen, and Lucy was already explaining with ferocious excitement that Linus was going to be their father too, and that Arthur and Linus were to be married. They would have to talk to him again about eavesdropping.

As the children jumped on the both of them, shouting their happiness with no small amount of tears, Linus found he wasn't upset at all.

Sometimes, he thought to himself in a house in a cerulean sea, you were able to choose the life you wanted.

And if you were of the lucky sort, sometimes that life chose you back.